THE
SACRIFIST

Other Books Coming from Anagram Press

Poker: A Sex Comedy

Ten Random Stories

Rise of the Rimms

Reading Kills

The Sacrifist

A Novel
by
T. Mason Gilbert

Published by Mjollnir Enterprises LLC

This book is a work of fiction. Names, characters, places, and incidents are either the product of the author's imagination or are used fictitiously. Some locations, businesses, and brand names are real but are used fictitiously.

Trade Paperback ISBN: 978-0-9863646-0-0
eBook ISBN: 978-0-9863646-1-7

Copyright © 2015 by T. Mason Gilbert

All rights reserved. No part of this book may be reproduced in any form or by electronic or mechanical means, including information storage and retrieval systems—except in the case of brief quotations embodied in critical articles or reviews—without permission of the author.

Printed in the United States of America

March 2015

Cover art by Jerone De Leon

For my Mother

Who taught me that a
quitter never wins and a
winner never quits.

And for Diana

Who never quit on me.

ACKNOWLEDGMENTS

The first person I would like to thank is Diana, my wife of over 35 years. She has always supported me, for better or ill. I would like to thank my kids, Morgan and Claire, and my brother, Tracy, for their suggestions and kind words.

I would like to thank my high school pal and linguistics expert Julie Tabler for helping me with language isolates and other language basics; Linda Porter with the Canine Training Academy in Canon City, CO, who helped me with dog tracking and trailing information; Courtney Streeter of Sorenson Forensics for her help with data on genetics and testing; and Professor Mark Donohue of Australian National University and Bhoj Raj Gautam of Tribhuvan University for their help with the Kusunda culture and language. I also would like to thank all the businesses who gave me permission to mention them or their product in my novel.

I'd like to give thanks to my editor, Susan Shepherd and my proofreader, Judith Seirup.

Lastly, I would like to thank all of my teachers in all the schooling I've ever had. Teachers work hard and should get a lot more credit than they do. Sometimes a teacher can have such an impact on a student's life that it changes the person's life and sends them off in a better direction. In particular, I would like to thank three teachers in my own life that had that kind of influence on me.

First, I would like to thank Mrs. Wilma Wimmer, my 4th grade teacher at J.C. Boyd Elementary. Because of her I spent less time in the principal's office and I'm quite sure she saved me from a life of delinquency. Second, I want to thank Professor Harry Murray of San Bernardino Valley College, who

taught me the basics of art, entertainment, performing, and professionalism. Finally, I would like to thank Charles "Chuck" Grande of Eisenhower High School, who had a profound influence on my life. I would not be who I am today without his teaching and guidance. I thank him from the bottom of my heart.

FOREWORD

When I started writing this book, people would ask me what I was doing. I told them I was "writing about the discovery of the yeti in the Himalaya and why it has remained hidden for so long."

Their follow-up question ninety-five percent of the time was always the same—and it always shocked me. They would ask, "Is it non-fiction?"

"No," I'd explain. "They haven't discovered the yeti. The book is a product of my imagination."

But a funny thing happened along the way. Even though I used my imagination to write the book, during the writing process I would research various things and found out the things I had 'imagined' often turned out to be factual.

The third highest mountain in the world, Kangchenjunga, which I decided to use as the location solely because there were already too many stories about Everest and K2, turned out both to be considered sacred, and to be the first place where the yeti was reportedly spotted. Hence, the term 'Kangchenjunga Demon' is an actual name used in Nepal for the yeti.

There were too many coincidences to comment upon but the book turned out to be based on more factual information than I had originally planned. In fact, if you skim while reading or speed read, you will miss important facts and may not be able to understand the story. Every word in this manuscript is important to understanding the whole.

And who knows what will be discovered in the future? As far as this novel is concerned, what we know currently is that the yeti has not been discovered ... *at this time.*

T.M.G.

The
Sacrifist

Quotations

"Monks, even if bandits were to savagely sever you, limb by limb, with a double-handled saw, even then, whoever of you harbors ill will at heart would not be upholding my Teaching. Monks, even in such a situation you should train yourselves thus: 'Neither shall our minds be affected by this, nor for this matter shall we give vent to evil words, but we shall remain full of concern and pity, with a mind of love, and we shall not give in to hatred. On the contrary, we shall live projecting thoughts of universal love to those very persons, making them as well as the whole world the object of our thoughts of universal love—thoughts that have grown great, exalted and measureless. We shall dwell radiating these thoughts which are void of hostility and ill will.' It is in this way, monks, that you should train yourselves."
~ *Siddhārtha Gautama Buddha*

"What we think, we become."
~ *Siddhārtha Gautama Buddha*

Ancient Tibetan Myth

Long before the Tibetan people were born, there lived a devil and a rock ogress who held sway over all the other living creatures and the country was known as the Land of the Two Divine Ogres. As a result of their union, fearsome meat-eating beasts were born.

One day the devil went away and the rock ogress, having no one to quench her lust, threatened to have her monstrous offspring devour thousands of other sentient beings unless the Monkey King agreed to satisfy her ravenous passion.

The Monkey King had been meditating in the snowy realms of Kangchenjunga and was torn between his compassion for his fellow beings and his vow of chastity. He was transported instantly to where the great Bodhisattva[1] Avalokitesvara looked out upon the world. Avalokitesvara bade him to marry the rock ogress in order to protect all of the other living creatures. So, the Monkey King consented to her demands.

Thus, the Tibetan people were born.

From the King, the Tibetans acquired the attributes of kindness, high religiosity, and their industrious work ethic. The rock ogress bestowed upon them quick tempers, passion, jealousy, and the strong desire to eat meat.

Such are their characteristics to this day.

But what became of the Two Divine Ogres' offspring—the meat-eating beasts? This is the great secret of Tibet, the Land of Snows.

And secrets never last forever.

---

[1] Bodhisattva: a person who has attained Enlightenment, but who postpones Nirvana in order to help others to attain Enlightenment.

CHAPTER 1

HE HAD NO mind. That was what made him different. That was what made them all different—all two hundred and sixteen of them.

As a five-year-old boy, his given name had always seemed odd to him—had seemed not to belong. After entering the *gompa,* or monastery, for his training, he had assumed a new name, one fit to be used at this time and place. Still, it had seemed incorrect, and the feeling had persisted through the years. Now he knew why. A moment ago, he had had a 'reminding.'

Those names were not his *real name.*

He recognized that his twenty years of training had led him to this one moment. The awakening occurred just after reading a phrase in a sacred text. He found it somewhat amusing that a simple phrase from a book had had the effect of revealing the truth of his existence. It was like a veil had been lifted.

He knew who and what he was.

If he did not know better, the reminding would have seemed like magic, because it had not occurred as a memory like a normal person would have had. It was more than a mere realization, more than a thought to be considered or evaluated. The *Epiphany* had changed him all at once into a new state of being—*a state of knowing.*

A person does not *remember* their own name. They just *know* it.

And so, he was himself again, with no additives—nothing blocking his abilities. Once again, he could do things other human beings could not do.

The first thing he noticed was that his thought process had changed. Vocal thoughts had vanished. The little voice in his head disappeared, no longer a distraction. His thinking was no longer internalized. This transformation meant that his attention remained on the exterior world rather than the interior world, inside one's head.

He had no sense of introversion, only a powerful feeling of personal serenity. He looked forward to fulfilling his purpose in this life.

The only thing limiting him now was his body, and the fact that all the memories of his prior incarnations had not fully returned. He could recall only bits and pieces. But he realized that that particular knowledge would be restored to him after he had performed his sacred duty. He estimated he had about five years until he would be needed. He would be ready.

Five more years—then, *the beast.*

CHAPTER 2

DANE NIELSEN RAPPELLED down the sheer rock face of a cliff he had descended many times before. The bluff gave the aspiring mountaineers he taught something they could learn on with a reasonable expectation of safety, it not being more than a two-hundred foot drop.

He halted his rappel and sat comfortably in his climbing harness. He knew that he was finally back in shape after what many of his friends had called *the Great Bender*.

The Great Bender had lasted for the three months of last year's winter. He had spent most of that time hiding out in his ranch house near Leadville, Colorado, and had refused to take calls from any friends or family.

Guilt does that.

His days had consisted primarily of visiting the local liquor store to pick up a case of scotch, then spending the rest of his time drinking it while watching ESPN. That, and lots of sex. Drugs, sex and death are great guilt-relievers. The first two give temporary relief, but the third works the best.

Single malt scotch had been his drug of choice during the Great Bender. He had trashed half his liver and was headed for the permanent relief option when the Fates intervened in the guise of a pretty blonde biathlete named Shelly Newton. She had been skiing near Leadville, and had stopped in at the Silver Dollar Saloon for a drink.

The Silver Dollar building had been standing since the 1850s and had been a saloon since the 1870s. Such notable Wild West figures as Doc Holliday, Tom Horn, Texas Jack, and Jesse James among others had stayed in Leadville and frequented many of the saloons in town. Holliday's last public gunfight took place just outside the Silver Dollar. He did not kill the man.

Whenever Dane got a hankering for the other sex, he would drive his 1969 Pontiac Firebird over to the Silver Dollar to try out his luck while partaking in their refreshments. His genes being of Native American and Danish descent, he had little difficulty attracting the attention of some of the snow bunnies who were staying at Leadville's inns while skiing the local area.

It always amazed Dane how simple it was to engage with a woman for a night of pleasurable exercise. There was nothing to it. Literally. The formula was simple. Ask a question, shut up, actually listen to their answer, repeat. Add a drink or two and that did the rest. Women will tell you everything, *if* you listen.

The first time, it had happened to him inadvertently. He hadn't even been thinking about sex. Beth was a dirty blonde. He found out later, her hair wasn't the only dirty thing about her. She had come in alone, wearing tight ski clothes—a white parka with a white fur hood and bright red ski pants. She sat down and ordered a Manhattan. She was mildly cute. Max, the bartender, brought her drink over and set it down on the bar napkin.

"Skiing the area?" Dane asked, just to chat.

She pretended to see him for the first time and tried to keep herself from looking at his muscular physique, and shoulder-length dark brown hair.

She couldn't help staring into his big, deep blue eyes which stood out against his light mocha-colored complexion. Dane could read her thoughts immediately. *She thinks I'm hot.* He laughed inside. He was hot, but he was not conceited about it. It was more like it was just a matter of fact. He'd been told he was unusually attractive by other (usually older) women in the past.

Two drinks later, she was telling Dane everything about her current boyfriend. She even showed Dane a photo of him, while revealing the size of his manhood, and how much she loved giving said boyfriend oral sex. Finally, she told Dane about her beau's propensity to cheat on her. That was it. Dane knew when women start talking about being cheated on, it usually means they want to cheat.

Dane listened with interest and nodded when appropriate. After her third Manhattan, she asked, "Ya wanna go have some fun in my room?" He kept himself from choking on his drink and nodded in the affirmative.

And it *was* fun, too. Beth turned out to be an expert in how to dance around the Maypole. Dane's main takeaway from that night was that the boyfriend must be some kind of an idiot. Until the Beth escapade, the name Kegel only had applied to the last name of a friend from high school. Until that time, Dane had not known women could actually *do* that with their Holiest of Holies.

And so it went with the Great Bender, a scene that repeated itself, with only minor variations, numerous times during that winter. Despite his guilt and self-imposed isolation, Dane was far from alone. There was scotch and—Beth, Kate, Robbin, Laraine, Julie, Desiree, Stella, Antigone, Rhonda, etc. Months later, Dane's good friend Smokes, who was an inveterate joker, would rename that period of time the Great Bend Over.

The night Shelly had walked in, he had not been particularly wasted. He struck up a conversation with the beautiful blonde and found out she had competed in the biathlon at the 2010 Winter Olympics. He had always thought shooting and cross-country skiing to be an odd event. *When would you use those skills at the same time? Hunting a moose?* After a bit of small talk, Dane introduced himself.

"Dane Nielsen," he said, holding out his hand.

"Shelly Newton," she said, scowling a bit as though his name had joggled something in her memory. A moment later, a look of recognition came across her face. "Lake Nielsen?"

He stared down into his scotch on the rocks. Only his friends called him Lake. At least, until the mountaineering media had picked up on it. It did not sound right to hear that name coming from a stranger.

"Guilty." He took a drink. He was mildly famous in the mountaineering community, he knew, but Dane was still surprised she knew his nickname. Few casual skiers did.

They had hung out the rest of the night and Dane had gone easy on the scotch for a change. For the first time in three months, he had really enjoyed himself. Shelly was intelligent. That was pretty sexy to Dane. She had had a good time as well, and told him she would be back the next night after another day of skiing. He figured she was lying. She was not.

And the rest, as they say, was history.

He stopped drinking the scotch and switched to an occasional beer. He had begun climbing again over a year ago. Since that time, he had taken on jobs teaching novices to climb, and as the months passed it turned into a steady business. He had a friend put up a website.

Shelly had become his fiancée two months ago. Besides

being an experienced skier, she was a good climber as well. Together they taught the basics of climbing and skiing.

Life was good again.

Dane looked around at the scenery. Shielding his eyes from the sun, which highlighted some copper strands in his hair from the Danish side, he could see Mt. Elbert in the distance. It felt good to be back in tip-top shape.

He closed his eyes and listened to the silence in between the sounds of nature, like his Ojibwe grandfather had taught him. The cool breeze felt good on his sun-tanned face and negated the heat of the sun beating down. Opening his eyes, the serenity of the scene reminded him of an old Ojibwe song his mother used to sing to him in her native language when he was a child.

See Mother Earth,
Behold her beauty.
The four grandfathers sit,
Watching from their home,
North, South, East, West,
Protecting her children,
So they may live to care
For their Mother Earth.

The song of a canyon wren—a musical cascade of descending liquid notes ending in a metallic buzz—filled the air. *Must be nesting nearby.* He made a mental note to watch where he placed his feet while pushing off the cliff face.

"Ouch! Shit!" a voice yelled from above, destroying Dane's scene of tranquility.

He looked up the rock face at his hapless pupil, then sighed and shook his head. Brad Comstock was a young Wall Streeter with too much money and not a lot of practical climbing experience. Sometimes Dane regretted teaching novices how to mountaineer, but at the same time he knew the job had helped him get back on his feet and regain his confidence in the climbing game.

Teaching beginners is easy. But it can't beat the majesty of standing at the top of an eight-thousander, he thought. A sudden pang hit him, reminding him why he had quit. His stomach got anxious. But months of practice had become habit, and Dane took only a moment to file the bad memory in a compartment labeled 'fuggedabowdit,' a term he'd learned from one of his climbing partners. He smiled, thinking about his former mountaineering friends and their shared exploits. The memories, as much as his own well-developed sense of self-control, drove his anxious feeling away.

"Dammit!" Brad said.

"Whatever it is, it's not babysitting stockbrokers," Dane murmured aloud. He refocused on his student. Brad was a fair distance above him, fiddling with his rappelling set-up.

"Okay, Brad. Now … easy does it," Dane called out.

Brad began his rappel again, starting off at a slow pace.

"Remember now, don't rush it," Dane said.

Brad did okay for the first ten feet, but then started picking up speed, dropping faster and faster.

"Oh, no!" Brad cried, plummeting toward Dane.

"Oh, boy," Dane muttered to himself. He kicked along the rock face, deftly moving his feet, swinging slightly to the right, and expertly maneuvering out of Brad's line of descent.

"Heeeellllp!" Brad screamed, as he plunged down the cliff, falling fast.

Dane pushed his feet against the mountainside, swinging back in the direction of his wailing client's flight path, while at the same time descending rapidly enough to somewhat match Brad's speed. Timing it perfectly, he reached out in the same instant that Brad whooshed by, and just managed to grab the right leg strap of his client's seat harness. His arm muscles straining to their limit, he struggled to hold onto his client as he braked to stop them both.

Brad's momentum inverted him quickly and he smacked the back of his helmeted head on the cliff face. The Wall Streeter came to a stop upside down.

Stillness had returned and all was okay. The sounds of nature filled the air once again.

"Owww," Brad moaned, after he realized he had been saved. "That hurt."

Dane began to secure Brad from any further danger of falling, and his cell phone rang, playing "Ride of the Valkyries."

Torleif's calling, he thought, hearing the familiar ringtone he had chosen for his former longtime climbing partner. Since the end of the Great Bender, Dane had talked with Torleif regularly, but Dane had not spoken to him since Torleif left on expedition.

Since his client was in no immediate danger, Dane left Brad hanging upside down for the moment and answered his phone.

"Hey, Leif. How's it going?"

"Not so good, Lake," Torleif said, sounding unlike his usual good-natured self.

"Really? What's up?"

"Hey, don't leave me upside down," Brad said.

"Quiet, you big baby," Dane said.

"Busy with a client?" Torleif asked.

"Hardly."

"Come on, Dane."

Torleif heard Brad's whine in the background and chuckled, sounding like himself again. "Living the easy life. Teaching amateurs for the big bucks."

"Hey! ... It's respectable work," Dane said, looking down at the inverted stockbroker. "And, trust me, not always easy. Sometimes, I actually *earn* my money."

Torleif laughed, and Dane laughed back. Turning serious, Torleif said, "Lake … I really need your help."

He doesn't sound right, thought Dane, hesitating a moment. He knew that for Torleif to ask for any kind of help, the situation must be serious.

Trying to sound more nonchalant than he felt, Dane heard himself say, "No problem."

"Thanks, buddy. I appreciate it. I'm going to be hopping a plane from London tomorrow morning. I'll see you and Shelly tomorrow, early evening."

Torleif's sudden rush to see him caught Dane off guard. He swallowed and said, "Okay. See you then."

Putting his phone away, he wondered, *What's happened?* He and Torleif had been friends for a long time and had helped each other many times while climbing. They had saved each other's lives as well. But Torleif had never *asked* for any help. Torleif was not someone who would ask for help. Neither was he cryptic—until now. *If he's flying out, it must be important.*

"Can we go now?" Brad asked.

Dane focused his attention back on Brad and put on his instructor hat. "What are the rules of rappelling?"

Brad began to drone robotically. "Number one: Always climb with a qualified supervisor. Number two …"

Brad continued to recite the rules of rappelling. Dane helped him turn upright and assisted him the rest of the way down.

But Torleif's call began to eat away at his inner calm. He could feel the deadliness of the Himalaya beginning to beckon. *Something must have happened on Kangchenjunga.*

Something did. But that was ten days earlier.

CHAPTER 3

A GUST OF cold wind hit Torleif Günner's face and blew his golden hair back as he watched his client, Randolph Barrington, Jr., make his way up the slope on the great Yalung glacier. They were southwest of the main peak of Mt. Kangchenjunga, the third highest mountain on Earth.

Depending on the weather, we'll be climbing the Face soon, Torleif thought. The Yalung Face's main feature was the Great Shelf, a large sloping plateau at around 7,500 meters which was covered by a hanging glacier. Almost entirely located on snow and glacier, the route also had one icefall, and it was widely considered the most difficult stretch before summiting the main peak.

That boy is a climbing fool, thought Torleif as he watched Rand up ahead. Young Master Barrington was neither likable nor unlikable. But Rand inspired admiration because his climbing skills were exceptional. By the time Rand turned twenty, he had already distinguished himself in the mountain climbing community. He had even had a mountaineering 'list' named after him.

Climbers had argued for years over which of the two Seven

Summit Lists qualified as the *real* Seven Summit List.

Two lists existed that detailed the highest mountains on each of the seven continents. The Bass List was named after Richard Bass, who was the first person to come up with such a list. The Messner List was named after Reinhold Messner, arguably the most famous mountaineer of all time. Messner was also the first person to summit all fourteen of the eight-thousanders.

The eight-thousanders were the fourteen independent peaks in the Himalayan and Karakoram mountain ranges with heights exceeding 8,000 meters. That's around 26,000 feet if you're from the USA, Myanmar or Liberia, the only three countries in the world still refusing to convert to the metric system.

The difference between the two Seven Summit Lists was the Bass List had Mt. Kosciuszko listed as the highest mountain in Australia, which actually was the case. The disagreement came from the climber's opinion of what made up the Australian continent. Messner lumped Indonesia in with Australia, so his list included Puncak Jaya, also known as Carstensz Pyramid, instead of Kosciuszko. Puncak Jaya is technically a more difficult climb whereas Kosciuszko is an easy hike. To cover their bases, most mountaineers usually climbed all *eight* of the 'Seven Summits.'

Rand bypassed all of that by completing what most mountaineering circles considered the seven most *technically challenging* climbs on each continent, thus creating the Barrington List. It contained challenges from Cerro Chaltén in the Southern Patagonian Ice Field—also known as Mount Fitz Roy—to the Nordwand, the North Face of Mt. Eiger in the Alps. The Germans nicknamed it the Morwand, which was German for 'murderous wall.' At least sixty-four climbers had died climbing it since 1935.

Torleif was concerned because Rand was way up ahead of

the rest of their expedition, something he continuously tried to stop Rand from doing. *I wish he'd slow down a little.* Not that Torleif's forty-five-year-old six-foot-five body tired easily. It did not. He just knew that getting too far ahead was not safe.

***

The morning darkness dissipated as the coming dawn lit up the area, bathing the Yalung glacier in blue semi-darkness. Anxious to get to the summit in a few days, Rand pressed on. At twenty-eight years of age, Rand would become the youngest man ever to summit all fourteen of the eight-thousanders. *Move over, Nielsen; there's a new world record holder. Dad will be proud.*

It had snowed during the night but the weather was clear now. The men in the expedition could increasingly see without artificial light, but most still had their headlamps burning. Rand and his crew had left several hours ago from main base camp at 5400 meters and only taken with them the best of the climbing Sherpas. All the others had stayed behind.

He had spent the last two weeks acclimatizing to the thin air, setting up higher base camps. Three of the four camps above main base camp had already been established. He was headed back to Camp 1, which was at 6200 meters. *Acclimatizing is a bitch,* thought Rand, wishing he had a Sherpa's physiology.

Despite living in the oxygen-depleted high altitudes, Sherpas had no more oxygen in their blood than other people. They did, however, have ten times more nitric oxide. Nitric oxide caused the blood vessels to dilate and effectively doubled the forearm blood flow to the extremities, which aided in the release of oxygen to tissues. Scientists had yet to figure out why Tibetans, and their related cousins the Sherpas, had this trait, and it was not yet known if it was genetic.

Acclimatizing aside, climbing for Rand was more comfortable than it was for most mountaineers. He climbed expedition style, instead of alpine style. Alpine-style climbers carried all their own equipment, shelter, and food, refraining from using Sherpa porters, guides or even supplemental oxygen.

Climbing alpine style was cheaper but more hazardous than expedition style, especially when climbing an eight-thousander where the air was so thin a person without supplemental oxygen risked experiencing life-threatening complications. Expedition style cost a lot more. But if you were the son of a multi-billionaire, expedition costs could be considered chump change.

The younger Barrington stopped trudging in his crampons for a moment and took in the clean crisp air, freezing his nose hairs momentarily. He gazed at the majesty of the five peaks of Mt. Kangchenjunga, its main peak topping out at 8,586 meters. *No crowds here. Unlike that tourist trap Everest. No prima donnas here, either*—his label for the Alpinists. Everest was so overcrowded with climbers, authorities were considering installing a ladder on the famed Hillary Step to ease congestion on the forty-foot rock wall near the summit of the world's highest peak.

When Rand had climbed Everest there had been twenty-nine other expeditions present. In contrast, at that same time on Kangchenjunga there had been only one. The truth was that Kangchenjunga was a much tougher climb, probably the toughest of the eight-thousanders, along with Annapurna.

Kangchenjunga, located on the Nepal-Sikkim border in the Himalaya, had five peaks—four of them over 8,450 meters in height. The name Kangchenjunga referred to the whole section and meant the Five Sacred Treasures of Snow, representing the five repositories of God—grain, gems, silver, gold and holy books. *People and their superstitions. Should I respect the Kangchenjunga tradition?*

The sacred tradition dictated that the climber should stop a couple meters short of the summit, out of deference to the Buddhist authorities of Sikkim, who regarded Kangchenjunga as holy. The custom started with George Band and Joe Brown, the two Brits who first summited the main peak.

Kangchenjunga was the second least summited eight-thousander, having only been ascended a little over two hundred times. All those mountaineers had honored the holy ritual. But Rand eschewed rituals. *Screw that. I'm not coming all this way without standing at the very top.*

Kangchenjunga had the highest death rate percentage since 1990, making it the most deadly of all the eight-thousanders to climb. Within the last year, five climbers—two from Hungary, two from Nepal and one from South Korea—had disappeared without a trace while descending the mountain. *One for each peak*, was the rumor around base camp. The Sherpas assumed the men had violated their hallowed tradition.

Rand ignored the rumor. He was not worried. Gazing back down at Torleif Günner leading the climbing Sherpas, he thought, *I've got it made. I have Günner, who's one of the most experienced climbers of all time, helping me. Soon I'll achieve the ultimate goal of every important mountaineer. Then in a month, I'll be back home in Miami Beach where the weather will be hot and the women hotter. Life is good.*

This ascent of Kangchenjunga looked like it was going to be a big success for everyone involved. A gust of wind hit Rand, rousing him from his self-absorbed daydream. He shivered from the sudden burst of frigid air. *Wake up, Stupid*, Mother Nature said. He turned around and continued his trek up the glacier.

***

No problems at all. That can't be good. No doubt part of that was due to Rand's (father's) money and the fact that Torleif, not having to worry about a budget, had been given free rein to prepare for almost any eventuality.

The expedition included eighty Sherpas (both climbing Sherpas and base camp Sherpas), cooks, cooks' boys, three doctors and several guides who had Kangchenjunga experience. Phurba Salaka Sherpa was the chief *sirdar,* or head guide, and was the most experienced Sherpa sirdar to be had. *Even the toll booth collectors were cordial,* thought Torleif, referring to the bothersome, roving Maoist rebels who collected a toll for each head in an expedition.

I don't like *everything going right. It makes people complacent, and then they forget to pay attention.* The Himalaya had a way of pulling your pants down when you got complacent. When everything went according to plan, it nagged at Torleif and made him feel like something bad would happen. He hated that feeling, and although he brushed it off as soon as he noticed it, the feeling kept coming back.

Although they had had more snow than usual for September, the weather had not been too bad, and everything else had been in their favor. *Maybe I should take it easy, like Dane,* he thought. *Too bad about what happened. Seems like Shelly has helped him recover though.*

The sun hit the tops of Kangchenjunga's five peaks, and he paused a moment to look at their natural beauty. He chuckled to himself. *What does Schmiddie say? Kangchenjunga's like a nasty blonde—stunning and treacherous but worth it.*

"Stop! Everyone! Look!" a voice yelled, speaking Sherpa.

Torleif spun around, looking to see which Sherpa had cried out. At the end of the line, one of them pointed to his left. The other Sherpas looked in that direction. Others walked back to speak with him. Torleif watched as their conversation disintegrated into arguing and then laughing, with a lot of gesticulating. More Sherpas walked down and joined in on the commotion. Their volume began to increase, so Phurba walked down to see what was going on.

Phurba arrived, and the others shut up. Phurba and the Sherpa who had cried out continued to talk. He pointed and spoke rapidly to Phurba. Some of the Sherpas listened with rapt attention, but a few others laughed. The frigid air blowing from their lungs made them look like a bunch of men standing around smoking and arguing. The sight reminded Torleif of his friend Smokes, who had always smoked while climbing the Himalaya. *Wish he was on this climb.*

"Hold up, Rand," Torleif shouted, not wanting him to get too far ahead, as Rand was already about fifty yards in front of him.

Torleif watched as Rand turned around and held up his hands as if to say, *What the hell?*

Torleif called out, "Hold on while I check out what's happening."

Torleif headed back to where the Sherpas had gathered around. Phurba was speaking with all of them. Torleif arrived, and Phurba stopped speaking. Torleif saw that there were two distinct groups of Sherpas. One group looked apprehensive. The other group was smiling, and a few of them were even chuckling underneath their breath. Phurba shot those laughing a stern look and they stopped immediately. Only one Sherpa looked terrified.

Torleif liked Phurba. He had climbed with him several times and was glad he had been available for this expedition. He considered Phurba an exceptional climber and a fearless companion. This was his second climb with Phurba on

Kangchenjunga.

"What is going on?" Torleif asked Phurba, speaking in Sherpa. Although Phurba could speak perfect English, Torleif wanted to show his respect to the other Sherpas by speaking their own language in front of them.

Phurba nodded at the terrified Sherpa and said, "Lhakpa, tell him."

Torleif looked at the frightened Lhakpa and stifled a chuckle. *Wednesday's child is definitely full of woe.* Many Sherpas were named after the day of the week on which they were born. The name Phurba meant Thursday, Lhakpa meant Wednesday.

Unlike most Sherpas, Lhakpa was known to be a chatterbox while climbing. Phurba had put him at the end of the line, where he would distract fewer people. He had been jabbering away at Nawang, one of Phurba's deputies, when the snow far to his left rose up and walked.

"Did you see that?" he had asked Nawang. But instead of looking in the direction where Lhakpa was pointing, Nawang had looked at Lhakpa. By the time Nawang had looked over, the shadowy figure had melted into the snow again. Lhakpa had then raised the alarm for the others to stop.

With the cold wind blowing in his face, Lhakpa stood there and glanced at the other Sherpas. He felt embarrassed and had a nervous feeling in the pit of his stomach. *Did I really see anything? Maybe it was just my imagination.*

Forced to admit it now to the chief sirdar and the head expedition guide, he was not so sure. He was extremely grateful to the man with the funny name. He and his fellow Sherpas were being paid a lot more money than was usual for this climb. The rich Englishman had desired the best Sherpas available, and he had been honored to be included in that group.

His outburst had made some of his fellow Sherpas anxious

as well. *I'm not a capricious person. I'm a responsible climber. I take my job seriously. I have a wife and two children. Quit acting like a superstitious old woman,* he told himself. He stared down at the ground, ashamed.

"Tell him, Lhakpa ... *Now,*" Phurba said.

Lhakpa looked up at Torleif and attempted to speak. He was glad he did not need to use his broken English with the man.

"I, uh ... I think I ... saw something. The snow stood up and walked," he said. "Over there." He pointed to his left.

Everyone looked at where Lhakpa pointed but saw nothing other than the bluish snow of the glacier. The Sherpas kept staring in that direction as Torleif addressed Phurba.

"I do not get it. What is he talking about?" Torleif asked.

"Tell him the rest," Phurba said without looking at Lhakpa. Phurba had his back turned to the group and was standing a few paces behind Torleif in order to keep an eye on Rand. He turned back to look at Lhakpa. "Tell him."

Lhakpa gave him one of those do-I-have-to looks and Phurba's harsh look back was his answer.

"I thought ... maybe ... I saw the ... *Mih Teh,*" he muttered.

Some of the Sherpas started talking amongst themselves. One of them said, "The demon guards the entrance to *Beyul Demoshong.*"

Mih Teh? Demon? Beyul Demoshong? Torleif had heard these words before, and now he sought to recall their meaning, or where he had heard them.

He turned to Phurba, who was still watching Rand.

"Phurba, help me out here," Torleif said in English.

"Beyul Demoshong is a hidden valley of immortality on the slopes of Kangchenjunga. It is said by some to be guarded by a Mih Teh—a yeti. Some call it the Kangchenjunga Demon."

Phurba turned back to keep an eye on Rand. Lhakpa saw the

realization on Torleif's face and waited for his reprimand, but it never came. Instead, Torleif burst out laughing. He remembered hearing the story about Beyul Demoshong.

In 1962, a Tibetan Lama had led over three hundred followers into the high snow-covered slopes of Mount Kangchenjunga to 'open the way' to Beyul Demoshong. Most were never heard from again. The monk, Tulshuk Lingpa, was a special kind of Tibetan Lama known as a treasure revealer. The name Tulshuk Lingpa meant 'crazy treasure revealer.' *How apt,* Torleif had thought upon hearing the story.

Lhakpa did not know whether to feel ashamed or angry with the golden-haired Scandinavian. The Sherpas who'd been laughing at him before, now joined in with Torleif's mirth, increasing Lhakpa's mortification. Now he wished he had been chastised instead.

Torleif's laughter was not meant to be demeaning. He just thought the whole situation was absurd, a kind of joke. The only problem was, Lhakpa was not joking.

***

Rand wondered, *What's so funny?* He took a couple steps back down the glacier.

"Do you need some help?" Rand asked, yelling out.

Torleif waved Rand off without turning around to look at him. Rand was going to shout again but a noise from behind stopped him. He turned to look but saw nothing. He was about to turn back toward the Sherpas when he noticed movement in a dip in the terrain, fifty feet in front of him. The snow moved. The wind whipped up and the cold air bit at his face.

That's odd. He was sure there were no crevasses in this area. Crevasses were cracks that formed in glaciers. They could range from just a few inches across to over forty feet wide, and could be as much as two hundred feet deep. Usually they were less than that because the deeper layers of a glacier often compressed into a plastic-type state which could flow over and around most obstacles without cracking.

Rand walked down toward the bottom of the dip where he had seen the movement. Snow fell into a small hole in the dip and steam emanated from the orifice. He drew closer. He had the absurd thought that he had discovered a hot spring. *Don't be ridiculous.*

He reached the area, removed his pack and kneeled down to peer into the cavity. He brushed aside some of the snow at the outer edges, and the hole increased in size as snow fell into the widening gap. He leaned forward to look closer.

Shock.

He froze, seeing the yellowed, fang-like teeth in a giant, fully extended maw. His mind said *run* but terror gripped his body and it did not respond.

The monster jerked its huge head upward out of the snow cover, clamping its massive jaws on either side of Rand's face—engulfing it. He tried to scream but the extreme pressure of the beast's teeth crushing his skull prevented him from moving his jaw. His adrenaline had taken his breath away. His head felt like it would explode. The putrid breath of the beast assaulted his nostrils. Its tongue licked his lacerated flesh.

Rand struggled to release himself from the beast's vise-like jaws. The monster relaxed its bite for a split second to more forcefully chomp down and finish off its prey. In that moment, Rand broke free, wrenching his face away from the monster.

Blinded by the blood in his eyes, he attempted to stand. He pushed off the ground with his left hand. The creature bit into his forearm—*crack!*—nearly severing it at the elbow. Rand managed to stand, the jagged and torn flesh of his arm dangling from his elbow.

The severed brachial artery sprayed Rand's blood onto the snowpack. His face, now the consistency of hamburger, dripped blood all over the chest of his down jacket. The monster's savagery had produced another monster.

Rand's shrill, primal scream pierced the cold thin air. He staggered, his mangled arm spraying blood in random directions. Swiftly, the beast rose out of its snowy grave, like a reaper towering three feet above Rand. The monster's arm swung around Rand's neck, and snapped it, bending his head at an impossible angle.

The life of Rand was over.

CHAPTER 4

SIR RANDOLPH BARRINGTON, Sr., awoke hearing a cry of intense sorrow. He sat up in bed and realized the anguished sob had been his own. He thought it was odd, because he could not remember dreaming.

He looked at his seventeenth-century grandfather clock, which occupied the corner of his spacious bedroom. It had been a gift from Prince Charles for defending the heir apparent to the throne. Sir Randolph had stuck up for the Prince in the press when architects had attacked his book *A Vision of Britain: A Personal View of Architecture*.

Sir Randolph watched the pendulum swing, producing its faint tick-tock. Every time its golden disc swung to the right it caught the light of the full moon shining through his window. The first four notes of the Westminster Quarters chimed, confirming the time as 12:15 a.m.

His wife had died eleven years ago, and he was used to sleeping alone in his ornately carved wooden bed, an antique which had once belonged to King Philip IV of Spain. Even so, he still missed her body being next to his, especially when he awoke during the night. His bed companions of late were rare, unless he paid for it, and even then the experience was not that enjoyable.

Sex with his wife had been wonderful. He had loved her deeply. She had been with him before he was a 'Sir.' Try finding someone to love you when you are a knighted billionaire. It is a crap shoot, and all you shoot is crap. Money makes some things easier, but love is not one of them.

Still groggy, Sir Randolph thought about where Rand was climbing—Kangchenjunga.

A creeping feeling of dread began to spread across his being, and it only grew stronger as the seconds passed. He thought the idea that he would know what was happening on the slopes of a mountain over seven thousand kilometers away was more than preposterous—but somehow he *did* know. His little boy was dead.

And he began to weep.

CHAPTER 5

AN EERIE WAILING came from the sky above and terrified the Sherpas. Torleif heard the harrowing scream and its cessation, but it took him a second to determine from which direction it had come. They had all heard men cry for help before, but it usually did not curdle their blood. When the howl ended abruptly, they realized it was Rand and looked in his direction, expecting to see some sign of him. But he was gone.

Torleif took off running toward where Rand had been, following Phurba, who was well ahead of him, heading fast in that direction. Fast was a relative term. Running through the snow of a glacier in boots and crampons was about ten times harder than running with bare feet through soft white sand on a tropical beach. It was slower, crunchier, and nigh impossible to achieve any kind of speed, especially in the thin air of six thousand meters above sea level.

Two other Sherpas and the climbing doctor followed behind Torleif. The rest of the Sherpas were paralyzed with fear. All of them looked at Lhakpa, who noticed they had drawn closer together and further away from him. Everyone knew it was bad luck to see a yeti. They did not want any of his luck rubbing off on them. For his part, Lhakpa thought, *No one is laughing now.*

Torleif ran to where he had last seen Rand. Thoughts of Lhakpa's explanation raced through his head—*Mih Teh, yeti, Abominable Snowman, Kangchenjunga Demon*—more *likely a black bear or even a snow leopard. Both unlikely at this elevation. Yeti? Don't be stupid,* he chided himself. Running toward possible danger made him think of his wife and kids. He wished he was home.

Torleif arrived after what felt like an eternity. The bloody patch of snow shocked him and made his heart sink. He did not expect to see blood, especially not like this—scattered everywhere, helter-skelter. From the amount of blood splashed across the snow, Torleif knew Rand must be dead. *But then, where is he?*

Rand's pack sat a few feet away, undisturbed. Phurba walked up. He had quickly surveyed the area prior to Torleif's arrival. Both men were winded.

"He's gone," Phurba said.

"How can that be?" Torleif asked in English.

Phurba shook his head. "I don't know."

The three others arrived. The two Sherpas paled, staring at all the blood in the snow. The doctor was puzzled. Dr. Meritt was an experienced climber who was married to a Nepalese woman.

"Where is he?" Dr. Meritt asked.

"We need to start looking," Torleif said.

They all looked around but could find no crevasse or opening in the snow. Torleif sent each of them in a different direction. He went forward about thirty feet, looking around, then went from side to side in the hope that a broader sweep would reveal something he had missed, but all he could see was snow.

Torleif pushed down his rising panic. *Keep a level head,* he thought, knowing that overreacting would get him nowhere and might well lead him to make a bad decision.

The memory of Sir Barrington's voice invaded Torleif's thoughts. *Take care of my boy.* The admonishment resounded in his head and became all he could think about. That statement had been the last thing Sir Randolph had said before they had left his estate in England. *Take care of my boy.*

"Maybe he's under the snow somewhere. Get out your shovels," Torleif said to all of them. "Let's dig where we find the most blood."

All of the men broke out their small snow shovels and began digging into the moist, blood-soaked snow. The snow yielded easily at first, making them think they might be on the right track. They dug for a while, until all of them were tiring from the thin air and heavy exertion. Torleif stopped and stood up straight, breathing hard. The Sherpas in the hole slowed their pace, then stood up. They all looked at Torleif. The hole was deep enough that the edge came halfway to Torleif's thigh and up to nearly all the Sherpa's waists. The snow had become more difficult to dig into, and was more akin to ice. Torleif realized digging further was pointless.

"That's enough," he said to Phurba with a look of resignation. He did not want the Sherpas or Dr. Meritt to start sweating too much and risk hypothermia.

"He's gone," Torleif said. Then he thought, *But* where *has he gone?*

The Sherpas climbed their way out of the hole and sat down to rest. Torleif walked a wide circle around the spot where they had been digging, poking the snow randomly with a probing pole.

Torleif found a huge crevasse way off to the left of their planned route. With the Sherpas' help, and roped in, he inched forward to peer down into the crevasse, hoping to see if Rand had been dragged into it.

"What the ..." he muttered.

Torleif looked left, then right. The crevasse was different than any he'd ever seen before. In this particular section of it, the wall was completely flat and sloped slightly outward. *It would be easy to climb,* he thought. The sheet of ice looked like a glass wall.

"Phurba, I'm going in," Torleif said.

Phurba and the others helped Torleif, who scaled down about one hundred feet. The wall was flat and it seemed stable. He could not get over the weirdness of it. *Odd, like Rand's disappearance.* He looked down into the increasing darkness. Nothing. No sign. *No telling how far it goes.*

He knew it was over.

The Sherpas pulled Torleif out of the crevasse again. The big man fell to his knees, removed his helmet, and held his head in his hands. Every Sherpa there felt sympathy for the tall Viking.

The thought kept pounding in Torleif's head—*What happened to Rand?* He felt like he was going mad. It was one thing to have a client be the victim of an avalanche or sustain a high altitude cerebral edema or some other fatal injury, but to have someone vanish into thin air, leaving only a blood splotch behind, seemed impossible.

He felt like an evil magician had played a horrible joke on him. *What else can I do? Nothing.* He made the decision.

"The climb is over. Let's get back to the others," Torleif said. The others needed no more orders. They turned and started to head back down the glacier. Torleif looked at Phurba, then at the Sherpas who were further down the slope and who wanted no part of searching for a man they believed had been taken by the Kangchenjunga Demon.

"Wait a minute," Torleif said. He walked over to the Sherpa who had Rand's pack and dug out a little black box GPS. He was glad Rand had spared no expense. He handed the device to Phurba.

"Take it to where we were digging and turn it on. Leave it there. It will transmit our exact coordinates. Sir Randolph will want to know where his son was lost," he said.

He watched Phurba kneel down and place the GPS and knew there was not anything else he could do.

Torleif plodded back down the mountain, and questions swirled in his head. *How do I explain this to Sir Randolph? Was it a bear? How else could there have been so much blood?* Torleif stopped and waited for Phurba to catch back up to him.

"What did you see?" Torleif asked him earnestly, in English.

Phurba shrugged his shoulders and said, "Probably the same thing you saw."

"He was gone. I saw nothing."

"Right," Phurba said, holding Torleif's gaze.

Torleif thought he understood what Phurba was saying. Phurba would back him up, no matter who was asking.

"Okay. Let's go home," Torleif said with finality.

Phurba watched Torleif walk ahead of him. He knew how he felt. *Now he must go home and tell Rand's father,* Phurba thought. He winced, thinking of the last time he had told a Sherpa's wife her husband was dead. Following Torleif, Phurba continued his trek down to base camp without saying another word. Of course, he would back up Torleif's account of what happened to Rand if need be, but Phurba knew better. The fact was, Phurba Salaka Sherpa had seen *everything*.

The other Sherpas were listening to Lhakpa speak to Torleif and had been looking over at the spot where Lhakpa had glimpsed the yeti. However, Phurba was the sirdar and he had kept his eyes on Rand. Rand was their benefactor, not Torleif. Rand was the one paying out all the money. Money that would feed Phurba's family for many weeks.

He had seen Rand walk down the dip in the snowy terrain and remove his backpack. Phurba had lost sight of him as Rand kneeled down. Not seeing Rand, Phurba had started to move forward. Then, only seconds later, Rand had wrenched himself up, his face covered with blood, forearm dangling and blood squirting everywhere. Phurba had begun running toward him as Rand screamed.

A moment later came the instant that was now frozen in Phurba's mind. He had seen the monster and hesitated. The giant white beast rose up out of the snow like a hairy white wave, looming two feet taller than Rand, and swung its arm down, snapping Rand's neck. Then the beast and Rand had disappeared into the dip of the snowy slope.

Phurba had seen clearly what Lhakpa only had glimpsed—the Kangchenjunga Demon.

He was torn about keeping it from Torleif, but thought it best not to do something he might later regret. Seeing a yeti and talking about it brought bad luck. He would not speak of it to anyone now. He must get back home first.

***

The beast heard their sounds drift further and further away. He lifted his great head out of the snow and looked at the tiny figures in the distance. He squinted. He did not like the sunlight. The brightness hurt his eyes.

He stood up and pulled Rand's dead body from the snow, scarcely fifty feet from where the men had been digging. He shook off the icy snow like a Labrador retriever spinning water from its coat after setting down its feathered quarry in front of its master. Reaching down for Rand's booted foot, he scraped his fingers on a crampon and growled his disapproval, jerking his hand away. Repeating the action more carefully, he grabbed Rand's ankle and began to drag the body back across Yalung glacier toward the peculiar flat-walled crevasse, leaving a wake of blood trailing behind him.

CHAPTER 6

A WEEK LATER, Phurba said goodbye to Torleif at Suketar airport. Torleif grabbed a flight to Kathmandu, where Sir Randolph had a private jet waiting to bring him to England. The airstrip at Suketar sat high on a ridge above Phurba's village of Taplejung.

Taple was the name of a medieval king who had ruled the area, and *jung* meant 'fort,' hence the name, which meant 'Fort of King Taple.'

Phurba passed the large water reservoir on his way down to his village. Taplejung had cobblestone streets, government offices, a police post and a small hospital. It was Saturday and the village's weekend bazaar bustled with lots of local people and tourists looking for bargains. Phurba made his way through the colorful bazaar, picking up some gifts for his wife and two boys.

Taplejung was one of the jumping-off points for scaling Kangchenjunga. North of Taplejung, the Tamur river diverged into its tributaries—the Ghunsa and Simbua Khola, which could be followed to the Kangchenjunga glacier and the Yalung glacier, respectively. Southern base camp was on Yalung glacier.

Phurba had ascended Kangchenjunga more than any other living Sherpa or mountaineer.

He made his way down the cobblestones of Taplejung, wondering how to tell his wife what he had witnessed. She would not be expecting him back so early. He got to his front door, and like all faithful Buddhists, removed his shoes before entering.

Phurba and his wife, Sunita, belonged to the *Nyingmapa*, also known as the Red Hat sect of Tibetan Buddhism. Most Sherpas did. This was the oldest Buddhist sect from Tibet, and *Nyingma* literally meant 'the Old School.'

Nyingmapa was founded sometime during the eighth century by a monk named Padmasambhava. He was known as Guru Rinpoche—Tibetan for 'Precious Guru.' Guru Rinpoche was regarded as the second Buddha after Siddhārtha Gautama Buddha, the originator of Buddhism.

The Nyingmapa emphasized mysticism and worshiped local deities that had also been worshiped by the pre-Buddhist *Bön* religion. Bön had many shamanic elements, and the Sherpas, as a group, believed in hidden treasures and valleys.

They had monasteries, called *gompas*, inhabited by celibate monks and nuns. Sunita's brother, Chodak, was a monk in the ancient Diki Chhyoling gompa. The four-hundred-year-old gompa was said to house great reincarnated spiritual leaders. It contained a butter lamp that had been burning continuously since the gompa's original construction.

Phurba did not mention what he had seen on the Yalung glacier to any other Sherpas with whom he might work in the future. That would not be good for business. *May the Lord Buddha help me if one of the other sirdars hears that I've seen a yeti.* First of all, it was bad luck to see a yeti. And second, he might never again get another important job.

But he told Sunita what he had seen.

"You have to tell Chodak," Sunita said.

"I've only arrived home and now you want me to leave again?"

He did not want to go on another long trip. He wanted to stay at home, rest, and relax for a while.

Sunita persisted. "The reason for going to Chodak's gompa is well known."

"To whom? Meddling old women?"

"All the women of Taplejung and other villages know that if one sees the demon, they should report it at Diki Chhyoling immediately."

"All the women know," he scoffed.

She nodded her head.

"Of course they know. They're rumor-mongering gossips," he said.

Sunita had told him this many times in the past when the subject of the yeti had come up. He had always ignored it because he had never expected to see one. Sunita believed, though. When she was twelve, her uncle had seen the Mih Teh.

Her aunt had insisted her uncle go and report it to the monks at Diki Chhyoling, the gompa nearest to Kangchenjunga. This was something she'd heard all her life from female friends and relatives. Women who gossiped about such things as the Kangchenjunga Demon all knew where to go to report it.

Phurba did not want to act like an old woman who listened to gossip. But he was as religious as his wife, and he knew, deep down, that he must go.

Sunita told their neighbors the cover story that Phurba was going to see Chodak at the gompa simply to pay his respects and pray for their family's good fortune. Phurba would tell Chodak what he had seen and be done with it. *Let* him *decide if it's important*, Phurba thought. Still, Phurba wondered for what possible purpose the monks would want this information. What could they do with it, other than pray for Lord Buddha's protection? It was a mystery. A mystery for which Phurba wished he had the answer.

Phurba would experience many regrets in obtaining that answer and the resolution to that mystery would change many lives, including his own.

CHAPTER 7

SHELLY NEWTON HAD not been doing much field work for Nielsen Mountaineering lately. Planning her wedding to Dane for the last two months had taken up much of her time.

Dane seemed to get a kick out of listening to her talk about their wedding plans, and she had made an effort to include him in the important decisions, which varied from where the wedding itself would be held to which of three different shades of aubergine he preferred. She was so excited, and it was great to be able to share her excitement with Dane. Shelly had no one—no immediate family. She had been an only child and her parents had both died a couple years ago, before she and Dane had even met.

It made her sad to think that her father would not be able to walk her down the aisle, and that she would not be able to see the joy in her mother's face during the ceremony. She had had other boyfriends, and her mom had always hoped that one of those relationships would turn serious. But none of them had been the *one*. Upon each break-up, her dad would always try to cheer her up by saying, "Your other half is out there, Bean. And the other half always turns up."

She missed hearing his voice and being called Bean. Thinking about it brought up bittersweet memories. But her dad had been right. Her other half *had* turned up. She thought her parents would have loved Dane. Her dad had been a blue-collar worker and had worked for the railroad. Her mother had been a stay-at-home mom, and Shelly and her mother had always been close. Through thick and thin, her mother was someone she could always talk to.

And then, with little warning, her father was gone. He had suffered a fatal heart attack a week after retiring at age sixty-five. Her mother had been devastated. Shelly's parents had been high school sweethearts, and had been each other's best friends for most of their lives. When Shelly's mother was diagnosed with an especially aggressive cancer, Shelly had done what she could to help, but it was not enough. Her mother had died less than six months after Shelly's dad. *The victim of a broken heart,* Shelly thought.

Shelly spent the next year in a depressive funk, regretting the times she had felt herself to be too busy to visit or to call or to reply to emails. At least they had gotten to see her almost win the bronze in the 2010 biathlon. She had missed winning the bronze when a girl from Belarus had beaten her time by a couple seconds, but that did not matter. What mattered was that her parents had gotten to see their daughter achieve her dream of competing in the Olympics. Bronze-winner or no, Shelly knew her parents had been proud.

The thing that had pulled her out of her malaise was that she had started to train again. Her parents both had life insurance policies and they had left her a large inheritance, so the depression had not harmed her finances irreparably. Even so, she was glad to be closer to her old self, and to have something special to look forward to.

She had an uncle, her father's brother, and eventually, when she had felt nearly back to normal, had asked him to walk her down the aisle. He had said he felt honored, and accepted. It was not the same as having her father there, but he was still family.

Shelly pulled her Toyota SUV up to Leadville Discount Liquors. She parked, and continued talking excitedly on her mobile to her chosen maid of honor, Nancy Villarreal. At twenty-nine years old, Shelly realized she was not getting any younger, and the year that she had spent in a funk was time she would never get back. But right now, she was deliriously happy about planning her wedding.

"I'm telling you, Nance, they will love it."

"Thank God! Send it to me."

"I just emailed it to you. Can you make sure everyone gets a copy?"

"I definitely will. Let me look at it … Okay … I'm looking at it right now … Awww, that's a beautiful shade of aubergine!"

"I know, right? I'll talk to you more tonight after Dane gets home. I want to talk about some different dress styles I saw online."

"Okay, Shel. Talk tonight."

Pocketing her phone, Shelly walked down one of the aisles, grabbed a four-pack of Stone Ruination IPA, and headed to the checkout counter.

"Hi, Whit. Thanks for letting me know this came in. Dane will be pleasantly surprised." Whit took her debit card and Shelly punched in her PIN code.

"Buying beer *for* Dane. Unbelievable," Whit said. "Do you have any sisters?"

"No." The question stung a bit. She had always wished her parents could have provided a brother or sister for her. They had had her too late in life and had not been able to have any more afterward. *I will have* at least *three kids, though,* Shelly thought. "What can I say, Whit? I'm in love."

"Me, too," Whit said, flirting as he bagged the ale.

"Ah, go on now."

"You don't get it. Women don't buy beer for their husbands. Their boyfriends or *fiancés*, maybe. That's how they trap ya."

Shelly frowned. "Pretty cynical."

"Really? I got reason. My *ex* used to throw my empty bottles at me."

"Ouchie! Better luck next time, Whit," she said as she headed out. "Thanks again."

"Say 'hi' to Dane for me."

"Will do." She hopped into her SUV and sang with the Fleet Foxes all the way home.

CHAPTER 8

THE FIRST-CLASS luxury of a private plane did nothing to lessen Torleif's anxiety. It had been ten days now since Rand's disappearance, and he felt dread well up in him as Sir Randolph's Canadair CL-600 Challenger landed at Bristol Airport. The jet taxied off the runway, and Torleif saw a large, black limousine and its chauffeur waiting on the tarmac, ready to whisk him off to see Sir Randolph at once.

After disembarking from the plane, Torleif explained to the chauffeur that he had other business to conduct in London and would need a rental. A small white lie; he just wanted to delay facing his employer, not wanting to explain all over again the confusing incident on Kangchenjunga. *Driving will clear my head,* he hoped.

His employer, Sir Randolph, had become wealthy by buying and selling the one thing that cannot be manufactured—land. He had been at it since he was eighteen years old. Having inherited a couple million pounds from his barrister father, he downplayed his business acumen, but he was a shrewd businessman nevertheless.

He went on to found the Barrington Group, which owned

over four hundred companies. He had turned his father's two million pounds into well over three billion. Torleif, reading about Sir Randolph's exploits, had wondered, *How many millionaires turn themselves into billionaires?* He doubted it was an easy feat, or that many other people could have done what Sir Randolph had accomplished.

Evidently, the Queen had agreed. Years before, Elizabeth II had conferred the honor of Knight Bachelor on Randolph Barrington for his 'services to entrepreneurship,' and he was knighted by Charles, Prince of Wales, on August 2, 1986, with the investiture done at Buckingham Palace, making him *Sir* Randolph Barrington.

On his way out to see Sir Randolph, Torleif stopped in the village of Barrington and had lunch and a pint of stout at the local pub. He sipped his stout and recalled his first trip to Barrington Court several years ago.

It had been a Saturday, the day when Sir Randolph opened up his sixteenth-century mansion for tours. Torleif was waiting for Rand in the library, there to discuss Rand's plans to complete climbing the last six of the fourteen eight-thousanders. While waiting for Rand to arrive, Torleif had listened to the tour guide, who was outside in the large foyer speaking to his current passel of tourists.

"Barrington Court is what's called a Tudor manor house. Construction began around 1538 and was completed in the late 1550s. It was the first manor house acquired by the National Trust in 1907," the guide said proudly. "It was then leased to Colonel A. A. Lyle in the 1920s. The Lyles refurbished the court house, renovated the adjacent Strode House, and arranged for the design of the three formal gardens on the property. When their last descendants vacated the lease in 1986, Sir Randolph took it over."

"So the house is not named after Sir Randolph's family?" a middle-aged female tourist asked.

The guide's tone indicated he had heard this question many times before. "No … Sir Randolph had been looking for an old English estate to live in, and it was during this search when he found Barrington Court in the National Heritage List. The name is simply a coincidence."

Rand had already told Torleif the story of his father leasing the great mansion called Barrington Court. Torleif, listening to the guide, grinned. He knew that Sir Randolph got some sense of mischievous delight from having tourists assume the village of Barrington and Barrington Court were named after his family.

After his lunch at the pub, Torleif headed out of the village down Eastfield Lane and drove up to the guard shack on the right where Eastfield turns left and becomes Broadmead Lane. Inside the small building were two guards. One came out, holding a clipboard.

"Torleif Günner to see Sir Randolph," he said. The guard checked his clipboard, then turned back to the other guard without saying anything to Torleif.

"It's okay," the other guard said. He turned back to Torleif as the gate swung open. "Mr. Günner, just follow the winding road to the right and on up to the house. Park in front."

Torleif drove through, following the familiar path. The grounds of the estate were lush and well kept. Greenery, colorful flowers and foliage were everywhere. On his right was a fruit orchard featuring plum, pear and apple trees. He turned right on the main drive, skirting a small forest to his left. He crossed another drive and could see, in the distance, through the trees on the left, a large mowing tractor cutting wide swathes of grass.

Gardeners were everywhere, trimming trees and pruning bushes. The thought crossed his mind that the landscape crew could cut the grass and trim trees all day, every day for a month and still not finish everything. He rolled up the drive. The great mansion's many out-buildings stood off to the right.

Sir Randolph had renovated and restored Barrington Court and Strode House to their former glory with the kind of wealth only a billionaire could provide. A large parking area sat in front of the house for tourists to park in.

Off to the left was a great, ornate fountain that had been placed there by Sir Randolph after he had sought the National Trust's permission to build it. Torleif glanced at it while getting out of his car and remembered how odd he'd thought the motif was when he first saw it.

He had later found out that the fountain was in the style of the interior of the main house—native Gothic combined with French Renaissance elements. It featured several gargoyles spitting water in a counterclockwise direction. The water coming from the mouths of the gargoyles served to fence in a beautiful but frightened young maiden who stood in the center of the fountain. Both times Torleif saw it, it had reminded him of the ale that Lake liked to drink.

Torleif drove up, and could see a number of tourists walking around the grounds and a few others entering the Strode House Cafe, a tea room and restaurant located in the old brick stable house. He parked in front of the grand manse, and noticed Barrington's tall, thin butler waiting at the front entrance to escort him inside.

"Hello, Montgomery," Torleif said.

"Good afternoon, sir. Nice to see you again, however unfortunate the circumstances."

"Thanks, Montgomery."

"Sir Randolph is waiting for you in the library, sir. Come this way," and Montgomery turned to lead Torleif inside.

They headed through the great, towering oak door of the entrance into a spacious, high-ceilinged foyer. They went to the right toward another great room before entering the library. Torleif glanced around and marveled again at the evidence of Sir Randolph's wealth—the room featured Chinese vases, tapestries, and other expensive museum-like furnishings.

Upon entering, Torleif was reminded that Sir Randolph had one hell of a library. Expensive Persian rugs graced the oak floor, and floor-to-ceiling oak bookcases lined three of the four walls, filled with an assortment of leather-bound books. Each bookcase had a wheeled wooden ladder to accompany it, allowing easy access to the upper shelves.

Torleif turned and spotted his host. Sir Randolph rose from a tan club chair to greet him and shake his hand.

"I'm so sorry, Sir Randolph," Torleif said again, having already apologized to him once on the phone. "We did all we could. He just disappeared. We searched for hours but couldn't find any trace of him."

"I understand, son. Thank you, Torleif. Capital of you to come so quickly to speak to me before heading home. Please sit down," Sir Randolph said, motioning toward a matching leather club chair.

Torleif noticed a change in Sir Randolph. Although Sir Randolph was sixty-three years old, the last time Torleif had seen the man, he had exuded a certain charismatic youthfulness. Now that youthfulness was gone. *The death of his son has weighed heavily on him,* Torleif thought.

"Can I offer you anything? A drink, perhaps? Some food?" Sir Randolph asked.

"No food, but water would be great. Thank you." It was not

that Torleif could not use another drink. He could. He just did not want to spend any longer than necessary detailing what he had seen and felt responsible for to the financier of his failed expedition. Montgomery brought some bottled water and a glass on a polished silver salver. Torleif took the bottle but left the glass on the tray.

"That will be all, Montgomery. We don't want to be disturbed any further," Sir Randolph said.

"As you wish, sir." Montgomery walked off, drawing the library doors closed behind him.

Sir Randolph took a deep breath. He started to speak, and a change came over him. It was not anger; it was a controlled expression of will. The words he spoke were not a command, but they felt like it when Torleif heard them.

"I want you to tell me, again, everything you can about what happened to my son," Sir Randolph said.

Torleif started from the beginning of that fateful day's trek. He went over all he could remember. He had not seen any animal attack Rand, but he told Sir Randolph about all the blood they had found in the snow and his efforts, along with the efforts of the other Sherpas and Dr. Meritt, to search for Sir Randolph's son. He told him his son must have been attacked by an animal, probably a bear or, less likely, a snow leopard, as that would account for all the blood at the scene.

He decided not to mention Lhakpa's supposed yeti sighting, but told Sir Randolph everything else. Torleif finished his story after what seemed like an hour but in reality might have been closer to thirty minutes. When he finished, there was a lengthy silence from Sir Randolph. Torleif said nothing, knowing the respectful course of action was to let him think it over, but his own discomfort was increasing by the minute.

"I'm confused about something," Sir Randolph said. "You

said you were behind my son, but you didn't see him get attacked by whatever animal it was." It was a statement, not a question.

"That's right," Torleif said, dreading what was next.

"Why?" Sir Randolph asked.

"I had my back turned because I was talking to one of the Sherpas," Torleif said. He felt that Sir Randolph could see there was something he was not telling him.

"What were you talking about?" Sir Randolph asked.

"It wasn't anything important. It was just something silly," Torleif said, and then immediately regretted his choice of words. "I'm sorry, sir. One of the porters thought he saw something."

"What did he think he saw?"

Torleif paused, not wanting to talk about a foolish subject, but he could see that Sir Randolph would not be denied.

"A yeti," Torleif said.

Sir Randolph heard Torleif, but the admission provoked no visible reaction as he contemplated the porter seeing a yeti.

"Well, that's ridiculous," he said finally.

"Agreed."

"I'm going to ask you for a substantially large favor, Torleif."

"Yes, sir?"

"Would you please …" He trailed off. "Would you go back to find my son's remains and bring him home?"

Torleif sat for a moment, thinking. He did not *want* to go back, but he still felt responsible for his failure to protect Rand from whatever had attacked him, and he knew Sir Randolph would make it worth his while—probably even be generous. Ultimately, he knew he was just helping a bereaved father find closure, and it might do something to help him deal with his own guilt as well. He decided that was enough for him.

"You know there is no guarantee we will find anything," Torleif said.

"Yes. But I have to try."

"Okay. Then yes, sir. I'll help you."

"Thank you, Torleif." Sir Randolph paused briefly. "Now, for the difficult part. I want you to ask Nielsen to go ... Money is no object."

Getting Dane to go was another story. Torleif had asked him to join a couple of expeditions after the Annapurna incident, but Dane had always turned him down flat. He would not even discuss the matter.

"Sir, you know he's retired from climbing the Himalaya," Torleif reminded him gently.

"Yes, I know," Sir Randolph said. "But we're not asking him to summit, are we? Just to search for Rand."

Torleif thought it over for a moment. *That's true*, he had to admit. *Dane just refuses to lead summit expeditions. This will be a search party.*

"What do you think he will say?" Sir Randolph asked.

"Hard to predict," Torleif said. "He's getting married in seven months."

Sir Randolph grabbed a pen and a small notepad off the side table. He scribbled in it, tore off the sheet, and handed it to Torleif. Torleif looked at the number and was shocked. He looked at Sir Randolph, who grinned.

"Everyone has a price," Sir Randolph said. "And I'm a good guesser."

"No doubt."

Torleif thought he understood now why the man was a captain of industry and how it was he made things happen that changed the world. He stood to take his leave, and Sir Randolph shook his hand. Torleif strode to the library doors and opened them.

"Oh, Torleif," Sir Randolph called as he approached the door.

Torleif turned around. "Yes, sir?"

"Just out of curiosity. What was the Sherpa's name who thought he saw a yeti?"

Torleif thought a moment, puzzled by the odd question.

"His name was Lhakpa, sir."

"Ah, Wednesday," Sir Randolph said, nodding his head. "Have a safe trip."

Before getting in his rental car, Torleif called Dane, who was saving Brad on the cliff face.

CHAPTER 9

AFTER DANE GOT Brad down off the mountain, they hiked back to their rendezvous point, which took about two hours. Once there, a sullen Brad headed for his Lexus SUV and peeled away.

"Don't go away mad, Brad," Dane said aloud to himself while stowing his gear in the trunk of his car. "Just go away."

Dane started his Firebird and listened to the 350 engine rumble. He loved his car. It was colored a metallic royal blue with a silver racing stripe down the center. He had had it painted by his friend Tom Lockwood at Tom's custom paint shop over in Thornton, and it shined like glass.

He switched on the stereo system hooked up to his iPod. Hank Williams, Jr. crooned his 'Family Tradition' song. He sang along with Hank and enjoyed the drive home. After an hour, he pulled onto the road that led to his ranch house, still singing along to classic country. His ranch house was about five miles west of Leadville.

Leadville had an elevation of over 10,000 feet, making it the highest incorporated city in the U.S. It was the perfect place to live if you were a mountaineer. He had chosen it because its elevation gave him a head start at being acclimatized for the big mountain climbs. Now that he was out of that game, he and Shelly had a business teaching newcomers the basics of mountaineering. He had been doing it on his own for the past few weeks while Shelly planned their wedding.

His business consisted of teaching clients the basics of rock climbing or leading hikes up nearby Mt. Massive or Mt. Elbert, the latter of which had an elevation of 14,440 feet, making it the second highest mountain in the contiguous United States.

Some of those clients were climbers trying to get a head start on acclimatizing before going to do some of the more difficult treks around the world, such as those in the Himalaya. Since Dane had already climbed all of the biggest mountains in the Himalaya, half his time was spent answering questions about where his clients were headed.

He was thirty-five years old and had reached a point in his life where he wanted to have some kids to whom he could pass along the things that had been passed down to him from his own father and grandfathers. His Himalayan career had brought him fame and some fortune. Taking rich people on what were, for him, easy hikes and teaching them basic climbing skills paid the bills. *Life is good*, he thought as he looked briefly out over the Colorado landscape.

He pulled into his garage but left the car running a moment so he and Faron Young could finish singing 'Hello Walls.' After his performance ended and the song's music died away, he got out and grabbed a soft rag to wipe the dust off his prized automobile. He left the music playing and his dog, a Samoyed named Duke, came running in.

"Hey, boy, keeping Shelly busy?" He bent down to rub behind Duke's ears. Duke barked, happy to see him. "Ready, boy?" Duke barked again. Dane reached into his pocket and pulled out a rag and held it down for Duke to sniff. Before he had left that morning, he had marked the rag with the scent of lavender oil, doing the same to a ball which he had then hid. It was a game he played every day with Duke, using a variety of scent sources to make it challenging. Duke sniffed the rag, and took off to find the ball. Dane knew Duke would start out by ranging around the house, trying to pick up the scent.

Dane and Duke were part of a search and rescue team. They had trained together at the Canine Training Academy in Canon City in its five-day foundation class. Each day, Dane had made the two-hour drive to the Academy, where they had learned the basics of tracking and trailing.

Dane learned things like the difference between an air scent dog, a trailing dog, and a tracking dog. He had picked a Samoyed because he had had one as a child and because he thought it would be a good breed to use in case the rescue was in subzero weather.

Samoyeds had double-layer coats that could withstand cold far better than the coats of most other breeds. They were originally bred to hunt, herd and work in freezing conditions by a group of Samoyedic people called the Nenets, an Asiatic group of nomads on the Taymyr Peninsula in the Far North of Russia, where the temperature rarely got above freezing.

Dane found out the hard way that Samoyeds were not the easiest breed of dog to train, so he and Duke took CTA's foundation class three times. Dane bought the training manual used at CTA and continued Duke's training at home, working with the dog one hour every day for a year. He discovered that when he made the training more fun, Duke responded better.

Dane went the extra mile and enrolled Duke in avalanche dog training, too. All the extra work paid off, because, although Duke had been difficult to train, his dog proved indispensable during emergencies, when they might be searching for people in subzero temperatures or trying to locate skiers who had been caught in an avalanche.

Dane and Duke eventually became part of the Lake County Search and Rescue Team. In their first rescue, Duke showed his worth by finding a climber buried six feet deep in an avalanche up near Galena Mountain. A massive avalanche had trapped three of the four skiers who had been in the area at the time. They had thought the area was safe and were taken by surprise when the snow upslope began to shift. Each trapped skier had an air bag and an Avalung breathing apparatus, but one of the skiers' avalanche beacons had malfunctioned.

When Dane arrived with Duke, two skiers had already been rescued, but the other one had been buried for almost an hour. Avalungs reliably provided enough oxygen from the surrounding snow for about an hour, or sometimes a little more if conditions were right. But time was running out.

Duke went to work and found the buried skier within eight minutes. When they pulled the skier out, one of the other rescuers told him he was lucky to be alive, because his beacon had not been working and there had been no way for the arriving rescue workers to know where he had been buried.

"How did you find me?" the skier asked.

"Duke," the rescuer told him, pointing at the dog.

The man took one look at Duke, then broke down and wept. The man's outburst of genuine emotion and gratitude made Dane feel truly thankful for all the time he had spent training his dog.

Over the past two years, they had been called out to a number of search and rescue operations, and Duke had helped save a few more lives. They made a great team.

"Sweet ride," a voice said from behind Dane, as he wiped

the dust off his classic vehicle.

He turned around and saw his comely, blonde fiancée Shelly holding out a bottle of his favorite IPA. He loved the gargoyle logo.

"Whit finally got some in?" he asked.

"Yep. He called. So I picked it up to surprise you."

"Thanks, Sugarpop," Dane said. He grabbed the ale and took a sip. "Aaaahh, you ruin me."

"Goofball."

They were in love. She had told Dane that she had had her sights set on him from the first night she knew him, when they hit it off so well at the Silver Dollar. They had been together ever since, and Dane was a much happier person because of it.

His iPod started playing a new song, 'Just One More' by George Jones. Feeling mischievous, Dane put down his ale.

"May I have this dance?" he asked, holding his hand out.

"Yes, you may," she said, grabbing a hold of his hand. They began to waltz, dancing around on the garage floor. They had taken lessons at a dance studio in Lakewood following Shelly's suggestion that they try something new. At first, Dane had not wanted to go, but after a while he got into it and found he was actually pretty good at it when he practiced and set his mind to it. Morgan, their instructor, had said they were made for each other.

Dane gazed into his fiancée's eyes. "You know, it's funny. I hated this music when my dad was alive, because he would play it constantly. But I guess it kind of grew on me."

"I love it. And you."

They kissed. They would be married in seven months. They (mostly Shelly) had planned it for the two-year anniversary of the day they met. And Shelly was busy over-planning, like most brides-to-be. Duke bounded in with the ball.

"Good boy," Dane said. He crouched down to pet his dog.

Shelly saw the pride for his dog in his gaze. "Dane, he's so good at that. You're such a great trainer, you know that?"

Dane smiled back at Shelly. He got up and took her in his arms. And they danced, as lovers do.

CHAPTER 10

WHEN PHURBA FIRST arrived at the Diki Chhyoling gompa, he stood there humbled. The ancient gompa had a small stream that ran nearby, and the rushing water from it spun twelve prayer wheels. Phurba walked over to the prayer wheels and stared at them for a bit. He could see that the Buddhist prayer 'Om Mani Padme Hum' had been inscribed on all of them.

All Buddhists were familiar with this prayer. The Buddhists believed that repeating this mantra over and over brought to them the benevolent attention and blessings of Avalokitesvara, the Bodhisattva that was the embodiment of compassion.

He closed his eyes and silently repeated the holy phrase to himself, aware of the ground under his feet and the cool breeze flowing past him. Something fluttered by and Phurba opened his eyes to see a colorful blue magpie land on top of one of the nearby posts. He felt he must be dreaming, as he had never seen a magpie at this elevation before. The bird pecked at invisible insects with its red bill while Phurba watched. It paused and looked at Phurba, cocking its head as if to say, *What are you doing here?*

"Good question," he said aloud to the bird. "I should ask

you the same thing."

The bird did not fly off, but began to sing. Phurba smiled at it and left the stream to go inside the gompa. The magpie's high-pitched flute-like song faded into a dissonant rattle as Phurba walked farther away.

Inside, the life-size golden-faced statue of Avalokitesvara stared down at him from its dais among the ancient, reddish-orange painted interior. Phurba paused to pay his respects.

"Beautiful, isn't it?" a soft voice said from behind him.

He turned and saw his brother-in-law, Jinpa Chawa Sherpa, now known as Chodak Sherab Yeshe. All Buddhist monks changed their names to remind themselves of the changes they made in their lives.

Phurba smiled and Chodak smiled back. They had been friends since boyhood and had done much climbing together as adolescents. When Jinpa decided to become a monk, Phurba was somewhat surprised, but he did not question his friend's chosen path.

"Namasté," Phurba said. Namasté was the customary Buddhist greeting, used both for hello and good-bye. It was always accompanied by a slight bow and made with hands pressed together in front of the chest, palms touching and fingers pointed upwards. The term was derived from Sanskrit and, translated, meant, 'the divine in me bows to the divine in you.'

Chodak bowed. "Namasté. Come with me for some tea. You must be tired after your journey."

Phurba followed Chodak down a corridor to a small room with a low table. They sat down on the floor and Chodak poured some tea. Each sipped their tea silently, and Phurba began to feel somewhat uncomfortable. He wondered how his brother-in-law would react to what he would tell him. *I'm stupid to believe in old women's gossip. Why did I listen to Sunita?* He wished he was scaling Mt. Everest instead of sitting comfortably in the gompa with his brother-in-law.

"Are you troubled, my brother?" Chodak asked. The question roused Phurba from focusing on his internal doubts. Strength of purpose returned to him. *It must be this place. Do the right thing,* he thought.

"I have something I need to tell you," he said.

CHAPTER 11

ELSEWHERE IN THE gompa, a little shaggy dog lay sleeping in the corner of a small room. It woke up with a start and sat up, pricking its ears as though it were listening to something. The dog began to pant with excitement and cocked its head from side to side, a motion it coupled with some intermittent growling at the only other occupant in the room—a slight young Asian man, who sat in the lotus position, meditating. After a moment, the dog's excitement waned. It stared at the man for half a minute longer, then lay back down and became quiet again.

   The room was furnished with a single cot-like bed against one wall and a desk and chair on the opposite wall. It was clean and neat, with no windows. An aging cloth hung in the doorway, covering the opening. The walls were a mottled assortment of colors. They had been painted many times over the centuries, and various layers of paint had worn off at varying rates, giving the wall an antique patina of the sort Fifth Avenue interior designers would kill for.

   Despite the near-freezing temperatures outside and the frigidness of the air within the room, the man was lightly dressed, wearing only simple black clothes and a pair of black canvas shoes. The man sat motionless; not even a shiver or a breath could be detected. His only remarkable feature was a shock of white hair just above his forehead which contrasted with the rest of his jet-black mane.

After a moment, the dog sat up again. Then the mongrel stood up on its hind legs and remained in that position, completely still, for several seconds. The odd behavior still failed to get the man's attention. The dog began to turn clockwise, looking like some strange canine Baryshnikov, until it had performed a full pirouette.

After its dance, the animal lay back down, closed its eyes, and appeared to go back to sleep. Silence reigned for a few seconds until the dog jumped a foot off the floor, yelped, and bolted from the room—like it had been shot from a cannon.

The man reacted not at all to this commotion, but continued his meditation, still sitting in perfect stillness in the center of the frigid room.

CHAPTER 12

THE HIGH LAMA, Yangji Norbu Rinpoche, listened as Chodak relayed Phurba's account of the yeti attack. The diminutive monk had a shaved head and laughing eyes that exuded compassion. He had expected to receive such a story for some time, but not one accompanied by reports of a human death. *Is this the first one?* Yangji wondered. *Or only the first to be reported?*

Yangji knew that people went missing on Kangchenjunga all the time. Five climbers had disappeared several months ago. It was assumed that there had been an avalanche, but he had no proof of that. Every twenty years or so, during the time of the Sacrifist, the High Lama of Diki Chhyoling had to be more vigilant. Yangji knew now that this time might be upon them once more.

Chodak continued his narrative, relaying every aspect of the story he had heard from his brother-in-law. Yangji remained impassive while Chodak explained the witnessing and existence of a Mih Teh.

But when Chodak described the color of the beast witnessed by Phurba, the elder monk's impassive demeanor changed.

Nonetheless, Yangji listened thoughtfully until Chodak finished relaying Phurba's account and went silent, waiting for further instructions from the High Lama.

"Go and thank your brother-in-law for bringing us this news, but tell him not to speak of it to anyone else," Yangji said. "Impress upon him the need to be extremely secretive. Have him tell his wife that he was able to see you, and that you relayed everything to me, and the Lord Buddha blesses them."

Chodak nodded his understanding and turned to leave, but another thought had occurred to Yangji, and the Lama added, "One more thing, Chodak. Tell him that we may soon need his help regarding another matter."

Chodak nodded again and left the room. The High Lama sat for some time, lost deep in thought. He knew that, most likely, Phurba would keep the secret; it was harder to guess whether his wife would also keep the secret but that did not matter. *It is good that women talk amongst themselves. They are quite an alert system for their husbands' exploits.* Although the news of the Mih Teh had been expected for some time, what had been *unexpected* about Phurba's story was the color of the beast. *White.* This was not good news at all.

Yangji remembered reading about the white beast. Its existence had been foretold in one of the ancient Sacrifist manuals. All the Sacrifist training texts were written in Kusunda, a language passed down from an ancient people that some academics now believed were once part of a social ecology that had held influence over a much more widespread area, perhaps stretching from Pakistan to Sichuan in China.

Over the ages, their urban influence dwindled and their descendants took to the forests, where they became the unparalleled hunters known as the *Ban Raja,* meaning 'Kings of the Forest.' The Ban Raja were followers of animism—the worldview which held that non-human entities, like animals, plants, and even inanimate objects or other natural phenomena, could be inhabited by spiritual beings. They referred to themselves as *myahq*, a word which in Kusunda meant 'tiger.'

Kusunda was a language isolate, meaning it was unrelated to any other language on Earth. Outside of the Diki Chhyoling gompa, Kusunda only had a handful of fluent speakers left, and was considered a nearly extinct language. The secret Sacrifist texts contained the only known writings written in the Kusunda language, and only the High Lama of Diki Chhyoling, his successor, and the Sacrifists were permitted to learn the ancient language or to read it.

Over time, the descendants of the Kusunda or Ban Raja had been nearly wiped out as a distinct ethnic group. In the 2001 Nepal census, there were only one hundred and sixty-four Kusunda reported.

Yangji remembered reading about the *Qolom Qasigi Duktsi*, or Bad White Son, in one of the Kusunda Sacrifist texts. The prophecy proclaimed that the evil spirit guiding the qasigi duktsi would be 'difficult to tame.'

And we have not conquered the beast before he has killed a human, Yangji thought. A yeti had not killed a human in twenty years, but Yangji knew it had been bound to happen sooner or later, given the increase in climbers on Kangchenjunga.

The monk rose to his feet and headed outside to clear his thoughts with nature. He had a lot to think about. He walked over to the twelve prayer wheels spinning near the stream. Their whirring sound had always been pleasing to him.

He closed his eyes and began to chant the ancient prayer. "Om mani padme hum, om mani padme hum."

CHAPTER 13

"YOU'RE A KOOK, girlie! And I have no problems in *that* department, anyway," a would-be customer declared.

"Whatever. Good luck with your sex life," Lily McCrowley said aloud, after the man had left, slamming her shop door shut. *Why do people lie to strangers they'll never see again?* she wondered. She could always tell when people were lying. Her father had even nicknamed her *cailín fhírinne,* Irish for 'truth girl,' because she could always tell when he was stretching the truth.

After the last tinkle of the shop door's bell ceased, Lily noticed her other two customers. A woman and her six-year-old towheaded child had been examining just the right color of Chinese finger trap to buy, but now they were staring at her. Lily just shrugged and smiled.

The irate customer had come into her Chinatown shop some minutes before, and she had watched him out of the corner of her eye while he looked at things he clearly was not interested in. She knew he was lying when he came to the checkout counter to pay for a trinket that only cost a couple bucks and told her it was for his kid.

He was middle-aged and had kept looking behind her, his

eyes roving over the shelf where she kept her homemade remedies. She assumed he had come in for her best-selling item—a liquid aphrodisiac for men. Middle-aged women had been buying it for their husbands ever since Lily had first stocked it. When word had gotten back to her that her customers were calling it *O-my-agra,* she had laughed out loud. She had been buying it in bulk from an old Chinese doctor ever since. The aptly named Dr. Dong was eighty years old and still practiced Tantric Buddhism. Naturally, she assumed the man had come for Omyagra but was too shy to ask about it directly. So she had offered it to him.

A kook, huh? Tesla was a kook, too. She took the moniker as a badge of honor. Although she did not put herself in Tesla's company, it made her feel better that such intelligent people could be thought of so derogatorily in their own lifetime.

Lily knew she was not like a lot of other people. Most people thought she had a few peculiarities. But to her, they were everyday, ordinary peculiarities.

She did not believe in the lone gunman theory. She tended to be on the side of most, but not all, conspiracy theorists. In fact, she believed there was a conspiracy to discredit conspiracy theories by calling them conspiracy theories.

Cute, maybe even pretty, standing five foot two without shoes, she had curves in all the right places and shoulder-length black hair, green eyes and full lips. She owed her looks to her Irish father and Tibetan mother.

Lily was a self-proclaimed Catholic-Buddhist. Which meant that, as a Catholic, she often felt guilty, but as a Buddhist, she was okay with it because feeling guilty was just another life experience to be enjoyed. She loved Catholicism's rituals, the confessional, and the beauty of their cathedrals, and embraced Buddhism's philosophy of life. But she attended neither church nor temple.

Besides Omyagra, behind her counter there were all sorts of jars containing teas, herbs and other natural remedies. No ingredients from endangered animal parts, though; she was against that abhorrent practice. Out front on her curio shop's big picture window were the Chinese characters for 'remedy,' 补救.

She felt that those characters were most appropriate for what she was selling. She sold *answers*. Sometimes it was a piece of antique furniture; sometimes it was an amulet, crystal or potion. Her motto was: *Sometimes people just want an answer, and any answer is better than no answer.*

Her mother, Dohna, who had Americanized her name to Donna, lived above Lily's shop and came down to see her daily. Every day, her mother would come in to drink some green tea and read the latest news from Nepal. She received the Sunday edition of the Himalayan Times, mailed to her by her brother, once a month—which was okay because it took her a whole month to read the entire paper.

Lily wanted to show her how to access it online, but her mother told her she preferred the feel of the newspaper and did not care how old the news was. Today was no different. Her mother walked in around 11:00 a.m. with her tea in one hand and a new copy of the Nepal newspaper in the other. Lily knew it made her mother feel good to have a connection with her adopted homeland.

Her mother had grown up in Kathmandu. Her parents had fled Tibet when Donna was two, along with her brother and two sisters, near the beginning of the Tibetan Rebellion of 1959.

Donna's father, upon hearing of the Dalai Lama's departure, gathered up his family and fled with thousands of others to

Kathmandu, leaving almost everything behind. It had been a long, difficult journey, and one of Donna's older sisters had died in route. In Kathmandu, they had stayed with her father's sister and had started life over again.

Usually, Lily's mother would grunt, groan and make other odd noises while reading. Today she had not made a peep. Lily noticed her mother's silence while she was helping a Japanese woman who had come in for a dose of Omyagra.

"Can I mix it with his evening cocktail?" the woman asked.

"Absolutely. It's tasteless and he will never know the difference," Lily said, assuring her.

"Velly good. That will help keep his honor."

"Let me know how it goes," Lily said, waving as the woman left the shop. The woman smiled demurely and left through the shop door, its attached bell jingling. When the bell made its last little tinkle, Lily set her eyes on her mother. *Where's the grunting?* She walked over to the little table by the storefront window where her mother was reading so intently.

Lily did not watch the news, considering it propaganda. She did not read any U.S. newspapers. Once in a while, she would read her mother's newspapers just to keep up on Nepal's news so she had something to talk to her about. Her mother spoke three of Nepal's numerous languages—English, Tibetan and Nepali. Lily spoke Nepali with her mother to keep it sharp. Her Tibetan was only so-so.

She read the headline of the article her mother was reading and saw why her mother had been so silent. The son of a famous billionaire had disappeared on Kangchenjunga.

This kind of story would not normally have been enough to affect her mother, but it had happened on Kangchenjunga. Lily's father had been an experienced mountaineer who had vanished climbing Kangchenjunga with two others in 1992.

Their bodies had never been found.

Until then, she had enjoyed growing up in Port Angeles, Washington. As a child, her parents often took her hiking through the Olympic National Park rain forest. During those trips, her dad would regale her with stories about Bigfoot that made her laugh and feel scared all at the same time, even though she could tell he was stretching the truth.

She had climbed Mt. Rainier with her father when she was ten years old. It was the last thing she ever did with him. His loss hurt her deeply, especially not knowing what had happened to him. After he disappeared, they had moved to San Francisco to live near relatives.

She touched her mother's shoulder.

"Mama," Lily said.

Her mother looked up and Lily saw the tears in her eyes.

"It's back," her mother said.

Lily knew exactly what her mother was talking about. She shivered at the thought.

Lily went to her computer to get more current info. Online, she found another article about the son of billionaire Sir Randolph Barrington being killed on Kangchenjunga by a bear, and being dragged off before his body could be recovered by his climbing crew. It contained a blurb, quoting his father, Sir Randolph Barrington, soliciting Sherpas for an expedition to find his son's remains. The article went on to say he was attempting to hire another famous mountaineer, Dane Nielsen, to head the operation.

They don't have any idea what they're up against. Who's this Dane Nielsen? I should warn him. A light bulb went off, and she thanked Jesus and Buddha for Google. *At the very least, I should tell him it's not a bear.*

CHAPTER 14

TORLEIF DROVE HIS Range Rover rental up the drive toward Dane's home while thinking about the climbs he and Dane had made together, and the times he had saved Dane's life—or vice versa. When you climbed together for a long time, it was bound to happen sooner or later.

Torleif knew he would do anything to help Dane if Dane asked a favor of him, and he knew that Dane would most likely help him since he had asked. It did not make Torleif feel better about dragging Dane into this. *I hate to use the friend card.*

Dane walked out of his home, which on the outside looked more like a mountain lodge with a standard rustic wood exterior. The sun set low on the horizon. Torleif exited his car and they gave each other a big bear hug.

"Good to see ya, B.G.," Dane said, grinning. B.G. stood for 'Big Guns.' Torleif had massive arms.

"You too, Lake Eyes," Torleif said, using Dane's full anglicized Ojibwe name. Torleif stepped back and looked Dane up and down. "Have you gained some weight?"

"Your mother," Dane shot back.

"Apparently guiding executives around some little tiny hills has made you more than just soft in the head."

Dane laughed and slapped Torleif on the back.

"Come on in. Shelly is looking forward to seeing you," Dane said.

Climbing the front steps, Torleif noticed two Ojibwe dreamcatchers hanging from the posts that supported the house's huge covered porch.

"Need protection?" Torleif asked, nodding at the dreamcatchers.

"My mother sent them to me. A little extra protection never hurts," Dane said, winking at Torleif.

Torleif had known Dane for fifteen years and had been climbing with him off and on for most of those years. They were both alpine-style experts, but they were not snobs, and had guided expeditions as well. He had not seen Dane since June of 2011, right before Dane's last climb on Annapurna. Dane had asked Torleif to be part of that expedition, but family matters had prevented Torleif from joining.

He knew the Annapurna incident was the reason Dane no longer went on Himalayan climbs. Dane had called him one night about two months after it had happened. Drunk and morose, Dane had ranted about how he blamed himself. He confessed to Torleif that while climbing the mountain he had disregarded signs of a possible avalanche because the financier of the expedition insisted Dane was wrong, persuading him to continue leading the climb.

When the avalanche hit, three people, including the financier, died. The Sherpas there knew it was not Dane's fault, but Dane felt that he had allowed himself to be talked into taking an unnecessary risk. A month after his drunken phone call, Dane had decided not to tempt fate any longer. Since he had made enough money to retire, he hung up his Himalayan crampons.

"Thirsty?" Dane asked, as he showed Torleif into the family room.

"Here you go," Shelly said, walking into the room from behind them. Torleif turned around, smiled and took the chilled glass of aquavit she offered, giving her a one-armed hug. He took a sip of the caraway-flavored drink, his favorite.

"Mm-mm, life's good. Feels like home," he said.

Torleif had met Shelly several months before, when he and his wife Antonia had paid Dane a visit prior to the Kangchenjunga expedition.

"Well, have a seat and tell us what's up with your mysterious, out-of-the-blue visit," Dane said.

Dane and Shelly sat together on their deep burgundy sofa. Torleif sat down in a matching chair. He looked at Dane and was about to launch into his story when the phone rang at a side table. Dane held up a finger, signaling Torleif to wait, then leaned over and answered it.

"Nielsen Mountain Climbing," he said. "This is him. … Okay. … Yes. … I didn't know him … Okay …" Dane listened to the caller.

Torleif stared at the blaze raging in the over-sized fireplace. His gaze traveled above the mantle. On the wall hung a lot of pictures of Dane with other climbers—Smokes Mitchell, Hank Schmidt, Tug Sanders, himself, and many others he also knew, either personally or by reputation.

On the other walls were Native American artifacts. A flag Dane's mother had given him, from the American Indian Movement was the most notable. It had four differently-colored vertical stripes—black, yellow, white, and brick red—going from left to right. In the center was a brick-red logo consisting of the profile of an Indian head and the two-fingered peace sign, the two fingers representing the head feathers.

Torleif remembered what Dane had told him about his parents over the years. They had been hippy radicals in the late 60s and had met each other at the Wounded Knee incident of 1973, where they had been part of the protest movement. Dane's brother was conceived during the protest, and his mother soon discovered she was pregnant. Dane's dad had been raised Catholic, so the pregnancy put an end to their radicalism. They found the closest Catholic Church to Wounded Knee in Rapid City, SD, and were married by a young priest at the Church of Michael the Archangel.

Dane had arrived seven years later. He was half Ojibwe. Dane's dad had some Native American blood as well, but Torleif could not recall if Dane had ever mentioned which tribe. He had said his dad was a Viking, like Torleif.

Dane's parents moved to Boulder, CO, where Dane was born. His dad got a job working for the Coors Brewery. As Dane grew older, his dad, brother, and sometimes his mom would go hiking or climbing in the Rockies, which was how Dane became involved in mountaineering.

Dane sounded like he was politely trying to finish up with a telemarketer. "Okay. Listen. I'm sorry for your loss. ... I bet your dad was a good climber, but what can *I* do for *you*?"

Dane listened to the other person and smiled. He looked over at Torleif, his expression amused. "Okay, what can you do for me, then?"

Dane's smile disappeared. "Yes, he's here. How did you ..."

The caller interrupted Dane, and he glanced at Torleif and shrugged his shoulders.

"You don't say ..." Dane shot another look at Torleif. "Really? Oh, well, there are no worries there, Miss. I'm retired. But why are you so concerned?"

Dane listened for a couple more minutes. He rolled his eyes as though he thought someone was pulling a prank call on him. "Did Smokes put you up to this?"

Torleif listened, eyebrows raised, as the call went on and on. "All right, thanks, Miss McCrowley … okay, Lily. Say, listen, *as you apparently know already*, I have company here and I'm awfully busy but thanks for all that information … I'm sorry. I don't have the time right now. Okay … *Okay*. Bye."

Dane hung the phone up.

"Who was that?" Torleif asked.

"Some crazed girl," Dane said. "So!" His voice turned artificially cheerful. "Sir Randolph wants me to go with you to Kangchenjunga to search for the remains of his son, right?"

Torleif stared at him with his mouth open. Dane's face fell.

"Well, maybe the caller wasn't completely nuts," Dane said.

"Who *was* that?" Torleif asked again.

"You ever heard of a climber named Roger McCrowley? Probably from the early nineties?"

"Yeah, sure. I climbed with him once on Lhotse. Very skillful, super quick. Good climber." Torleif paused to dredge up details; he had not heard that name for a long time. "Went missing on Kangchenjunga, I think."

The words *missing on Kangchenjunga* stung Torleif even as he uttered them.

"Right. Well, that call was from his daughter. She told me about her father being lost on Kangchenjunga and wanted to warn me against going there. That wasn't all she said. The rest was crazy stuff … but is that truly why you're here? You know I've quit the Himalaya."

Torleif told Dane what had happened on the climb with Rand Barrington. He omitted the part about Lhakpa's supposed yeti sighting. He told Dane some animal, probably a bear, had dragged Rand away, but admitted he was mystified at how fast the animal and Rand had disappeared. Torleif told Dane he felt responsible, and noticed Dane's frown. He went over everything just as Sir Randolph had asked him, and summed it up by saying, "It's not like we're summiting. Rand's disappearance occurred at around 6,000 meters."

Torleif handed Sir Randolph's offer to Dane. Dane and Shelly looked at the little sheet of paper. Torleif added, "He doesn't only want your skills as a climber. He wants a good tracker. I don't know if he knows about Duke, but he sure seems to be well informed in general."

"You've got to be kidding," Shelly said, still staring at the small piece of paper.

"I can assure you, Sir Randolph doesn't kid around," Torleif said.

"With the weather, there won't be anything left to track. Besides, it would be best to have a cadaver dog," Dane said.

"You know of one?" Torleif asked.

"Yeah. Lolo and Snoops," Dane said.

"I completely forgot about them."

"Who's Lolo?" Shelly asked Dane.

"Lolo is the guy with Snoops. Snoops is a cadaver dog. A damn good one, too."

It was not often that Lolo and Snoops were used. Because of the extreme conditions of the Himalaya, most deceased climbers were left wherever they perished. But when the searching was doable and the recovery efforts were backed by money, it was a different story.

Lolo and Snoops had found the three dead bodies in Dane's ill-fated Annapurna expedition, and Torleif noticed that Dane seemed uneasy at the idea of bringing them in.

"This money is Dane's whether he's successful or not?"

Shelly asked.

"Yes," Torleif said. "Well, Lake?"

Dane took a deep breath and exhaled. "That's a lot of money. I'm not sure I'm *worth* that kind of money."

"Doesn't matter what you think. It's what Sir Randolph thinks."

Dane turned to his fiancée. "What do you think, Shell?"

"The offer sounds too good to be true," she said. "And when something sounds too good to be true, it probably is. No offense, Torleif."

"None taken," Torleif said.

"It won't take that long. I'll be in and out quickly. No big deal. We can do a lot with that kind of money." It sounded like Dane was trying to persuade himself as much as his partner.

Shelly noticed it, too. "Okay. It's up to you. I've told you what I think, but the final decision has to be yours."

"Can't pass it up, then." Then, to Torleif: "I'll do it."

"You mean, *we'll* do it," Shelly added.

"Really?" Dane looked from Shelly to Torleif and back again, his expression surprised. "What about planning the wedding?"

"You don't think I'm going to let you out of my sight before we get married, do you? Think again, Mr. Nielsen. I'm going. We'll only be climbing to around 6,000 meters. It'll be like when we climbed Denali together," she said, using the Koyukon name for Mt. McKinley. "Remember, *you're* the one who said, 'No big deal.'"

Torleif grinned as Dane started to speak, then reconsidered.

Dane looked at Torleif. "You see what I have to put up with?" He leaned over and gave Shelly a smooch. "Okay. No big deal."

CHAPTER 15

CRUNCH! BLOOD SPRAYED across the icy snow, giving the landscape the appearance of a red and white Jackson Pollock painting. The beast's razor-sharp teeth chomped with ease through the man's thigh bone, his guttural screams lapsing into gasps for air.

The beast tore into his prey's belly and began devouring the man's vital organs, hoping to pacify his voracious hunger. Feeding on the guts would make him feel satisfied and content, the way most people felt after eating a T-bone steak. Guts were comfort food.

Aching with hunger, he ravaged the viscera, blood splashing in every direction. The beast had not eaten for days, and hunger pangs drove him. After gorging awhile, he began to wonder why his aching hunger was not dissipating, and he paused his binging.

He considered the matter, and then the demon heard some faint sounds off in the distance, distracting him for a moment. He lifted his enormous head up to listen, but was interrupted as his meal came back to life and started to shriek again. He looked down at the terrified man and tried to lift his arm to silence him but found that he could not move. This puzzled the beast.

The sounds in the distance intruded again into his awareness. The beast ignored the man's anguished cries for a moment, attempting to discern from what direction the sounds were coming from. The man's screams made it difficult. He tried again to move his arm and, successful this time, he raised his giant clawed hand to stifle the cries of his zombie-like lunch. However, the man had disappeared. The beast looked up to see the man hopping away on one leg, guts trailing behind him.

If he had known how to laugh, he would have. Instead he just grunted his bewilderment and wondered how his food could get away in such a state. The monster reached down to grab some of the entrails and stop the man, but as he reached down they disappeared from sight. He looked up for the pogoing meat-stick, but he was gone too.

The beast awoke from his dream.

Dreams confused the beast. He had few other thoughts about them. He listened for the sounds that had intruded on his slumber. He realized the sounds came from the two-legged creatures that were easy to kill. They tasted good. He roused his muscular eight-foot frame and stood up, rubbing the sleep from his eyes. Breathing deeply through flared nostrils, he felt the promise of food in the pit of his stomach.

Even underground, the giant beast could sometimes hear prey moving above him, and he knew the sounds he was hearing now belonged to men. Men were oblivious of being tracked, especially at night. The beast could easily sneak up and crush them—could kill them before they even *saw* him, in most cases. He preferred to prey on humans. Other animals were harder to catch in the snow. They were more nimble, and could smell the beast's approach unless he came from downwind.

It had been a week since he had last eaten. The bones and

tattered clothing of Rand Barrington lay on the floor of the large cavern room. Four torchlights gave the scene the eerie look of a cannibal's dungeon. By each torchlight was a tunnel that led to one of the cave's exits.

The scent of remains filled his nostrils. The beast hoped there would be fewer men this time. Although he did not fear humans, he felt it better to not be seen by them. Something about humans reminded him of the Others. Anxious to kill and eat, the beast headed toward a tunnel exit.

He began to lope through the pitch-black tunnel, making his way unerringly through the passageway to the exterior world. Though his eyes were capable of seeing in unusually dim light, he did not need them to find his way through the dark tunnels, having traversed them from infancy. He could find his way with his eyes shut if need be.

The cavern-like rooms, lit with torches, provided the only light in the tunnel system. The beast used the lighted rooms as places to eat, but he left the torches alone. They had been lit by the Others, whom he feared. The Others were different, and the beast wanted no contact with them. Sometimes they came as the beast slept, lighting new torches or removing any remaining animal bones upon which the beast had feasted.

He neared the exterior world and felt a quickening of his pulse. The bloodlust intensified within himself. He arrived at the tunnel's end, the exit blocked by snow and ice. His massive hands tore into the snowpack with sharp, one-inch claws, shredding the ice like a monster blender.

Nearing the surface he felt the air temperature drop. His pure white coat of hair protected him from the severe cold and his physiology accommodated sharp changes in temperature with ease. The beast paid no mind to the internal changes. He only had one thought. Soon, he would eat.

The beast broke through the outer ice wall, creating an opening on the flat-walled crevasse Torleif had scaled down looking for Rand. With his sharp claws the beast easily climbed up the icy wall to the snowy slope above.

Above ground it was still dark, which was how the beast preferred it. At night, he did not have to hide in the snow. Seeing the two climbers in the distance was easy because of their headlamps, which illuminated the snow in front of them. He decided he would take the one from behind first.

CHAPTER 16

JOSEF DAHLBERG AND his long-time friend Alex Reinhold were German alpine-style climbers. They climbed without supplemental oxygen and carried all of their own equipment. Purists in the extreme, they felt disdain for expedition-style climbers and even for other alpine-style mountaineers who associated with expedition-style climbers.

They did not ever pay Sherpas to carry equipment for them. If mountaineers were not physically and mentally able to climb the toughest mountains in the world, like the eight-thousanders, without help, Josef and Alex thought they should go climb Mt. Kilimanjaro or something even less difficult.

For Josef and Alex, it was all about being accountable for their own ascent. This meant climbing with each other and *with no other help*. It gave them a sense of accomplishment and satisfaction. In their view, those who paid Sherpas were relying on someone else's skill and help to make it to the summit.

In their opinion, expedition-style climbers had ruined the field of mountaineering. Mt. Everest had become overcrowded with rich part-time climbers who could not have summited even lesser peaks on their own. It was pathetic. Paying Sherpas to help them make it up the mountain proved nothing but the considerable skill of the Sherpas and the depth of the part-time climbers' pockets.

Another sad fact was that Chomolungma, as the Sherpas called Everest, had become scattered with litter. A recent effort at trash removal had brought out about eight tons of garbage—all of it left behind by expedition-style climbers. The alpine mountaineers packed out all of their own trash.

Josef and Alex knew Sherpas took advantage of the rich climbers, but who could blame them? A Sherpa could be supporting not only his own family but also his extended family. By helping expedition climbers, they made good money that went a long way toward feeding their families for some time. It was a tough job carrying heavy equipment for clients in one of the most ruthless environments in the world.

For these reasons, Josef and Alex customarily made their base camps away from the main base camps used by expedition climbers.

It was 10:30 p.m. They had just left their base camp and begun their climb up the Yalung Glacier. Nighttime was a common start time when climbing in the Himalaya. The lower temperatures ensured avalanches would be less likely to occur.

This was especially important when climbing mountains like Kangchenjunga. Unlike Everest, Kangchenjunga did not have stationed *avalanche doctors*—experts that could tell when an avalanche might be imminent. This made it a more risky mountain to climb. Experienced mountaineers such as Josef and Alex usually only climbed through the night and early morning to minimize risk.

Josef and Alex trekked through the snow and up the slope. They had started well before the expedition climbers below them. Josef was twenty feet behind Alex. A shuffling noise behind Josef interrupted his concentration on climbing. He turned around and his LED headlamp flashed the area like the beam of a lighthouse. The only thing visible was his own frosty breath in the headlamp's light path. A frigid burst of wind hit him from behind. *I'm imagining things,* he thought. The temperature of the air was well below freezing.

Josef switched the headlamp to wide-angle mode and lit up a bigger area. Nothing was unusual or out of place, except for their own footprints. Far below, the lights belonging to the headlamps of climbers moving around the expedition base camp indicated to him that they were preparing to start their own trek up Kangchenjunga. His wariness bothered him, as it was unusual for him to be nervous about anything. He'd heard about Rand Barrington's death by a possible bear attack. Although it was surprising for animals to attack climbers at this elevation, he was armed, just in case.

He turned back, saw Alex up ahead, and continued his trek. After walking several more feet, the shuffling noise came again from behind. He quickly jerked around, his headlamp still on wide-angle mode, and took a couple steps back down in the direction from which he'd come.

Half-turning back toward his friend, he called out over his shoulder, "Alex!"

But there was no immediate reply from his partner. Josef continued to survey the snowy landscape. He kept turning his headlamp to and fro, searching the area for any movement, but saw nothing.

"What the hell?" He knew he wasn't imagining it.

Turning his head again back upslope toward Alex, he called out, louder this time, "Alex!"

No response.

Dread came over him. He turned slowly around to look for

his climbing partner. The light of his headlamp flashed across the bloodied face of Alex, who stood but five feet away. Deep gouges across his cheeks oozed blood, and his left eye was missing. Alex staggered toward him.

Josef freaked out. *"Sheisse!"*

Alex moved his mouth, trying to speak. A gurgling noise was all that emanated from him. Josef noticed his friend's throat had been slashed, and gushed blood. He panicked as blood spewed from his friend's choking coughs and splashed onto his own face, warming the spots it hit. Alex reached out for his boyhood friend and lost his balance. He gasped his last breath as he fell into Josef's arms.

Josef knew Alex was dead. He laid him down on the snow. Looking into his friend's blank right eye, Josef heard a deep, low growl. A chill that had nothing to do with the weather overcame him. Nearly paralyzed with fear, his thought went to his holstered gun.

Josef moved his hand to draw his gun. Looking up slowly from his friend's body in a long drawn-out movement that would hopefully not provoke a hungry bear's rage, the shock overwhelmed him. The thing staring down at him intently from only a few feet away was not a bear. His headlamp flashed into the monster's blazing eyes, blinding it briefly. It roared and charged. Terror gripped Josef as he frantically tried to draw his gun.

"Oh, fick mich!"

He struggled to undo the snap holding his Walther PPX in its holster. The beast's clawed hand came down across his neck.

Josef felt nothing.

He was surprised, not even a sting or slap across his neck. *Did the beast miss me?* His body collapsed and fell into the snow. The icy snow on his cheek turned warm as blood from his wound pooled near it. He became light-headed and drifted in and out of consciousness. His life drifted away, but he was unconcerned. The pain disappeared. He sensed his right leg being hoisted up and his body being dragged through the snow.

His headlamp shone briefly on the dead eye of Alex, who was being dragged along beside him. Josef was glad his friend was with him.

A light snow began to fall. Each snowflake made a musical note upon hitting the ground, producing an ethereal melody.

The whole scene was glowing. *It's not night at all*, he thought as the lyrical notes continued all around him. He wondered why a large white rabbit was helping him and Alex across the snow pack. He passed away thinking, *How silly life is to have such a thing as death.*

CHAPTER 17

PHURBA ARRIVED BACK home and did as Chodak had instructed. He explained everything to Sunita while eating her *rikikul,* a Sherpa dish made of potato pancakes served with nak (female yak) butter and hot sauce. In between bites of his wife's tasty food, he told her that Chodak had relayed everything to the High Lama.

"See. I told you they would want to know," she said.

"But *why* do they want to know?" he asked, expecting no answer.

Sunita shrugged. "Maybe they pray to Lord Buddha for help."

Phurba was religious, but not stupid. *Then why would they need my help?* he wondered.

"Mmm, this is good," Phurba said, wishing to change the subject.

"I haven't said anything about the sighting to any of my friends," Sunita said. She knew if she did, it would get around and hurt Phurba in his chosen profession as a Sherpa sirdar. "However, Lhakpa's wife not only told me everything he saw, she's spreading it around to anyone else who will listen. Of course, he saw a great deal less than you."

"Okay. Let's talk about something else," Phurba said.

Phurba knew his wife could tell that something had been bothering him ever since he had arrived home. She just did not know what it was. The last thing Chodak had said nagged at Phurba. *The High Lama may need your help soon.* If so, why? How could he, an ordinary sirdar, help?

The door burst open and Phurba's two boys, Lopsang and Ringbo, aged twelve and ten, tumbled into the room. They were arguing. Phurba was grateful for the interruption. Lopsang held a black and white futbol over his head, and Ringbo was trying to grab the ball without success.

"What's going on here?" Phurba asked. The two boys quieted down at once.

"He won't let me kick the ball or let me play with it," Ringbo said.

Phurba gave Lopsang a stern look. "Sang?"

"But, Pop, he hogs the ball too!" Lopsang said.

"You can play together, or shovel some nak dung, since you have so much energy to fight," Phurba said. The boys looked at each other, resigning to cooperate. Lopsang handed his brother the ball. "Now go outside."

Seeing the boys skulk off made Phurba smile and momentarily forget his dilemma. Soon, though, he started thinking again about how he could possibly be of service to the monks. *Monks don't go on expeditions. At least, I don't* think *they do.*

"You think they may need your help?" Sunita asked.

"What?" Phurba asked, surprised. "Are you a mind reader?"

"Something is bothering you, I can tell. When have you not finished a plate of my rikikul?"

Phurba laughed. "You're right. I'm concerned about it. I can't figure it out, either. Chodak told me the High Lama might need my help. When I asked him why, he said he had no idea. I feel in my gut the Lama knows about the existence of the yeti. What else he knows, I can't even guess."

"Do you think they'll ask you to help locate it?" Sunita asked.

"The thought crossed my mind. I hope I'm wrong. Why would they?" Phurba asked.

Sunita shrugged. Phurba just hoped that, if the High Lama did need his help, it was not in the capacity of looking for the Demon. *I love the Lord Buddha, but that is* not *something I would like to be doing.*

However, he had the awful feeling that this might be exactly what he would be called upon to do. The thought of such a job gave him chills on the back of his neck that then traveled down his spine and ended at his feet.

"Let's hope that's not what they want," Sunita said.

"Agreed. Let's pray," Phurba said, smiling at her.

Phurba knew his job had always been risky, especially when he was guiding inexperienced climbers. He had risked his life proving that fact. He had generally been unafraid despite the risks, but he was careful and did not take unnecessary chances. But searching for the Demon? No, thank you.

His mobile phone rang. He looked down and saw that it was Prakash, owner of one of the main expedition agencies Phurba liked to work with. *Good. Some new work to take my mind off things.*

Little did he know.

CHAPTER 18

HIGH LAMA YANGJI Norbu Rinpoche sat on a dais in the gompa's meeting hall. Usually reserved for public services, the room was now entirely empty save for Yangji himself. He waited for someone important—Dzangbu Lingpa Rinpoche—the Sacrifist.

He thought back twenty-five years to when he had first met the boy, who was now known as Dzangbu. Yangji had been part of a legation of three monks who'd gone to see a young boy named Tashi at the home of his parents.

Tashi was one of a list of six boys (all named Tashi) who were possible candidates to be identified as the next reincarnated Sacrifist. Yangji had been the head of the delegation, charged with identifying the correct candidate.

The three monks had been sent to Kathmandu by Chonyi Tulku Rinpoche, who was the High Lama of Diki Chhyoling at the time. Chonyi had had a dream about the reincarnated Dzangbu. In his dream, he had envisioned a young boy with a red, blue, green and yellow *yungdrung* on his forehead, living in or near Kathmandu.

A yungdrung was a symbol for eternity in Buddhism and

looked similar to a counter-clockwise *svastika* or swastika, a Sanskrit word meaning a lucky object. The yungdrung symbol meant good fortune to Buddhists and was said to symbolize the footprints of the Buddha. The symbol was sometimes seen in Buddhist art and was often used to mark the beginning of some of its ancient texts.

Yangji recalled Chonyi being overjoyed about his dream of the boy with the colorful yungdrung. He had hoped and prayed for the sign for ten years before the dream came to him.

Chonyi had consulted an ancient text with the list of Sacrifists ten years earlier and five years before the approximate time of the next Sacrifist's birth to see who was next in line for rebirth. From the list, he knew that the name of the next Sacrifist was Dzangbu Lingpa.

Sacrifists were not monks. Their purpose was unknown to everyone except the High Lama of Diki Chhyoling and his successor. Sacrifists only received guidance on their instruction from the High Lama. Other monks of the gompa rarely interacted with a Sacrifist.

Each Sacrifist stayed at the gompa for twenty-five years and then left it to achieve their purpose in life. They were never heard from again once they departed the gompa. It was stated in an ancient text that their next rebirth would occur two thousand, one hundred and sixty years from the time of their last rebirth.

Since Yangji had been slated to be Chonyi's successor as High Lama upon his death, Chonyi had instructed him to read the ancient Sacrifist manual dealing with their identification. The identification manual contained the names of all one hundred and eight Sacrifists. It also noted each Sacrifist's specific identification symbols.

Yangji smiled, remembering when he had read that there

were one hundred and eight Sacrifists. This matched the number of prayer beads in a Buddhist monk's *mala* or rosary. Reading that a Sacrifist was reborn every twenty years, he finally understood the reason for the two rooms at the gompa which housed two 'special' individuals.

On the day when the senior Sacrifist left the gompa, Chonyi had called Yangji in and revealed the secret regarding Sacrifists. And when the time came, fifteen years later, Chonyi had asked Yangji to put together a legation that must include himself and two other monks. Chonyi had calculated Dzangbu's rebirth date according to instructions in the ancient Sacrifist manual.

He had interpreted the colorful yungdrung in his dream to mean that the boy's name would be Tashi, meaning 'good luck.' Therefore, Yangji was only to search for boys with that name who had been born during the range of dates Chonyi provided. The legation found six boys named Tashi born within the specified time frame.

When Yangji first saw the Tashi who would later become Dzangbu, he had already seen four of the five other Tashis. All had failed the stringent Sacrifist identification exam. The examination was administered in five parts. Each part corresponded to the 'Five Sacred Treasures of Snow,' Kangchenjunga's five repositories of God—grain, gems, silver, gold, and holy books.

The test had twenty-four unique items to choose from. Each of the one hundred and eight Sacrifists had their own specific combination of seven correct items. Even if a boy matched any one of the one hundred and eight different combinations, the legation would only be looking for the exact combination of items that fit the Sacrifist who was to be reborn at that particular time. The odds of an impostor assuming the role of a Sacrifist were impossibly remote.

However, each candidate's parents made every effort to have their child become a chosen one. Although they would never hear the word 'Sacrifist' or be told what their boy or girl would ultimately be doing, they knew that being chosen by emissaries of the High Lama of Diki Chhyoling was a particularly high honor, one accorded to only one boy or girl every twenty years. The honor would bring prestige to the child's entire family for many decades afterward.

Yangji remembered Dzangbu's test well. Only Yangji knew the correct combination, having studied the Sacrifist manual given to him by Chonyi. To properly carry out the test, only the three-monk legation and the boy had been permitted in the room.

When this particular Tashi entered the room, Yangji noticed that, rather than looking scared or confused the way the other boys had been, he looked uninterested and bored. Yangji watched as Pasang, one of his deputies, spoke to the child.

"You will be shown some things to look at," Pasang said, keeping his instructions simple. "Each time, Lama Yangji will ask you to choose one or more of the things laid out. When he does, you are to point to the one you feel is the right one. Do you understand?"

The boy nodded his head and yawned, glancing at Yangji, who sat watching him with a benevolent smile on his face. Yangji nodded at Pasang and at the other monk, Khenpo, signaling them to proceed with the ritual.

Each monk grabbed a vial containing a different type of grain. They poured a little of the grain out onto the table in front of Tashi. Then they stepped back and stood on either side of Yangji. Tashi fidgeted in his seat and swung his legs, which hung from the chair, back and forth.

"Choose," Yangji said.

When Yangji spoke, Tashi stopped kicking his legs. He looked at the two varieties of grain sitting in small mounds on the table. Pasang had poured out some Tibetan purple barley and Khenpo had put plain wheat on the table. Tashi looked up at Yangji, but the monk did not move.

"Choose," Yangji repeated.

Tashi put his hand on the table and pointed at the wheat.

"Very good," the Lama said.

Tashi relaxed and went back to swinging his dangling feet. To Yangji's eye, the boy did not much care about what was going on.

Yangji motioned for his deputies to perform the next part of the test. The monks removed the grain and set out three gemstones—Tibetan black quartz, blue turquoise, and pink Himalayan ice quartz.

Yangji nodded at the items. "Choose one."

Tashi yawned and took no time at all in choosing the black quartz. In fact, he did not even examine the other gems. Yangji saw that the boy had chosen correctly, and felt surprised but excited. The prior four Tashis had picked up each gemstone and had looked at each one closely before making a decision. This boy did not hesitate.

Yangji motioned for the next phase of the test to begin. His two assistants laid out four silver figurines—a horse, a snowlion, a peacock, and an elephant. All were sacred animals in the shamanistic Bön religion, and represented the four cardinal directions. Tashi watched as the monks placed the items on the table. When done Yangji nodded his head toward Tashi.

"Choose one, please."

Tashi began yawning again and immediately picked up the snowlion, wasting no time in looking at the other choices. Again, he had chosen correctly. He had now gone further in the

Sacrifist examination than any of the four prior candidates. Yangji was pleased.

The two monks cleared off the silver objects and replaced them with five golden figurines of Lord Buddha—a Laughing Buddha, a Serene Buddha, a Standing Buddha, a Reclining Buddha, and a Sleeping Buddha.

Before Yangji could tell the boy to choose, the still-yawning Tashi pointed at the Sleeping Buddha.

Yangji thought that, if this was truly the real Sacrifist, the Sleeping Buddha was an apropos identification symbol for him.

Just to be sure, Yangji asked, "Is that your choice?"

Tashi nodded his assent and again he had been correct.

It was time for the moment of truth. The fifth part of the test was the toughest. For this part, the boy would have to identify three particular holy books from a total of ten holy books. Choosing the correct three would identify him as the reincarnated Sacrifist, Dzangbu Lingpa.

Prior to this Tashi's test, Yangji had decided to make the fifth part of the exam even more challenging than usual. Now, seeing how bored and nonchalant the boy acted during the entire examination, he was glad he had done so.

Instead of having Pasang and Khenpo lay out the ten holy books, he had instructed them to lay out only eight, with six of them being decoys. Each of them was to hold onto one of the other two books throughout this part of the examination. Khenpo held the correct third book. Pasang held another decoy. The candidate had no way of knowing that there should be ten books on the table.

The monks laid out the eight holy books on the table in front of Tashi. They went back and stood on either side of Yangji, each monk holding their own designated book in front of them.

"Choose three," Yangji said.

Yangji watched and hoped he had not made it too difficult. He watched the boy quickly identify two of the three correct holy books. Yangji saw the boy hesitate as he looked for the third book. Tashi stopped yawning—a spark had occurred.

The boy was finally interested.

Tashi looked at all the remaining books on the table in front of him, touching none of them. Yangji projected no visible emotion, so as not to dissuade him from making the wrong choice.

The six remaining ancient texts were in many different colors and sizes. Tashi could not yet read. His choice could only be made from his own innate memory of his specific combination.

Confused, the boy looked up at Yangji. The High Lama was stoic, not willing to influence Tashi in any way. The boy looked at the monks to either side of Yangji.

Tashi saw they were each holding a book.

When the child saw the book held by Khenpo, his eyes lit up. He got off his chair, walked up to Khenpo, and held out his small hand. The monk looked at Yangji, who nodded. Khenpo handed Tashi the book. Tashi studied the book and looked satisfied. He traced a small index finger over the silver lettering on the blue cover. He turned and held the small text out to Yangji, who accepted it.

A warm smile spread across Yangji's face. The Lama looked down at the small child, ordinary in appearance save for a shock of white in his black hair. The Lama pressed his hands together.

"Namasté." Then Yangji winked and said, "Welcome back."

CHAPTER 19

THE DOORS IN the back of the hall opened and Dzangbu entered the room. He kneeled to perform three prostrations. After doing so, he arose and was motioned forward by Yangji. He came forward, kneeled, and performed three more prostrations.

The High Lama beamed at the young man. He loved the boy, who was now a grown man of thirty, and Yangji would be sad to see him go. However, his departure was for the greater good of all, and it was necessary if they were to prevent more lives from being lost.

Dzangbu's training had progressed well, and Yangji was astonished at the Sacrifist's capacity to relearn things. The more Dzangbu learned, the more he recalled things about his purpose and reacquired skills from his prior incarnations.

But even now, the Lama knew that there were some truths Dzangbu had not revealed to Yangji. He was a Sacrifist. And some things only the Sacrifist could know.

Each Sacrifist was mentored by a senior Sacrifist for the first five years at the gompa. Dzangbu had been mentored during his first five years by Kaya. Dzangbu had helped mentor Tendzen, the next Sacrifist in line after him. When Dzangbu left the gompa, Tendzen would become the senior Sacrifist and the next junior Sacrifist in line would have to be found.

The lamas did not know how long this process had been going on, but they knew it had been going on for at least twenty-five centuries—since the time of the first Buddha, Siddhārtha Gautama. It was their belief that Gautama Buddha had trained all one hundred and eight Sacrifists.

Dzangbu greeted his master. "Namasté."

Yangji nodded. "Namasté. How have you been?"

"I am well, Rinpoche." Rinpoche was the respectful form of address for one's own master lama or for any other important lama.

Yangji said, "It is you who should be addressed as Rinpoche."

"I'm honored you believe so, but I am a fleeting moment every two thousand years."

Yangji nodded. He was somewhat saddened, but his expression did not show it. A short silence conveyed their regard for each other. Dzangbu knew it was time for him to leave. And Yangji knew that he knew.

"How goes your practice?" Yangji asked.

"Very well, thank you. I have been ready for some time."

"That is good. Arrangements have been made. I will miss you."

"I will return again ... in about two thousand years."

Yangji smiled and some of his sadness lifted. He knew that Dzangbu's time at the gompa was limited. But he and the other High Lamas of the past did not really know how powerful they were as human beings.

Yangji paused a moment, debating on whether to discuss the information about this yeti being the Qolom Qasigi Duktsi. The ancient texts revealed this beast would be 'difficult to tame' but did not include instructions for any special way of doing so. Yangji assumed Dzangbu knew the significance of the White Bad Son.

"The creature is white."

Dzangbu nodded. "Ah. Thank you for telling me. I will be honored to fulfill my purpose. Namasté."

"Namasté."

Dzangbu got up and walked toward the door.

Yangji said, "Good luck, Tashi."

Without looking back, Dzangbu smiled and walked out.

CHAPTER 20

DANE, SHELLY, AND Torleif were in Sir Randolph's great library awaiting his arrival. Shelly was looking at all the books on the walls.

"I wonder if he has read them all," she said, her gaze taking in the oak bookshelves that reached all the way to the ceiling. Torleif and Dane glanced in Shelly's direction.

"About half of them, young lady," Sir Randolph said, striding into the room.

"Hello, Sir Randolph. I'm Dane Nielsen," Dane said, holding out his hand. "But my friends call me Lake."

Sir Randolph shook his hand. Dane noticed the handshake was firm and certain.

"Pleased to make your acquaintance, Dane," Sir Randolph said. "I know Torleif. You must be Shelly—Dane's fiancée."

"Shelly Newton, Sir Randolph," she said.

"Yes. You were a marvelous competitor on the U.S. Biathlon team," Sir Randolph said.

"You did some homework," Shelly said, sounding impressed.

Sir Randolph held up his hands in polite protest. "I've

always been interested in the biathlon. As a young man, I even tried out for the British team, and my interest in the event never faded." He paused. "In truth, it was my interest in cross-country skiing, I think, that spurred my son Rand's interest in mountaineering. It's been quite a while since I've done any of that myself. Please, sit." He motioned them toward the seats arranged around the central area of the library. "Why don't we all have a chat? Can I offer any of you some refreshments?"

All three of them declined, and Dane sat with Shelly on the tan leather sofa. Torleif and Sir Randolph took matching club chairs opposite the sofa. Sir Randolph paused a moment before he spoke.

"I'm not particularly good at small talk, Dane, so I'll cut right to the chase," Sir Randolph said. "I understand you've agreed to try to find my son's remains. Torleif relayed my terms and has told me that you are in agreement with them."

"Yes, sir. If you want me to do this, I most certainly will do all I can. However, I wish to caution you that it will most likely be a futile endeavor."

"Thanks for that, son. I realize there is only a remote possibility of finding him, and I don't care about that," Sir Randolph said. "The attempt must be made. Your integrity is well known and your skill in mountaineering is legendary. If you can't find my son, I'm sure no one else will be able to, either. I am trusting you to make your best attempt."

"I'll do my best, sir," Dane said.

"I had thought maybe your dog would come in handy, but I understand that by the time you arrive and acclimatize it will have been a little too long for him to be of use. So, I understand you plan to have a cadaver dog with his handler at base camp?"

"Yes, sir. Lolo and his dog Snoops are veterans of Himalayan search parties. They live in Nepal and are an excellent team with a lot of experience," Dane said.

"I called ahead and found out they are available," Torleif said.

"That's excellent. I want to spare no expense. If you need anything else, please let me know. Good luck," Sir Randolph said.

"We'll do our best, sir," Dane reiterated.

"I'm sure you will, son. I'm sure you will."

They spent the rest of the meeting discussing their plans. Sir Randolph told them they would be flying in his private 707. They all left in the limousine that had brought them there and headed for the airport.

After Dane and company left, Sir Randolph went through his cell phone contacts, looking for a number. Dane would be looking for his son's remains, and that was all to the good. But Sir Randolph wanted a different kind of closure, and though Dane was a fine mountaineer, he was not a hunter who could help Sir Randolph find his son's killer.

Rand's killer appeared to be some kind of animal, so the person Sir Randolph was looking for had to know animals and how to find them. And he knew just the person for the job. *He's a self-serving bastard,* Sir Randolph thought. *But he'll be perfect.*

CHAPTER 21

PHURBA HAD JUST sat down to his usual breakfast, consisting of Tibetan tea and a bowl of gruel made from nak milk and *tsampa*—a type of roasted flour—when there was a knock at his front door.

He had been dreading an unexpected knock ever since receiving Yangji's request from Chodak. Now it had finally come. Sunita opened the door. Phurba listened to her excited exclamation.

"Chodak! How wonderful to see you! And you have brought a guest. Namasté. Please come in."

Chodak came into the room and Phurba stood up.

"Namasté," Phurba said. "Please sit down, Chodak." Phurba studied the man who had entered with him. Chodak wore a monk's robes, but this man was dressed in typical Sherpa garb and carried a small knapsack. He watched the man walk into the room. *He doesn't move like a monk*, Phurba thought. The man appeared to almost glide into the room without taking a step, his eyes up, and surveying the area in front of him. When he looked into Phurba's eyes, it made the sirdar feel naked, as though the man knew everything about him, and understood all of his thoughts.

The stranger sat down across from where Phurba had been about to start eating. "Namasté."

Phurba returned the salutation and sat back down.

"This is Dzangbu Lingpa," Chodak said, introducing the man.

The name Dzangbu meant 'one who has attained spiritual perfection.' Phurba regarded the man with the shock of white hair. Dzangbu smiled benignly, closed his eyes, and bowed his head slightly, as if to reassure Phurba that everything was all right. Phurba noticed a change in how he felt. He could feel his anxiety leaving him and a sensation of peace spreading across his being, as if he had just meditated for an hour. The sudden shift to a pleasant state of being shocked him and the release of all his suffering took him by surprise, at least for the moment. Phurba wondered what he had been worried about in the first place. *Dzangbu. Good name for him.*

Sunita bowed slightly. "Our home is your home. Are either of you hungry? Or would you like some tea?"

"Tea is fine," Chodak said.

Sunita set about getting them some.

Phurba was glad the High Lama had sent his brother-in-law with Dzangbu, but he still wondered, *What is he doing here?* He assumed the answer would have something to do with his last expedition.

"To what do we owe the honor of your visit to our modest home?" Phurba asked.

Chodak glanced at Dzangbu, who nodded. Chodak faced Phurba. "As you know, the High Lama, Yangji Norbu Rinpoche, requested your help, if needed."

"Yes. How may I be of service to the High Lama?"

Sunita glanced at Phurba over her shoulder while fixing tea. Phurba saw the look on her face turn from one of warm interest to one of slight worry.

Chodak began to speak. Phurba watched Dzangbu and forgot about Chodak. Besides being motionless, the man seemed emotionless as well, his face impassive. Phurba wondered how an ordinary man could become a man like Dzangbu. He could not imagine it. *I couldn't even make it as a monk.* Phurba knew monks were special, but there was something far different about Dzangbu. *He's no ordinary man.*

"Phurba?"

Phurba looked at Chodak. "Yes?" He realized he'd heard nothing that his brother-in-law had said.

Chodak repeated himself. "Can you find a spot for Dzangbu on your next expedition to Kangchenjunga? He would like to see the spot where the yeti attack occurred."

Phurba wanted to ask why, but instead heard himself say, "That will not be a problem. I have just been retained for such an expedition. Coincidentally, it is the expedition to search for the lost climber's remains."

"That is most fortuitous. The Buddha smiles upon us," Chodak said.

"Yes," Phurba said, still feeling serene. "Lucky."

Sunita brought the two visitors their tea.

"Thank you very much, Sunita." Chodak sipped the tea. "I'd forgotten how perfect your tea is."

"Yes. Wonderful," Dzangbu said.

Dzangbu's calm and peaceful demeanor came across in his speech, and Sunita, hearing him, blushed with pride.

"When does this expedition begin?" Chodak asked.

"Very soon," Phurba said.

Phurba wondered why this man needed to see where Rand

had been attacked. He looked physically unable to carry a standard Sherpa load. Phurba wondered if he should even ask him to carry one. Whatever Dzangbu's purpose, Phurba was sure he should not ask. He felt that, whatever it was, it must be for the good of the gompa.

"Please stay with us until the expedition is ready," Phurba said.

Dzangbu bowed slightly. "Thank you. The High Lama appreciates your assistance."

Phurba bowed back. "I am only happy to be of service." But then Phurba thought, *I think he knows what I really think and feel.*

And Dzangbu did.

CHAPTER 22

LATE IN THE afternoon on Sunday, Lily returned from climbing Mt. Shasta—a monthly ritual she performed from mid-May to mid-September to keep in shape, as a supplement to her daily yoga and meditation sessions.

After shedding her climbing clothes and taking a hot shower, she slipped on her preferred casual wear, clothing in a style she called gypsy chic—a cross between Boho-chic and peasant chic—lots of scarves with colorful flowing skirts. She wore boots or sandals. No pumps or platforms, thank you.

After taking over her shop from her mother, who minded it when Lily took her little trips, she perused the Internet. She was still a little miffed by Dane blowing her off, and she wanted to keep up on the current news in Nepal.

Lily looked through the website of the Himalayan Times. The bell hanging from her shop door jingled. The middle-aged Japanese woman, who had bought the Omyagra remedy the week before, strolled in. She had three other Japanese women in tow. Lily guessed they were all in their early-to-late forties.

"How did everything go?" Lily asked.

"Good. *Velly* good," the woman said in her Japanese accent, smiling. She translated what Lily had asked her for her friends. They all giggled. "I bring you more customer."

Lily laughed to herself. *They all want their own bottle of Dr. Dong's remedy.*

She sold them all some of her 'magic potion.' *If this keeps up I'll have a whole cottage industry going. There's nothing like good word of mouth.* The women walked out. They were all yammering back and forth in Japanese and laughing at one another.

Lily went back to the Internet to look for any news on Kangchenjunga. She found an article about two other missing climbers, but did not consider it noteworthy until she had read that some members of an expedition following them reported finding their abandoned backpacks with some blood on them.

Climbers went missing on the eight-thousanders from time to time, but there were usually witnesses explaining that it was due to avalanches or falling ice or bad weather, et cetera. When those things happened, the equipment went missing too.

The famous English mountaineer George Mallory had disappeared on Everest with his climbing partner in 1924, and his remains had not been found until 1999. So mountaineers disappearing was not unusual. Many missing mountaineers, like Lily's father, were never found again.

Blood evidence is another thing. The two had been climbing alpine style by themselves, so the chance of anyone even realizing that they had gone missing had been low to start with. They might not have been reported missing for days or weeks if it had not been for the discovery of their bloodied packs.

She surfed the Internet for another half an hour and saw an article about how "the well-known Dane Nielsen has agreed to come out of retirement to help search for the missing Rand Barrington." The article mentioned that his long-time climbing partner, Torleif Günner, was going too. But what made Lily mad was the fact that Dane's fiancée was also going along.

What an ass. It's so foolish and irresponsible. The more she thought about it, the more upset she became. She tried to put it out of her mind by surfing StumbleUpon, but the situation kept gnawing at her psyche.

To hell with him. I warned him and now it's on him. She busied herself in her shop, but her conscience would not allow her to do nothing.

She had been researching the yeti and Bigfoot for years, starting as a child growing up in Washington. She had even gone looking for Bigfoot in various places with her father. In her shop, she sold maps to people interested in looking for Sasquatch, showing all the locations of sightings in the Stanislaus National Forest in California.

She was a great believer in seeing things for yourself and making up your own mind. She knew there was a Bigfoot. She believed she had seen one as a child in Olympic National Park. She had told her father about it at the time, and he had not scoffed at the excited ten-year-old's story. After all, she was cailín fhírinne.

I must do something *to get them to reconsider the danger they're in,* she thought. *What can I do?* She pondered the problem for a little while and an idea came to her—an idea that made her laugh out loud. She wondered why she had not thought of it before. *I'd love to be there to see the look on their faces.*

CHAPTER 23

GEORGE ARMSTRONG HAD just landed in Kathmandu with his cameraman, Harry Tisdale. He pulled out his mobile phone, scrolled his contacts, and pressed Send. He mentally cursed international mobile rates, even though he was wealthy, and waited for Typhon Hirsch to answer. Typhon was the producer of his TV show, 'Big Game, Big Times,' on the Discovery Channel.

Typhon picked up. "Hey, George."

"Just landed."

"Excellent. When do you interview the witness?"

"Depends on how long it takes to find him. How are the promotions coming together?"

"We are using some stock footage with ominous music. Your idea about tracking down the yeti was genius. Bigfoot is so big right now. It's much better than tracking down a boring black bear."

"Tracking down an animal in the Himalaya is not boring. It's pretty rough. But Harry and I have been here before. On Everest, remember?"

"I remember. Do me a favor and stay away from that nut

Nielsen. He's a hot head and has a short fuse."

"We probably won't even see him."

"Let's hope so. Now you're pretty sure this Sherpa thinks he saw the yeti?"

"Yup. That's the report. But, you know, he's probably just full of it because he's superstitious and suggestable."

Typhon giggled with glee. "Doesn't matter. The only thing that matters is that he *believes* he saw it. People love Bigfoot shows and keep watching. Not one of those shows ever videos a genuine Bigfoot."

"I know. I get it. Who knows what he'll describe or how believable he'll be? I have to find him first. All I have is a first name and the name of the expedition agency that Rand used. As I remember, a lot of those Sherpas have the same name, so it might be a while."

"You'll find him. Call me if you need anything."

"Will do."

Armstrong hung up. *If it's on TV, it must be true,* he thought cynically. *People will believe anything.*

CHAPTER 24

"**WHAT'RE WE HAVING?**" Shelly asked, sitting down at the table on Sir Randolph's private 707.

The steward/cook came out and handed Shelly and Dane a menu. Shelly looked at Dane sideways and said, "I could get used to this." Then, to the steward: "Eggs Benedict and orange juice."

"I'll have the same," Dane said. Then to Torleif: "Any idea where we're staying?"

"The Royale," Torleif said. "Rand and I stayed there in between expeditions."

"Sweet. Did you send word to Prakash? We should tell him to get Phurba. He's the best sirdar I've ever worked with, and since he was there when it happened, it could be more helpful."

"I called Prakash before I came to see you in Colorado. I told him when we'd be arriving and to hire Phurba. He said he'd also do his best to get as many of our usual crew as possible."

"That's why I love ya. One step ahead all the time." Dane paused, then his eyebrows lifted as the realization hit him. "Wait a minute. You called Prakash *before* you came to Colorado? Pretty sure that I'd be going, huh?"

Torleif grinned and winked. "Hey, I was going with you or without you."

Dane thought a moment. "I don't want to overdo it, but since Barrington can afford it, even though we aren't summiting, we should take a bigger crew plus a couple of doctors. Just in case."

"I thought so, too. We do have a bigger crew and two doctors. We're meeting up with them near Phurba's village."

"Who's flying us into Suketar?"

"Guess." Torleif twirled his index finger in the air.

"Rocky and Beauwinkle?"

Torleif nodded.

Dane shook his head. "Did I say you were good? I take it back. You're awesome."

Shelly chimed in. "Rocky and Bullwinkle? What are you guys talking about?"

"Rocky is a helicopter," Torleif said. "The Ecureuil B3e is a French-made high-altitude helicopter. *Ecureuil* means 'squirrel,' so Lake named it Rocky. And it's not *Bull*-winkle, it's *Beau*-winkle. Beau Chabret is a pilot for Mockingbird Air. Hence your impish fiancé's progression."

Shelly looked at Dane. "You're a goofball."

"This is the thanks I get for putting us into the mile-high club." Shelly smacked him in the arm. "Ouch!"

The steward brought out their breakfast. They spent the rest of their breakfast making small chit-chat about past expeditions and other climbers. Landing in Kathmandu, they got off the plane and were met by a representative of Sir Randolph, who directed them to their taxi. The driver of the prepaid taxi took off and weaved his way through familiar streets to the Royale.

Following their taxi, unnoticed by anyone, was a late model Toyota Land Cruiser. Their taxi pulled up to the Royale Hotel.

The driver of the Toyota pulled over to the side of the road, exited, and walked toward the hotel.

Dane and the others disembarked from their taxi. The driver and bellboy helped get their things from the trunk. The man from the Land Cruiser made his way into the hotel, unnoticed by the group, whose attention was fixed on getting their things from the taxi.

The Royale was one of the best hotels in Nepal. The hotel was made of terracotta brick and wood, and built using the Nepali architectural style, which included an inner courtyard or *chowk* surrounded by a vertically oriented building structure. The builders had integrated quite a bit of ornate, antique woodwork and carvings into the décor throughout the hotel and its rooms.

Shelly was quite impressed with its beauty. "Wow. This is gorgeous!"

"Wait till you see your suite," Torleif said.

They checked in while the man tailing them sat in the lobby pretending to read a newspaper. He listened in as the clerk told the bellboy their room numbers and watched them leave the lobby as they were shown to their rooms. After they left, he got up, went back to his car, and watched the hotel entrance/exit.

The bellboy took the group down a long hall on the third floor, wheeling their packs and equipment for them. He dropped Torleif at his suite first. Torleif tried to tip him, but the bellboy waved him off.

"We have already been tipped in advance, sir," the bellboy said, unloading his things.

"Boy, that Sir Randolph is sure detail-oriented," Torleif said to Dane.

"Apparently," Dane said. "See you in a bit."

The bellboy settled Dane and Shelly in their own room. They looked around the rooms as the bellboy unloaded their cart. A king-size four-poster canopy bed made of deep reddish-brown teak filled part of the room and was flanked by matching night stands made of the same material. The bed canopy consisted of white shears and matched the stark white bedspread, which was of a quilted design. Design patterns were sewn inside each square of the quilt. On the bed were throw-pillows bearing a blue, black, and white geometrical design. The floor was rich terracotta tile, and there were luxurious Oriental rugs throughout the large room.

"I can get used to this, too," Shelly said.

"Yeah. This is just how I roll," Dane said. "If you want the best, you have to pay the big bucks." Shelly laughed at him and gave him a kiss. "You don't only love me for my money, do you?"

"No. Just your looks. But money doesn't suck."

Dane laughed, then joked, "How about we test out this bed?"

A knock at the door interrupted Dane's playfulness.

"Too late," Shelly said.

"Damn," Dane said in mock disappointment, opening the door. It was Torleif.

"Ready?" Torleif asked.

"Yup," Dane said. "Let's go see good old Pray-for-Cash."

CHAPTER 25

THE MAN DOWN the street in the Land Cruiser sat up as Dane and Torleif came out of the hotel. Shelly had decided to stay at the hotel and soak in the fancy bathtub.

A white taxi with a tiger painted on its side rolled up to the two men. Many of the taxis in Kathmandu did not have meters, and even if they did, they would not be used with tourists or mountaineers. Dane knew enough to get the price of a taxi ride in advance, but he loved negotiating.

Dane leaned in the passenger window. "Speak English?"

The driver nodded.

"Do you know where Sharwa Himalayan Treks & Expeditions is located in the Thamel district?"

The driver nodded.

"How much one way?"

"Three hundred rupees."

Dane laughed and said, "What's your name?"

"Aadi."

"Okay, Aadi. I know you can do better. It's not our first rodeo in Kathmandu." Dane grinned at the driver, who looked confused by the rodeo reference.

Dane continued. "But because you have an honest face, I'm going to assume you want to do the right thing and take my generous offer of one hundred rupees." Dane knew that he was still overpaying.

Aadi nodded. "Okay. Deal."

Dane squeezed into the back of Aadi's small 1993 Suzuki Maruti.

Torleif, who was six foot five, squeezed in with much more difficulty. "Wish they had bigger taxis."

Dane laughed, noticing Torleif's cramped position. "Piss and moan. Piss and moan."

Aadi took off with a jolt, giving the two men mild whiplash. Riding in a taxi in Kathmandu sometimes could be like riding Space Mountain at Disneyland, depending on how fast the driver wanted to go. The streets were rarely straight for any significant distance and sometimes they could get pretty tight. During their wild ride, Dane and Torleif realized that Aadi fancied himself the Dale Earnhardt of Nepali taxi drivers. The two men kept stepping on non-existent brakes from their seats in the back as their reflexes screamed at them to avoid hitting other cars or pedestrians.

In the midst of this, Torleif looked over at Dane. "You see where negotiating gets you? Next time, how about we let our *billionaire* pay for a pleasant ride back to the hotel?"

Dane nodded. "Agreed."

The taxi pulled up in front of the storefront for Sharwa Himalayan Treks & Expeditions. Torleif and Dane got out. Dane tipped Aadi, who grinned, thanked him, and peeled out.

The man following them in the Toyota parked down the street and exited his car.

Dane and Torleif walked in and were greeted by a pudgy, cheerful-looking Nepali man.

"Hello, gentlemen! Good to see you together again."

Dane grinned and embraced him. "Hello, Prakash. Good to see you, too. Have you lost a little weight?"

"Stop kidding an old man, Dane. My wife wishes and prays to Buddha that I lose weight, but she cooks too well to have her prayers answered."

"Have you got our itinerary and our tickets for Mockingbird?" Torleif asked.

"Yes. Please sit down." Prakash motioned to the two chairs facing his desk. He sat down as well and rummaged through the papers on his cluttered desk. A moment later, he handed a paper and three tickets to Torleif. "Phurba is getting as much of your old usual crew together as possible."

Dane and Torleif looked over the itinerary sheet.

Dane looked up at Prakash. "I recognize most of those names. Nice job on getting Phurba. Anything unusual we should know about?"

"Yes," a heavily accented voice said from behind them. The man from the Toyota had entered the shop. "Beware of the Kangchenjunga Demon. We are in his time. He protects the Five Sacred Treasures of Snow. There is much danger."

Dane and Torleif turned to look at the man, who was taller than most Nepali men; Tibetan, perhaps. His salt-and-pepper hair and wizened face made him appear like he had seen much hardship. The reference he had made to the Demon made Torleif uneasy, both because of Rand's death and because of Lhakpa's story. This time the reference gave him chills down his spine.

Prakash shook his head. "Pay no attention to him." Then, to the man: "Get out of here! Leave my customers alone."

Dane held up his hand to forestall Prakash. "What do you mean, we are in his time?"

Prakash sighed. "Don't encourage him."

"Every twenty years the Demon reappears to wreak vengeance upon those who trespass on his mountain." The man came forward and began to pray in Tibetan over Dane and Torleif. But it sounded more like an incantation for a spell.

The man finished his prayer, took a necklace from his pocket, and pressed it into Dane's hand. The necklace had colorful beads and a crystal amulet that dangled from it. "Give this to your fiancée. It will protect her."

Dane tried to give it back, but the man would not take it, so he put it in his pocket. "How did you know about my fiancée?"

"Dorje the Humble knows all, sees all."

Dane stood up. "Don't bullshit me, pal. Out with it. Who sent you?"

The man held up his hands. "Okay, okay. Jeez, Americans. No faith. My name is Dorje Andrutsang, but you can call me DJ." His English was perfect, without a trace of any accent at all. "I am at your service. I am Lily McCrowley's uncle."

The name took a second to register with Dane. Then he nodded, recalling the crazy girl on the phone. "I should have guessed. I recognize the family resemblance."

DJ looked puzzled.

Dane turned to Torleif. "She's the kooky girl who called me at the house."

"Listen … Uncle DJ. I told your niece there is nothing to worry about. Aside from the fact that the notion of a Demon is just silly superstition, we'll only be on the mountain for a short time, searching for the remains of a climber who was lost. Soon as we find him, we'll be off the mountain."

DJ persisted. "How will you be able to distinguish his remains from the others?"

Dane looked at Prakash. "The others?"

DJ pressed the point. "After Rand Barrington was killed, two other climbers were attacked and killed by the Demon."

Prakash had had enough. "There is no proof of that!"

DJ went on. "There was blood on their trail and their abandoned equipment had blood on it as well."

Dane looked over at Torleif. "That *is* odd." Dane noticed the concerned look on Torleif's face.

Prakash began to speak to DJ in Nepali. An argument ensued, and Prakash got up and motioned for DJ to get out of his business establishment. They argued all the way outside. DJ left, but he yelled, "Beware!" again through the storefront window as he walked away.

Prakash came back inside and sat down. He was out of breath and sweating. He pulled out a handkerchief to wipe his brow.

"Sorry for the interruption. Pay no attention to him. He is a madman who masquerades as a shaman."

"You know him?" Torleif asked.

"Unfortunately, I do know him. He is someone who the old women visit for psychic readings. I know this because my wife has seen him many, many times. Thank the Lord Buddha she was not here. I would be in *deep feces* as you say. *Randiko choro,*" he added under his breath. "Son of a bitch. Do not get me started. Where were we?"

Prakash was still flustered.

Dane and Torleif looked at each other and burst out laughing at the bizarre set of circumstances.

But Prakash was not laughing. "It is just too much. That was the second strange thing this week." But before they could ask him about the first 'strange thing', Prakash changed the subject and began to go over their itinerary, and the matter was dropped.

CHAPTER 26

DANE PAID A different taxi driver extra rupees for a leisurely drive back to the hotel. The return trip was made without incident. Once they had arrived, they walked up to Dane's room. Shelly looked calm and refreshed when they walked into the room. They found her lounging on the couch with a magazine, wearing a colorful blouse, well-worn jeans, and tennis shoes.

"What're we doing next?" she asked.

Dane looked over at Torleif. "The pub sound good?"

"Sounds good to me," Torleif said.

Their taxi driver let them out near the Kelly green store front of an Irish pub. They walked inside, and it took their eyes a moment to adjust to the dark surroundings. They made their way to the bar, and a voice spoke from off to their left.

"Well, well. Look what the cat dragged in," the voice said.

Dane and Torleif looked over and saw who it was.

"Custer," Torleif said.

"Custer," Dane spit out, like the name disgusted him.

George Armstrong blanched at hearing Dane's nickname for him. He hated hearing it once, much less a second time.

"C'mon, boys, don't be nasty. Come on over and sit down and let's be friends," Armstrong said, motioning them toward his table where he was sitting with Harry and several empty pint glasses.

"Listen carefully, *Custer*. We ain't friends, and we ain't gonna *be* friends," Dane said, leaning forward. Shelly, taking note of his tone, reached over and grabbed his arm, squeezing it.

"Okay. Okay," Armstrong said, waving him off. "No reason to go '*all Injun*' on me. I heard you were looking for Rand Barrington, and I happened to be here on business. Let me know if you need any of my help, is all I'm saying." He looked at them, then started cackling and took a sip of his beer.

Dane snorted dismissively at what he considered an insincere offer of help. He, Shelly, and Torleif made their way to the bar and grabbed three stools. Dane ordered an IPA. Torleif and Shelly each ordered a stout.

Shelly turned to Dane. "Who is that guy?"

"George Armstrong," Torleif said.

"The TV adventurer?" Shelly asked.

"One and the same," Torleif said.

Shelly turned back to Dane. "You never told me you knew him."

"He's a dick, Shel."

"Oh, come on. He's a household name. In the US, his TV show, 'Big Game, Big Times,' is the longest-running adventure series on cable TV. It's a bit like Croc Hunter meets Survivor. He travels around the globe going through different adventures, usually ones involving menacing animals or exotic expeditions of one kind or another."

Torleif was enjoying the fact that Shelly was goading Dane a little and decided to join in. "You sound like a fan."

The bartender brought over their refreshments. Dane and

Torleif took sips of their beers. Dane wondered why Armstrong was in Kathmandu.

Shelly stared contemplatively at George Armstrong. "I didn't recognize him with his beard. Think he'll give me his autograph?"

Dane looked at her like she was crazy. "Not everybody is *'as seen on TV.'*"

Shelly started laughing. "Okay. I get it. You guys have some sort of history." She glanced back at Armstrong. "But why do you call him 'Custer?'"

"I gave him that name," Torleif said.

"Is it because of the George Armstrong name?"

"Well, partly. … That and, uh …" Torleif trailed off and looked past Shelly at Dane.

Shelly glanced at Dane, then her eyes went back to Torleif. "And what?"

Still looking at Dane, Torleif continued, "… and the fact that Lake went off on him. In fact, it happened in this very pub. After guiding Custer on his Everest adventure…. You could say Lake went 'all Injun' on him."

Dane was staring down at his half-empty pint glass. Guilty. After Torleif's last comment, though, he cracked a little smile. Dane gave Shelly a sidelong glance and saw her returning look of disapproval.

"What? He almost got Smokes and Torleif killed. Tell her."

Torleif nodded. "It's true. He did."

Shelly paused a second, then said, "Okay. You don't like him. But try to keep calm. And just in case, go easy on the firewater … *Lake Eyes.*"

Torleif started laughing.

"Very funny," Dane said. Torleif laughed harder. "Go ahead; get it all out." He glanced over at Armstrong and saw that the man was staring at them. He kept staring until Armstrong's mobile phone rang, playing some horrible song from the eighties.

***

"This is Armstrong," he said, still eying Dane.

"Have you made any progress?" It was Sir Randolph.

Armstrong disregarded Dane and his friends for a minute.

"The guy I bribed at the expedition agency gave us Lhakpa's village. It's Taplejung. We went there, but it's crazy. I found seven Lhakpas, but not *our* Lhakpa. Tomorrow we're going back. We should be able to find him."

"I'm positive he knows something," Sir Randolph said. "Something that should not have been ignored. Find out what he knows. Do whatever it takes." Sir Randolph hung up.

"Aye, aye, Captain Bligh."

Armstrong looked down at his dead mobile and felt annoyed. *People with money always feel privileged and expect that others will do what they want,* he thought. But then he remembered how much Sir Randolph was paying him. He felt better.

CHAPTER 27

THE NEXT DAY, Shelly, Torleif and Dane checked out of their hotel and made their way to the Kathmandu airport. Disembarking from their taxi, they made their way to Mockingbird Air. Dane introduced the pilot, Beau Chabret, to Shelly. *Wow,* she thought. *Is he handsome or what?*

"So, you're Beauwinkle," she said.

Dane and Torleif stifled their laughter as Beau gave them a dirty look. They had neglected to tell Shelly that Beauwinkle was not a nickname they used in his presence, which was embarrassing, although at least Beau seemed to understand that it had not been an intentional dig at his name on her part. She elbowed Dane after they boarded, but he just snickered. Mockingbird had Nepali pilots, too, but Dane had explained that Beau was their best and most experienced pilot, having saved hundreds of lives in high altitude rescues, which is why Torleif had hired him.

They watched Kathmandu disappear in the distance and turned their attention to the majestic Himalaya. *Never thought I'd be here again,* Dane thought. He estimated that they would need about a week of acclimatization before they began searching for

Rand's remains.

Usually climbers would need more days acclimatizing before ascending to such heights. But since Shelly and Dane had been living at Leadville's 10,000 foot (3,048 meter) elevation for some time, and they climbed the 14,400 foot (4,401 meter) Mt. Elbert regularly, they would only need a little more than a week of acclimatization in order to climb higher in safety.

Phurba would meet them at Suketar airport and guide them to the rest of the expedition. Within a week they would be at base camp. In the meantime, Shelly was content to stare out the window at the beauty below them, enthralled by the Himalayan scenery.

After a while, she noticed that Dane was staring at her. She smiled at him, glad to be along. "Stunning."

Dane nodded. "Yes. It is."

Dane looked out the window of the helicopter toward Kangchenjunga, but although he had not voiced his concerns directly, Shelly could guess his thoughts. Dane would not relish the idea of finding the mauled carcass of young Mr. Barrington; he was doing this because it was the right thing to do, but it was still unpleasant work. They had brought a body bag in which to put the remains if they were successful, and had even brought extra bags just in case Lolo and Snoops found more than one body, but being physically prepared was not the same as looking forward to completing their grisly search.

The Ecureuil Eurocopter they were in was used mainly for sightseeing trips and high altitude rescues. It had a maximum altitude range of 23,000 feet. From the stories Dane had told her, Shelly knew that Beau had rescued stranded or injured climbers from as high as 20,000 feet. The record for the highest altitude rescue was even higher, though Beau was not the record holder. At that altitude, a pilot and an EMT could usually only rescue one person at a time, because the thin air would prevent the helicopter from flying with too much weight, for multiple people to be retrieved at the same time.

Beau started the approach into Suketar airport. Shelly looked out the window and was surprised to see how much snow had already fallen on Kangchenjunga.

Dane must have noticed it as well, because he lifted his head from the window and asked Beau, "How's the weather been?"

"It's been odd. We've had snow much too early. As you can see."

Dane nodded at that. Then he said, "Oh, well. No worries. I've seen snow before."

Beau touched the helicopter down on the landing area. Torleif opened the door and he and Shelly got out first. Dane got out and said to Beau, "Hopefully, we'll see you back here sooner rather than later."

"Okay, Dane. *Bonne chance*," Beau said, yelling so that his voice could be heard above the noise of the helicopter.

The three companions got their gear out of the cargo hold and Dane gave Beau the thumbs-up sign.

Beau waved, lifted off, and started back toward Kathmandu. They watched the blue, white, and red helicopter go, and were soon met by Phurba, as they left the landing area.

"*Boozhoo, Zaaga'igan Nishkiinzhigoon,*" Phurba said, greeting Dane in a language Shelly recognized as Ojibwe. Dane had mentioned to her that he had taught Phurba a few phrases in their many expeditions together, and since then, Phurba had made it a habit to always greet Dane in Ojibwe.

"*Halo Phurba. Thangburang?*" Dane continued their ritual by speaking Sherpa, asking, *Are you fine?*

"I am well, my old friend. But I wish that we were climbing the Northwest Ridge of Cho-Oyu, instead of searching for a dead man." Phurba said, referring to the easiest eight-thousander to climb. "*Nisidotaw?*" he added, using the Ojibwe word for 'understand?'

Dane nodded. "Yes. I do."

Even though Shelly had deduced the stranger's name from context, she nudged Dane for an introduction.

"Oh, I'm sorry. Shelly, this is the great Phurba Salaka Sherpa. The finest sirdar in the Land of Snows. Phurba, this is Shelly, my fiancée."

"Namasté. Congratulations to you both," Phurba said to Shelly. "Dane honors me by asking for my help."

"Namasté," Shelly said, returning his salutation. "Dane has told me all about you so many times, I feel as if I know you already."

Phurba smiled and bowed his head. "Dane is too kind. Unfortunately, he tells many tall tales. Yes?"

"Yes, he does," Torleif said, grinning. "Hi, Phurba." Torleif shook hands with the sirdar. "Phurba's right. Lake Eyes speak with fork-ed tongue."

"Me? It's you guys that do all the exaggerating." The three comrades laughed at each other.

"Well, let's get a move on and check out the troops," Torleif said.

"Yes. It'll be good to see some of those guys again," Dane said.

Within a half hour, they had met up with most of their expedition party. It was clear to Shelly that Dane recognized many of the others from past expeditions, and he was pleased to have such a competent group of people working with him.

"Thanks for getting all these guys together, Phurba," he said after meeting the crew. "I recognized a lot of them. It's good to have experienced people. Even though it's only a short ascent, it may take some time to find Rand's remains."

Phurba nodded, but to Shelly's eye, the sirdar seemed uneasy. "Yes. It may."

Dane glanced around and then stopped, a curious look on his face. "Who's that?" Dane asked, pointing.

Shelly turned to follow Dane's gaze and noticed a porter with a shock of white hair. He was standing still only a short distance away and peacefully gazing at the scenery. Shelly thought it was odd how lightly the man was dressed.

Phurba saw where Dane was pointing. "That is a friend of my wife's brother."

"Isn't he cold?" Shelly asked.

Phurba shrugged. "Apparently not."

Dane shrugged too. "Oh well. It takes all kinds, I guess. Let's get this show on the road, Phurba. Take me to Lolo and Snoops?"

CHAPTER 28

"I NEVER WANT you to climb Kangchenjunga again," Amala said.

"Okay, okay," Lhakpa said, happy to agree.

He sat with his wife, Amala, at the kitchen table, eating a breakfast of gruel. They had just received news of the deaths of the two alpine climbers on Kangchenjunga. *Again, blood was found in the snow,* thought Lhakpa; it was one of the reasons he was more than willing to swear off ascending Kangchenjunga ever again.

Their conversation was interrupted by a knock at the door. Amala and Lhakpa shared a glance, and they both remained seated, waiting to see if the visitor would go away.

Neighbors had alerted Lhakpa that two men were looking for him. He did not know what they wanted, so he decided to wait until they found him. Normally, Lhakpa would have been on an expedition by now, and not at home. But because he had a talkative nature, and because seeing a yeti was considered bad luck, he was considered *persona non grata* to most sirdars at the moment.

The one exception was Phurba, who had offered him a job

with the expedition searching for Rand's remains. Lhakpa, however, had declined it. He had been lucky once; he was not at all certain his luck would hold for a second time. *Three deaths on Kangchenjunga in less than a month,* he thought, *and none from an avalanche or anything else that can be understood.*

In Lhakpa's mind, these were kills, not accidental deaths. The realization that his first sighting of the yeti was correct gave him little satisfaction, however, since he needed to work to survive. But he could not get the monster out of his head. He had been having nightmares, and he thought the news of the two alpine climbers' deaths would make it worse.

Whoever was at the door continued to knock. *He's not going away,* Lhakpa thought. He got up from the table and opened the door. Two Caucasian visitors stared back at him.

"Are you Lhakpa Pinasa Sherpa?" one of the men asked.

"Yes," Lhakpa said in English.

"You've been served," the man said. Lhakpa looked at him, not understanding the joke. The man laughed as though he had said something hilarious. "Just kidding. We want to talk to you."

Lhakpa looked puzzled. He glanced back at Amala, who was hovering a few feet behind him, looking curious.

"My name is George Armstrong," he said, introducing himself. "Speaky Englishy?"

"A little," Lhakpa said.

"Damn," Armstrong said. "Does anyone in your household speak English?"

Amala walked to the door. "I speak English."

"Excellent," Armstrong said.

"Ask him if he was on the expedition with Rand Barrington."

"He wants to know if you were on the Rand Barrington expedition," Amala translated, speaking Sherpa.

"Should we tell him yes?" Lhakpa asked.

Amala looked at Harry, who had a camera, then back at Armstrong. "They look like they want to film you. Let's see what they want."

Lhakpa nodded.

Amala turned back to Armstrong. "He says that, yes, he was on that expedition."

"Ask him if we can speak privately and on camera."

Amala relayed this to Lhakpa.

"What do you think?" Lhakpa asked. He frowned, studying the visitors' equipment and manner of dress. "They look like Americans but act a little different than others I've met. They're not climbers. Too flippant."

"Maybe they will pay? Let's see what it's for, before we refuse them," Amala said.

Lhakpa nodded.

"What's this for?" Amala asked.

"I have a TV show in America. Tell him I'll make it worth his while," Armstrong said.

Amala relayed this to Lhakpa, who nodded again. Amala invited them in.

"Namasté," both men said.

They removed their shoes, as was the custom in Sherpa households, and walked inside, greeting Lhakpa with the same salutation. Amala shut the door. She had them sit down at the kitchen table. Lhakpa asked her to fix some tea and she went about making some, though she kept one ear turned toward the table so she could follow the conversation well enough to act as a translator.

"Can I offer you food?" Lhakpa asked in his best English.

"No, thanks. We won't be long," Armstrong said, Amala translating after every sentence or two. "If he can just sign this release form, we can begin."

Amala read it carefully, then explained what the form said to her husband. Lhakpa looked reluctant.

"What does he want?" Lhakpa asked Amala. She repeated the question to Armstrong.

"I want you to tell me exactly what you saw near the Yalung glacier during the Barrington expedition," Armstrong said.

Lhakpa listened to Amala's translation. He knew that Rand and the other two climbers were probably victims of a yeti attack, but he did not like the idea of telling an outsider about either his sighting, or Rand's death.

It was not that he would not talk about it at all. Unlike Phurba, Lhakpa was not a leader of men whose job depended on discretion. He was only a porter. He was also known as a chatty Cathy, so, naturally, Lhakpa's story had grown in the telling.

Once he had gotten back home from the fated expedition, he had amused his friends with his story several times after drinking too much *chang*—a beer made from maize. By the fifth recounting, the beast had grown to over twelve feet tall, and Lhakpa had attempted to save Rand but had arrived too late at the scene of his demise. But in his present unemployed state, Lhakpa lamented shooting his mouth off.

"Should I tell him?" Lhakpa asked Amala, nodding at Armstrong. He felt leery. It was one thing to discuss such matters with his friends or Amala, and another to repeat his tale to strangers.

Armstrong, seeing Lhakpa's hesitation, took out a hundred dollar bill and laid it on the table.

Lhakpa was about to reach for it when Amala told him, "Wait."

Armstrong pulled out another, identical bill, and then a

third. Lhakpa looked at his wife. She nodded her head. With that, Lhakpa signed the release form and picked up the three hundred dollars, which Amala took from him and stowed away.

Lhakpa took a deep breath and began to put his thoughts in order as the Americans prepared their equipment to record him.

***

Armstrong's assistant, Harry, got his video camera out of its shoulder bag and turned it on. Lhakpa waited until the man was pointing the camera at him. "Okay. Go ahead," Harry told Armstrong.

"What exactly did you see on Kangchenjunga?" Armstrong asked, and Amala translated.

Lhakpa paused to collect his thoughts, and then began to tell them his story. The two men listened to Amala's translation of Lhakpa's words, and they knew that although he was exaggerating, they were sure he had seen *something*. Armstrong decided while listening to Amala that the description definitely was not that of a snow leopard. The porter's fear came through on camera, and it seemed unlikely that an experienced mountaineer would mistake a four-footed predator for a two-legged one.

Still, it never hurt to ask. "Do you think it was a snow leopard?" Armstrong asked Lhakpa, and Amala translated.

"No," Lhakpa said, shaking his head. "Snow leopards usually attack livestock, and are rarely seen by anyone. This animal was huge and it walked erect."

Armstrong had anticipated this answer. Snow leopards rarely attacked unless provoked. A snow leopard was more closely related to the tiger than the common leopard, but the latter two were more likely to attack humans. Armstrong knew that snow leopards had a peaceful temperament by comparison. Man-eating leopards and tigers were well documented, though rare, but there had never before been a case of a snow leopard attacking a human unprovoked.

Armstrong had already been thinking that a Himalayan black bear was the most likely possibility. Himalayan black bears were aggressive, and could go up on two legs and walk if they wanted to, although that was not their normal way of walking. However, such bears were black, not white. *It's also unusual for a black bear to be up at that elevation. What could account for its change in behavior?* Armstrong's mind raced for answers. That is, until Amala translated Lhakpa's description.

"It was as white as the snow," she said.

Of course! It's an albino, Armstrong thought. He became excited. An albino bear answered all of his questions. An albino's white color would camouflage it in a snowy environment and make other animals or people easier for it to catch and kill. Moreover, an albino's eyes would be extremely sun-sensitive, so it would only hunt at night. Even better, since climbers of the eight-thousanders always began a day's climb at night to avoid avalanches, they would become the most likely target for a hungry bear. It all fit. *But if that's the case, it has to have somewhere to go during the daytime. A hiding place located out of the sun and away from the light.* He realized that all three victims had been killed in the same general area. *I bet there's a cave or underground den somewhere in the kill area.*

Lhakpa finished his story. Harry turned off his camera. Armstrong thanked Lhakpa and Amala, then he and Harry put on their shoes and left. They walked back to their rented vehicle and got in. Harry started the car as Armstrong punched a number into his cell phone.

"Hello, Sir Randolph. Good news. I interviewed the porter,

and from his story I think the animal is a remarkably large Himalayan black bear. And get this—it's an albino. At least, I'm pretty sure it is. It's the only thing it could be, based on what the porter had to say. I think we can locate it for you, but we will need some ground penetrating radar equipment to do it, and some night vision equipment as well. And guns. Big guns."

"Whatever you need, you've got it," Sir Randolph said. "Just order it and have it delivered to me. I'll see that it gets to you."

"Okay. Sounds good." Armstrong hung up the phone, put it away, and rubbed his hands together with glee. "I love working with billionaires. Money is never a problem when they want something." His eyes were bright as he thought about what the future would hold.

"Getting an albino black bear on camera will be worth a bundle."

"No kidding," Harry said. "It'll be awesome."

"It will be one of our greatest shows ever. On the trail of an albino, serial-killer yeti that turns out to be an albino bear. My ratings will soar, and we'll sell a fortune in prime-time advertising!"

George Armstrong smiled, dreaming of ratings and dollar bills.

CHAPTER 29

DANE AWOKE AND looked at his watch. *We should get up in another hour. If this were a normal expedition, we would already be climbing.* But he knew better. Nothing was normal about this expedition.

The expedition's trek to south base camp had been uneventful. Dane had had fun because he had gotten to show Shelly many of the beautiful features of the Kangchenjunga area. After the first day of trekking, they had stopped in Lali Kharka, a village known for its *tungba*—a millet brew served in a wooden churn and topped off with a straw. Shelly had made a face while drinking it, but all in all she had been a good sport.

They had come across some Maoist rebels halfway to their destination, but with all the money they had, their 'toll' had been easy to pay. The rebels would probably have asked for more had they known, so Dane was glad that they had settled the matter without incident.

Phurba had sent much of the expedition ahead to set up base camp, so by the time they got there at midday everything was ready. The rest of the day, they had just relaxed and talked about their trek, which Shelly had enjoyed. Then they had slept, and he, at least, had dreamed.

Now it was 2:00 a.m. Dane lay there looking at Shelly in the moonglow that shone through a partially opened window in the tent. One of the advantages of working for a billionaire was access to state-of-the-art equipment. They had fallen asleep in a spacious one hundred and twenty-five square foot dome tent, one which could sleep eight but was currently sheltering three. Torleif and Shelly were still sleeping. Shelly looked beautiful, wrapped up in a down sleeping bag. Dane lay back and stared up at the tent's ceiling. *Phurba got base camp set up nicely and everything's ready to go. We've all the personnel and equipment we need. Now all we have to do is find Rand.*

"What are you thinking about?" Shelly whispered.

Dane turned to face her. "Nothing but how pretty you are."

"You're the sweetest man."

"*G'zaagi'in,*" Dane said, meaning 'I love you' in Ojibwe.

Dane leaned over in his bag to kiss Shelly. Dane heard someone's plodding footsteps outside the back of the tent.

"Phurba? ... That you?" Dane asked.

He unzipped his sleeping bag, switched on the lantern, and crawled toward the tent entrance. Shelly struggled to unzip her bag, but the zipper got stuck.

"Oh, crap," she said, sitting upright and fiddling with the zipper.

Torleif's eyes flickered, as he became aware of the hushed voices interrupting his slumber.

"Phurba?" Dane repeated. No response.

A ripping noise came from behind.

Dane looked over his shoulder at Shelly, who was still sitting up in her sleeping bag, trying to unstick the zipper. Behind her, massive, pinkish fingers, sprouting white hair and tipped with yellowed claws, sliced through the tent. Shelly heard the noise, looked back, and saw the claws. They were flecked with dried blood. She screamed, trying frantically to free herself from her sleeping bag. When the zipper remained immobile, she squirmed toward the entrance of the tent.

The beast tore open the tent like it was a flimsy plastic bag. It roared, and attacked. Everything moved in slow motion for Dane. He sprang forward, reaching for Shelly, who was still in her bag. The beast swung at him, and Dane raised his left arm up to shield himself. The beast's claws slashed his upper arm deeply, nicking the bone, and gashed his left cheek. The force of the blow knocked Dane off his feet, and he flew backward.

Shelly tried to wriggle away, still stuck in her bag. The monster stabbed down at her back, breaking her ribs and puncturing a lung. She gasped as she fought to breathe. The tent came apart in shreds and moonlight lit the horrific scene.

Torleif shed his sleeping bag and grabbed his ice ax. He dashed at the animal, racing to protect Shelly from further attack. The yeti backhanded Torleif, opening three gashes on his cheek and sending him to the ground. The Scandinavian lay semi-conscious on the tent's remains.

Dane had recovered his wits enough to know that he would not make much headway if he attacked the animal barehanded. He searched feverishly through his equipment, looking for his Bowie knife. *Where is it?*

The beast sprang upon the helpless Shelly. In the same instant, Dane found the sheath of his knife sticking out beneath Torleif's leg. He grabbed it and, unsheathing it in one smooth motion, he turned to lunge at the monster. He pivoted to attack, the beast's barbed fingers rip through Shelly's throat and carotid artery. She grabbed her neck and looked at Dane, blood pulsing through her fingers. The light in her eyes began to fade. She mouthed something. The words had no sound.

Dane's nightmare was real. "NO!"

Shelly collapsed and lay unmoving on the tent floor. For an instant that stretched endlessly, Dane heard nothing. His world narrowed, focused only on Shelly's limp form. He could not move, could not think. He was paralyzed.

The moment ended. A surge of adrenaline pulsed through Dane as the beast reached down to grab Shelly. Dane did not think. He charged the demon, knife held high.

"Aaaaaaaahhhhh!"

Diving for the beast's throat, he missed his target but opened a long gash in the beast's outstretched arm. Angered by pain, the monster swung at him, striking a solid blow. Dane flew sideways through the air, landing unconscious in the snow ten feet away.

The rest of the camp had been alerted by the noise. The beast heard yelling and recognized the sound of human voices. Putting the limp Shelly over his shoulder, the animal ran from the destroyed tent, only to encounter another human.

The beast stopped short. Torleif stood in the monster's way, an ice ax gripped in each hand. The beast hesitated.

"Hold on, big boy. I need a dead animal at my funeral," he said.

Awakened by the commotion, many Sherpas began leaving their tents. Phurba ran to where Dane's tent had been, seeing it had been ripped to shreds and that Dane lay unconscious on the ground nearby. He wondered if the mountaineer was dead.

Something moved in the darkness. The great beast stood there with Shelly slung over its shoulder, looking at Phurba. The hairs on the back of his neck stood up and he shivered. Torleif blocked the beast's path, then charged with lightening speed, swinging his ax and hitting the arm that held Shelly. Before he could swing the other ax, the animal jerked its arm away, taking the offending ax out of Torleif's hand. Shelly's body fell to the ground. Phurba knew that she was dead, seeing her throat had been torn apart.

The ax hung from the beast's arm for a split second, embedded in the wound, then fell to the ground as the animal shook it loose. Phurba hesitated, awed by the animal's inhuman strength. Aggravated by the pain from Torleif's strike, the beast swung its other arm in an uppercut aimed at Torleif. The animal's clawed fingers connected under Torleif's jaw, skewering him in the neck and lifting the six-foot-five, two hundred and sixty pound man four feet off the ground.

Phurba ran to help his friend. Torleif dropped the other ax and grabbed the beast's wrist with both hands, trying to free himself, his legs kicking. The monster tossed Torleif aside like a sack of potatoes, snapping his neck. Torleif's limp body flew into Phurba, knocking him off his feet. A few Sherpas now ran toward the scene. Torleif lay limp on top of Phurba, bleeding from his neck wound. Phurba rolled Torleif off of himself, and turned just in time to see the beast pick up Shelly's body and lumber off into the darkness.

Phurba watched it disappear into the night, Shelly's blonde hair trailing over his shoulder, her blood staining the beast's backside. He thought about chasing the beast, but he could not make himself move. *What would be the point? We have no weapons other than ice axes or knives. We came to search for Rand, not to hunt a monster.* Phurba was the sirdar, and he was in charge. He wanted no one else getting killed. He knew death when he saw it, and following the beast was death. *Nothing can be done. She's gone. Karma.*

He looked down at Torleif, his long-time friend and climbing companion. Torleif's dead eyes stared at nothingness. Other Sherpas came upon the scene, and after a moment

Phurba got up and rushed to Dane's side. Dane's arm gushed blood, but he was alive. If he was not bleeding internally, it was possible that Dane might live. Phurba began applying pressure to the wound using a T-shirt from Dane's pack. Some other Sherpas arrived.

"Get a doctor," Phurba said. One of the Sherpas nodded and ran off.

Dzangbu ran up with more Sherpas and knelt down to speak. "Which way did it go?" he whispered to Phurba. Dzangbu's look was urgent.

Had it been one of his normal men, Phurba would have forbidden any attempt to follow the beast. But Phurba knew Dzangbu was not an ordinary man, and he knew he should not try to stop him. Without speaking, he pointed in the direction the yeti had gone. Dzangbu stood up and gave chase, carrying nothing more than a light pack of climbing equipment. Phurba watched him go. *What's he going to do?*

"Get the sat phone for me. We need to get a med-evac in here quick," Phurba told another Sherpa, who ran off for the phone.

"Hold on, my friend," Phurba said. Dane started to come back to consciousness, his eyelids fluttering as though he were rousing himself from a terrible dream. One of the doctors, Dr. Meritt, arrived a few seconds later and started to examine him.

"Phurba," Dane said, barely audible.

"I'm here, Lake."

Dane went on weakly. "Check on Shelly." Dr. Meritt looked around, but could not see Shelly. He looked at Phurba, who shook his head mutely at Dr. Meritt.

"I'm sorry, Lake. She is gone," Phurba said.

"No, no, no. Noooooo!" Dane howled in anguish. He attempted to rise, but his arm would not support him. "Let me go! We have to go …"

"Hold him down. He probably has a concussion. He needs to lie still if we're going to keep him from bleeding too much," Dr. Meritt said. Phurba held Dane down. "I'll give him a sedative." Dr. Meritt pulled out a syringe from a pack of medical supplies and prepared the sedative.

"Hold on, my friend. The doctor is going to give you something."

"No," Dane said, struggling semi-consciously. "We have to go after Shelly." Dr. Meritt administered the sedative.

"We have to get you off this mountain, Dane," Dr. Meritt said. Dane's struggles grew more sluggish as the sedative took hold of his weakened body and sent him toward sleep. Blood, probably Shelly's, had pooled on what remained of the shredded tent. Phurba flashed back to all the blood he had seen in the snow during Rand's disappearance.

"Where's Leif?" Dane mumbled.

Phurba did not know what to say. Dane had lost his fiancée and a great friend in less than five minutes. He hesitated, finally the sedative took hold. Phurba sighed, grateful that he would not need to say anything else to his friend. Dane continued muttering something. Phurba leaned closer so that he could hear the words.

"I should've listened. Shudda listened, shudda liss …" Dane drifted into unconsciousness.

CHAPTER 30

HIS CRAMPONS GAVE him good traction in the snow as he ran. The Sacrifist was right on the beast's heels, but even the moonglow was not enough for him to glimpse the beast ahead. Even though he was only lightly clothed, the freezing air bothered him not at all.

Sacrifists had many skills aside from their specialized Sacrifist training. Like yogis, they could adjust their body's temperature at will. They had also been trained in the basics of mountain climbing in snow and ice.

The yeti was faster and had inhuman strength, but it was still carrying extra weight. Even though he was downwind, Dzangbu felt sure the yeti would sooner or later sense that it was being pursued, which would prevent it from slowing down. He left his headlamp off so as not to be detected.

Dzangbu stopped and listened for a moment. A shuffling noise drifted out of the darkness ahead. He continued to move through the snow. After another fifty yards, his target came into view. The beast slowed down, carrying its victim's body across the snow. Dzangbu gained ground as the beast abandoned the normal climbing route and headed to the left, walking another hundred yards toward the edge of a large crevasse.

Dzangbu slowed his pace. The beast dropped the body and kneeled down. Dzangbu thought it was going to start eating, but instead the yeti moved Shelly's body forward and it disappeared into the snow. Dzangbu crept closer, moving with care so as not to alert the beast. The yeti turned in Dzangbu's direction and sniffed the air. Dzangbu lay down flat in the snow to avoid being seen, his head flat against the snow. Waiting a few long seconds, Dzangbu took a risk and looked up. The beast had disappeared. Dzangbu looked around, but the creature was nowhere to be seen.

Dzangbu rose up and continued forward to where he had last seen the beast, keeping careful watch in case of an attack. The bright moonlight shone on the bloodied snow where Shelly's body had lain. He studied the area and saw a large hole. It was close to the crevasse and would likely be mistaken by climbers for part of the crevasse if they had come this way. But it was in the opposite direction of the path to the summit, so the area would have been avoided by climbers.

He kneeled down and looked into the blackness, but he could see nothing. He switched on the headlamp of his helmet. The hole went a long way down, the light glinted off some snow or ice at the bottom.

He took out two ice axes and began to make his way down into the hole. About halfway down, his right foot's crampon failed to make good contact with the snow wall and he slipped. Falling, he managed to slow his descent by dragging the axes along the sides of the hole. A pile of fresh snow broke his fall. He brushed the snow off and got up to see what he could see.

Shining his headlamp around the ice chamber, another dark opening revealed itself. He walked several feet inward, wary that he may encounter the beast at any moment. The ice cave led him into a stone tunnel. The headlamp showed him that the tunnel descended steeply. He stepped into the snowless tunnel and realized the crampons were a hindrance on the stone floor. He removed them and began to walk further down the tunnel.

He smiled, recognizing that he was in the home of the yeti. Sniffing the air, he could not detect any specific odor of the beast, just the invigorating freshness of mountain air. He descended into the depths, staying on high alert as he crept forward into the darkness outside of the area that his headlamp could light up. He kept his eyes to the floor to follow the droplets of blood shed by the beast's victim and prayed for her swift rebirth.

CHAPTER 31

"**SIR? ... SIR RANDOLPH!**" Montgomery said, louder than he had intended.

"Wha—" Sir Randolph had just fallen asleep when the butler addressed him. "What is it?"

"It's Jack Whitman, sir," Montgomery said, handing Sir Randolph the phone. "Calling from Kathmandu."

Jack was the pilot of his 707. Sir Randolph had told him to stay in Nepal until after the completion of the job. Jack was reliable.

"What is it, Jack?" Sir Randolph asked, rousing himself and sitting up.

"We don't know much, sir. I just got a call from a Mockingbird helicopter pilot asking for our assistance. Dane Nielsen was attacked and has been wounded. How badly we don't know. The Mockingbird pilot thought it would be faster if he flew him to Suketar airport. We can pick him up there and get him to a hospital in Kathmandu."

"Did he say what happened?"

"He didn't have a lot of info, sir. Just said Dane was attacked and was bleeding badly. He had to get going in order to take off before dawn."

"Okay. Meet the helicopter, and if possible, take a doctor along with some blood and transfusion equipment just in case. Get him to whatever the best hospital is in Kathmandu."

"Will do, sir," Jack replied. "He said one more thing, sir."

"What's that?"

Sir Randolph thought the line had gone dead when the pilot finally said, "He said Dane's fiancée is dead."

Sir Randolph sighed. "Sweet Jesus. You'd better get going, Jack."

Jack hung up the phone. Sir Randolph handed the phone back to Montgomery. He was in deep thought as Montgomery stood there waiting for his next command. *This confirms that people are being attacked by a vicious animal that only attacks at night. Maybe that jackass Armstrong is right.*

"Montgomery, bring me my mobile."

"Yes, sir." Montgomery left to retrieve the mobile.

I hope Torleif is okay, Sir Randolph thought.

Montgomery returned with the phone. It contained numbers for Prime Ministers and Presidents, as well as celebrities of all kinds, and even a few shady characters. He scrolled through looking for Armstrong, not thinking he would still be asleep.

"Hello," a groggy Armstrong said.

"More attacks have occurred," Sir Randolph said.

"More attacks? Who?"

"Unfortunately, Dane Nielsen and his fiancée Shelly Newton. Do you know them?"

"I know Dane. Didn't know his fiancée. Are they okay?"

"Dane is injured. We don't know how bad it is. Shelly is dead."

"Oh ... I'm sorry to hear that. That's too bad."

"Yes, it is," Sir Randolph said. "How are you coming along

at finding a guide and some porters to take you to base camp?"

"Not great. There's a lot of competition in the trekking business, and with the three recent unexplained deaths on Kangchenjunga many of the Sherpas are declining to go there. It'll be worse now with another death. Word is sure to get out."

"Keep me posted. Find some porters," Sir Randolph said.

"All right, Chief."

CHAPTER 32

WHILE THEY WAITED for the rescue helicopter, Phurba tried to calm down the Sherpas who had briefly spotted the yeti and were in a state of alarm. Most were concerned that the beast might come back. Or worse, *beasts,* plural, might attack. *Shelly and Torleif are dead. Dane is hurt badly. Their concern is warranted,* Phurba thought.

Phurba looked at the shredded tent with blood splattered everywhere. They had no guns, only ice axes, and a few Sherpas had seen what effect Torleif's ice ax had on the beast. Word traveled fast through base camp. The Sherpas' logic was—who wins between ice ax versus man-eating beast? Man-eater wins.

Phurba picked up and looked at Dane's bloodied knife. *He must have wounded the beast.* He threw it inside Dane's pack with his other things. Phurba could not believe he had seen the yeti *again.* He had now seen it twice when most people had never seen one their whole lives.

I should have told Torleif the truth. Then maybe they would never have come back and none of this would have happened. The other Sherpas clamored at him, rousing him from his thoughts. Most of them wanted to leave.

"That's enough!" Phurba yelled. "Are you a bunch of cowards? We have the injured leader of our expedition to look after. We will wait for the helicopter. Once Dane is on the helicopter, we will wait to hear from Sir Randolph, who is paying for you to be here. We will not leave until he says so. Is that understood?"

No one wanted to challenge Phurba. He was by far the best sirdar to work for. The Sherpas all nodded their heads and skulked back to their respective tents, occasionally looking over their shoulders for any sign of monstrous animals storming into camp. Phurba breathed a sigh of relief when the other Sherpas had quieted down.

He went back inside the large medical tent, where they had moved Dane after the attack. Dr. Meritt was with him. Dr. Lobsang Meritt was a rarity. He was half-English and half-Tibetan and could speak Sherpa fluently. He made his living attending the high-end expeditions.

"How is he?" Phurba asked, as Dr. Meritt took Dane's blood pressure.

"Okay for now, but we need to get him off the mountain. It was a pretty deep wound and I'm sure he has a concussion as well," Dr. Meritt said.

Phurba closed his eyes and prayed to Lord Buddha.

"Did you see it?" Dr. Meritt asked.

Phurba opened his eyes and looked at the doctor, but said nothing.

"You saw the creature. Didn't you?"

Might as well tell the truth, Phurba thought. "Yes. Yes, I did."

"What did it look like?"

"Like nothing you've ever seen before. It was covered with white hair and ferocious beyond belief. Eight feet tall, at least. It skewered Torleif by the neck with one clawed hand then lifted him in the air, and tossed him aside like he was some rag doll."

Phurba gestured with his hands and explained what he had seen to the doctor, and a huge guilty weight came off his shoulders. He did not care anymore. Two more people were dead, one of them a great, longtime friend, and it felt good to finally tell the truth to another human being who was not related to him by blood.

He wanted to tell Dr. Meritt that he had seen it kill Rand too, but he stopped short of doing so. He did not want Dr. Meritt to think he had withheld valuable information which might have prevented the expedition from occurring. He justified it to himself by thinking, *Lhakpa warned Torleif and he ignored it. He laughed at the possibility. In fact, he ignored it* twice.

When Dane and Phurba were catching up during the trek to base camp, Dane had relayed the story of how Lily's Uncle DJ had met them at the expedition agency and warned them against going. It was difficult to imagine that Phurba's warning would have done much better. *They were warned, and ignored the advice each time. Torleif and Shelly paid the steep price for not heeding it. Bad karma.* He silently thanked the Lord Buddha for keeping him alive.

"So ... what was it? A yeti, like the crew is saying?" Dr. Meritt asked.

"A yeti? ... I don't know. What do they look like? Have *you* ever seen one?" Phurba asked, making the obvious point that no one had ever positively identified one or even gotten this close before. "Ever since I was a child I have heard many stories of the Kangchenjunga Demon. And make no mistake, this *was* a demon. So, yes, I'll say that it exists. And I'll say that the demon's mountain is not safe to climb anymore and the sooner we leave this place, the better it will be for everyone."

The two men locked eyes for a moment. Dr. Meritt nodded his head and went back to tending Dane. Phurba walked out, heading back to his own tent.

A young Sherpa named Chamba peeked out from behind the medical tent and watched Phurba go. Chamba knew it was bad luck to speak about the Mih Teh. He wondered if he should say anything about the sirdar's story. Surely, this was important information but Chamba did not know to whom it would be valuable. If he mentioned it to his fellow Sherpas they may think he was lying or would be liable to tell the sirdar, and Phurba would think that Chamba had been eavesdropping on him. Which, in fact, he had been. Or the Sherpas may believe him and decide to leave base camp, as some were already whispering about doing. He was not altogether sure that he should continue to stay himself. It would be worth staying if he knew who needed this information. *But who would pay for this information?* he wondered.

CHAPTER 33

BEAU ARRIVED AT first light. Dr. Meritt had done all he could for Dane, and now he and Phurba loaded Dane onto the copter, along with Dane's personal things. Beau had also brought an EMT along, so there would be someone to look after Dane in case his condition worsened during the helicopter ride to Suketar.

Dane drifted in and out of consciousness while they made their way to Suketar airport to meet Sir Randolph's jet. *Bless the Madonna I reached Randolph's pilot,* thought Beau. *It will be much faster, and every moment counts when you don't know how bad a person's condition might be.*

All Beau knew was that Dane was in grave danger. As they flew, the EMT kept watch on Dane's vitals and alerted Beau when Dane's blood pressure dropped. Beau wondered if there was some internal bleeding Dr. Meritt had not been able to detect.

"The jet better be waiting for us. He should get to a hospital as quickly as possible," the EMT shouted over the engine noise. "Radio Suketar air traffic control and let them know the jet needs to be first in line when we get there."

Beau got on the radio and let the airport control staff know that they had a medical emergency.

Suketar Airport came into sight, and Beau noticed that Sir Randolph's jet had indeed made it in time. The transfer was quick. Beau brought the copter in for a landing right next to the jet and shut it down mere seconds later. He opened his door and was met immediately by Jack, Jack's co-pilot, and a doctor they had brought along with them. The EMT briefed the doctor as they moved Dane, who was still unconscious, onto the jet. The jet taxied out for take-off.

"Hope he makes it," the EMT said to Beau.

"C'est un coriace. Il va survivre. He's a tough guy. He'll make it."

***

On the plane, Dr. Sanduk Kharel determined that Dane should receive a blood transfusion immediately. He set the equipment up and began the transfusion. Checking Dane's blood pressure at regular intervals afterward, he was glad to see it had improved significantly before stabilizing. This was a sign that Dane was not suffering from internal bleeding, much to Dr. Kharel's relief.

The co-pilot came back to see the doctor, a satellite phone held up to his ear.

"Sir Randolph wants to know his status," the co-pilot said.

"He's going to be fine, but I would like to look at his wound more closely to see if it needs to be surgically repaired," Dr. Kharel said.

The co-pilot relayed Kharel's info into the phone, then listened. "Sir Randolph wants to know whether Dane can safely fly to England, if you accompany him."

"I can't go to England."

"That wasn't the question. Sir Randolph wants to know, if you accompany him, could Dane safely go to England?"

The doctor thought a moment.

"Yes. Theoretically, he could be transported there safely. I examined his wound, and though it's deep, the main artery doesn't appear to be nicked or cut. We have enough medical supplies on board, and he can safely make the trip provided he has someone here to attend to him. He might have a concussion, but he can still fly."

The co-pilot repeated what the doctor had said into the phone, then listened without speaking. After a moment, the co-pilot handed the phone to Dr. Kharel.

"Sir Randolph wants to talk to you," he said with a smug look on his face.

The doctor took the phone.

"Yes, sir?" He listened for a minute. "Yes, I'm sure. There is no danger. But I can't—" Sir Randolph cut him off, overriding his protests with an offer that made the doctor's eyes widen and his jaw drop open. "Yes. ... Okay, sir. Thank you, sir. Yes, sir."

He handed the phone back to the co-pilot, who listened to Sir Randolph for a moment before nodding.

"Yes, sir. We'll get right on it," he said, ending the call. He looked at Dr. Kharel and said, "So, I guess you're going to England ... *theoretically*."

Dr. Kharel gave him a crooked smile and shrugged his shoulders. "What's a week or two?"

The co-pilot laughed and walked back to the cockpit.

CHAPTER 34

DZANGBU FELT LIKE he had descended about a hundred feet when the tunnel leveled off. He kept his headlamp pointed toward the floor to help him track the beast. Deeper underground, he noticed the air temperature was milder. He realized the oxygen level had changed too. He did not think much about why, as he did not care, but he did take note of the change.

By the headlamp's light he could see fresh blood droplets that had fallen from Shelly when the beast retreated this way. Flashing the light onto the tunnel walls, the surface appeared unnaturally smooth. He ran his hand along the wall. It felt like stone, not earth, and appeared to be man-made. Of course, he knew he had been there before, but he was not fully cognizant of his exact location. He looked upward, and the headlamp showed that the tunnel ceiling had a smooth arch to it.

He came to a point where two more tunnels split off—one to the left and one to the right. He shone the light down each side tunnel, but saw nothing. He decided to search each side tunnel before passing them up, and he went down the left tunnel first.

Creeping forward, he studied the tunnel floor for any evidence that the beast had gone that way. Reaching the end, he found himself in a circular room, but there was no beast. Walking back, his headlamp brightened the wall near the entrance to the branch tunnel. Some markings graced the wall there, consisting of straight lines, dots and circles.

He had learned five languages at the gompa—Tibetan, Nepali, Sherpa, English and Kusunda—but the symbols bore no resemblance to any of them. Though he thought they looked familiar, he could make no sense of them. The tunnels also seemed familiar and although he knew he must have been here during his last lifetime, he could not recall a memory of it with any clarity. He repeated a similar search in the opposite tunnel and found another circular room with a dead-end.

He continued down the original main tunnel. After going a short distance, he got down on his haunches and examined the floor. A few fresh blood droplets told him that he was traveling in the right direction. The noise ahead made him quicken his pace.

The goal of achieving his life's purpose was at hand. He was ready to make the supreme sacrifice to save others and honor the sacred pledge. He was not afraid, he was excited.

Looking down the long tunnel, he noticed a faint light shining in the distance. Drawing closer to the lighted area, he came across two more sets of left-right branching tunnels. Instead of exploring the side tunnels and wasting any time, he looked for evidence in the main tunnel first, and each time he found more blood drops. The beast had stayed in the main tunnel.

The tunnel opened into a large square-shaped cavern room. He moved to the entrance and peeked inside the room. It was empty but lit by four torches, each of them stuck into one of the four walls. He assumed the torches must have been lit by the other Sacrifists.

He entered and switched off his headlamp. The walls had the same unnatural smoothness as the tunnels.

Shaped somewhat like a pyramid, the room had four triangular walls curving upward to a central point. Each wall had a tunnel opening that led away from the room. A torch next to each exit revealed more markings there. The symbols were similar to those he had seen in the two branching tunnels he had explored.

Staring in wonder, he walked about the space, looking up at the strange markings. He was wondering what they meant, when he fell over a dead body. He recognized the body of the woman who had arrived at base camp the day before. Her dead eyes stared back at him. He closed her eyes and said a prayer for her swift rebirth.

Next to her body lay two others—one of them human, with its face mauled into the consistency of hamburger. The other set of remains obviously belonged to a black bear. Both had been devoured, but the beast had not yet begun to eat the woman.

Getting back up, Dzangbu prayed for all of them. "Om mani padme hum, om mani padme hum."

The beast had not begun eating her, and Dzangbu realized that the yeti would come back for her. He decided to wait for the beast. He made his way back to the tunnel from which he had come and sat down in a meditation posture.

He *assumed* that the beast would return from one of the three other tunnels. But as he meditated, he reached out beyond his body and his attention began to permeate the space around him. His attention grew wider and wider, into a growing sphere.

And then he knew—his assumption had been wrong.

CHAPTER 35

LUMBERING DOWN THE long tunnel with Shelly's body over his shoulder, the beast found the wound on his forearm nagging at him. He had never been wounded before. He continued to bleed, but the wound was not deep. The beast perceived he was being followed. Besides the Others, no other living creatures had ever entered his realm before.

Even the Others could not enter his domain without the beast knowing it. His evolved sense of hearing told him that this was an unknown intruder. Unaccustomed to being followed, he quickened his pace, noticing the intruder's odor was similar to but different than that of other prey he had attacked in the past. He recognized the scent as coming from one of the creatures that walked erect, but there was an element missing from it.

The footsteps grew fainter and then stopped for a time, and the yeti recognized that the trespasser must have gone down a side tunnel, but the sound of footsteps resumed in the main tunnel after a few minutes. The animal lay his food aside in the lighted cavern room and retraced his steps, heading back up the passageway and toward the trespasser. A pinpoint of white light appeared much further up the channel. The sight reminded him of the lights the climbing creatures carried on their heads.

The monster ducked down a nearby side tunnel, crouched, and waited. Watching the tunnel opening, the yeti saw the headlamp of the creature get brighter and brighter as it came closer. The beast readied itself to attack the intruder if it turned into his tunnel. But its shadow walked by, accompanied by the light shining from its head. After the intruder passed by, the beast heard it pause for a few moments, then continue its trek toward the cavern room.

Alarmed at the thought of losing the food he had left behind in the room, the animal crept to the entrance of the side tunnel and peeked down the main tunnel, then watched the intruder step into his food pantry. It disappeared into the room. The giant yeti moved down the passageway toward the interloper.

The monster knew something was wrong. This was *his* domain, and any creature that he attacked, or which became aware of his presence, had a specific odor—the scent of fear. This was the element missing from the interloper's essence, and the beast was wary.

The yeti prowled down the tunnel toward the feasting room, but stayed far enough away from the ambient light so as to be shrouded in darkness. From there, he watched the intruding creature's movements. The creature stumbled, then got up and began to repeat a series of sounds over and over. A moment later, the sounds stopped, and the beast watched as the intruder backed into the tunnel near where the beast was hiding in the darkness. The beast took his breath in slowly through his nostrils—even now, no scent of fear emanated from this small creature and the beast knew—the little creature waited to attack him.

The yeti's fledgling intellect tried to process the situation. He had never been the prey before, and he had no experience with predators. This small being was stalking him. Disturbed, the beast did not move or breathe. The intruder's dark outline against the light of the cavern room sat completely still, flat on the ground, only about twenty-five yards away from the beast. The beast crept forward softly. At fifteen yards, he made the decision to attack.

Bounding forward and roaring, the beast readied himself to attack, seeing the trespasser clearly—black hair with a splash of white, like his own. The yeti bore down to crush this trespasser of his domain. But the little creature did an odd thing.

It did nothing. It did not even move.

In a split second, the yeti changed his mind and swung at the being's head, knocking it senseless. Without looking back, the beast gathered up the freshly killed human's body and left the room via the nearest tunnel, relieved to be away from the odd creature.

It was the first time the beast had opted not to kill when the opportunity had presented itself to him. He could not understand how he knew it, but he sensed that killing the tiny invader would have been harmful to him.

CHAPTER 36

PHURBA AROSE THE day after the attack to the sound of heated arguing coming from outside his tent. He went outside and saw his deputy, Nawang, arguing with several other Sherpas who were packed up and ready to leave.

"What's all this about?" Phurba asked.

"They want to leave," Nawang said. The others all started clamoring at once.

"One at a time," Phurba said, holding up his hands. He pointed to the oldest man in the group. "Pemba."

"Sorry, sirdar, but we respectfully ask to be allowed to leave. Many others left in the middle of the night," Pemba said. Phurba looked at Nawang, who nodded his head.

The elder Sherpa continued. "We respect you as our sirdar, and we won't run away like cowards in the night. We will tell you now and to your face. There is danger here. *You know* there is."

Phurba nodded at Pemba and turned to Nawang. "How many are left?"

"About half."

Phurba could not believe so many Sherpas had left. "How

many more want to leave?"

"These few," Nawang said, pointing at the five Sherpas requesting to leave.

I'll have to send Nawang off to get replacements and weapons for protection, he thought, realizing that the men who went with Nawang might not come back either. *Better to get some men here who haven't experienced the horror of a nighttime yeti attack.* Phurba could not afford to lose any more men. Since he'd been unable to reach Sir Randolph, Phurba had to decide how to keep the expedition together.

"I want a list of everyone who has left. Tell everyone who stays that there will be extra pay as a reward for completing this expedition," Phurba said. "Go tell them now."

Nawang smiled and ran off to spread the word. Phurba suspected that Nawang was laughing on the inside and would know what Phurba was doing. Phurba had been climbing with Nawang since they were both seventeen. They were best friends. Their wives were best friends. Nawang had often seen Phurba lead other men and get them to do what he wanted them to do.

They had lost many expedition members, and they might soon lose some more, but Phurba knew that Nawang would not be among them. Even though Nawang had seen the monster with his own eyes, it did not matter. He had no choice. *You don't desert your best friend.* Phurba thought he was lucky to have such loyal men with him.

Phurba wondered how long they would be staying on Kangchenjunga, given the two fatalities and the head guide severely injured. He hoped it would not be long, but knew it was not up to him. If someone was willing to pay for them to stay, they would stay.

Phurba sighed and turned back to the five Sherpas who

wanted to leave.

"Go ahead and leave if you want. Don't expect any more work on my expeditions, though." Phurba began to walk away.

The other Sherpas started jabbering at Pemba. Pemba shushed them all and called out, "Phurba!"

Phurba stopped and turned around.

Pemba nodded. "We will stay."

"Thank you," Phurba said. "You are good men."

Phurba was not smiling even though he had gotten his way. *I hope I don't regret making them stay,* he thought.

CHAPTER 37

DZANGBU BECAME CONSCIOUS again, and he felt his cheek against the cold, gritty cavern floor. The silence told him he was alone but alive. He sat up slowly. His head nearly exploded with pain and began to throb. Brushing the tiny dirt particles from his cheek, he stood up and began to slap the dust from his simple black attire. He wondered how long he had been unconscious.

He checked himself over, finding no open wounds or injuries other than his splitting headache. Retrieving his headlamp, he noticed that the beast had taken the woman's body away. He explored about twenty yards down each one of the four exit tunnels, hoping to determine where his target had gone. Each passage's floor had huge footprints leading into and out of the room, but he could find no blood or hair evidence in any of them, leaving him with no clue as to which route the beast had taken. He also had no idea how long the beast had been gone.

He felt disappointed at not completing his mission, but he was not defeated. He thought about what to do next. From the number of offshoot tunnels, it appeared there was an entire network of tunnels here. His previous incarnation's recollection of the tunnel system had not returned to him.

He looked at his options: look for the demon, find the other Sacrifists, or return to the gompa. He decided to search for the other Sacrifists. He began by searching the six offshoot tunnels that branched from the main tunnel he had entered. Each offshoot tunnel entered into a small circular room with no exits.

He went back to the cavern room and entered the first tunnel on the right. He crept down the dark tunnel but saw some light at the end and ran quickly toward it. He entered an empty circular room with only one exit, but the exit was not straight ahead. It was off to the left. Dzangbu thought this was odd. He had been good at mathematics. He considered the circular nature of the room, and estimated the exit to be located about one hundred and twenty degrees from the other tunnel entrance.

He continued out the exit, and entered into another dark tunnel. Another light shone in the distance. He ran toward it and was soon in another square cavern room that looked like the one he had already been in. Besides the tunnel through which he had entered, there were three other exit tunnels. Rather than take a tunnel on the left or right, he decided to take the tunnel directly ahead.

He soon came to another circular room that was identical to the first room he had entered. It also had an exit on the left, located one hundred and twenty degrees away from the entrance. From that, he guessed that there would be four more circular rooms, for a total of six.

He soon proved himself correct. The complex had six cavern rooms and six circular rooms. The only variation was that in the last circular room he entered, the one immediately before the cavern room where he had started, there was an immense spherical boulder sitting in the center of the room. It had been partially sunk into the floor. Otherwise, all the rooms had been empty aside from the torches set into the walls.

In the boulder room, a concave track led out from the boulder. He wondered what it represented, but could find no hint of its meaning within the room itself.

After he had circled back to the original cavern room, he knew that one tunnel in each cavern room led to the center of the complex. He entered that tunnel, and running as fast as he could, he dashed into the center room. Completely lit by many torches, the room was enormous and resembled a circular amphitheater with three rows of seats and six exits.

But the oddest sight was a tall statue depicting a woman and a beast with small horns who were sharing an embrace. The statue stood in the center of the room. The statue jogged his memory and he recalled being there before, not alone but in the company of many other Sacrifists. But the memory was too vague to help him with his search.

He had searched virtually everywhere and had not located the beast. He was quite sure the beast was on the same level of the tunnel complex, but he suspected the beast's attuned senses would prevent him from catching it. He needed a different strategy, but he would need help, and he had found no other Sacrifists. Without their help, his mission might fail.

One thing bothered him above all others. The beast had not attacked him with the intent to kill. The implications of this were dire indeed.

From his training, he knew this had never happened to a Sacrifist before. A Sacrifist had never returned to Diki Chhyoling without completing his or her mission. He decided that he would be the first, as he thought maybe Yangji would have some counsel to offer him.

He headed back up the entrance tunnel. It took about five minutes to reach the snow cave area. Fortunately, the shaft upward had not sealed over with snow. He put on his crampons and got out both of his ice axes. He free-climbed the ice chute and made it back topside.

It was daylight when he emerged from the cave. The sunlight initially hurt his eyes, making his headache pound even harder. Putting his pain into a compartment, he headed back to base camp, which he could see in the distance.

He walked into base camp, and noticed many of the Sherpas who had begun the expedition with him had vanished. Those that remained were visibly surprised to see him. Most had apparently assumed he had deserted the camp, and a few of them made comments as he passed, saying he only had returned because word had reached him about the increase in pay.

One of the Sherpas even shouted at him. "Look, the rookie wants to make the big money!" The other Sherpas joined in and laughed at Dzangbu.

Phurba walked out of the communications tent and the Sacrifist spotted the sirdar and turned in that direction. Seeing Dzangbu getting razzed by the others, Phurba gave them a stern look, and they went about their business.

"How long have I been gone?" Dzangbu asked.

"You left last night," Phurba said, giving him an odd look. No doubt he was wondering why Dzangbu did not know.

Phurba invited Dzangbu into his tent and gave him a protein bar to eat. Dzangbu looked at it. He had seen others eating them, but he had never had one before. He had rarely eaten at the gompa. Part of his training as a Sacrifist was to go without food or water for long periods of time, subsisting on meditation only, a process known to some as Breatharianism.

Breatharians could not really exist for long in human form,

since the human body needs food and water to survive. Yet there had been rare instances of human Breatharians going for months without food and water. Most recently, Ram Bahadur Bomjom of South-Central Nepal, also known as the 'Buddha Boy,' had gone for at least ten months without food or water, meditating in the hollow of a tree.

A film crew filmed him meditating, and he remained unmoving for ninety-six hours straight. The average human being could only last three or four days without water. During the filming Ram was observed for longer than four days and showed no signs of dehydration. Many witnesses believed he was the reincarnated Buddha, but he denied this, claiming only to have become enlightened like the Buddha through meditation.

Dzangbu partially unwrapped the bar and took a bite. Its label declared that it was chocolate chip with peanut butter. He did not know what to think. It tasted different from anything he had ever eaten before. He did not know if it was okay or sinful to be eating the sweet bar, but he knew it tasted good.

Phurba watched him, apparently deducing Dzangbu's thoughts from his facial expressions, and started laughing.

"Tastes good, huh?" Phurba asked.

"Yes," Dzangbu said. Phurba gave him some water. The Sacrifist drank it down, pocketing the protein bar after one bite.

"Did you find the beast?" Phurba asked.

"Yes."

"What happened?"

"Not what was supposed to happen."

"I'm sorry," Phurba said, although he did not know what was supposed to happen.

"I must return to the gompa and consult with my master."

"Of course."

"I will be leaving now."

"Okay. We'll be here for at least a couple weeks if you come back this way," Phurba said. "Do you need an escort for your return to the gompa?"

"No. Thank you. No one would be able to keep up."

Phurba looked puzzled, then briefly incredulous. Dzangbu understood. Phurba had some of the fittest Sherpas in the world working on his team, but he had certainly never encountered another Sacrifist.

The Sacrifist got up. "Thank you for your help," he said to Phurba. "Namasté."

"Namasté," Phurba said. They walked outside. Carrying his light pack, Dzangbu waved at Phurba as he started back down the mountain. He was walking out of camp when the Sherpa who had been ribbing him started to chide him again.

"Oh, have you changed your mind?" he said.

"You're going the wrong way," another yelled. They all laughed, but Dzangbu paid them no mind.

"Leave him alone," Phurba said. "Do you need some work to do?" The other Sherpas heard their sirdar and shut up and dispersed. A cold breeze hit Phurba as he watched the still lightly clothed Dzangbu begin to run down the mountain. *Running. Unbelievable. I'd love to know your whole story.*

CHAPTER 38

THE BEDROOM AT Sir Randolph's home, with its ornate oak paneling and priceless antiques, looked like anything but a hospital room. A Louis XV cartel wall clock chimed, waking Dane. A voice spoke to someone and Dane kept his eyes shut.

"He could wake at any time," the voice said. "How he reacts will determine if we need to sedate him again."

The first day at Sir Randolph's, Dane had woken up yelling that it had all been his fault and that he should never have allowed Shelly on the trip. Still under the influence of heavy pain medication, he wanted to get out of bed, but was restrained and sedated by those who had been attending him. He vaguely remembered flipping out. The thought he could not get out of his mind was seeing Shelly mouth 'I love you,' blood seeping through her fingers as she held her own throat.

"He's lost his fiancée. That's enough to wreck anyone," Sir Randolph said. Dane recognized Sir Randolph's voice.

"Yes. That's why I'm worried about his reaction when he learns his Norwegian friend was killed. It could be too much. Physically he's fine, but I don't think he should be told more until he's more stable emotionally."

Torleif's dead, too. This horrifying news had the opposite effect on Dane. Instead of plunging him into despair, it brought back a memory.

***

Dane was seven. He had gone back to Minnesota for the summer to visit his grandparents on the reservation for the first time. Later in life, he found out his mother had refused to see her parents for so long because they were angry with her for marrying outside of the tribe. When they finally met her husband, Mack, they were surprised to find out he was a quarter Yaqui—a tribe from the southwestern United States.

While visiting them, his dog, King, a Samoyed, had been hit by a car and killed. His grandfather, Mingo Wakonabo, a medicine man or *midewinini*, found him crying in his bedroom. A midewinini was a practitioner of Midewiwin, the secretive religion of the Ojibweg. The root word *mide* had many meanings, but was mainly related to 'spiritual mysteries.'

"What's all this, then?" Mingo asked.

"King is dead, Nimi," Dane sobbed, using the shortened version of the Ojibwe word for grandfather, *Nimishomis*.

"Okay. But why are you crying? His spirit lives on. Are you Ojibwe or aren't you? The Ojibweg are a strong people who do not cry at the death of the body. Even our little *babies* don't cry."

"What? How?" Dane asked, his tears subsiding.

"As babies, the Ojibweg are taught not to cry. If the tribe is hiding from danger and a baby cries, it could expose the whole tribe. So why are you crying? You don't want a Wendigo to know where we are, do you?"

Dane shook his head, remembering the *Wendigo*—the

Ojibwe monster of legend.

"Can you be strong, like an Ojibwe, and protect us?"

His grandfather stared down at him, waiting to see what he would do. Dane swallowed his grief, digging deeply within his soul for the strength not to cry for the loss of his dog, though his sadness continued. His grandfather saw him stop crying and smiled.

"You're a good boy. A strong Ojibwe boy. Very brave. Thank you for protecting us."

It felt good to hear his grandfather's praise. Later that day, Mingo told his wife, Margie, and Dane's mother, Mitzi, about the young boy's courage.

"His eyes were like waterfalls. But this Ojibwe boy became very brave and stopped the water from falling. He has real strength," Mingo said.

"Thank you, Dane," his grandmother said.

His mother had an idea after hearing her father's story of Dane's deed. She thought it would be a good idea to perform a name-giving ceremony for Dane.

"Mom, why not give Dane an Ojibwe name? Can you give him one even though he is older?"

Margie was a name-giver for her Ojibwe tribe. Name-givers were considered special people, and not just anyone could become one. It was a gift. Not having been born on the reservation, Dane had never been given an Ojibwe name. Usually the ceremony was done within four months of a baby's birth, but Dane had grown up in Colorado.

"I will meditate about it to see if the spirits agree to give forth a name," Margie said.

A week went by. One morning, his mother came to wake him.

"The spirits visited your grandmother in her dreams last

night. A ceremony will be performed later in the week."

All that week, Dane looked forward to hearing his new Ojibwe name. A name-giving was done with great ceremony, and many other people from the tribe would come to the ceremony and its accompanying feast. The ceremony was done with its participants speaking only in Ojibwe. Fortunately, Dane understood Ojibwe because his mother had spoken it to him since birth.

He knew his grandparents' English first names were just alterations of their Ojibwe names. Margie's real name was *Migwaans*, meaning 'Little Feather.' Mingo's was *Miskwaa Ma'iingan*, meaning 'Red Wolf.' His mother, Mitzi, was *Migiziins*, meaning 'Little Eagle.'

During the ceremony, Dane's grandmother thanked his parents for honoring her as the name-giver. She accepted a gift of tobacco, which was traditionally given to the name-giver during the ceremony. She talked about how and where she had gotten the authority to give the name she was giving to Dane.

She told those assembled the story about the passing of Dane's dog that his grandfather had relayed to her, so the tribe knew she was being truthful. In her dreams, the spirits told her the event was to be commemorated by Dane's name.

Then his grandmother pronounced his Ojibwe name for the first time as she faced each of the four cardinal directions in turn—*Zaaga'igan Nishkiinzhigoon*, meaning 'Lake Eyes.' Each time she said it, the name was echoed by the rest of the congregation.

This was done both so the Spirit World could accept and recognize the child as a living thing for the first time and so his ancestors would protect him and prepare a place for him when his life ended. Many at the feast nodded in agreement at the wise choice of the name, and some remarked upon the coincidence created by Dane's blue eyes.

Afterward, his grandmother kissed him on the forehead and took him to meet his eight *we-ehs*—four men and four women. Before the ceremony, Dane's parents had chosen them. We-ehs were like godparents. Each we-eh kissed his forehead and welcomed him to the tribe by calling him by his Ojibwe name.

His grandmother asked if any of the we-ehs wished to give him a different name, which was their right. None of them thought that changing the name was a sensible idea, so the name became permanent, sealing the ceremony as complete. Afterward, there was a feast to honor his new name.

The name-giving ceremony made Dane feel like he was part of something bigger than himself. He felt a foot taller, like a real man, and knew he was now part of the great heritage of the Ojibweg.

***

"Tell me when he wakes up," Sir Randolph said.

"I'm awake," Dane said, sitting up in bed. The look on their faces told him they were wondering if he had heard them talking. "Yes. I heard. Leif's dead. No more sedation; I have work to do. I'm going back. Has anyone notified Torleif's wife?"

"Yes. I took care of it, and I've made sure that Torleif's remains were flown home," Sir Randolph said. "I couldn't locate any next of kin for Shelly."

"She had an Uncle. Besides that, Shelly only had me." When he said it, there was a silence in the room. *I let her down.* He looked from Dr. Kharel to Sir Randolph. It was clear from their expressions that they understood how he felt. "Thanks for contacting Torleif's family. I'll need to pay my respects before I do anything else. Can you help get me where I need to go?"

"Of course, Dane," Sir Randolph said, pausing a moment. "I had a couple of men looking into what kind of animal was attacking the climbers."

"Did they come up with anything?" Dane asked.

"Yes. They think the beast is an albino Himalayan black bear that uses the snow as camouflage and must have a den underground," Sir Randolph said. "They've asked for some ground penetrating radar."

"It's not a bear," Dane said.

"You're sure?" Sir Randolph asked.

"Yes. I wounded it."

"Wounded? How?"

"Cut its arm with my knife."

"What is it?"

"It's an albino, all right. I looked into its eyes. Red eyes. I was only a few feet away from it. It's not a bear, though. It's more like a man-ape but much bigger than either. Its face was huge, but more human-like than ape faces, and its hands were closer to a human's hands than to a bear's or an ape's. Its body was mostly covered in white shaggy hair, so I think you're right about how it uses snow as camouflage."

They stared at Dane in evident disbelief.

"Unbelievable," Sir Randolph said at last. "Are you absolutely positive? It may have been a hallucination from extreme stress. Or perhaps nightmares have affected your memory of what you saw."

Dane became serious. "I know how this sounds. A week ago, I would have blown off anyone who told me this, dismissed them as crazy." *I did blow someone off,* he thought. "I don't say it lightly. But what I'm describing to you is true. Phurba and maybe some others at base camp may be able to confirm it."

"The Kangchenjunga Demon," Dr. Kharel murmured under his breath.

"Exactly. It must be the yeti," Dane said.

"Unbelievable," Sir Randolph said. He met Dane's gaze, and Dane saw the moment when disbelief turned into acceptance, then hardened into resolve. "My boy, I'm going with you. While you're paying your respects, I'll spend my time getting acclimated and trekking to base camp. If we can prove the yeti's existence, it will go down as of one of the biggest finds in the history of anthropology."

"Fine with me. You can go down in history books if you want. I don't want to confirm its existence to the world. I want to kill it and confirm its death. So we'll need to bring big guns. Lots of them."

CHAPTER 39

YANGJI MEDITATED, AND there was a polite knock at his door.

"Come in," he said.

Chodak entered the room, bowing. "Namasté, Rinpoche. Sorry to disturb you. Dzangbu has returned."

Yangji was shocked but did not allow his expression to show it. "Show him in immediately."

Chodak left to retrieve Dzangbu. *This is distressing. What could have happened to force him to return?* Yangji knew there had never been an instance of a Sacrifist returning to Diki Chhyoling once they had left to fulfill their mission. *Not one has ever returned. Not until their next incarnation, at least.*

Dzangbu came into the room and performed a prostration before his master. Yangji motioned for him to sit nearby.

"What has happened?"

"I have failed."

"You've quit?"

"No. Of course not."

"Ah. So you've just delayed your success."

"Yes." Dzangbu smiled slightly at his Master's observation.

Dzangbu was not a monk and had not been trained as one. He had a specific skill, for a specific task, and that was all.

"Tell me what happened."

Dzangbu nodded and began to explain what happened in Kangchenjunga's subterranean tunnels. *I've suspected there must be some underground sanctuary for the yeti to hide in, but there has never been a confirmation of this,* Yangji thought. Listening to Dzangbu tell his story, Yangji was astonished. He realized that the information Dzangbu was providing would help future Sacrifists.

Dzangbu dropped the bomb.

"I believe it's thinking rationally," Dzangbu said. "I can think of no other reason for the yeti's refusal to engage me."

If the yeti refuses to engage Dzangbu, he will not be able to complete his mission, Yangji thought. The implications of this were alarming. Yangji and Dzangbu both knew that this factor could be the *actual* meaning behind the Qolom Qasigi Duktsi prophecy: "The White Bad Son will be difficult to quiet."

"When you regained consciousness, did you explore any of the other tunnels?"

"Yes, I checked through much of the tunnel system and found that one of the larger tunnels forms a hexagon. Then there are other tunnels that branch out from the hexagon. My guess is the yeti sensed my presence and stayed one step ahead of me. I thought it best to come back here and see if there was any more knowledge available, any more information that could help me in my task."

The term hexagon began to stimulate Yangji's memory of something that he could not quite recall. "I'm sorry, my son. All the Sacrifist knowledge has been provided to you. There is no more. Is there anything else you can tell me about the beast or the tunnels?"

Dzangbu thought a moment.

"Yes. There were some symbols near each of the tunnel entrances that branched off, and I noticed a few in the cavern room, as well. I believe it was a type of alphabet or code. They seemed familiar to me, of course, but I don't know their meaning. They were variations of circles, lines, and dots."

Again something stirred in Yangji's memory, images from when he was a young student with a master of his own. The full memory came back. Yangji rose to his feet. "Come with me."

The Sacrifist followed his master. They walked down a long hallway and into the gompa's library, a room containing all the Buddhist holy books and additional, esoteric knowledge. Many of these books looked as though they had never been opened. When he was young, Yangji had spent many a day in the library. A voracious reader, he had soaked up as much knowledge as he could find.

Dzangbu followed Yangji closely. In the corner of the room sat the large wooden and leather chest, containing all the books of Sacrifist-related knowledge. The chest had two locks. One key was held by the senior Sacrifist; the other key was held by whoever was the present High Lama of Diki Chhyoling. Dzangbu had surrendered his key to Senge, the librarian, the day he had departed the gompa. Therefore, the chest could never be opened by only one person alone.

Yangji walked to the bookshelf that looked to have the least use and the most dust collected on it.

"Here," Yangji said, pointing at two books on the top shelf, out of their reach. "Senge, please retrieve those two books for us."

Senge got up from his small desk in the corner, where he had been studying, and walked over to them. Towering at least a foot over both of them, he easily retrieved the two volumes for

Yangji. The books were eight inches tall and five inches wide, but not thick, at less than half an inch each in width. They were similar, but the older of the two was leather bound.

"Thank you, Senge. Please unlock the trunk. I want to put this leather one inside."

The gompa's librarian, Senge, would be the keeper of the senior Sacrifist's key until such time as the new apprentice arrived to fill Dzangbu's absence, thus making Tendzen the senior Sacrifist. It would be another ten years before Yangji would send out a legation of three monks to locate a girl named Chesa, who would become the new junior Sacrifist.

Senge opened one lock on the trunk. Yangji retrieved a key from around his neck and opened the other lock. Lifting the lid, he deposited the older text inside, then closed and locked the trunk.

"Thank you, Senge."

"My pleasure, Rinpoche. Namasté."

Dzangbu and his master headed to Yangji's room and shut the door behind them. Yangji sat down at his desk and motioned for Dzangbu to sit next to him. Dzangbu had spent many years sitting with Yangji in his room as part of being trained as a Sacrifist, and was accustomed to it.

Yangji laid the book on the table. The book's cover was made of blue cloth. It had no writing on it. Although it looked fairly new compared to the one Yangji had stored in the Sacrifist trunk, it had some wear and tear from use.

"The book in the trunk is quite old," Yangji said to Dzangbu. "It may be one of the oldest books we have at the gompa, or even in our existence as Buddhists. The author is unknown and no one has been able to decipher what the pages mean. Therefore, it has never been used in any way at all. This one is an exact copy that I had made."

Yangji handed the book to Dzangbu, who opened the book to the first page with writing on it. The words were Tibetan. The short script read:

The following symbols have been copied directly from a terma in the form of an ancient leather scroll discovered in a treasure chest I found at the bottom of the burning lake, Membartso, in Bhota-anta. It is one of the one hundred and eight treasures of Guru Rinpoche. I had a dream that a gompa should be built near Sewalungma [Kangchenjunga] *to house this text. In the dream, the text comes into the hands of the revealer by way of Sewalungma. I sent the butter lamp I used to discover this terma, along with the text itself.*

It was signed by Pema Lingpa, the foremost of the Five Great Tertön Kings. Tertöns were the finders of *terma*, meaning 'hidden treasure.' A terma could be an ancient text or a ritual instrument, and could be hidden in the earth, or in a lake, a tree, a rock, a crystal, or even in the sky. The Nyingmapa scriptures were updated by terma discoveries, and terma teachings guided many Buddhist and Bön practitioners.

"Is Pema Lingpa writing about your gompa's butter lamp that has been burning continuously for the last four hundred years?" Dzangbu asked.

Yangji nodded his head. "That is what past scholars have believed."

Dzangbu turned the page. On the next page, were the same kind of symbols he had seen in the tunnels—a series of circles marked with lines and dots. The page only had five symbols on it, and it appeared to Dzangbu's eyes to be a title page. The next page was filled with symbols. He scanned it but saw nothing there that he could understand.

The symbols were in some kind of geometric progression. The circle acted as a base for the placement of the lines and dots. The circles with no lines only had zero to five dots, with dot placement restricted to the center and the four cardinal directions. Even with those limits, this allowed for many combinations.

The circles with lines had one to four intersecting lines and zero to eight dots—a dot's placement being permissible inside the sections created by the intersecting lines. This yielded many more combinations.

"These are the same symbols I saw in the tunnel system," Dzangbu said.

"That's what I suspected when you told me what they looked like," Yangji said. "Monks and Buddhist scholars have attempted to understand these symbols several times over the centuries, but all of them have failed."

"Perhaps their success has just been delayed," Dzangbu said, smiling.

Yangji bowed his head. "Of course."

Dzangbu slowly turned several pages in the book, and he began to have the idea that he knew, or once had known, the meaning of the symbols. Each page was filled with them. He did not have time to concentrate upon their individual meanings, although he thought that their significance might return to him at some point in the future.

Presently, he came to another page that was nearly blank, save for four symbols.

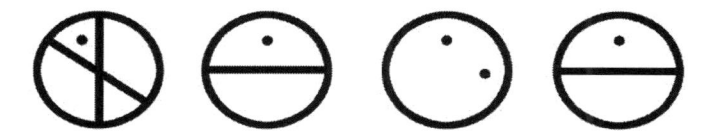

"So few symbols on this page," Dzangbu said.

"A title, perhaps," Yangji said. He shrugged.

Dzangbu turned the page. The next page was unlike any of the preceding pages. It was a large, carefully drawn decorative hexagon symbol that looked like a snowflake with six branches. It appeared to be perfectly symmetrical. A large circle was in the center of the hexagon and a smaller circle was located at each of the six points. Between each point were smaller squares. Lines connected all the circles and squares.

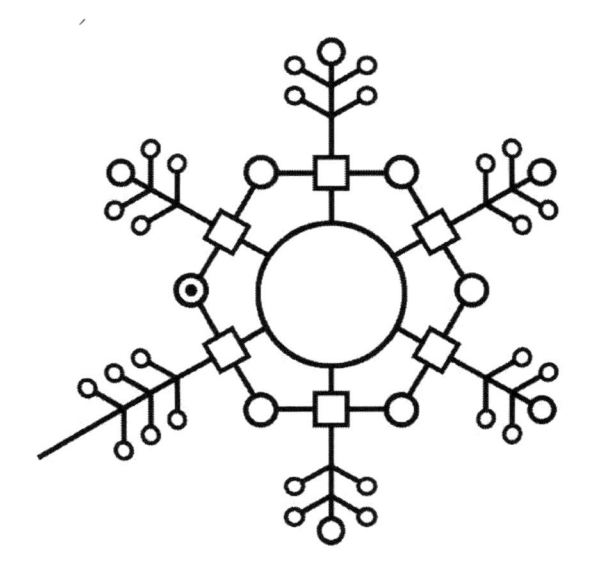

"Quite unlike the others," Yangji said. "A beautiful symbol, is it not? Like a snowflake."

Dzangbu did not hear Yangji at first. He was transfixed by the figure on the page. He realized that it showed where he had already been. He wondered at the intricacy to the demon's lair. But the map gave him hope of eventually locating the other Sacrifists.

"This is not a symbol, Rinpoche. It's a map of the tunnel system I was in. Do you see the hexagon?"

Yangji's face lit up at his student's observation. "Ah, yes."

"These lines represent tunnels, and the squares and circles are rooms," Dzangbu said, pointing at the features.

"The student teaches the master. It appears I was mistaken. There *is* further Sacrifist knowledge. I apologize," Yangji said in mock deference.

They smiled at each other.

Dzangbu continued. "Here is the problem. I searched almost the entire tunnel system, and besides finding no beast, I found no other Sacrifists."

"None?"

"None."

"I think I know why. Turn the page," Yangji said.

Dzangbu turned the page and saw a few symbols there.

"Again."

Dzangbu turned to the next page which was another snowflake diagram. He kept turning the pages. There were six diagrams in all, and Dzangbu had an epiphany. He knew again what he had known before.

"There must be five more of these sanctuaries," Yangji said.

"Where do you think they could be?" Dzangbu asked, but he believed that he already knew the answer and where the other Sacrifists might be located. The problem would be getting to them.

"Unfortunately, we can't know, since we can't translate the text. You must find them. Maybe there are other passageways?" Yangji asked.

"Perhaps," Dzangbu said.

Dzangbu did not want to divulge too much information to Yangji. He realized that the knowledge was not something for people other than Sacrifists to know. "Yes. I will widen my search to the outer tunnels. This map may help me track down the beast more methodically."

"Take the book if you think it will help you locate the Qasigi Duktsi. We have the original here, and there may be more information in the book that is only useful once a reader is inside the tunnel system. I will have more copies made of the original volume, as a resource for future Sacrifists."

Dzangbu looked at his former master, a man whom he had thought he would never see again, and felt compassion. At that moment Dzangbu recognized how much he was really going to miss him.

"Thank you, Rinpoche. I shall not return again. Namasté." He smiled and bowed.

"Namasté."

Dzangbu packed the book in his small backpack and left the gompa immediately. He knew from the map that the boulder room was the key to locating the beast.

CHAPTER 40

SIR RANDOLPH CALLED Gus Darby into his office. Gus was not one of his half dozen secretaries. Gus was a boyhood friend of Sir Randolph. Son of a U.S. Air Force Colonel, Gus was a U.S. Citizen, but his mother was British. He was Sir Randolph's trusted right-hand man, and totally loyal.

Most people got things done for Sir Randolph when he wanted something done. But when he wanted it done quickly at one of his four-hundred-odd companies, he sent Gus. If you were a CEO at one of the Barrington Group companies and Gus Darby arrived, you listened and then followed orders—*now*, not when it was convenient for you.

"Gus, I've got a job for you," Sir Randolph said, as Gus took a seat across from him.

Sir Randolph opened up a large metal briefcase. "I own a biotech company named Bar-Gen Research. They're in New York. I want you to go there and have them identify the kind of animal blood on this knife and coat." He held up two plastic bags containing the items. "Tell them that some of the possibilities are an Himalayan black bear or a snow leopard. I want to know *yesterday*."

"No problemo, Randy," Gus said, using the name he had used since they were seven. Gus was the only one who could use it, but he only used it in private. Gus got up and grabbed the bags. "Anything else?"

"Yes. And this is just between you and me. There is a possibility the blood comes from a new species. The knife belonged to Dane Nielsen, and he swears he saw a yeti and wounded it. Don't tell anyone this, but I believe him, and I'm betting the blood will not be identifiable as any known species."

The mention of a yeti had no visible effect on Gus. "Got it. I'll make sure the results are kept under wraps."

This was one of the reasons Sir Randolph liked Gus. Nothing shocked him. "Thanks. As soon as you learn the results, let me know. A car is waiting for you outside."

"I'll call you as soon as I know anything," Gus said.

Gus grabbed the briefcase and left the room. Sir Randolph picked up his cell phone and dialed the secretary who oversaw his businesses in the eastern half of the U.S.

"I'm sending Gus Darby to Bar-Gen on a project. Call ahead and grease the wheels for him."

CHAPTER 41

PHURBA HAD JUST finished dinner and was speaking to Sir Randolph via satellite phone.

"Dane is paying his respects to the family of Torleif and Shelly's Uncle. Then he'll be back to continue the search for Rand and the beast," Sir Randolph said. "I'll be coming in a couple of days."

Dane must have told him what he saw, Phurba thought. He was surprised that Sir Randolph would be joining the expedition.

"I heard you had some people desert," Sir Randolph said.

"Yes. But I was able to replace most of them," Phurba said.

Phurba had sent Nawang and six of the Sherpas back to get more supplies and to hire Sherpas to replace those that had chosen to leave. Five of the six had refused to come back. However, Nawang was able to sign on twenty more to accompany him back with more supplies, even despite the 'monster stories' circulating in the Sherpa communities. *No doubt enticed by your hazard pay, Sir Randolph,* Phurba thought.

Along with Nawang came Armstrong and Harry. Ironically, Armstrong was the one who had helped Nawang sign on more Sherpas. He had allayed their fears of the mythical monster and had gotten them to believe it was not anything more than a Himalayan black bear. When he arrived at the encampment, he discussed his albino black bear theory with Phurba.

He had told Phurba about the soon-to-arrive ground penetrating radar that might be able to help locate the bear's den. Since Armstrong was so excited at the prospect of filming an albino Himalayan black bear, Phurba did not bother trying to burst his bubble by telling him that the beast was anything but a bear. It would have been a waste of effort.

"Did the shipment of guns come in?" Sir Randolph asked.

"Yes, sir," Phurba said.

Sir Randolph had his crew bring in the guns and shotguns on a Mockingbird helicopter so that they could defend themselves if attacked. In this way, they avoided encountering the pesky Maoist rebels who always stopped climbers, making them pay a toll to continue their climb. If the rebels had found guns on the Sherpas, they would have taken them for themselves.

Phurba had the guns distributed to those Sherpas with gun licenses, of which he was one. During the day, he posted two armed sentries for base camp, and he posted four at night. Phurba put all the other Sherpas in base camp on high alert. Any bear—or anything else—that showed up would find them ready.

"Good. I'll be hiking in right away and getting acclimated," Sir Randolph said. "Let me speak to Armstrong."

It took a minute or two, but Phurba quickly found Armstrong in his tent, passed the phone to him, and left. He had not bothered to listen in, but went on about his business. Later, he noticed that Armstrong, whom he had gotten to know in the last few days, was not his usual annoying self. He appeared more thoughtful.

He's up to something, Phurba thought. *But who cares if Armstrong wants to make a TV show out of our search? It's none of my business. My business is keeping base camp intact until Dane and Sir Randolph arrive to assist with tracking down the beast.*

When Phurba reflected on the fact that he was not on a climbing expedition anymore, but would instead be helping to hunt down the legendary Kangchenjunga Demon, he just shook his head. *How did I get wrapped up in this mess?*

He had a hard time believing what he was doing. Namely, searching for, instead of running from, a man-eating beast. *I probably need to have my head examined*, he thought, chuckling to himself.

Nawang, who stood nearby, heard him laugh. "What's so funny?" Nawang asked.

"I was just thinking that we all must be crazy to still be here, looking for the Demon."

"We are not crazy," Nawang said, deadpan.

"If we are not crazy, then what are we?"

"We are Sherpas."

They both started laughing.

CHAPTER 42

DANE LOOKED AT the Northern Lights Casino to his right as he drove up Highway 371. His mother, Mitzi, dealt blackjack there. She had moved back to help her parents on the Leech Lake Indian Reservation, *Gaa-Zagaskwaajimekaag*, when Dane's father and brother had died eighteen years ago. The casino revenue had done some good for the Leech Lake Band of the Ojibwe, but it was not as profitable as Ojibwe casinos closer to the Twin City area.

Any help is better than no help, he thought. His mother, with Dane's help, had purchased a better home for his grandparents to live in. Mitzi stayed there with them, as now they were both seventy-eight years old, albeit a young seventy-eight, as his grandfather would say. In the cold season, Mingo would still chop wood every day for the family fire.

Dane drove down the long driveway toward their home on the shore of Walker Bay. He was glad he had been able to help his grandparents financially, as he had gained much from being their grandson.

Mingo referred to the house as the *chi-wiigiwaam,* meaning 'great lodge.' His mother and grandmother came out of the house to greet him. His mother gave him a hug and just held him a little longer. It was enough to tell him that things were going to be okay. That he would be okay.

"*Aaniin*, Mama," Dane said. *Aaniin* was Ojibwe for 'hello.'

Dane hugged his grandmother, Margie. "*Aaniin, Nookoo*," Dane said, using the shortened name he had called her since he was a little boy. *Nookoomis* was Ojibwe for 'grandmother.'

"*Aaniin, Zaaga'igan Nishkiinzhigoon*," Margie said.

"Are you okay, Dane?" asked Mitzi. She touched the new scar on his face. "Oh, my poor boy."

"I'm okay, Mama," Dane said. And he felt, this time, that he actually was. "Where's Nimi?"

"He's inside, watching the game," Margie said.

They walked into the wood and stone house. It was about three thousand square feet. Dane's endorsements for some mountaineering equipment had helped pay for it. Dane walked into the big family room and remembered the difference between this house and his grandparents' small home on the reservation. His grandfather sat in a recliner watching a golf tournament.

"Turn off that boring game," Margie said. "Say hello to *goozhishenh*." The word was Ojibwe for 'your grandchild.'

"How many times must I tell you, woman? Golf is not a game. It's a skill," Mingo said.

Dane laughed and greeted his grandfather. "*Aaniin, Nimi.*"

"*Aaniin, Zaaga'igan Nishkiinzhigoon*," Mingo said. "I watch her cooking shows all day. Or worse, her talk shows. How much gossip about meaningless celebrity activities can you take before your mind turns to mush?"

Dane laughed again. His grandfather studied him, and from Mingo's expression Dane realized that his grandfather could see that he was only laughing on the outside. Dane had endured a terrible misfortune. Not the first. But this was one he might relive every time he looked in the mirror.

"Come with me," Mingo said. He got out of his recliner and took Dane into the den. On the walls were many black and white pictures. Dane had never seen many of them before and went over to look at them.

Dane saw that one was a photo of ten Ojibwe men. Four were seated and wearing traditional Ojibwe garb. A handwritten label on the picture read: *Leech Lake Ojibwe delegation to Washington – 1899.*

His grandfather pointed at the man seated on the far right. "That is my grandfather, your great-great grandfather," Mingo said.

"He went to Washington? What did he do there?" Dane asked.

"Listened to a lot of white people lie," Mingo said. "If there's one thing you can depend on, it's that the white man will go back on his word. Not once, in Native American history, has the US government ever kept its word. Like they say: same shit, different day. That's the only thing the white man is good for—his aphorisms and cuss words."

Dane forced a smile.

"What's really bothering you, Zaaga'igan Nishkiinzhigoon?" Mingo asked.

The residual smile fell away from Dane's face. He had never been able to fool his grandfather. The man was a *midewinini*. Spiritually gifted. Dane loved and admired Mingo's ability to see beyond the illusory surface to the heart of things. He looked into his grandfather's eyes and his own eyes began to fill with water. But no water fell. He smiled at his grandfather—a smile of love and devotion. Besides his father, Mingo was the greatest man Dane had ever known.

"Can we sit?" Dane asked.

Mingo motioned for him to do so. They sat down. Dane detailed his harrowing story of what had happened to Shelly and Torleif, and he kept his emotions in check. Afterward, his grandfather sat thinking for several minutes. Dane waited patiently for him to speak. When he did speak, it was about the great man-beast of the Ojibwe, known as the Wendigo.

"A Wendigo is inhabited by a fierce, evil spirit. When he engages in cannibalism, this makes him even more insane and murderous. He craves more blood to quench the never-ending hunger he has created," Mingo said. "To defeat a Wendigo, such as this, takes a warrior of great strength and will. One must be of the Great Spirit to defeat such a beast. The chosen warrior must dance with ghosts."

Dane smiled at the reference. When he was a child, his grandfather had told him many stories about the great warriors of the Ojibwe Clans who *wiijishimotaw jiibayag,* meaning 'dance with ghosts.' As a child, he had loved hearing his grandfather tell him the Ojibwe's stories of pure bravery in the face of terrible odds. And even though he had never quite understood what it meant to 'dance with ghosts,' he loved listening to his grandfather talk about it, because it always made him feel better.

Mitzi poked her head in the door. "Dinner's ready, you two."

"Okay," Mingo said. "We'll be there in a second." Then to Dane: "What will you do?"

"I will track the beast to its lair and shoot it." Dane made a shooting gesture with his hand.

"Be careful, grandson. Wendigos are tricky. Sometimes they are not what they seem. Think before you aim, and if you must shoot, then shoot twice. But make sure your purpose is true and honorable, for revenge is a slow death all by itself. Sometimes, the best thing to do may be to let it go and do nothing."

He knew his grandfather was right but it did not change things. He could feel the intense, emotional sickness of desiring retribution for Shelly. He knew that it was unhealthy but he was in grips of the monster, the beast called Revenge. One monster had changed him outwardly, the other began to change him inwardly.

Dane nodded solemnly. "I understand, Nimi."

"Good. I'm starving. Let's go eat your grandmother's duck and wild rice."

CHAPTER 43

COURTNEY KAUFMAN ONLY had been working at her dream job for seven months. She'd been hired as an entry-level Research Assistant for Bar-Gen straight out of Texas A&M University, having just earned her PhD in Genetics. She was an oddity—an American at the top of her class. Most foreign students put kids from the U.S. to shame, especially the Asians.

She did not know how many people had applied for her job, but she was ecstatic when she was hired. Even though being an entry-level RA sometimes meant cleaning up other people's messes or running here and there on errands for 'real scientists,' at least she looked the part in her white lab coat.

She was doing some paperwork detailing the findings of her immediate superior, a Senior Research Analyst, when the CEO of Bar-Gen, Dr. John Bean, walked in followed by a stocky fellow with a briefcase who looked to be about sixty years old. Dr. Bean spoke briefly to her SRA, who nodded, looking unhappy with whatever he had been told.

Dr. Bean and the stocky man walked over to her.

"Dr. Kaufman, I'm Dr. John Bean," he said.

"Yes. I know," she said, trying not to be nervous.

"No need to be nervous. But I'm going to need your help with something immediately. I asked Dr. Collins who we could use full-time on a project." Dr. Collins was the boss *above* her SRA.

"Okay," Courtney said.

"This is Gus Darby," Dr. Bean said. "He's come straight from Sir Randolph Barrington's estate and has some artifacts with some blood on them. He needs to know as quickly as possible the species of animal whose blood is on the items. You may have heard about Sir Randolph's son being killed in the Himalaya. They think the blood may have come from an Asiatic black bear, a snow leopard, or perhaps something else. But the blood on the knife came from some kind of animal."

Courtney's memory went to work. As a child, she'd had an eidetic memory that allowed her to remember novels word-for-word. But where most such children eventually lost that ability, Courtney never had—and as part of her work, she often found herself recalling useful facts from scholarly articles she had read months or even years before. *This should be easy. The Asiatic black bear has seventy-four chromosomes and the snow leopard has thirty-eight chromosomes. It'll take additional tests to confirm a positive match, but I can knock false candidates out of the running in less than an hour.*

"How quickly is this information needed?" Courtney asked.

"Yesterday," Gus said.

Dr. Bean nodded. "Yes. As soon as you can provide it. You are to work on nothing else. Mr. Darby will stay with you until you find something out."

"Okay," Courtney said. *I guess I'm not going home tonight.* Dr. Bean walked out, leaving Gus with her.

Gus put the large metal briefcase on the counter, turned the dials on the combination locks and opened it up. Gus stepped back so she could see, and she looked inside. The bloodied knife in the plastic bag lay on top of another plastic bag containing a thick down jacket—perhaps a skier's or mountain climber's gear.

"We want you to test the DNA from the blood on the knife and the jacket. There's blood on two areas of the jacket—the upper left arm and lower right sleeve. Test those samples against the sample on the knife."

"I read that they hadn't found Sir Randolph's son. Is that correct?"

"Yes. These are from the man who was sent to look for him."

Courtney eyed the jacket and saw that part of it had been torn. "Is he okay?"

"Yes. But two others are dead. So, we need some answers. Quickly."

"Okay. I'll get right on it."

Courtney's stomach had butterflies, but she felt honored to have been singled out as a competent worker by the CEO. *Don't blow this. This is a free ticket to improving your career. I feel like I'm on CSI!* She was giddy and nervous all at the same time. She would come to find out that her thoughts had been an understatement.

CHAPTER 44

THE LIGHT OF the computer screen was beginning to blur Lily's vision. It was near closing time and she had been reading one of her favorite conspiracy theory websites. It fed her appetite for news that showed that the power-elite politicians were only out for themselves and couldn't care less about those they were allegedly serving.

When will people wake up? she asked herself. But she knew the answer—*never*. She shook her head, then remembered that she had just received a fresh batch of Dr. Dong's remedy. She decided to transfer the big bottle into multiple tiny bottles thus turning it into her own Omyagra potion.

In the last month, the formula had created such a stir in Japantown that even the women of Chinatown had started coming in to buy it. *Nothing like good word of mouth.* She wondered how these women were getting their husbands to drink it. *Here's your cocktail, honey,* she thought, laughing to herself. *Maybe I should go global.*

Before shutting down her computer and locking up, she clicked over to the Himalayan Times website and began to scan through it. They had a page on mountaineering in the sports section, so she clicked through to that. The headline read: *Two Killed on Kangchenjunga.* Her heart sank. The article said the victims were Torleif Günner and Shelly Newton.

Torleif Günner was Dane's friend and climbing partner. She remembered his name from the earlier article she had read before calling her Uncle DJ. *Oh no! The other victim was Dane's fiancée.* She really felt bad for him, and the guilt was even worse because she had been unable to keep them from going on their ill-fated expedition. She read on. *Of course, there's no mention of the yeti. Just some stupid speculation about an oversized Himalayan black bear.* The article ended.

She knew it was no black bear. *The poor man. I hope he'll be okay. But how could he be?* Slowly, she felt her own emotions about her father begin to well up and overflow. She started to cry.

The bell on her shop door jingled as someone came in. She looked up, wiping her eyes quickly, and was about to say, "We're closing." But she stopped. The man who walked in looked out of place, not at all like one of her usual customers.

He's got a unique look, she thought, feeling a stir in her loins she had not felt in some time. *I guess we can take one more customer. Don't gawk,* she added, mentally scolding herself for wanting to stare at the man a little longer.

He had light mocha skin and medium-length dark brown hair. His physique looked tight under his light jacket, T-shirt and jeans. But what really struck her were his deep blue eyes. *What's he looking for? It isn't handsome pills, that's for sure. Definitely not my specialty item.* She realized she was still staring. *Get a grip on yourself.* But when the man came closer, his features were flawed. A scar ran across his left cheek. *Looks recent.*

"Er, can I, uh, help you?" *Nice. Real friendly. And personable. Dope.*

"I'm looking for Lily McCrowley," the man said.

She hoped he was not with the FBI, CIA, IRS, or any other three-letter organization. *Buddha and Jesus, I promise to stop looking at conspiracy websites,* she prayed. *The NSA is probably watching.*

She took a deep breath. "That would be me." But it dawned on her, just before he spoke.

"Hi, Ms. McCrowley. I'm Dane Nielsen."

Speechless, she eked out, "Lily."

He smiled and nodded. "Hi, Lily."

She felt her legs wobble a bit, and forced herself to smile back.

***

Dane looked around the shop, taking in its unfamiliar ambiance. He thought the shop's décor looked like something you would expect to see in a Chinatown curio shop. Although he could see it was clean, it had the appearance of being old and dusty since there were all kinds of books on shelves, curio cabinets, several types of antique furniture, and other odds and ends strewn about in no particularly organized fashion.

She's attractive. I was right there, too. Smokes's law, no doubt. His friend Smokes had contended that crazy women were always beautiful. But Dane was not attracted. He only had returned a couple days ago from Shelly's memorial, which had been organized by her Uncle and a few of her friends.

"I just read about what happened to you. I'm so sorry for your loss. It reminded me …" She stopped short. Dane saw that some emotion was overwhelming her.

"This a bad time?"

Lily visibly suppressed her grief and shook her head.

"No. I'm okay. … Please. Sit down."

Lily beckoned for him to take a seat at her mother's usual

table and they sat down across from each other. He was watching her, still wondering if she was okay.

"I'm sorry. Your story reminded me of something else. I'm not usually this emotional," she said, getting her composure back.

"*Really?* I wouldn't have guessed that from our last phone call," Dane said. He chuckled.

He winced a little, remembering her attempt to warn him about the yeti. Shelly had been sitting next to him at the time. He watched as Lily laughed in spite of her stifled grief. It felt good to make someone laugh. He had not had much opportunity for laughter while he was attending two funerals.

"Right. I'm sorry. What can I do for you, Mr. Nielsen?"

"Call me Lake. My friends call me Lake."

He held out his hand and she shook it. He smiled and she smiled back.

"Okay, Lake. How can I help?"

"I want to know everything you know about yetis."

"How much time do you have?"

"Unlimited."

Lily's stomach growled. "I'm hungry. You like Chinese? I'm buying."

"All right. That's the least you could do after sending your Uncle DJ," Dane said.

"Sorry about that," Lily said, smiling.

No, I'm sorry I didn't listen to him, Dane thought as Lily locked up her shop.

They walked a couple blocks down the hill in Chinatown, passing hordes of Asian people, tourists, and a small number of restaurants. Turning left, a few more steps took them to the red latticed windows of her favorite restaurant, the Nankin.

"Why are Chinese restaurants always painted red?" Dane

asked.

"In Chinese culture, red corresponds with fire and symbolizes good fortune and joy," Lily said, without looking at him. A few seconds later, she noticed Dane's surprised look. "Oh, I'm sorry. Was that a rhetorical question?"

He nodded and smiled. She blushed a little. Dane opened the door and they walked inside. Dane looked around, wondering, *Where are we going to sit?* The restaurant had more tables and chairs than it had room for, and there were more patrons than chairs. A short, rotund Chinese man came bustling up to greet them.

"How are you today, Lily?" he asked in his heavy Mandarin accent.

"I'm fine, Po," she said. "Two."

Po quickly shoe-horned them in between two parties of four.

"How's business?" she asked him.

"Slow. But it slow all over."

"I'd hate to see it when it's busy," Dane said, looking around at the packed restaurant in an exaggerated manner. Lily laughed. Po noticed him for the first time.

"Ahhh, you finally bring man-friend," Po said.

"Yes. This is my friend Lake, from Colorado," Lily said. Dane shook hands with Po, whose handshake matched that of a dead fish. Po winced. Dane had forgotten that Chinese people preferred weak handshakes.

"You lucky. She good girl. Never come in with man. Had lost hope for her," Po said, prattling on. Lily flushed with embarrassment. *Maybe she bats on the same team. I am in San Francisco.*

Dane enjoyed just sitting there with a stranger. He had spent the last week attending two memorials with many people he knew and loved. Lots of people, all sharing their grief, and it did not help that Dane felt partially responsible for causing it. He pushed those thoughts from his mind.

"Ready to order?" Po asked.

"What's good?" Dane asked Lily.

"We'll have the sizzling rice soup and the sesame chicken," she told Po.

"Good choice," Po said and turned to get their order in. A skinny Asian busboy brought them two glasses of water and a pot of hot tea with two small cups. Dane poured Lily some tea, then poured some for himself. They sipped a bit and took a moment to relax in the noisy silence of the packed restaurant.

"So, tell me about yourself. Live here long?" Dane asked, making small talk.

"Since I was ten."

"Do you like it?"

"It's one of the great cities of the world. I love it. Went to college here at UCSF. Majored in Anthropology. You?"

"No college. Loved to play sports in high school. Got the mountain climbing bug from my dad, and when he died, I got some life insurance money that allowed me to climb the Himalaya, which he had always wanted to climb. Buried some of his ashes on Kangchenjunga, which was my first Himalayan climb. Started making money guiding others on expeditions and eventually became the youngest man to climb all fourteen of the eight-thousanders. Have you ever climbed an eight-thousander?"

He waited for her to reply, but after a moment it was clear that her mind had wandered. A few seconds later, she glanced up at him.

"I'm sorry. What?" she asked.

"I said, have you ever climbed an eight-thousander?"

"No. But my father did."

"Oh, that's right," Dane said. "Torleif told me he climbed with your father once. Said he was very skillful."

An awkward silence ensued. They had both reminded themselves of dead people.

"He was," she said quietly.

Dane changed the subject. "How was college?"

"It was fun for a while," Lily said. Then she added, "Until the study thing."

"I'm sorry?"

"The study. I was part of a long-running study called the Wizards Project, which was originally called the Diogenes Project."

Dane raised an eyebrow. "You mean like the Greek guy who went around with a lamp looking for an honest man?"

"Very good." Lily was impressed.

"I didn't go to college, but I can read."

She laughed.

"Anyway, some friends of mine told me about two doctors who were looking for people who could tell when people were lying. They said I should go see them. So I did."

"And?"

"I'm a Truth Wizard."

"A Truth Wizard, huh?"

"Yes. My father used to call me cailín fhírinne, which is Irish for 'truth girl.' I used to always catch him in a fib."

"What is a Truth Wizard, anyway?"

"Most people can't tell when other people are lying. The study tested twenty thousand people and most were only correct fifty percent of the time. No more accurate than a coin flip would be."

"And Truth Wizards?"

"Eighty percent or better."

"Wow," Dane said, genuinely impressed. "That's a big difference. How many Truth Wizards were there, out of the twenty thousand people in the study?"

"Only fifty. And forty-six of those were in a field that already dealt with trying to spot deception. You know, like the Secret Service, FBI, sheriffs, police, attorneys, arbitrators, and psychologists. Most people showed no more aptitude than a college freshmen, which I was at that time. Secret Service agents turned out to be the most skilled."

"Well, that's because every day they have to listen to the President."

Lily started laughing. "You're funny."

Dane smiled. "So you were one of the four people who was just good at it without having a profession that forced you to deal with liars. That's pretty impressive. How did that make college less fun?"

"Well, it's one thing to *think* you know when people are lying and another thing to have it confirmed by academics that you are one of the few who actually *do* know when people are lying. Once the information got out, going out on dates became a chore and most of my so-called 'friends' stopped hanging out with me."

"Ouch. I see what you mean. That's too bad." Dane changed the subject. "How did you get into the yeti business, Miss Truth Wizard?"

"I saw a Bigfoot when I was ten and I have been interested ever since," Lily said with a straight face.

She's serious. If I'd heard her say that a month ago, I would have thought she was delusional.

"I'm sorry for thinking you were a nut job when you called me that day," he said.

She looked away, embarrassed. "Don't worry about it. I have people call me crazy every day."

"I ... I should have listened to you ... and your Uncle." He paused a moment and reached into his pocket. "Here. This is for you. Your Uncle gave it to me. I forgot to give it to my fiancée."

He handed her the colorful beaded necklace and crystal amulet that her Uncle DJ had given him for Shelly to wear. Dane was not superstitious, but the thought had crossed his mind that he had been the one with the necklace in his pocket during the yeti attack.

Lily took the necklace from Dane and noticed the sadness below his façade. *He's having a hard time living with the guilt of having ignored two warnings.*

"You know, I saw it—the yeti," Dane said.

She nodded slowly. "I figured." And although Dane might not have the self-knowledge to realize it, Lily had noticed that he was not in the habit of lying. It was what had startled her into losing track of the conversation just as Dane was talking about climbing the eight-thousanders.

In a world where nearly *everyone* was deceitful, to one extent or another, Dane simply *was not*.

He rolled up the left sleeve of his T-shirt and showed her his stitched-up arm. "It did this to me before killing my fiancée and one of my best friends. And this." He pointed at the scar on his cheek. "I guess, it could've been worse." Lily looked away a moment and Dane waited for her to face him again. When she did he said, "I need your help."

"Okay," she said, without hesitation, wondering how she could help.

"I need to find this thing. Is there anything, anything at all, you can tell me about it?"

"Possibly," she said. Po brought out their Sizzling Rice soup. They ate briefly without talking.

"Soup's good," Dane said.

Lily stopped eating. "What are you going to do if you find it?"

"Kill it."

I understand why you want revenge. But she was sorry to hear him say it. Even though she'd always assumed that a yeti had killed her father, she did not want to see one of the creatures get killed. In the Yeti/Bigfoot world there were two schools of thought—those who wanted to kill them, and those who wanted to protect them. She was in the latter camp.

"Will you help me?" Dane asked.

She thought about it. *If I don't help him, he'll find someone else to help him. On the other hand, if I do help him, maybe I can change his mind.*

"Okay. Yeti School starts after dinner."

CHAPTER 45

WHEN DANE AND Lily got back to her shop, she went behind her checkout counter, which was actually an antique oak Wild West bar, complete with antique cash register. Behind the bar were all the things most people came in for—Omyagra, amulets, medicinal herbs, crystals, et cetera. She grabbed some old books from under the counter.

"Have a seat," she said, motioning Dane toward another small table in the back of the shop.

Near the end of the bar was her Tarot table. It had a deep blue velvet table cloth that was spotted with silver crescent moons and stars and trimmed with a golden fringe. A deck of Tarot cards sat in the middle. He gave the table cloth the once-over as Lily sat down with her books.

"You also read fortunes?" he asked.

"Only if people want me to. Not everybody wants to know their future," she said.

Dane looked skeptical. "What? The cards do the talking, not you?"

"A girl's gotta make a living," she said smiling.

He held up his hands. "I get it. I get it." He picked up one edge of the fancy tablecloth and pointed at it. "Do you have a matching pointy hat?"

"That costs extra."

Dane laughed.

"Okay. This is one of the best books I have on the yeti. It is no longer in print. It was written in the late 1920s." She opened the book up and turned to a spot she had bookmarked. She turned the book around for Dane to read and pointed at a passage she had highlighted in yellow. "There."

Dane began to read aloud. "The most recent sighting of a yeti was by a British geological expedition on Kangchenjunga in 1925. They asked the locals about it and were told it was the Kangchenjunga Demon. Living on one of the tallest mountains of the world—Kangchenjunga—the yeti remains hidden and rarely seen. It's thought to live in hidden valleys or caves, venturing out only seldom to feed on smaller animals."

He looked at Lily. "Sort of makes sense. Torleif said Rand disappeared and he couldn't find him. Small animals, though? This yeti is different. It's killed at least three people, and maybe as many as five people. All of them were above ground."

"One second." She grabbed a different book and flipped through it for what she was looking for, then gave it to him. "Read the highlighted part."

"The reason has not been determined, but it is factual that the yeti sightings follow a pattern of an increase in reports every twenty years. These clusters of reports are one reason a theory has been put forth that the yeti hibernates for a period of twenty years, like some primatial cicada." Dane rolled his eyes at this last part.

"Okay. I get it, the primatial cicada theory sounds dopey, but the facts are that about every twenty years a yeti appears. Another thing is, the people reporting the sightings always mention only seeing one. No one ever sees two together."

Dane's face clouded. "Trust me. One is enough."

I bet, thought Lily, but she did not say so. "There are many different kinds of theories about the yeti. I've read theories saying he's an alien being or a pre-human, or even a spiritual adept. Others have put forward even more fantastic theories, like he's a thought form or a ghost."

"Where do you find this stuff?"

"Trust me. If you can imagine it, it's already on the internet."

"If it's in an ice cave, we'll need to find an entrance. We know the general area it's in, from its attacks. Someone at base camp already theorized that it could be hiding underground. Sir Randolph is bringing some ground penetrating radar with him that may help us locate spaces underground."

Lily spent two more hours showing Dane everything she had collected about the yeti. Finally, when they had finished reading the last of Lily's collective store of knowledge, Dane stood up and held out his hand.

"Thank you, Lily. It's been nice meeting you. You have been extremely generous and helpful."

Lily did not want to shake hands. She felt like this was the opportunity she'd been waiting for all her life. She was not going to let it pass her by.

"Take me with you."

Dane was visibly taken aback by her request. "This is an unusually dangerous operation."

She was desperate. "I know. But I have experience mountain climbing. I summit Shasta every month. So I won't be a burden."

"Every month? Why in the world would you?"

She looked down at the floor, slightly embarrassed, then peeked up at him. "To stay in shape and … to look for

Bigfoot."

He shook his head. "I can't really risk anyone else getting hurt or killed."

"Please. I have to go. I can pay for it."

"You don't get it. There's a beast that eats people and has the strength of ten men. It doesn't care who it kills. This isn't *for* you. It's not mountain climbing. We're hunting it to kill it. *You can't go!*"

He stopped. Lily fought back tears.

"Listen," Dane said. "I can't let another person …"

She interrupted. "It killed my dad when I was ten."

Dane stopped speaking. He looked away from her.

"It probably killed him," she said.

Tears dripped down her cheeks as she waited for him to think it over.

"I'm sorry that happened to you." His voice was quiet. "But I have been responsible for five deaths because I allowed people to dissuade me from avoiding what I knew was a dangerous situation. I'm not letting it happen again."

Lily had a different view of life, so her response was immediate and hardened. "If people dissuaded you, it's on them. People are responsible for their own conditions. And besides, you don't get to decide what I do, *I do*. If you won't take me, I'll fly over and follow you anyway."

Boom.

She could see that her words had had an effect. A tiny effect. But the sorrow etched into his features softened slightly, as though dissipating.

He sighed. "Do you have a passport?"

She wiped the tears from her face and half-smiled. "Does Bigfoot shit in the woods?"

CHAPTER 46

TERRY MITCHELL HAD the hood of his 1965 Ford pickup open and was in the middle of changing the spark plugs. A Camel non-filter hung from his mouth. He was tightening the wrench when it slipped, skinning his knuckles.

He spit out his cigarette, shook his hand and looked it over. "Damn it, Smokes, you idiot."

He grabbed an open can of beer off the fender and took a long swig, then rested the ice cold can against his scraped knuckles. Off in the distance, an SUV cruised up his drive. His ranch backed up to Canyon Ferry Lake, just outside of Winston, Montana. Which was like saying it was just outside nowhere. Winston had a population of one hundred and forty-seven.

When he bought the place, he told his friends he had bought forty acres and a mule. The mule was his Ford pickup. Its prior owner offered to include it in the sale as an enticement to buy the ranch. Smokes stared at the SUV. *Must be Lake.*

He had gotten a call from Dane, who had told him that he was in Terry's neck of the woods and wanted to see him, to offer him a proposition to make some good money. Since Terry 'Smokes' Mitchell was running low on cash, he had decided to listen to what Dane had to say. *Besides, it'll be nice to see that Injun anyway,* Smokes thought.

He liked climbing with Dane. He had heard about what had happened to him from his friend Hank Schmidt, one of their climbing companions. *Damn fucked-up thing,* he thought. He did not know Shelly, but he had climbed with Torleif and Dane many times and had gained a lot of pleasant memories over the years.

Terry went inside to wash his hands and splash some water on his face. It was eighty-two degrees outside, so he had been sweating. He thought briefly about throwing on a clean T-shirt but nixed the idea. *It's only Lake.*

He walked back outside just as Dane drove up to the house. Dane was smiling, and Smokes was smiling back until he saw that Dane had a passenger. Dane and the passenger got out of the car. Smokes looked the woman over. *Wow!*

"First ya surprise me by sayin' yer in my neck o' the woods. Then ya surprise me with some hot girl ridin' shotgun," Smokes said. "Sweet Jesus, Lake."

Lily started to blush. Dane spoke up.

"Pay him no mind. He's harmless. He says that every time he sees a girl."

"I do not. Besides, where are yer manners?"

"I'm sorry. Lily, this is the great Terry Mitchell. Smokes, Lily McCrowley. Smokes is one of my oldest friends."

Lily walked forward and held out her hand for him to shake. "Hi, Terry."

Smokes removed his Los Angeles Dodgers baseball cap and tossed it over his shoulder. He took her small hand in both of his hands, bent down while gently raising it to his lips, and gave it a light kiss.

"Enchantay, mad-mwa-zell. An' it's Smokes. Everybody just

calls me Smokes."

Dane rolled his eyes.

"All right. Leave the woman alone, horndog." Dane shook his head. "Can we go inside now?"

"This way, mad-mwa-zell," Smokes said, and beckoned to Lily, ignoring Dane. He led them both into his house. They walked into the family room and sat down on the sofa.

"Can I get ya anythin'?

"Water," Dane said.

"Water would be great," Lily said. After Smokes had gotten them their waters and procured another beer for himself, he sat down in his recliner and reclined halfway.

"Sorry to hear about Shelly and Torleif, Lake."

"Thanks, Smokes. Thanks for the flowers you sent to the memorial."

"That's the least I could do, man. So wassup?"

"I got a little job for you," Dane said.

He explained everything that had happened thus far and what he intended to do about it. He told him it might be treacherous, but said he needed somebody dependable.

"Don't feel obligated, Smokes. Hank said that if you don't want to go, *fuggedabowdit,* and let him know and he will try to reschedule his appointments. I also called Tug, but haven't heard back yet."

Smokes sat there, thinking. He took a long drink, finishing his beer, burped, and crushed the can. He forgot that Lily was there. "Pardoh-nee mwa."

To Dane, he said, "Wow. That's some fucked up shit ya just explained." To Lily: "Sorry, Lily, 'scuse the French." He winked at her.

"It's okay. I'm bilingual," she said.

Smokes laughed, then said, "Fuck it. I'll go. And tell Hank

and Tug, if he calls back, I said I'd better be the one to go, because they're pussies and I don't want anyone gettin' hurt."

Dane laughed. "Will do."

"When do we leave?" Smokes asked.

"After we pick up the most important member in our party."

"Who's that?"

CHAPTER 47

"LADIES AN' GENTLEMEN, thank you for flying with Barrington Airlines," Smokes said, winking at Lily. They had just landed at Suketar. "Going to hit the head."

"Me too," Lily said.

"Ladies first," Smokes said.

Lily whisked past him. The different intentions of the people around her caused her great concern: Dane's need for revenge; Smokes's desire to help Dane; Sir Randolph's desire to elevate his reputation by making a discovery of great historical significance. *I need to think of a way to stop all of them.* She was there to protect the yeti, not kill it, and she did not want it harmed or captured or exploited.

Dane seemed anxious to get to base camp. He and Duke (the most important member of their party) got off the plane as soon as they could manage. Their little group was meeting a half dozen Sherpas who would trek with them to base camp. *Thanks to Sir Randolph's contacts, they don't need to spend any time acquiring firearm licenses,* she thought, mentally cursing the British consulate for helping arm them.

Lily came down off the plane and stared at Dane and Duke,

wondering what she could do to stop them from killing the yeti. She paused, contemplating her dilemma. Dane gave her an odd look.

"You coming?" he asked.

"Yes," she said.

"C'mon, darlin'. Time's a wastin'," Smokes said, walking past her.

"Is anything wrong?" Dane asked.

"No. Sorry," she said, walking forward.

He refrained from asking her anything further. She was relieved. She hoped he could not tell that she had a different purpose for the trip. If he knew, Dane could try to prevent her from coming along. *I have to think of a way to change his mind.*

They had packed lightly, as most of the gear they would need had been brought in by Sir Randolph and his crew. They began their trek to Kangchenjunga base camp.

CHAPTER 48

COURTNEY WAS STARING at the results of her third DNA test—the Ouchterlony Immunodiffusion test—and she still could not believe it. She knew she had not made any mistakes.

She had performed the Hemastix test first. It had quickly shown that the samples were indeed actual blood samples. Then she had performed the HemaTrace test on all three samples and had rechecked the results twice. After the results of the Ouchterlony Immunodiffusion test came back, Dr. Bean's comments seemed increasingly misguided. *This is no bear, and certainly no leopard,* she thought.

"Is there a problem?" Gus asked.

Courtney jumped, startled.

"Oh! You scared me," she said, putting her hand on her ample chest.

"I get that a lot. Sorry. But you looked confused."

Courtney shook her head, started to speak, then hesitated.

"Well, no … but sort of," she said. "It was just that Dr. Bean said the samples were possibly from an Asiatic black bear, or snow leopard, or some other sort of … animal."

"Okay. And …?"

"I assumed we would be looking for an animal of some type. I performed a Hemastix test, a HemaTrace test and the Ouchter—"

"English, honey. What's the bottom line?"

Courtney was startled by Gus's gruff demeanor.

"All the samples are human or from some other higher primate," she said flatly.

"Really? Higher primate?"

She nodded. "It is probably human. There are no other higher primates in the Himalaya."

Gus paused a few seconds to think. "Did the blood on the knife match the coat?"

"Well, it tested as human or higher primate, but I can't tell if they're from the same donor yet. We will need to do some karyotyping. Using gel electrophoresis, we can separate and count the chromosomes, then do some rapid genome sequencing. I can access BLAST, the basic local alignment search tool, to compare it to different genomes ..." She trailed off, noticing that Gus looked uninterested because of the jargon she was using.

He said, "Yeah. Right. Go ahead and do ... whatever. Sir Randolph will want to know all the details."

Gus turned to leave Courtney to her work, then stopped. "Dr. Kaufman. No one is to know what you find out."

"No one?"

"No one. Not your superiors. Not Dr. Bean. *No one*. Do you understand?"

She said, "I understand."

But she did not.

CHAPTER 49

IN THE EARLY evening, Dzangbu arrived back at base camp. Phurba saw him walk into camp while he was engaged in conversation with Sir Randolph, who had just arrived with Lance Jones and a small party of Sherpas. Lance operated the ground penetrating radar equipment they had brought along.

Phurba excused himself to talk with Dzangbu.

"Namasté," Phurba said, approaching him.

"Namasté. Have there been any more attacks?" Dzangbu asked.

"None since you left."

"Good. Be vigilant. The creature may be hunting again soon. His killings have been occurring in one week intervals."

"Yes. I'd noticed that as well. I've posted four sentries for each night and two during the day. They are good men, and alert, but I'll remind them to be extra watchful. Was the High Lama able to help you?" Phurba asked.

"Yes. May I stay the night? I want to get going first thing in the morning."

Phurba wanted to ask how the Lama had helped him and where Dzangbu would be going, but instead said, "You are welcome to share my tent for as long as you need."

"Thank you. You are most helpful. One night should be sufficient."

"There is one other thing you should know," Phurba said.

"What's that?"

"There are people who have arrived in camp who wish to hunt the beast, and they have guns. A few more are coming and they are bringing a tracking dog with them."

Dzangbu nodded, but Phurba could not tell if he was distressed or not. *Do you ever get distressed?* Somehow Phurba doubted it.

"This particular dog is trained to work in snow. His master is my friend, Dane Nielsen, a great mountaineer. Dane's fiancée was one of the two who were killed by the beast when you were here last," Phurba said.

"How will it pick up the scent?"

"From smelling other items the beast has touched."

"Are there items for the dog to pick up the beast's scent?"

"Yes. We have saved the shredded tent from the attack, which possibly has the beast's blood on it. Plus some hair was found."

Dzangbu nodded. "I will need your help, then."

How can I possibly help him? "Okay. What do you need?"

"No one can be allowed to track down this beast. The High Lama has sent me for one express purpose and for this purpose only. I need to be alone with the beast to achieve it. The hunters must not be allowed to find the beast before I do. Do you understand?"

"I understand your words, but not the reason behind them."

"All I can tell you is that people such as myself have been dealing with these beasts for thousands of years. That is all I'm able to tell you. I need time to carry out my mission. I'm not asking you to stop them. Merely delay them. Will you help?"

Phurba felt conflicted. But he knew that if his religious wife was there, she would tell him to follow Dzangbu's request, whatever it was, so he decided to help. "What do you want me to do?"

"Hide or destroy the items being saved for the dog."

Phurba knew that helping Dzangbu would violate the trust Dane and Sir Randolph had placed in him. But he also knew that with Dzangbu involved, the purpose must involve some higher religious objective. *His purpose must be more important than seeking revenge for the loss of a few lives,* Phurba thought. He knew where the items were. They were not guarded. There had been no reason to guard them.

"Okay. It will be done."

Phurba directed Dzangbu to his tent, then left to dispose of the items as requested by Dzangbu. After Phurba had done so, he went back to his tent. But instead of entering right away, he peeked through a crack in the flap covering the entrance. He could see Dzangbu staring at a diagram in a book. The design resembled a snowflake. Phurba wondered what it was for. He entered, and Dzangbu immediately put the book away.

"Did I interrupt your study?"

"No. Not at all. It was just a map of the area."

Phurba knew it was not true, though he did not want to say anything to contradict the holy man. But it did make him wonder. *What kind of holy man are you?*

CHAPTER 50

THAT NIGHT, MINGMAR Topche Sherpa kept watch as one of the night sentries. He was one of the replacement Sherpas who had returned carrying supplies with Nawang. He had heard the stories about the Kangchenjunga Demon causing havoc on the mountain, but he did not believe them, thinking they were ridiculous. As a child, he had listened to his grandfather tell stories about the Demon many times.

"I saw him once on expedition with the first men to summit Kangchenjunga. It had brown hair covering its entire body and looked like an ape but walked like a man. But it was much larger than either a man or an ape. The Demon is ten feet tall, Ming!" his grandfather had said, grinning a smile that was missing more than a couple of teeth. "It guards the way to Beyul Demoshong."

His grandfather's stories had always terrified him. But now, at twenty-three years old, Ming thought they had just been his grandfather's way of entertaining his young grandson.

Ming lit a cigarette. He drew in the satisfying smoke. A crunching, squishing sound in the snow behind him sent chills down the back of his neck. Quickly he turned around, his headlamp flashing across the area, but there was nothing but darkness.

"Anyone there? Pemba? Is that you?"

Pemba, who was in charge of the other sentries for the night, did not answer. Ming walked slowly toward where he thought he had heard the sound.

"Dachen? Kipu?" he said, calling out the names of the other sentries. Ming heard more crunching and squishing, except the source of the sounds had moved. The noises emanated from behind the doctor's large medical tent. It sounded like someone was digging in the snow.

He crept slowly toward the sounds. Nearing the corner of the tent and preparing to take a peek, he felt fear build in the pit of his stomach and his heart started to beat faster. *Get a hold of yourself.*

He lowered his shotgun. At the corner of the tent, he began to stick his head out to take a look when two huge, vice-like hands grabbed both of his biceps and yanked him backward, pulling him to the ground. The surprise attack caused him to drop his shotgun. He struggled violently, flailing his arms wildly with his eyes closed. He began to scream for help and a hand quickly covered his mouth, stifling his screams. Ming heard uncontrollable laughter and opened his eyes. Dachen and Kipu were bent over and laughing heartily.

Dachen teased Ming by flailing his arms. "Help me! Phurba, help me!"

Ming got up and retrieved his shotgun. "It isn't funny."

Kipu poked Ming. "Admit it. You were scared."

Dachen laughed, then said, "Did you shit your pants?"

Ming ignored the question. "Was Pemba the one making those sounds?" Ming turned toward the direction of the sounds. "You can come out, Pemba."

Kipu shook his head. "We haven't seen Pemba."

Dachen's laughter subsided. "What sounds?"

"The sounds behind the med tent," Ming said.

Dachen looked at Kipu. "We didn't hear anything."

"Okay. No more kidding, guys."

"We aren't kidding," they said in unison.

Ming grew tired of their lies. "That's enough. Pemba, you can come out now. Show's over."

Another loud crunching noise rent the air followed by a loud pop, similar to the cracking a knuckle. Ming looked at the two others, "I told you …"

The looks on their terrified faces told Ming that his friends did not know where *or from whom* the sound was coming. The sounds ceased. They all froze and stared into the darkness. A large object hurtled through the air, landing about ten feet from where they stood. It bounced once and rolled toward them, coming to rest at their feet.

Staring up at them was the head of Pemba—his dead eyes bulging and a maniacal grimace on his face.

They ran away as fast as they could, shooting their guns in the general direction of the origin point of the flying head.

Their commotion awoke everyone in base camp. Phurba, who had been sleeping lightly as of late, was first on the scene with his shotgun. The sentries ran up to him and were jabbering all at once while pointing in the direction of Pemba's head.

Phurba noticed the head and ran over to it. Looking down, he recognized it was Pemba. He sneaked over to the corner of the medical tent and peered around it, switching his headlamp on to see better. On the ground behind the tent he could see a huge patch of blood in the snow, but no body—and no beast. Only Pemba's purple beanie with its white Nike logo remained. *The shooting must have scared it off.* He flashed his beam around the entire area, but the creature had vanished.

By now, others had arrived and were talking to the sentries in the center of camp. They all watched Phurba walk back.

Phurba spoke to all three sentries. "What happened?"

They all looked at each other. None of them wanted to speak. Phurba chose Ming. "Ming, what happened?"

"I heard a noise behind the medical tent and went to investigate. Just as I was about to look around the corner, Kipu and Dachen stopped me for a moment." Ming paused, looking at the other two sentries. "Then, before we could look to see what the noise was, Pemba's head came rolling out. Then we raised the alarm."

Raised the alarm. I'll bet they were scared shitless, Phurba thought. Ming's choice of words were a bit self-serving. He wanted to laugh at them, but refrained from making light of their encounter because another good man was dead.

Armstrong, Harry and Sir Randolph came running up.

Sir Randolph saw the head. "Oh, good God."

Armstrong pointed at it. "Harry, get some pictures of this."

Harry began snapping away. His camera flashes lit up the camp.

Armstrong walked up to Phurba. "Where did the animal go? Did anyone see it?"

Phurba ignored him. *This man is an annoyance.* "Ming, grab some cloth, wrap Pemba's head, and put it in some sort of container. Nawang, double the sentries to eight. Everyone, *stay alert!*"

After this order, some verbal rumbling went through the camp. Phurba could see that Armstrong was listening to the Sherpas. The term 'Mih Teh' was mentioned several times. Phurba wondered if Armstrong knew that the Sherpas were talking about the fabled yeti.

Sir Randolph walked up to the sirdar. "Phurba, what happened?"

"Another attack. That is the head of our lead sentry."

The grumbling from the Sherpas continued. "Excuse me, sir," Phurba said. He turned to address the Sherpas in their own language. "Quiet! This is what you signed on for. You are being paid extra. If anyone leaves, there will be no pay for any time served. And anyone who wants to leave can do so *now.*"

Phurba looked around at everyone. No one said a word. Sir Randolph was impressed.

Armstrong persisted. "Where did it go? Does anyone know what happened here?"

All the Sherpas ignored him and walked back to their tents. Nawang made sure five more men were armed, making a total of eight sentries.

Armstrong shook his head and spit. "These people are useless." Harry nodded but kept photographing Pemba's head from every angle. Finally, Ming arrived and gathered it up, wrapping it in cloth.

Sir Randolph had apparently had enough of Armstrong. "Pipe down, Armstrong. You aren't going to chase it, are you?"

"Well, no. But—"

"But what? What does it matter where it went? If you aren't going to chase it, then shut up, man. Someone is dead. Show some respect."

Armstrong stared at Sir Randolph, but the man seemed to know better than to retort to his benefactor. "Come on, Harry. Let's get back to our tent."

Phurba saw Dzangbu walk up and went over to fill him in on what happened. "The beast killed one of our sentries."

"Then I must leave immediately." Dzangbu turned and hurried back to get his knapsack. Phurba followed him to the tent and met him as he emerged.

Dzangbu paused. "Good-bye. Thank you for your help. I know I have put you in a bad position. Namasté."

Dzangbu turned to leave.

Phurba's curiosity was more than he could bear. "Are you going to kill it?"

Dzangbu paused a moment, thinking about how to answer the sirdar. But all he said was, "No."

Phurba watched the Sacrifist disappear into the dark, realizing he was still in the dark himself.

CHAPTER 51

THE GUNSHOTS HAD scared the beast into retreating from base camp before he had intended to, and he quickly made his way through the long entrance tunnel carrying his prey's headless body. He sensed someone following and paused for a moment to pick up the scent. He recognized that the scent belonged to a man, but there was not the usual scent of fear. The beast quickened his pace. He felt that the man intended to do him harm, and his rudimentary mind tried to think of how he might avoid the man.

Arriving at the square cavern room where he usually resided (because of its proximity to the exterior world and food) he made a left turn and went down another long tunnel. This took the beast to a large, circular, torchlit room. It was the room with the large sphere of stone that appeared to have been partially sunk into the floor.

Extending out from the sphere was a curved concave trench. The trench led from the tunnel opening to the spherical boulder. The entrances to the room were at a one hundred and twenty degree angle to each other. The yeti placed the headless body of Pemba on the floor. He had always tried to avoid this circular room in the past.

Over the years he had seen the Others occasionally traverse through the tunnels lighting new torches, and he had noticed that they would often return in the direction of this room. Several times the beast had followed one of the Others and watched them enter this room. But when loud noises began to emanate from the room, the beast would go no further and instead would retreat.

Afterward, when the noises subsided and the beast checked the room, it would always be empty and the Other's scent would be gone, leaving the beast confused.

The beast smelled the man's scent getting stronger, and knew the man was getting closer. He realized that he would have to do something quickly to protect himself. He gazed at the huge stone sphere in the middle of the room. Then he looked toward the entrance where the man would soon appear.

A memory returned to the beast.

He stood at the entrance as a young yeti. His mother moved the sphere toward where he stood at the entrance, making loud scraping noises as the boulder moved. The sphere sealed off the entrance with a loud crash, separating him from his mother. The beast remembered using all his strength in trying to push the sphere back, but at that time he could not move the huge stone. He had lain down at the foot of the boulder and felt the pain of his mother's desertion. He had fallen asleep.

When he awoke, the boulder was back in the center of the room. The beast had searched for his mother for days but could not locate her. Until that time he had seen the Others on a regular basis, but now they had all but disappeared.

The human was closing in. The beast stared at the boulder, then at the opening. Then he put his shoulder to the sphere and heaved with all his might. Pushing it up slowly, he dislodged the sphere, which began traveling easily down the trench toward the entrance. The beast stepped back reflexively and saw the hole in the floor where the sphere had been resting. Stepping around it to avoid falling in, he continued to push the sphere toward the entrance.

The entrance's opening was circular in nature, and when the sphere landed with a smash, it fit like a glove. Seeing the sphere safely in place, the beast walked back to the hole and gazed down. Stone stairs led a long way down to another torchlit room. He realized this must be where the Others were living. He picked up his prey's body and cautiously went down the stairs, wary of his own kin.

CHAPTER 52

DZANGBU KEPT HIS headlamp pointed at the tunnel floor so he could follow the blood trail left by Pemba's mutilated body. Entering the square cavern room, he followed the blood trail into the tunnel on the left.

Before entering, he looked at the map and noticed that the tunnel led to the next circular room. This time he noticed a dark dot in the center of the circle and knew what that meant. He began to sprint, seeing faint light at the end of the tunnel.

He was about halfway down the tunnel, when a loud scraping noise shattered the silence, followed by a crash that echoed loudly in the tunnel. At the same time, the light coming from the end of the tunnel was extinguished.

He arrived at the entrance to the circular room. It was blocked by the huge spherical boulder. Light shone through some gaps near the bottom of the sphere. He tried moving the gigantic smooth boulder, but it would not budge. He marveled at the beast's brute strength, to have been able to have moved such an object.

He got down on the floor of the tunnel and looked through the two gaps for the beast. Through the gap on the right, he could see the other tunnel was not similarly blocked. He reopened the book. His headlamp illuminated the map. He looked at the circle on the map that represented the other room and quickly reviewed the route he needed to take to reach it. He turned and ran as fast as he could toward the other entrance.

CHAPTER 53

SIR RANDOLPH WAS falling asleep just as his satellite phone rang. Perturbed at being prevented from sleeping, he picked up the phone. "What is it?" he asked, not bothering to keep the annoyance he felt out of his voice.

"Come on, Randy. You're the one who wanted to be kept apprised of the DNA testing."

Sir Randolph grinned. "Sorry, Gus. I thought it was from someone unimportant."

"That's more like it."

"You have some news?"

"Every sample of blood tested as coming from a human or higher primate."

Sir Randolph was surprised. "Okay. Were they all from the same donor?"

"We don't know yet."

Sir Randolph thought a moment. *Human or primate. If Dane is right, then that could make sense.* "Anything else?"

"The gal is going to do more tests to see if there are any differences between the blood samples. If I was a younger man, I'd ask her out. She's stacked."

Sir Randolph chuckled. "Okay, you dirty old man. Keep it professional. I want this followed all the way down. Tell no one. This girl is to talk to no one else. Understand?"

"She has already been so instructed."

"Good." *This is why I use Gus. He doesn't need orders.* "Tell Dr. Bean she is not to be disturbed or bothered by anyone, including him. This is our top priority."

"Done already."

"Let me know more when you do."

"Okay. No problem." Gus hung up.

This is great. We'll need to figure out how to bring a body back, dead or alive. Photographs or video won't be enough. He began to think about the logistics of capturing and hauling back one of the creatures.

CHAPTER 54

THE YETI DESCENDED the stairs, quickly reaching the floor below. The room had four walls and four exits, each of them lit by torches. The sound of the Others reverberated down from all the other tunnels. He had no way out. He waited on his haunches in one of the corners of the room, ready to protect his food. From one tunnel, four huge yetis emerged—at least nine feet tall, a foot taller than the white beast. One had black hair, while the other three had sandy brown hair.

From another tunnel emerged three more yetis, all with dark brown hair. The seven yetis walked slowly toward the beast. The beast roared loudly, guarding his kill. The seven did not flinch or move. They showed no fear. The white yeti stopped roaring. The Others stood still, watching him.

The white beast rose to his feet slowly, throwing his headless prey's body over his shoulder. The other yetis watched him carefully. They positioned themselves so as to block any path of escape. The beast would have to break through them to get away.

The beast took a nervous step toward one of the blocked tunnels. The yetis blocking him looked at the black yeti, who nodded. Then they slowly parted to make an opening wide enough for the white yeti to walk through easily. The beast walked slowly through the opening unmolested, and once he had gone past, he hurried away down the tunnel.

CHAPTER 55

DZANGBU RAN BACK to the square cavern room and took the tunnel to his left. Sprinting now, he headed for the large amphitheater room in the center of the complex.

Once there, he made his way to the first tunnel on the left and sprinted down the length of it to the next square room, checking the floor for blood as he ran. Its absence told him that the beast had not come this way. Reaching the square room, he checked the tunnel on the left for blood traces to make sure he had not missed the beast. Seeing none, he sprinted the length of the tunnel, heading toward the boulder room he was seeking. He slowed his pace as he drew near.

He stopped short of the entrance and peeked to either side to see if the beast was inside. No beast. Only the giant, smooth boulder blocking the only other entrance.

He walked in and saw that what he had recalled, when he reviewed the manual Yangji had provided, was indeed an actual fact. The other maps were floors. The boulder covered a passageway. Walking over to it, he peered down and saw a set of stairs leading downward. He flipped the book open and looked at the first map. A black dot was in one of the circular rooms. He flipped to the next map and noticed a circle in one of the square rooms and another black dot in a circular room. He realized the circle represented the entrance to a lower level and the black dots represented sealed exits, just as he had suspected. He flipped to the other maps and confirmed that there were five levels below the one he was currently in. Luckily for him, the beast had failed to reseal the room, and Dzangbu could still pursue him.

He crept down the stairs and noticed a few drops of blood. Arriving at the bottom of the stairs, he looked around the room. It had four lighted torches and four exits. He turned on his headlamp to see if there was any more evidence of a blood trail. He checked each tunnel exit, and the second one he checked had a couple drops of blood in the passageway. The tiny amount of blood told him he was running out of time.

He pulled out the book and turned to the map he had been using. From there, he turned a couple of pages to the second snowflake diagram. The map showed that there were many different directions in which the beast could escape from in that particular tunnel. He took off in a sprint with no more delay.

After a few minutes, Dzangbu heard a crash like stone falling on stone. He surmised that the boulder had been moved back into place. Dread hit him as it became quiet again. He assumed he had been tricked and was now trapped below. But a moment later, a second, equally loud crash burst from the silence.

Dzangbu became confused. "What is happening?"

CHAPTER 56

ARMSTRONG BECAME CURIOUS after Pemba's death, having concluded from the evidence that the attacking animal could not be a bear. Bears were strong, but they did not rip heads off bodies and throw them at people. *But what else could have attacked the Sherpa like that?*

He went around questioning other Sherpas, but he could find no witnesses willing to talk about the incident. Frustrated, he walked back to his tent.

"Psssst!"

One of the Sherpa sentries beckoned him from behind the medical tent. He walked over to the young man, who was clearly afraid to be seen talking to him.

"You want story of Mih Teh? The Demon. Pay money," the young Sherpa said, in broken English.

He's probably trying to shake me down, Armstrong thought.

"Chamba," the Sherpa said, pointing to himself, "heard the sirdar speak to doctor when golden hair man killed."

"What did he say?"

Chamba held out his hand. Armstrong reached into his pocket and pulled out a wad of bills. He placed several in

Chamba's hand, which apparently satisfied the younger man. *This had better be good.*

"What did the sirdar say?"

"He said the demon is eight feet tall and his mountain is not safe to climb."

Armstrong assessed the young Sherpa for a moment. *He's scared. Definitely scared. And he's telling the truth.*

"Thank you, Chamba."

Armstrong walked directly to Dr. Meritt's tent to confirm everything that Chamba had just told him.

"What do you think?" Armstrong asked.

Dr. Meritt shrugged. "I think Phurba saw something unusual, and he can't explain it because he'd never seen it before. Whether it was *the* actual yeti, I don't know. What I do know is that most Sherpas are honorable, brave, and don't lie. And Phurba is one of the most honorable you are ever going to find."

This news made Armstrong extremely excited. He ran back to his tent and Harry. He had to plan how to ensure his own fame and fortune.

"You know what this means for us, Harry?" Armstrong asked. "We'll be famous beyond belief."

Harry nodded. "Yes. If we can get good, clean video of it, it will be like the goose that laid the golden eggs. It will keep on giving forever."

"Right. We need to get good video. That's the key. All the videos of Bigfoot have always been crap. Shitty video is the same as fake video. Worthless."

They both went to sleep, dreaming of possible riches.

The next day, Armstrong asked Sir Randolph if he and Harry could take Lance, the GPR operator, out to 'scout' the area.

Sir Randolph shook his head. "You're going to have to wait for Dane and his dog. Trust me. With the dog it will be easier to find the yeti."

Armstrong tried to feign surprise. "Yeti?"

Sir Randolph laughed. "You think I don't know you've been asking a lot of questions around the camp? Don't worry about losing your shot at fame. You and Harry will be the only ones to get video. Dane doesn't want any credit. He only wants to kill the monster."

Armstrong was not so sure. *That's what Dane says, but if he changes his mind, I'm screwed.*

"Kill it? Isn't there some law against that?" Harry asked.

"Technically, the yeti doesn't exist. So there is no law," Sir Randolph said.

"I don't think we should kill it. Think of how much better it would be for the world if we captured it," Armstrong said. "An entirely new species of primate!"

"Don't get any ideas. This isn't King Kong," Sir Randolph said.

Armstrong was already thinking of ways to capture the beast. He had brought along a tranquilizer gun just in case the animal they were hunting turned out to be an endangered species, such as a snow leopard.

"Dane should be here later today," Sir Randolph told him. "You won't have to wait long. Tomorrow we'll start the search."

Armstrong walked dejectedly back to his tent and sulked for the next hour.

CHAPTER 57

DANE AND HIS crew were only a short distance from base camp. The trek had been good for him. Since it was Lily's first time in the Himalaya, he and Smokes had shown her local sights along the way that they thought she would like to see. It reminded him of his trek with Shelly less than a month ago. He had shown Shelly many of the exact same things.

The Kangchenjunga area was one of the more beautiful areas in the Himalaya. The beauty of it always put Dane into a different, more peaceful state of mind. He could see why the Buddhists considered it a sacred mountain. Despite what had happened to him, he felt a bit better every day of their trek. He was also impressed by Lily's stamina.

The first day, they stopped in Lali Kharka and Smokes introduced Lily to tungba. They made the mistake of having a second churn and things got a little silly. Smokes did his James Brown impression during karaoke, and Dane and Lily laughed so hard their heads hurt. It felt good.

Finally Dane and the others arrived at base camp. Everyone came out of their tents to greet him and Smokes. Phurba was clearly pleased to see Smokes; Dane had not told Phurba he was bringing him. They walked over to Sir Randolph, Phurba, and Nawang, and the other Sherpas assembled there. Dane introduced Lily to Phurba and Sir Randolph.

"Glad you're here, young lady," Sir Randolph said, shaking Lily's hand. He watched Smokes light a Camel non-filter. "And you must be Smokes Mitchell."

Smokes shook hands with Sir Randolph. "The one *and only*."

Sir Randolph turned to look for Armstrong. "George? Where are you?"

"I'm back here," Armstrong said, standing behind a crowd of Sherpas. He was taller than all the Sherpas and he and Harry were clearly visible from the shoulders on up.

"Dane, this is George Armstrong. You may have seen him on TV. He's going to be recording our little adventure for his show—'Big Game, Big Times.'"

Dane and Smokes glared at Armstrong. Dane turned to Smokes. "You ever seen that show, Smokes?"

Smokes recognized Dane's set-up and blew out some smoke. "Can't say I have. That on the Home Shoppin' Network?" Smokes spit off to one side.

Armstrong rolled his eyes. "Okay. Let's try to get along. How long does a man have to pay for his mistakes? I apologized at the time. And I'm still sorry. What do you want from me?"

Sir Randolph arched an eyebrow. "You all know each other?"

"Not me. Hi, I'm Lily McCrowley." She shook hands with Armstrong. "I've seen your show. I really like it." She glanced at Dane, and she must have seen the distaste he felt for Armstrong, because she gave him a WTF look.

Sir Randolph clearly also felt the tension between the three men. "Okay, boys. Let's all be friends. I'm paying you all to be professional. Act like it. Shake hands." They hesitated. His voice hardened. "It is *not* a request."

Reluctantly, Dane and Smokes shook hands with Armstrong.

Sir Randolph nodded. "Okay. That's better. Dane, come into my tent. Phurba will get you all up to speed on what's happening and our plan of action."

CHAPTER 58

PHURBA HAD RISEN about two hours before dawn to check with the sentries, wanting to see if they had observed anything in the night, but all had been quiet. The temperature was just below freezing, but the sky was clear. The moon shone brightly.

Phurba woke all the others. Dane came out of his tent followed by Duke, who was wearing his tracking harness. Phurba worried about the dog messing up whatever plan Dzangbu intended to carry out. He had destroyed the scenting items as Dzangbu had asked. *That should slow them down long enough to give Dzangbu time for whatever he needs to do.* Phurba still wished he knew what that was.

Phurba, Dane, Lily, Smokes, Sir Randolph, Lance, Harry, and Armstrong all gathered at the center of camp. Lance had the GPR equipment in case they needed it. Their breath billowed out like steam in the frigid air, especially Smokes's, whose breath was mixed with tobacco exhaust.

Dane kept shoving Harry's camera out of his face, telling the cameraman to back off while Dane spoke to his crew. Harry recorded the movement of all the expedition members talking about last minute protocols.

***

Lily knew what Harry was up to because she'd seen a lot of similar Bigfoot 'reality' shows on cable TV. She hated those shows because they were always the same. A camera crew would go out at night with their green glowing night vision. All the 'investigators' in the show would hear noises, but no one ever got a picture or shot a clear video of a Bigfoot—or any other scary monster, for that matter—and all the accounts of someone seeing a Bigfoot were always second or third hand. In her opinion, those shows were a rip-off and likely staged to make bucks for advertisers.

She found being part of the 'Big Game, Big Times' show exhilarating. The show was reality-based. George Armstrong did not just look for things that had never been seen. His show captured real true-to-life occurrences.

Lily was excited.

We're on a real adventure. The fact that we'll be searching mostly during daylight hours adds credibility.

Lily knew that the lack of night vision meant she was not part of a hoax-type show. *That and all the deaths.* The deaths were the real reason she knew it was not a hoax. Other shows did not have deaths as part of their investigation.

Everyone was pumped up to search for the beast. Phurba and seven other Sherpas were all armed. Two of the Sherpas had high-powered Remington 870 shotguns. All the others had Smith and Wesson .357 magnums, courtesy of Sir Randolph's pocketbook.

Dane had told Sir Randolph to get revolvers for the Sherpas because revolvers had no safety, and he knew well that in the heat of being attacked, most people tended to panic and forget to disengage the safety on a semi-automatic. Sir Randolph, Dane and Smokes were armed with Glock 21s and shotguns.

Dane addressed the group. "Okay, everyone. Let's be careful. We don't know what we are going to find, if anything. Phurba, do we have those items for Duke?"

Phurba turned to Nawang. "Go get the items."

Nawang ran off to retrieve them. Harry ran with him to shoot video. They went into a nearby tent. After a few minutes, both men emerged.

"They are gone," Nawang said.

"What?" Phurba asked, sounding surprised.

Lily saw Phurba's face, and his expression caught her attention. *He already knew,* she realized.

Phurba walked over to the tent and went inside, followed by Dane, Sir Randolph, and Lily, who watched Phurba closely. Phurba pretended to search, but to Lily's eyes, it was obvious that he was merely playing a role.

Phurba looked up at Dane and Sir Randolph. "The things are gone."

"How can that be?" Dane asked.

"I don't know."

Lily knew something was up. She knew Phurba was lying.

Sir Randolph intervened. "Should we search the other tents and see if someone took them?"

Dane shook his head. "Why would anyone take them? I'm not going to accuse anyone by searching their tent. I know most of these men. They're honorable. The items must have been misplaced."

Lily wanted to pull Dane aside, but waited. Dane's comment had plainly stung Phurba, and it was possible he would admit what he had done without Lily intervening. Nawang came into the tent.

Sir Randolph persisted. "If the items aren't here, they must be in one of the other tents. Either that, or they have been disposed of. The only way to find out is to search the other tents."

"It's unnecessary," Nawang said.

Dane regarded Phurba's deputy. "Why is that?"

"We have fresher evidence."

"What evidence?" Phurba asked Nawang. Then his eyes widened. "Oh. Pemba's head."

"And his beanie," Nawang said.

***

Phurba could hardly believe it. It had slipped his mind that Pemba's head could be used to track the beast. And a head was something Phurba could not dispose of. *Karma,* Phurba thought, resigned. *Dzangbu will have to deal with them if they find him.*

Everyone looked at Sir Randolph like it was up to him to okay using Pemba's head. He nodded. "Go get it."

They all walked outside. Dane had Phurba lead them to the scene of Pemba's demise. Nawang left and came back with the head wrapped in cloth. He set it on the ground. Everyone's headlamps shone down as Nawang carefully unwrapped the cloth and set Pemba's head down on the snowy ground.

The jagged bloody neck was visible to all. Lily let out a gasp at seeing Pemba's cloudy dead eyes staring into space. His death grimace remained frozen on his face. Harry videoed the entire scene.

Phurba had not seen Mingmar wrap the head up, but it looked oddly comical because Mingmar had apparently retrieved Pemba's purple Nike beanie, recovered at the scene of his demise, and put it back on Pemba's head.

Armstrong grinned when he noticed the beanie on the decapitated head. "Nice product placement, Nike."

Harry laughed.

"Come on, Duke," Dane said. He led his dog over to smell Pemba's head for a few seconds. "Phurba, bring that beanie with us."

Phurba removed Pemba's beanie and put it in his pack. Nawang quickly wrapped up the head and handed it to one of the Sherpas who was to remain at base camp.

Dane looked down at Duke. "Find 'em!"

Duke smelled the ground, then ranged around the nearby area picking up the scent, and at last, the dog took off.

Dane let Duke tug him along on the thirty-foot trailing leash. Everyone else followed, and one by one made their way up the sloping terrain through the snow. Their headlamps, flashing to and fro as they made their way up the slope, made them look like miners on their way to work.

Dane had total confidence in Duke's ability to lead them to Pemba's body, and maybe even to the beast.

Their fifteen member, plus dog, mini-expedition moved slowly through the snow, but they made their way following Duke, who was certain of his path. When the lead got tight at points, Duke would wait for Dane to catch up a little to slacken the lead. At other points, Duke would check left, then right, to make sure he was going on the right path.

***

Lily saw that Phurba had stationed himself at the end of the line of the expedition members. If she was going to speak to Dane away from Phurba, now was the time to do it. She passed a couple Sherpas and finally reached Dane at the front.

"How long have you known Phurba?" she asked as quietly as she could.

"A long time. Why?"

"Because he lied about the things that were missing."

Dane looked at her with disbelief on his face.

"Can't be. He's a trusted friend. You must be mistaken."

"Sometimes I am. Ten to twenty percent of the time. But this time, I'm not. I'm certain."

"I don't believe it," Dane said. "Even if it's true, which I doubt, it doesn't matter because we had fresher evidence for the scent."

"I understand. But I'm not wrong."

"What reason would he have?"

"I don't know. I just wanted you to know."

"Okay. I'll keep it in mind."

She dropped back to where she had been in the line. Dane would think about what she had said. Beyond that, she was not certain what else she could do.

After a long while, the coming dawn light made it easier to see. They reached a spot where the normal summit route for climbers went to the right. Duke, however, went to the left. Dane knew the area and knew that if they went too far, their route would lead them dangerously close to a large and deep crevasse in the glacier. But as they approached, Duke stopped just short of it and started to bark—normal search dog behavior to signal the rescue crew to start digging. Instead of digging, Sir Randolph told Lance to scan the area with the Ground Penetrating Radar.

Turning on his equipment, Lance walked over to the area where Duke was barking and started to scan. Holding the transmitter/receiver in one hand, he scanned the area. All the while, he watched the reading on the PDA (personal digital assistant).

The electromagnetic instrument looked like a board with paddles at either end. The paddles contained two sets of coils located on opposite ends of the board. At one end, a set of coils transmitted a primary magnetic field, which generated an electrical current into the ground. The induced current then generated a secondary magnetic field, which was sensed by the coils at the receiver end of the instrument. Data was then displayed on the PDA unit, indicating the conductivity of the earth below.

Lance slowed, passing the four-foot instrument over a specific area.

"Interesting. There is about ten feet of snow, then an open space here," Lance said, without glancing up from his PDA. Phurba ordered three Sherpas to start digging. The three Sherpas pulled out their snow shovels and prepared to dig where Lance was indicating. Dane stuck the dog lead onto his ice ax and jammed it in the ground.

"Stay, Duke." Duke lay down in the snow.

"Hold up a minute," Smokes said. "We are a little too close for comfort to that crevasse. Tie off first." Smokes pulled out some orange nylon rope. Dane took it and attached it to the harnesses of all three Sherpas. Then he attached two more Sherpas, Phurba, himself, and Smokes at the other end. Lily knew that way there would be plenty of help if there was a large collapse into the crevasse.

It was dawn. Harry videotaped everything that happened without artificial light.

Armstrong spoke into his digital recorder.

Lily watched the Sherpas, wary of all the weaponry. She did not know what she could do if all the testosterone around her erupted at a yeti sighting.

The Sherpas dug vigorously, and the snow collapsed. Two of them scrambled back, and narrowly missed falling in.

The one nearest the crevasse, Nyima, was not as lucky, and fell into the crevasse along with the collapsing snow. The rope jerked twice and then went tight as the two other Sherpas he had been digging with lay on the ground to prevent themselves from being pulled in. Dane, Phurba and the other Sherpas had the rest of the rope line and dug their heels in to prevent anyone else from being dragged over the side.

Sir Randolph and Lily had been standing somewhat further back, next to Armstrong and Harry. The host of the show and his cameraman were delighted at the unfortunate mishap. Harry had captured it all on video. They high-fived each other. Lily glanced at them in disgust. Armstrong looked back, still grinning. "Hey, no one died."

***

Hanging from the rope in the crevasse, Nyima thanked the Lord Buddha for Smokes and his forethought. He had fallen about twenty feet down, and now he dangled against the crevasse wall. Preoccupied with falling into the abyss, he looked down and noticed that he could not see the bottom. *That's a long way down.* He noticed the collapse of snow had opened up a channel in the side of the flat-walled crevasse. At the bottom of the channel there was a ledge, and what looked like an opening about thirty feet farther down from where he hung.

"I see something!" Nyima yelled.

Nyima looked up to see Smokes peep over the side and look down at him. Nyima pointed down. Smokes looked down the ice chute past Nyima and saw a small outcrop covered with snow from the collapse.

"You see it?" Nyima asked.

"What the hell," Smokes said. He turned to Dane. "Ya gotta see this. This is the strangest crevasse wall I've ever seen. It's flat. The collapse made an ice chute which leads down to some sorta ledge down yonder. It looks like there may be a cave or somethin' down there. If we can lower Nyima down a little further, he can take a look."

Smokes laid down his ice ax handle under the rope to prevent it fraying on the icy snow on the edge of the crevasse.

"Nyima," he called out, "we're going to lower you down a touch to that ledge."

Suddenly Nyima regretted mentioning having seen the opening. He braced his feet against the crevasse wall. His crampons bit in. He steadied himself as the others lowered him down to the ledge.

Nyima landed in a pile of snow on the ledge. He knew Smokes would be relaying the situation to the others.

Smokes called down to him. "See anything?"

Nyima looked up. "An ice cave. Let out some line and I'll take a look."

Smokes relayed the request.

The others let out some slack, and now Nyima was able to move freely. He started shoving the snow off the ledge to make it more navigable. After he had cleared it off enough, he crept into the cave to have a look. It was pitch black. He turned his headlamp on. Trepidation set in.

Nyima was tall for a Sherpa at five foot eight, and nearly had to stoop to negotiate the ice cave. From the headlamp light he could see that the cave went much further in. At four meters in, the ice cave became a stone cave that went swiftly down, but how far it went, he could not tell.

He had reached the end of the slack in his rope. He began to walk back to the outcropping to ask for more slack and a noise echoed up from the stone tunnel. *"Grrrrrr! Rawrrrrrrr!"*

The roar chilled him to his bones. He did not turn back to look; he just started running as fast as he could in his cramponed boots. The beast's snarls grew louder and louder. Nyima panicked. He pulled his gun out but dropped it, leaving it behind.

Nyima's new wife flashed into his mind. He started to get some traction as he neared the exterior. Fear gripped him as he felt the beast almost upon him. Swearing in Sherpa, he exited the ice cave and leaped off the ledge into the thin air of the crevasse, screaming in English: "Hellllp!"

Smokes heard Nyima's cries and looked down to see him come flying out of the ice cave and into the abyss without stopping. Smokes yelled to the others. "Brace yourselves!"

Too late.

Nyima's fall reached the end of his rope's slack, and the weight of his body jerked the other two Sherpas off their feet unexpectedly, nearly dragging them both into the crevasse.

Dane and Phurba reacted and strained at the rope. Sir Randolph and Lily came to help them. The other two Sherpas recovered and dug in too. The yeti burst out onto the ledge. The beast blinked its sensitive eyes in the morning sunlight as Nyima screamed uncontrollably below.

Smokes looked down at the top of the beast's head, amazed at how large it was. "Well, looky there."

The beast looked down at Nyima, then followed the orange rope upward and saw Smokes peeking out over the side. Their eyes met.

Smokes could not believe it. "I'll be damned."

"What's going on, Smokes?" Dane asked.

Smokes shouted, "We got a big ol' hairy monster over here."

"Can you get a shot at it?" Dane asked.

"Nyima's in the line of fire. I better move over and get a safer angle."

Armstrong and Harry looked at each other, grinned and began to gingerly walk toward Smokes and edge of the crevasse.

Smokes reached for his gun and noticed Armstrong and Harry coming toward him. "This ground may be unstable. Take another step an' I'll shoot *you* insteada *it*."

Duke picked up the yeti's scent and ran to the edge of the precipice, taking up the slack of his leash, which was still attached to Dane's ice ax, stuck in the snow. He started barking.

Dane looked at Lily. "Lily, can you get Duke away from the crevasse? He must be scenting the animal. Duke, stay!"

The dog sat down. Lily reached down, grabbed his trailing leash and began to reel him in.

Armstrong and Harry retreated, making their way back around Dane and the others who were holding on to Nyima. They headed over to the other side of the lifeline.

In the meantime, Nyima kept traversing to his right along the ice wall to keep his rope away from the monster's reach. With tears running down his face, he kept screaming, "Get me out of here! Please, get me out of here!"

Like impending doom, gravity kept bringing the hysterical Sherpa and his rope back toward the yeti's grasp. The beast swiped at the nylon cord several times and it began to fray.

While the beast looked down at Nyima, Smokes took up a position further left to get a better angle for a shot at the monster. He did not want to hit Nyima by mistake. He was a good shot, but not a great one. Taking his time, Smokes took careful aim at the animal's head.

BLAM!

The shot rang out. But it was not from Smokes. Everyone

looked over and saw Lily to their far right, lying near the edge, giving herself a good angle from which to view the beast. She had grabbed one of the revolvers the Sherpas had set aside while they had been digging and had crept over to get a look.

Dane blew up. "Dammit, Lily! Get away from that edge. You aren't tied in and you coulda hit Nyima."

The yeti looked at Lily when the gunshot got its attention. Its piercing eyes radiated evil. She shivered in spite of herself. She had aimed away from it, only wanting to scare it back into the cave. The bullet had not even come close, but her shot had the desired effect. The beast retreated immediately into its lair and out of sight. But something else about the encounter bothered her.

Smokes failed to get off a round before the beast disappeared back into his cave. Armstrong and Harry arrived near Lily, but were too late to witness it themselves or get any video footage of the beast.

"You three fools get away from that edge," Smokes yelled.

"Everyone, let's get Nyima back up here," Dane said. He got up and immediately rigged up a boot-ax belay to help recover Nyima safely. To do this, Dane jammed an ice ax shaft into the snow at a slightly uphill tilted angle and put his uphill foot against the downhill side of the ax for support. He then looped the rope over his boot and around the shaft of the ice ax. The ability of a boot-ax belay to hold strongly was related to the firmness of the snow and to the strength of the ice ax's shaft. Wrapping the rope back around the heel of his boot would act like a brake when pulled on.

The men pulled Nyima up near the top and then Phurba and Smokes hauled him back up over the edge of the crevasse. Harry and Armstrong videoed everything and high-fived each other when the others were done rescuing the terrified Sherpa.

Dane looked at Armstrong and Harry. "You two could help a little."

"Then who would do play-by-play?" Armstrong asked.

Dane faked a step toward the TV show host, making Armstrong's smarmy smile turn into a flinch.

Sir Randolph intervened. "Come on, boys. We have a much more serious problem here."

He pointed at Nyima, who was chattering to all the other Sherpas they had brought with them. They all looked aghast. They had not seen the monster, but Nyima was doing his best to paint a picture for them.

Phurba walked over to them as Nyima finished and they all started yakking at him at once. He held up his hands to quiet them down and nodded his head. He said a few words to them and then came toward Dane and Sir Randolph.

"They say they will go no further. They want no part of the Kangchenjunga Demon. They will not go into his home underground and they want to get off his mountain as soon as possible."

"Will they assist with lowering us down and assist pulling us back up when needed?" Dane asked. "We will be back well before sundown whether we find the beast or not."

Phurba turned and spoke to Nawang, his second in command. Nawang spoke English, but Phurba spoke in Sherpa for the benefit of some of the other Sherpas there. Armstrong and Harry looked worried. Lily was surprised at what Dane was considering.

"Are you crazy? Go underground?" Lance asked. He turned to the others. "He's nuts."

After speaking with the other Sherpas, Phurba explained the outcome to Dane. "They will assist in lowering any of you who wish to go down into the cave, but they will only stay here while there is sunlight. They want no part of his darkness."

Dane nodded. "Okay. That's fair."

Phurba spoke some more with Nawang.

"Nawang says he can be trusted to keep the others here as long as we get back before sundown. I will follow you down to help you find the demon—for Torleif."

"You're a good man, Phurba."

Smokes flicked his chrome Zippo, lit another short Camel, and looked over at Armstrong and Harry. "What about *you* two? Are you good men? Wanna shoot some pictures o' the big, ol' bad yeti for yer TV show? Or are ya *yella?*"

Armstrong and Harry looked at each other. Lily watched them to see what they would say. Armstrong looked like a child backed into a corner. Lily felt sorry for him. At last, Armstrong straightened his stance.

"Let it never be said that George Armstrong is a coward." Harry looked unsure.

Smokes picked some tobacco off the tip of his tongue and flicked it away. "That's the spirit, Custer."

Sir Randolph retrieved the gun from Lily. "I'll take that back now. I'm guessing you're not Annie Oakley reincarnated."

Lily shrugged her shoulders. "Guess not."

She did not feel guilty in the least. She had saved the yeti from being killed. She only hoped she would not regret it. The truth was, she actually was a great shot.

The Sherpas started to set up for lowering the search party down to the cave.

Lily spoke up. "Wait. What about me? I'm going, too."

"Why don't you and Sir Randolph stay top side?" Dane asked.

Sir Randolph bristled. "Wait a minute, Dane. This is my party and I'm definitely going."

Dane pointed at Lily. "Okay, but she stays."

Lily shook her head. "I'm going too."

Dane looked at her. "No. You're not."

Lily gave him an incredulous look. "You aren't the boss of me."

"Uh … children," Sir Randolph said. Then to Dane: "Dane, she's a grown woman. We shall not be chauvinists here."

Dane sighed and muttered, "*Ikwewag,*" the Ojibwe word for *women*. Then, to Smokes, "That woman is a pain in my ass."

Smokes spit. "Ain't they all."

Lily just smiled back at Dane, triumphantly.

Dane shook his head. "Okay. Give Wonder Woman a gun too."

CHAPTER 59

THE LIGHT OF Dzangbu's headlamp shone on the map of the lower level. For many hours now, he had conducted a methodical search following Pemba's blood trail. He had come to the conclusion that he had indeed been fooled by the beast and was trapped below the floor where the beast was actually located. The blood trail had disappeared. He had nothing left to follow.

He went back, checked the room with the stairs, and saw that the boulder above was still lodged in place. During his search of the lower floor he had discovered another room with a spherical boulder leading to level three.

His spirits began to sink, as he knew that without help he had no way of moving the giant boulders that were separating the floors.

He decided to head to the most likely place, for the level he was on, where the beast might show up. He knew that on each floor all the tunnels eventually led to a large room at the center of the snowflake tunnel system. He made his way there quickly.

In the center room of level two was another statue. This one depicted two yetis back to back. And again, there were six seating sections and six exits, but not much in the way of places to hide. He extinguished one of the six torches, ducked into the adjacent tunnel exit, and waited.

Half an hour passed. A faint pop-pop-pop-pop-pop-pop broke into the silence of the tunnel he inhabited and puzzled him. A few minutes passed. He heard another loud crash, the sound of the spherical boulder falling into place.

The noise made him hopeful that the yeti had returned. He began to hear loud shuffling noises that echoed from the other end of the tunnel where he was hiding. They became louder and were coming toward him. He ran back into the amphitheater room. Shuffling noises echoed from all six tunnels.

He backed into the center of the room against the double yeti statue that towered above him. The yetis invaded the room, pouring in from every tunnel. They padded calmly to their adjacent seating section and sat down. The yetis were of different colors, being sandy brown, reddish-brown, medium brown, dark brown, black, and grey.

Each of the six seating sections held eighteen yetis—each top row held eight, each middle row held six and each bottom row held four. All of the sections had been filled, except one section that was missing three yetis on the bottom row, which meant there were a total of one hundred and five yetis present.

A reddish-brown yetess got up and walked toward him. She towered above him, taller by at least four feet. These yetis were taller than the white yeti. She looked down upon him with kind, green eyes.

Dzangbu looked around the room. The sight of the yetis filled him with great joy. He had finally found all the other Sacrifists.

Or rather, they had found him.

CHAPTER 60

DANE HAD INSISTED on going first, and the Sherpas had lowered him down into the ice cave. When the entrance came into view, Dane emptied half a clip of his Glock 21 into the pitch-black void. He explored into the ice cave all the way to where the stone tunnel began. He picked up Nyima's gun and stowed it in his pack.

Smokes followed Dane down and helped to steady the party—Phurba, Sir Randolph, Lily, Armstrong, Harry, and Duke—as each member hit the cave's floor. Dane kept watch and ushered everyone inside.

Inside, they all turned on their headlamps. Dane, with Duke on his trailing leash, led the way. Harry scrambled around to the front, where the stone tunnel began, and kneeled down to video their descent into the yeti's labyrinth.

Everyone's crampons slipped on the smooth stone surface. Lily fell and her butt hit the floor. "Ouch."

Dane stopped. "Before we go any further, everyone remove and stow your crampons. No need for them down here."

Smokes stepped over to help Lily. She looked up and the light from her headlamp lit up the ceiling. "Look at that."

Everyone followed her gaze and their headlamps revealed the arched character of the tunnel. Harry kept shooting video.

Dane removed a glove and touched the wall. "Looks and feels man-made. Smokes, check this out."

Smokes removed a glove and touched the wall. "Smooth. That ain't all. Breathe deep."

Dane and the others paused a moment, just breathing.

"There's more oxygen in here," Armstrong said.

"Custer's right. Plus, the temp is higher," Smokes said.

"How is that possible?" Sir Randolph asked.

"Being underground would explain a little temperature change, but not this much. I don't know. It's odd. Maybe further in we'll find some answers," Dane said, although from his tone it was clear he had his doubts.

The tunnel was wide enough that three people could easily walk abreast. Much wider than the ice cave entrance.

Armstrong continued to run his hand along the smoothness of the stone. "This is bizarre. I've never seen anything like it anywhere else in the world. This is not indigenous stone. I'm not sure it even *is* stone. I'm going to take a sample."

"Good idea," Sir Randolph said. "I'll have it analyzed."

Armstrong pulled out a knife to chip off some of the wall but the knife just glanced off the rock. He tried again, then a third time. He looked closely at the wall. "Not even a scratch. This stuff is unbelievably hard."

"Forget about it for now. Let's get going," Dane said, as he took his coat off and stowed it in his backpack.

Smokes followed suit. "It's downright tropical in here."

Everyone took off their outer coats and packed them. Although milder here, the air was still frigid.

"Yeah, and the closed environment should help Duke. Phurba, let me have Pemba's beanie."

Phurba removed the item from his pack and handed it to Dane. Dane kneeled down and let Duke smell it. He knew they had a good chance now of at least finding Pemba. With any luck, the beast would still be with the body.

Duke sniffed the beanie and Dane handed it back to Phurba. He turned to Duke. "Go find him, boy."

Duke took off. The party had no snow to hinder their speed and plenty of light from their headlamps. They moved quickly along the tunnel. Before long they came to the first junction of left-right offshoot tunnels.

Duke ignored the offshoots and attempted to keep going forward, but Dane held him up. "Smokes, I think you and I should check these tunnels first. The rest of you, keep an eye in every other direction. The beast could come from anywhere."

Sir Randolph assumed control. "Will do. How will we know if you need help?"

Smokes lit a smoke. "If ya hear shootin', we need help."

Sir Randolph and Armstrong looked at Dane for confirmation.

Dane grinned. "What he said." Dane handed the trailing leash to Lily. "Hold onto him." Then to Duke: "Duke, stay."

Dane and Smokes went down the tunnel. The tunnel went about fifty yards in and led to the opening of another, larger space. They crept closer with their guns drawn. They sneaked to either side of the opening and peeked in. Their headlamps lit up the area. It was a circular room that was about thirty feet in diameter. It was empty. They walked inside and saw that there was no other exit.

Dane was satisfied. "Let's get back."

Dane and Smokes came back and saw Sir Randolph and Armstrong examining the symbols on the wall near the offshoot's entrance, while Harry shot video.

Sir Randolph beckoned to Dane. "Look at this. They appear carved but are decidedly precise. Like they were made with a machine. Have you ever seen anything like this before?"

Dane and Smokes looked closely at the symbols.

Dane shook his head. "No, sir. I haven't. This whole place is … well, out of place."

"Ditto," Smokes said.

Armstrong took out an ice ax. "No telling how old this place is. We need to get a sample of this stone."

Armstrong took a big swing at the wall. The ice ax bounced off the wall and nearly struck him in the head. The ax had no effect on the wall. "The stone is impervious. The ax didn't even scratch it, and it felt like it shocked me."

"Let's move. We have limited time," Dane said. Dane resumed control of Duke. "We don't know how far these tunnels go. We don't want to have to climb out by ourselves. We can do it, if we have to, of course. But it'll be safer with the Sherpas' help."

Dane, Duke and Smokes explored the five other side tunnels and all led to different but similar circular rooms. All of the rooms proved empty. In the main tunnel, Duke picked up the scent again and led them to the torchlit square cavern room.

"Fire denotes intelligence. Only humans light fires. Look, more symbols," Lily said. She pointed at the symbols near each torch and walked around the center platform to the far side of the room. She gasped. The remains of two mangled carcasses littered the floor.

Sir Randolph went past her to inspect them. Dane followed, not wanting to see Shelly but determined to recover her remains if at all possible. Harry stood on top of the center platform, videoing. Sir Randolph knelt beside one of the corpses. It was Rand. With a quick glance, Dane saw that the other remains belonged to a black bear, not a human.

Tears began to form in the billionaire's eyes. His voice cracked. "My boy. My poor boy." He attempted to stifle his weeping.

The others' collective thought was, *Money can't change death.*

Harry zoomed in on Sir Randolph's grief. Dane looked at the cameraman. He said, softly, "Shut it down, Harry."

Harry ignored him. A moment later, Dane heard a shotgun pump behind him. Glancing over his shoulder, Smokes pointed the shotgun—either at Harry, or at the camera. Given the angle, Dane doubted Harry could tell which.

"Ya heard him, Spielberg," Smokes said.

Harry turned off his camera. Dane walked over to Sir Randolph, who was holding a ring he had removed from what little remained of his son's ravaged corpse. Dane put his hand on Sir Randolph's shoulder.

"His mother gave this to him when he graduated high school. She died shortly after. He never took it off."

Dane looked down at the grieving father. "Let us collect him. Gather up the bones."

Sir Randolph nodded his head and rose to his feet.

Dane looked at Phurba. "Phurba, you got this?"

Phurba nodded and removed a body bag from his pack. He and Smokes gathered up the bones of Rand. Sir Randolph leaned against the platform in the center of the room. He took several deep breaths.

Dane watched him wrestle with his emotions. "Sir, do you want me to have Phurba lead you back out of here?"

Sir Randolph shook his head, catching his breath through his grief. "I'll be okay."

Dane nodded. "All right."

Sir Randolph turned to face Dane. "Thanks for finding my

boy."

Dane sensed the man's heartfelt gratitude. "You're welcome, sir. But we're not done yet."

Sir Randolph nodded.

Dane addressed everyone. "Okay, listen up. We'll leave the remains here until we go back up topside. We'll have to rely on Duke. But keep watch behind you. Duke is most likely scenting only Pemba, not the beast. So from now on we are only going to follow Duke. No more side trips. There are three more exits here. I'm guessing there may be a whole system of tunnels, and we have no way of knowing how many."

Dane kneeled down next to his dog and had him sniff Pemba's beanie again. "Okay, Duke. Ready? Go find him."

Duke sniffed around the entire platform, then took the tunnel over to the left from where they had entered. Their headlamps' light flashed off the darkened walls as they all followed Duke into the tunnel.

Dane saw a lighted room in the distance. "I see something far ahead."

Soon they came to a circular room with a spherical boulder in the center. Duke began to range around the room. He went up to the boulder and sniffed it where it met the seam in the floor, all the while whining and attempting to dig at the stone floor.

Dane kneeled down. "What's the matter, boy?"

Duke barked like he would have if he had found a buried skier in the snow.

Armstrong kneeled down and examined the trench leading from the tunnel to the boulder's resting place. "What's going on with your dog?"

"He's saying Pemba's underneath the boulder," Dane said.

"This trench looks like a track for moving the boulder,"

Armstrong said. "Let's see if we can move it."

Dane, Smokes, Phurba, Sir Randolph and Armstrong began to push on the boulder. It did not budge. Lily helped. It still would not budge.

"Harry! Put down the damn camera and lend us a hand," Armstrong yelled.

Harry put down his camera, being careful to situate it so it would record their actions. He lent his shoulder to their effort.

"Ready? On three," Dane said. "One, two, *three!*"

They strained with all their might. The boulder started to move up an inch, then two, but it was too much weight for all of them and came back down with a thud.

"One or two more people ought to do it," Dane said. "Phurba, use the low-freak to call Lance and see if we can get some Sherpas down here to help move this rock."

Sir Randolph had brought along the low frequency radio, suspecting they might need it underground. The radio system had originally been devised for deep cave rescues because the signal it used would go through solid rock.

Phurba radioed Lance. "Let me speak to Nawang." Phurba started speaking Sherpa. He listened for a moment, then looked at Dane and shook his head.

"Tell them I'll pay two thousand extra to every man who comes to help," Sir Randolph said.

Phurba gave Nawang Sir Randolph's offer and listened as Nawang relayed the offer to the other Sherpas. Phurba heard someone reply. The others could hear Nawang speaking Sherpa from the radio speaker. When Nawang finished, Phurba turned to Sir Randolph. "Nawang said they all agree that dead men cannot spend money. They will not come down for any price."

"Then have Lance come down," Sir Randolph said. "Hopefully, he'll be enough. Have him bring the GPR equipment, too. Maybe he can get some readings before we head down."

Phurba got back on the radio and told Nawang they were coming back for Lance and to lower him down with his equipment.

"Smokes, go with Phurba. Keep your eyes open," Dane said. "Bring Lance back straight away."

Smokes lit a cigarette, picked the loose tobacco off his tongue and flicked it away. "Roger that."

Phurba left with Smokes. Harry followed them, since all of the others were just waiting. Everyone except Dane sat down against the wall, slightly tired from their attempts at heavy lifting.

"The beast must have some unbelievable strength to move that thing," Armstrong said.

"Either that or it had some help," Dane said.

His comment gave them pause. Until that point in time, it had not occurred to any of them that there might be more than one yeti below.

CHAPTER 61

COURTNEY HAD LOST track of time. She had been up for more hours than she could ever remember, including times she had stayed up all night cramming for tests in college. She was not even tired. She sat at her desk, staring at her results, fascinated. She had never before seen DNA like the sample she had been examining. It was definitely human DNA, but like none she had ever seen.

Thoughts swirled in her head.

"Find anything else out?" Gus asked.

She jumped and turned around. Gus smiled down at her.

"Quit sneaking up on me." She nodded her head in answer to his question. "Too much. I can't believe what I'm seeing."

"Okay. What ya got?"

Courtney took a deep breath and got ready for a long-winded explanation, but Gus held up his hand.

"Nutshell it, honey. I had to take a nap after our last conversation."

"Okay. Both samples of DNA are human, but ..." She smiled and paused for effect, proud of herself.

"But what?"

"But the blood on the knife and the blood on the right sleeve ..." She paused again, she was enjoying herself. Gus rolled his eyes and put up with it. "... are a different species of human."

Gus thought a moment. "Okay. I'm not going to ask you how you know that, because I probably wouldn't understand it anyway. But what does that mean? What are we dealing with? I thought you said a higher primate was a possibility?"

"It was, but the more in-depth tests showed that both samples are definitely human. It's just that one of them has variations that aren't found in the normal human genome. I found some genes that were previously unknown. I sure would like to meet this person and do more tests."

"Uh, ... I don't think that's going to be possible."

"That's too bad, because this is Nobel Prize type stuff."

"Okay, Einstein. Continue."

"All right. I'll keep it simple, Mr. Gump."

"Very funny."

Courtney giggled. "It's definitely human DNA. There are twenty-two pairs of autosomes and one pair of allosomes—the sex chromosome. He's male, by the way. Forty-six chromosomes in total. That rules out a bear or a leopard, but we already knew that. However, there are about a dozen different mammal species with forty-six chromosomes, most of them from the orders of Rodentia (rodents) and Artiodactyla (hoofed animals). And there are very few species with forty-six chromosomes in the order of primates besides humans—Titi monkeys from South America and the Crowned Lemur from Madagascar. Neither of those would attack and kill humans, and they don't live in the Himalaya. This species has some variations, but is very close to the human genome. Closer to human than a Chimpanzee, which was, until now, the closest. It is so close, in fact, that I would classify it as a Homo sapiens."

Courtney paused, expecting Gus to show some excitement or enthusiasm to match her own. But he only said, "Anything else?"

She was a little miffed that he was not more excited. "Well, it's too bad he's a murderer, because I would like to meet this person."

Gus sighed. "Yeah. Like I said, I don't think that's gonna happen, Sweetie."

Gus noticed she looked tired and looked at his watch. "Okay, you've been up for over forty-eight hours. Why don't you go home and get some sleep? I'll need you sharp in the morning if you're going to be able to pick up on anything else you might find out."

"I've been awake over forty-eight hours?"

Gus smiled. "Yeah."

His affirmative answer made Courtney extraordinarily tired. She picked up her purse and headed for the door.

CHAPTER 62

THE BEAST SAT on his haunches in the tunnel opposite from where the party of men had gone. He watched them enter the left-hand tunnel across from his hiding place in the right-hand tunnel. He smelled their scent, which dissipated as they moved away in the other direction.

He stayed put. The gunshots had frightened him and irritated his keen sense of hearing. He rested a while, and his ears stopped ringing. The sound of men's footsteps came from the opposite tunnel.

He watched three men re-enter the room and exit into the tunnel that led to the opening in the crevasse. The beast heard their steps get fainter and he decided to follow them partially up the exit tunnel. Leery of them, he stayed a good distance back and waited to see if they would return.

After some time, the men re-entered the tunnel. The beast ran back to the room and hid once more in the right-hand tunnel. This time he detected a fourth scent and knew the men had added another to their number. The new person smelled of fear. The beast began to salivate for his blood.

He readied himself to attack once they entered the room.

CHAPTER 63

LILY, ARMSTRONG, AND Sir Randolph sat with their backs against the wall of the circular room. Armstrong had his knife out and was making symbols in the dust of the room's floor like the ones they had seen on the tunnel walls. Duke lay next to Lily. She scratched him behind his ears.

Lily watched Armstrong write the symbols. "I wonder what they mean."

He looked up. "No telling. I've never encountered anything even remotely similar."

Sir Randolph looked over. "Neither have I."

Dane walked around the room. He had been watching Lily talk with Armstrong and noticed that he felt slightly jealous and wondered why. He watched her laugh at something Armstrong said. *She's flirting. So what? She can do what she wants.*

Dane walked over to the tunnel they entered by and shone his headlamp inside. *What's taking those guys so long?* They had been gone about an hour. Dane walked across to the other side of the room and entered the opposite tunnel. His headlamp shone down into the darkness. *No movement of any kind. Good.* He walked back out and went back to eavesdropping on Lily's conversation with Armstrong.

"What did it look like?" Armstrong asked Lily.

"Honestly? Not anything like I'd thought he would look."

"*He?* How did you know it was a he?"

"Have a clue, Armstrong," Dane said.

Armstrong looked at Lily. She nodded.

"Oh," Armstrong said.

Lily continued. "Anyway, I was expecting something more like Bigfoot."

Armstrong laughed and then kidded, "Oh, and you've seen Bigfoot? Come on, now."

Lily became indignant. "Well, I have. It was a long time ago. When I was ten."

Armstrong smiled at her. "Ten? You're still a ten."

She slapped his arm. "Quit it." She glanced at Dane, who averted his gaze.

Armstrong failed to notice. "Okay. So it didn't look like Bigfoot. What *did* it look like?"

She thought a moment. Something about the sighting had bothered her but so much adrenaline had been pumping through her body during the moment before she fired the gun, she had not evaluated the details.

"I only saw Bigfoot briefly and from a distance. The yeti had white hair. So that was different. And the yeti was much closer. He looked right at me with his evil eyes. That's it!"

"What's it?"

"When he turned around to look up at me, something had bothered me. It was the way he twisted his body. Like a human being would. Right now, thinking back, even though he was easily eight feet tall, he looked like what a human being would look like if he was covered with a lot of hair."

"Oh, come on. Like a human?" Armstrong asked. "Well,

maybe it's Professor Up-to-No-Good dressed up as a yeti, and Duke is Scooby-Doo, and you're Daphne." He laughed at his own joke. "That would make Dane ..."

A distant, blood-curdling scream pierced their quiet moment, followed by several gunshots. Everyone rose quickly to their feet in the silence that followed. Several more gunshots exploded in the distance.

Dane ran to the tunnel from which they had entered. He looked back at Armstrong. "Custer, with me. Draw your gun. Sir Randolph, you and Lily stay here. Draw your guns and watch both exits. Lily, hold onto Duke."

Dane ran off down the tunnel. Armstrong paused and looked at Lily. His expression said, quite plainly, *What have we gotten ourselves into?* He hurried to catch up with Dane.

Lily grabbed Duke's harness. She began to regret her decision to come underground. *I hope no one is hurt badly.*

Sir Randolph walked down the concave trench toward the tunnel entrance and watched the two men go. "Lily, you watch the other exit. I'll keep an eye on this one."

Lily switched on her headlamp and shone it down into the passageway on the other side of the room. Its beam shone a long way down the passage, but all she could see at the other end was more darkness. *Jesus and Lord Buddha, please protect everyone.*

CHAPTER 64

IT HAD TAKEN Smokes a while just to *convince* Lance to come underground. Lance kept pleading that it was "not in my job description" to go down into the caves.

Finally, Smokes said, "Ya can go down there conscious or unconscious. *You* decide. I'd recommend conscious. Because if I have to drag yer unconscious ass down there and I run into Mr. Yeti, the first thing I'm doin' is throwin' yer carcass over to him for lunch."

Lance sat on his pack, still hesitant.

"Well?" Smokes asked.

"Conscious."

"Good choice."

They began their descent down the long tunnel to the square cavern room. They walked by each offshoot tunnel, and Smokes shone his headlamp down each one as a precaution against the beast lying in wait. They reached the cavern room and Harry ran to the front and got on top of the platform in the center of the room to get video of them entering.

Smokes was in a hurry to get back to Dane and the others. "Come on. Let's pick up the pace." He lit a non-filter as he walked toward the tunnel on the left, intending to head for Dane and the others. He was followed by Phurba, then by Lance.

Lance asked Phurba, "How does he smoke at this elevation?"

"I do not know. It is amazing. Smokes, are you part Sherpa?"

Without looking back, Smokes said, "My daddy was a locomotive and mama was a ragin' fire."

Smokes heard a vicious growl from behind and turned around to see the yeti storm from its hiding place in the right-hand tunnel and jump onto the platform. Harry wailed as he turned toward the beast. The camera's bright spotlight blinded the beast momentarily. The yeti swung its claws, narrowly missing Harry's throat but knocking his camera from his hands. Harry gashed his head on the floor as he fell off the platform, momentarily stunned. Smokes sprinted past Phurba and Lance and re-entered the room. Phurba drew his gun and ran to follow.

The yeti jumped off the platform toward Harry, and Smokes began blasting away at the beast. His first shots hit the wall near the beast and sent sparks flying, showering the beast and Harry. A shot grazed the beast's shoulder, and it speedily retreated to the tunnel where it had been hiding.

Phurba entered the room firing. Sparks flew every time a bullet hit a wall and the noise stung everyone's ears. The beast disappeared down the tunnel.

"Check on Harry," Smokes said.

Phurba kneeled down at Harry's side. Smokes sprinted to the beast's tunnel and began unloading the rest of his clip into the darkness. He reloaded, then shone his headlamp down the corridor, but could not see anything of interest.

The beast was gone.

Smokes ran back to Harry, who was dazed from his near brush with death. Phurba took out a first aid kit and cleaned Harry's wound. When he was finished, he wrapped gauze around Harry's head.

Lance, who had been hiding in the opposite tunnel, came over to the other men. He looked down at the ground and Smokes saw him pick up something.

"Whatchya got?" Smokes asked.

Lance showed Smokes that a small piece of the wall had been chipped off. The edges seemed to glow briefly.

"Guess it ain't indestructible. Ya got yerself a souvenir," Smokes said.

Lance stuck the stone chip in his coat pocket and zipped it closed.

"You okay?" Smokes asked Harry.

"Look at my camera," Harry whined. "What am I going to do now?"

The camera had scuff marks on it and the lens was cracked. He turned it on and looked in the viewfinder. A line showed across the screen.

"Hey, it still works. We'll take the line out in post!"

"Yer okay," Smokes said, answering his own question.

"Oh … yeah. I'm okay. Thanks for coming back," Harry said.

"No problemo, Coppola."

Dane and Armstrong burst into the cavern room with their guns drawn.

"Look, boys. The cavalry's here," Smokes said.

Armstrong helped Harry up.

"Everyone okay? What happened?" Dane asked.

"The beast tried to make a meal outta Harry," Smokes said.

"Where did it go?" Dane asked.

Smokes gestured at the opposite tunnel. "Down yonder."

Dane ran over to the tunnel and shone his headlamp down it with his gun drawn. Behind him, he could hear Harry updating Armstrong on what had happened.

"Lens is cracked," Harry said to Armstrong. "But it still shoots. Look."

Armstrong watched as Harry showed him the damaged camera.

Satisfied that the beast was no longer nearby, Dane walked back to Smokes. "I don't get it. Duke was sure it had gone under the boulder. Maybe there is another entrance from underground. Did you get a good look at it? Was it the animal you saw at the entrance?"

"Yup. Had the same weird-looking grey eyes," Smokes said.

"You mean red eyes," Dane said.

"He means grey. Come look," Armstrong said.

Harry and Armstrong were looking at the camera's playback screen. Dane and Smokes walked over. On the small video screen was a paused close-up of the beast's face from right before it slapped the camera from Harry's hands. Staring back from the screen were the creature's grey eyes.

"That's the sucker," Smokes said.

Dane shook his head. "How can that be? When it attacked Shelly and me, it had red eyes. I'm sure of it. It's not possible. Unless …"

Armstrong chimed in. "There are two."

"Custer's right. Sounds like we got an Edgar and Johnny type of situation … without the good music," Smokes said.

Everyone took in the prospect of there being two albino yetis. A woman's shrill scream broke their silent pondering. The shrieking ended abruptly, punctuated by a loud crash.

Dane looked over at Smokes. "Oh, no. Lily and Sir Randolph!" He sprinted back in their direction.

Smokes yelled out. "Everyone! Double time. Let's go."

Smokes ran after Dane, followed by Phurba and the others. *I hope they're all right,* Smokes thought. But he had a sinking feeling of dread. He began to think that they had bitten off more than they could chew.

In front of him, his headlamp flashed intermittently on Dane's backside as they ran. But something was odd. The light emanating from the boulder room had gone out.

"Stay alert, partner. The torches are out!" he yelled to Dane.

CHAPTER 65

FINISHED WITH GORGING on Pemba's body, the red-eyed albino yeti heard the shots above and recognized the loud crash of the spherical boulder. He decided he should escape to another area. But the only area he felt safe in was the section where he had grown up. The Others would sometimes visit his level to light the torches but usually they stayed away. When they came, he stayed in the tunnels that surrounded the center room, avoiding contact with them.

He carefully passed through each torchlit room, getting closer and closer to the room with the exit to the level he considered home. The sound of the Others' footsteps made him stop and listen. He sniffed the air.

He smelled the Others, and knew there were more than one. He scented the blood of a two-legged creature as well. A third type of scent he was not familiar with. He decided to go no further and ducked down a side tunnel until the Others had gone. He did not have to wait long. After they left, he went forward cautiously. He reached the square room with the set of stairs leading up. He sniffed the air and smelled the faint scent of the hairless creatures. He noted several distinct voices. He backed down off the stairs and began to retreat from them. Their loud explosions (gunshots) back at camp had frightened him.

He was about to exit the square room when he sensed a drop in temperature coming from one of the four exits. He walked over to that exit and noticed it was much cooler than the others. He began walking down that tunnel, and the air around him grew colder and colder. A bluish light shone at the end of the tunnel which, as he got closer, turned out to be an opening to the outside world. It was daytime, but the sun had not risen far, so the area remained in shadow.

The beast stuck his head out of the opening and saw the deep crevasse below. He looked up and saw the top of the crevasse about a hundred feet above him. Getting a foothold was no problem because of the beast's razor-sharp claws, which provided an excellent grip for his hands and feet.

Knowing that there was an opening to his home level up above, he decided to scale the wall to get to it. He began to climb the crevasse wall but then heard noises (voices talking and laughing) above. He sniffed the air and knew the noise came from the two-legged beings (men). He decided to retreat but then the other white yeti appeared from out of the cave on level one—his home. This was not the first time he had seen the other white yeti. But he had never had any interaction with him. The other yeti had always seemed to want to avoid him as well.

The other white yeti began to scale the wall in the direction of the Sherpas. He sniffed the air and looked back down at him. They looked directly at each other for the first time, frozen for a moment. Slowly, the red-eyed yeti climbed up toward the grey-eyed one, not feeling threatened, but wary nonetheless.

The grey-eyed yeti waited without making a threatening move as the red-eyed yeti came to a level even with him. They stared at each other, seeing a reflection of themselves. Both of them, having seen the Others, knew they were unique. Until then, they had both assumed that the other white yeti was part of the Others. But they were twins, and now that they were close enough to see each other's eyes, they felt a bond.

Laughter from above interrupted their examination of each other. They grunted. Together, they scaled the rest of the wall on their way to the top.

CHAPTER 66

DANE'S HEADLAMP SHONE forward as he ran back to the room with the boulder. He raised his Glock to fire, seeing movement in the darkness ahead.

"Dane! Help!"

Recognizing the voice of Sir Randolph, he lowered his weapon. Dane arrived and saw that Sir Randolph was trying to push back on the boulder. "What happened?"

"I re-entered the tunnel to keep watch, and something moved the boulder against the entrance so quickly I couldn't get back in time. Lily screamed ..." Sir Randolph looked crestfallen. "There wasn't anything I could do."

Dane knew the feeling and felt sorry for the older man.

Smokes arrived. "What happened?"

"Something moved the boulder and got Lily," Dane said.

"Can we move it?" Smokes asked.

"I've tried," Sir Randolph said. "Couldn't budge it."

Dane squatted down and looked at the bottom of the boulder. "Still, it's no longer in a hole. Let's try to shift it. With some help, we might be able to roll it."

Phurba and Armstrong arrived and the five of them gave the

boulder a push. It slowly began to move. Harry had his camera recording the action.

"Not too hard," Dane said. "We don't want it rolling back down into its resting place."

Harry and Lance watched as the five men let up on the boulder. It came to rest halfway between the entrance and the hole in the floor.

Dane walked around it and looked down at the floor. "This floor must be perfectly level. Another oddity."

Smokes picked up Lily's abandoned handgun. He noticed a lot of blood on the floor. "Lake."

Dane walked over to where Smokes was standing and followed his gaze down. The blood made him grimace and his stomach fluttered. He had failed to protect someone under his charge again, and even though she had come on the expedition of her own accord, it hurt him. He looked at Smokes.

Smokes looked back with sympathy. "Nothin' we coulda done, Lake."

Dane said nothing.

Armstrong looked at the perfect sphere of stone. It looked like a giant billiard ball. "You're right, Dane. It must be perfectly level here, for so much tonnage to be moved by only five men. The engineering for this alone would be impossible for a primitive race."

Dane left the scene of blood and crouched by the hole in the center of the room. "Duke!"

Dane pulled out his dog whistle and blew into it—no response from Duke. Everyone stared into the room below, and they saw it was torchlit like the one they were in. Despite the torches, they could see no signs of life or movement.

"Dammit. Someone's lightin' these torches, and I'm just guessin' it ain't Edgar or Johnny," Smokes said.

"Edgar or Johnny?" Sir Randolph asked.

"Yeah. We're pretty sure there are *two* white-haired yetis," Dane said. "One with red eyes and one with grey eyes."

"Oh, I get it," Sir Randolph said, understanding Smokes reference to the two albino rock and rollers.

"Harry just had a run-in with Johnny," Smokes said.

Sir Randolph turned to Harry. "You okay?"

"Yup. Just a scratch." He continued to shoot video.

Dane kept staring into the room below, thinking. He finally stood up. "I'm going down. Who's coming?"

"I'm all in," Smokes said. "We know Johnny's up here. So Edgar's down yonder. He's probably the one who had Pemba. And now …"

"Lily and Duke," Armstrong said. To Dane: "You know, she's dead. Your dog, too."

Dane looked at Armstrong. *I know he's right,* Dane thought, but he did not care. "I'm going anyway."

Sir Randolph put his hand on Dane's shoulder. "Dane, I know how you must feel, but you know Mr. Armstrong is correct. People haven't survived a yeti attack. Let's go back to base camp and stay there until I can call in some reinforcements with more weaponry. We don't know what might be down below, and we don't want to be reckless."

Dane knew that Sir Randolph and Armstrong were right. He silently recited to himself the question he had asked himself many times before when climbing the Himalaya. *What do you do when you can reach the summit, but not with enough time to make it back down safely? Answer: Don't be stupid. Turn around.*

He had seen enough mountaineers make foolish decisions and never return. But the correct decision here tore him up inside. *Is it any different? No. It isn't. But it doesn't make me feel any better. She was a good girl. Now she and Duke are dead.*

CHAPTER 67

NAWANG LAUGHED SO hard his sides ached.

"It's true," Nyima said. "Three times. Every night."

"He's Superman," Chamba said.

The others laughed, too.

"Better enjoy it while you can," Kundun said, the oldest Sherpa there. "When you're old like me you'll be lucky to get into the golden pagoda once a week. You newlyweds are all the same."

Everyone laughed, but their laughter was interrupted by the low frequency radio.

"This is Phurba. Nawang, come in."

"This is Nawang, Phurba."

"Nawang, we're coming up. We've figured out that there are *two* white yetis. We need to get some more help. The woman and the dog have been killed and one of the men was attacked. We're coming up. Stay alert. Prepare to go back to base camp."

"Okay. We'll be ready when …"

A loud roar came from down the slope near the crevasse. The Sherpas scrambled to their feet and turned as one to see the grey-eyed yeti charging at them. They frantically dug into their packs for their guns, but before most of them could arm themselves, another roar came from opposite direction from up the slope. Several of the men looked in that direction, only to see the red-eyed yeti coming down toward them at full speed.

"The beasts!" Nawang yelled into the radio. "Phurba, help!"

Nawang dropped the radio, pulled out his gun and began shooting wildly at the yeti coming up the slope.

"Nawang! What's that?" Phurba's voice yelled from the radio. But Nawang was not listening.

Edgar reached the Sherpa crew first and slashed the back of Nawang's neck, nicking his spinal cord, knocking him down and paralyzing him. Johnny arrived, shoving his clawed hand into Kundun's gut, then ripping his bowels open and spilling them onto the snow. Kundun fell to his knees as Nyima and Chamba took off running down the slope. Kundun's blood spray landed on the face of another Sherpa, blinding him momentarily, and Johnny ripped the blinded Sherpa's throat open.

Edgar swung at another Sherpa who'd drawn his gun. The swipe nearly severed the Sherpa's arm and he dropped his gun, his appendage now useless. Before he could pick it up with his good arm, Edgar ended his life by tearing his throat open, and nearly decapitating him. Blood drenched the snow and sprayed onto the other fallen Sherpas.

Nyima and Chamba ran as fast as they could in crampons, heading toward base camp. Looking over their shoulders, they could see both of the beasts gaining on them—Johnny in front and Edgar several paces behind. Frantic with fear, they had left their guns behind, unable to retrieve them in time before fleeing.

Nyima was slightly in front of Chamba, who Johnny caught first.

"Nyima! Help!"

The grey-eyed yeti made short work of Chamba, whose last living sight was the monster's jaws as they clamped down on his throat.

The time Johnny spent on Chamba gave Nyima the chance to make it to the edge of the crevasse. He watched grey eyed yeti finish off Chamba, then saw the red-eyed yeti stalk his way toward him.

He thought of his young wife—and the children they would never have. He thanked Lord Buddha for his life and prayed his next life would be longer.

The beast walked slowly toward him.

Nyima finished his prayer. The hairy monster stopped a few feet away. Nyima jumped and flew into the thin air, feeling briefly like Superman, then plummeted into the abyss. The yeti walked to the edge of the crevasse and peered down, but could not see anything. A moment later, he walked back toward his brother.

Kundun, semi-conscious and bleeding profusely from the mortal wound to his gut, looked around the landscape. Blood was everywhere—sprayed over the snow and all over the four other Sherpas.

He looked at his mangled innards laid out on the snow and thought it made him look like a samurai who had just committed ritual suicide. He wished he had a 'second' samurai present to take his head off quickly and end his misery. *All honorable samurais have a second to help them into the beyond.* He knew that he was going to die. Death was all around him.

But he noticed life.

One of the seemingly dead Sherpas—Nawang—opened an eye. Kundun had thought he was dead because his face and body were covered with blood and he was not moving. From their vantage point, Kundun and Nawang could see the two yetis coming back up the hill. Nawang shut his eye—no doubt praying he would be left alone.

The grey eyed yeti stepped over a dead Sherpa that was lying on top of another one and then reached down for Nawang. Nawang, paralyzed but still alive, looked over at Kundun with terror in his eyes as the grey-eyed monster picked him up and slung the helpless Sherpa over his shoulder.

Kundun reached slowly for the gun Nawang had dropped and picked it up, aiming carefully at his captor. But the clawed hand of the other yeti came down and sliced Kundun's forearm off at the elbow, his brachial artery spraying even more blood onto a dead Sherpa's face that poked out from beneath another's dead body. Kundun fell down onto his spilled innards, finally losing consciousness.

The whole attack had lasted no longer than four minutes.

The red eyed yeti picked up Kundun and slung him over one shoulder. The two beasts walked up the slope toward the crevasse, with the two Sherpas they carried slumped over and bleeding onto their white hair. Nawang could do nothing but watch his yeti's backside as it trekked up the slope.

Once the two beasts reached the crevasse, they scaled it easily, using their claws like natural crampons, and balancing the Sherpas on their shoulders like they were mere sacks of potatoes.

Unable to move, and knowing he would soon be eaten, Nawang began to wail uncontrollably.

CHAPTER 68

PHURBA RAN BACK down the exit tunnel as fast as he could, Dane and the rest right behind him. They reached the exit to the exterior world, and everyone put their crampons back on. Luckily, the climbing ropes were still anchored and usable.

Phurba and Dane were the first to begin the climb back up. Unable to summon the attention of any Sherpas when they called to those above, they climbed as quickly as they could. Phurba felt a sick feeling of doom as he made his way up. He kept shouting for Nawang, but heard nothing in response.

It took an eternity of twenty-five minutes to get back topside. Phurba crested the edge of the crevasse, and he became sick at seeing the mass of bodies lying fifty feet away in the snow. He looked away and concentrated on helping Dane up over the side.

Once up, Dane saw the carnage. "Go, Phurba." Dane stayed to help Smokes over the crevasse's edge. Phurba walked slowly toward the scene of the massacre. At ten feet away, the sirdar could go no further. He dropped to his knees. He felt numb. The whole area was doused with blood and three dead Sherpas lay in a heap. The sight overwhelmed him. Stifling the urge to weep, he bowed his head and prayed. *This is my fault, Lord Buddha. Help me understand.* He had seen men lose their lives before, but not like this.

Seconds passed. He felt Dane's hand on his shoulder.

He knew Dane would know how he felt. Death. Friends killed violently. No words needed to be spoken for the two men to understand one another.

After a pause, Dane stepped away, leaving Phurba with his thoughts.

Dane and Smokes helped the rest of their party up and over the edge of the crevasse. One by one they arrived, only to see what had happened to their small expedition.

Harry began to get his camera ready to record the slaughter. Sir Randolph put his hand over the camera lens. "Sit this one out, son," his voice breaking.

Lance saw the carnage and began to retch, remembering how he had been forced by Smokes to go underground and leave the 'safety' provided by these men, now dead.

Smokes had seen a lot of blood and guts during the Gulf War, but seeing it juxtaposed against the austere beauty of the Himalaya gave him a surreal feeling. He searched the scenery outside the main bloodbath area. Further down the slope, a body lay in the snow. He walked down to it.

"Chamba," he called out.

Phurba watched as Smokes crouched down and examined Chamba for any sign of life. Smokes looked back at Phurba and shook his head.

Smokes saw two sets of tracks that headed toward the crevasse—one large, one small. *Somebody jumped.* He walked back up to Dane and Phurba.

"We're missin' three," Smokes said.

"Nawang, Kundun and Nyima," Phurba said, still sounding

dazed.

Smokes continued. "I think one of 'em jumped into the crevasse. The two others must have been taken."

Phurba stared off into space. "Nawang and I grew up together. He was my best friend. Our wives are best friends." Tears were in his eyes. "How do I tell Opame what has happened to her husband?"

Dane had no answer for his friend. When you were leading a group of men, you were responsible for their safety. You were the one giving the orders, surveying the landscape for danger, and looking out for everyone else's well-being. *But this is different. Phurba had no way to predict this.*

Phurba wept. "This is my fault."

Dane looked at him. "No, Phurba. This is no one's fault."

A scream startled everyone and guns were drawn. The pile of dead bodies began to move. A bloodied Sherpa named Dawa pushed the two dead men off of himself and began to frantically crawl away. He stood up and waved his gun at everyone, screaming in his native language. Smokes quickly tackled him, wrestling him to the ground. He grabbed the gun, taking it from Dawa's hand before he shot anyone.

Phurba rushed to his side. "Dawa, it's okay. We are not delusions. We are real. You are okay. Somebody, get him some water."

Phurba looked Dawa over and determined that although the terrified man was covered in blood, he had received no wounds of any kind. Dane handed Phurba some water. Phurba made Dawa drink some even though he was still delirious and in shock. It took several minutes for him to calm down. When he became rational again, he explained what had happened.

"When the animals attacked, I tripped and fell. One of the beasts killed Nawang. The other beast killed Kundun and

Ketsun and then took off running after Nyima and Chamba. The one that killed Nawang killed Gulu, who fell on top of me and Ketsun. I saw the beast catch Chamba, but Nyima jumped to his death before the other one could reach him. When they walked back up, I closed my eyes and prayed to Lord Buddha that I might be spared. I heard the beasts pick up two bodies, and walk away. I kept my eyes shut and made no moves. When you arrived, I was afraid they had come back for me."

Smokes began to walk in a wide circle around the area, and soon spotted a blood trail and some tracks going up the slope. "Over there," he called, gesturing to the evidence he had spotted. He headed toward the footprints.

Everyone came over to look and saw the tracks. Smokes pointed out a blood trail that accompanied the tracks from the edge of the massacre up to the edge of the crevasse further up the slope. Dane, Smokes and Phurba followed the trail of blood, which led to the crevasse.

"On the radio, Nawang said, 'Beasts,'" Phurba said.

Smokes whistled. "Attacking together. Bad news."

"They must have another entrance hidden somewhere down in this crevasse," Dane said. He noticed that Phurba looked hesitant, and guessed that it must be because Phurba might not want to return to the caves. Dane could not blame him.

"Lake, I have been keeping something from you. There is another man down in the tunnels, searching for the yeti."

"What? Who?" Dane looked startled.

"A holy man, I think. He asked me to delay the expedition until his work was done. So I helped him." Phurba paused. "I am very sorry. That is why Nawang could not find the items for Duke to scent. I do not know if it matters now. The holy man is probably dead, too. Maybe if I had not slowed us down ..."

"But you didn't slow us down, Phurba. We had Pemba's

head and beanie." Dane appeared thoughtful for a moment. "This is not your fault. What was this holy man's mission?"

"I do not know. He never told me. He was very secretive. But I think he had a map of the tunnels below. I saw him looking at a diagram in a book which he tried to hide from me."

"What sort of a diagram?"

"I could not see it clearly, but it looked like a snowflake. I am sorry for causing you trouble. I will have to live with that."

Seeing Phurba's regret, Dane felt no anger, only sorrow for his friend.

"Phurba, don't beat yourself up. Get back to base camp and take Dawa and these men back to their families." *Lily had been right about Phurba,* Dane thought. But he would never have the chance to tell her so.

The three men looked back down the slope at where the dead Sherpas lay. Sir Randolph was walking toward them. Dane thought about all the senseless death he had seen in the past few weeks. Their whole expedition felt like a surreal nightmare from which he could not wake up. Rand, Shelly, Torleif, Lily, Duke, Nawang, and the other Sherpas, many of whom he had worked with in the past. *Dead. All of them, dead. They are all ghosts now. Things could not have gone any worse.*

Sir Randolph addressed the three of them. "Gentlemen, we need more help and more fire power. We need to ..."

Dane heard Sir Randolph talking, but the words held no meaning. He began to feel disconnected from everything like he was drifting away. The cold wind blew steadily and gusted in his face, but he could not feel it. A sound filled the air like the roar of a freight train and then ended abruptly, leaving only an eerie silence. He could not feel his hands or feet and had the passing thought that perhaps he had frostbite. But he knew innately that it was not so.

His conflicting emotions began to dissipate and vanish. He had no more thoughts about death.

Or life.

He did not feel bad anymore. He did not feel anything at all. His emotions were nonexistent, as if they had floated away into the ether.

He had no sorrow. No regret. No fear. Nothing ...

An immense feeling of serenity washed over him, and the calmness of simply *being* felt exhilarating. He had never experienced anything like it before. He felt bigger than himself. A voice whispered to him out of the silence.

"Wiijishimotaw jiibayag."

Dance with ghosts, he thought. *Grandfather?*

A memory appeared that was more vivid than any other he had ever had. He felt transported to his past and was once again reliving it, feeling every minute detail of the moment as it had truly been. His grandfather's words were crystal clear.

"The great warriors danced with ghosts and so became like them. And by becoming ghosts themselves, they became fearless and invincible. As a ghost, they could not be killed. And only as a ghost can a warrior feel the true power and serenity of the Great Spirit. Remember, Zaaga'igan Nishkiinzhigoon: to be a great warrior, you must be as a ghost."

"But how do I become a great warrior, Nimi?"

"You must banish all emotion and cast it aside as a sin."

"How do I do that?"

"It is not something you do. It is something you are. *And when the time comes, you will know."*

Dane finally understood.

Sir Randolph's voice came from out of the ether, like someone talking to him while he was still dreaming. He did not want to depart his dream state, but he needed to. His decision had been made. *I'm a ghost,* he thought, and felt at peace.

He could understand Sir Randolph again. "Let's get the hell off this mountain and bring in some hardcore hunters. Dane? Let me get some more help ... Dane?"

Dane came out of his reverie. He gazed at Sir Randolph, but Dane was not really seeing him at all. Dane sighed deeply.

"I know you're right, sir. We *should* go get some help. But I think, this one time, I'm just going to have to say ..." He paused and looked over at Smokes. "... fuck help."

Smokes smiled at his friend, nodded, and said, "Light up yer barbecues, ladies! Me and Lake are goin' to get some supper."

Dane and Smokes started back down the slope, heading to where the ropes hung over the side of the crevasse.

"Are they crazy? Where are they going?" Lance asked.

"Back to the tunnels, I guess," Armstrong said.

Sir Randolph was beside himself. "Dane, please. Don't do this."

Dane stopped and looked back at Sir Randolph. "Sir, you paid me to bring back Rand's remains. He's still down there. We'll do our business and then we'll bring him up directly."

Guilt radiated from the billionaire's expression. Sir Randolph appeared to have only now realized that they had left his son's remains below in their haste to resurface.

Sir Randolph hesitated not knowing what to do for the first time in his life. Smokes picked up their two shotguns and threw one to Dane. Harry began videotaping the two men as they prepared themselves to return to the tunnels.

Sir Randolph recovered. "Okay. But please, Dane, Smokes, don't go alone. Let me call in some help."

Dane shook his head. "Sir, no offense, but children need help. I'm a man."

"Zaaga'igan Nishkiinzhigoon," Phurba called out, using Dane's Ojibwe name.

Dane looked over at his friend.

"*Giga-waabamin naagaj,*" Phurba said in Ojibwe, giving Dane a thumbs-up sign.

Dane grinned and returned the thumbs-up. He had always liked the fact that the Ojibwe had no word for 'good-bye,' only the phrase, *giga-waabamin naagaj,* which meant 'see you later.'

"Giga-waabamin naagaj, Phurba."

Dane rappelled over the side, followed by Smokes, who paused a moment and looked at those assembled. "Anyone else comin'?"

"Is he kidding?" Lance asked, speaking to no one in particular.

Harry looked over at Armstrong, who frowned and shook his head quickly.

Smokes noticed Armstrong's refusal. "No? Okay. But remember, *yer* responsible for the side dishes."

With that, he disappeared from view.

CHAPTER 69

ONCE BACK INSIDE the second level of tunnels, the twin yetis made their way to an outer room where they could tear Nawang and Kundun to pieces. They sat there in silence, devouring their kills, occasionally stealing glances at each other. Neither one had ever eaten meat with another yeti before, nor could they recall having shared food with any other creature. They were twins, but they had been separated most of their lives and only had recently become aware of each other. Both were still wary.

Neither one of them had ever seen the Others eat food. They knew the Others were different somehow, and had been cautious on those rare occasions when they had come in contact with them. But they knew the Others would not harm them because they had never been challenged by even one of the Others. The Others were peaceful.

Both had been raised by surrogate mothers. All yetis had been raised this way for thousands of years—a yeti, once weaned, was raised by surrogates. When they were too small to hunt on their own, the surrogates would kill small animals and feed them. When the young yetis grew larger, they would kill larger animals on their own—yaks, bears, snow leopards, et cetera.

Until the arrival of the twin white yetis, humans had never been on the regular menu. It would happen once in a while, but not often. However, something about these two yetis was different. They not only killed humans, they *preferred* killing humans. And the more humans they killed, the more humans they wanted to kill.

Because of the unusual circumstances, in particular the unprecedented invasion of the tunnel system by armed humans, their survival instincts had taken over. The twins, thrown together in a battle for survival, were now killing not only to acquire food, but to vanquish an enemy.

The attack on Harry and then on the Sherpas was the first time they had attacked anything for any reason besides a need for sustenance. During the attack on the Sherpas, both had felt a sense of protecting the other, as if they were truly *one*. They could not understand their relationship, having only a base thought process and little understanding of the wider world. Nevertheless, they knew there was a bond between them.

They sat in a circular outer room in the dark and ate the fresh Sherpa flesh, oblivious to the fact that they were still being pursued, not only by Dzangbu, but by Dane and Smokes as well. Whichever one found them would determine their fate.

CHAPTER 70

DANE AND SMOKES made their way, sans crampons, down the entrance tunnel of the top level. Both were aware that an attack could come at any moment. They had no idea of whether there were more than two yetis in the tunnels, and the top floor was a labyrinth of passageways. As a result, they were careful to check around every corner.

They reached the first cavern room, the room that held Rand's remains. Dane got an idea. "There are two entrances to that boulder room. Let's see if we can't find the other route in."

"Okay, pardner."

"We know the tunnel on the left leads there. The tunnel to the right leads away. It may eventually lead there, too, but I'm betting we can get there quicker by taking the tunnel straight ahead. Let's do a little exploring."

"Roger that."

Dane led the way down the alternate tunnel, which appeared to be a continuance of the main entrance tunnel, being interrupted only by the platform in the cavern room. They crept down the tunnel and soon noticed that there were not any more offshoot tunnels. Before long, they could see dim light at the other end.

"Light at the end of the tunnel. How cliché," Smokes said, lighting a Camel.

Dane grinned and was glad Smokes was with him. In Ojibwe, there was a word for 'braver than brave' or 'beyond fearless.' *Aakode'ewin*. It literally meant 'the state of having a fearless heart' and applied to any person who would do the right thing even though the consequences for doing so might be dire or unpleasant.

He complimented Smokes about it once. But Smokes shrugged it off with his usual flippancy, and said, "Yer mistaken, Injun. I ain't no 'Oca-do-in' or whatever it is. The truth is, I just don't give a shit, and ya know I ain't got nothin' better to do anyway." Then he had added, "'Sides, who's gonna save yer crazy ass if ya get in trouble?"

They made their way to the end of the tunnel and slowly entered the lighted amphitheater room. The sight enthralled them. They could not take their eyes off the forty-foot statue in the center.

"Look at the precision and detail of that statue. That wasn't sculpted by primitives," Dane said. His voice was low, almost a whisper. "In fact, I don't think it was sculpted at all. There is more happening here than we can see. This is almost otherworldly stuff."

Dane had had this feeling since Armstrong had tried and failed to get a sample of the tunnel wall. He looked around the room, noting the locations of the other five exits. "It's like a miniature Coliseum."

Smokes's attention was still riveted on the statue, which depicted a voluptuous naked woman embracing a horned yeti-like creature. "Is it just me, or does that look *unnatural?*"

Dane laughed. "It's not just you. Let's take the first exit to the left. I bet it leads to where we want to go."

This place cries out to be explored and investigated, but we need to stay on target, Dane thought. He took a couple steps to his left, and something that had been obscured from view by the statue caught his eye.

Blonde hair.

Dane forced himself to walk over to it, despite his trepidation. Smokes watched him go and kept a lookout. Dane stared down at his fiancée's mutilated body. It was nearly unrecognizable, save for the remnants of Shelly's clothing and hair. Dane stared at the remains for a few moments. He had understood that finding Shelly's remains was a possibility, and had prepared himself for the effect it might have on him. Now the moment had arrived, but the overwhelming emotion he had expected to experience was missing.

The experience of serenity after the Sherpa massacre had changed him. He felt different. *How long will it last?* he wondered. By spending so many years with the Sherpas, who were Tibetan Buddhists, he had learned that karma was karma. It was not a penalty as many people thought. Harsh as it sounded, karma was right and just—a balancing of things, without emotion.

Memories surfaced.

Death is not the end, his grandfather had told him. Although some of the Ojibwe had converted to Christianity, Dane's grandfather Mingo had not. Mingo's beliefs stemmed from a car accident.

A drunk driver had run a red light, killing Dane's father and older brother when Dane was seventeen, and putting Mingo in the intensive care unit at the nearest hospital. Mingo was in a coma for a week. When he came back to consciousness, Dane was the first person to speak to him. Dane broke the news about the deaths to Mingo, struggling to suppress his grief.

"Don't be sad, Zaaga'igan Nishkiinzhigoon. During the coma I saw many things. I saw your thoughts. I saw loved ones. Your father and brother, my mother and father, even my old dog. They glowed with light and spoke to me without words. I was drawn to their light. The attraction was one of overwhelming beauty and love. Impossible to resist. I wanted to stay with them, but they told me I could go back if I wanted to. So I've come back to tell you that death is not the end."

His grandfather's words had not lessened the pain of losing his father and brother, but they had made Dane think differently. Any fear about death or dying had disappeared for him personally and faced with death, Dane could accept it. He suspected he would not have been able to, without the serene experience he had had during his 'dance with ghosts.'

Smokes walked up behind Dane. Though he was one of Dane's oldest friends, he had no words. "We'll come back for her, when we're done," was all he could muster.

Dane nodded. "Yeah. When we're done." *If we get done,* he thought. A feeling of revenge started to fester inside of him. But the emotion of hate seemed far away and foreign to him after his epiphany earlier. The idea struck him that he did not really know what he would do when he located the two albino yetis.

A sound began—low and deep.

It started faintly at first, but then, as it went on, it became louder. It emanated from the exit they had been about to enter.

Dane looked over at Smokes. "That sound familiar to you?"

Smokes stamped his non-filter into nothingness. "Yeah. It sounds a bit like the ol' didgeridoo my Uncle Mogo used to play down under in the outback."

"It sounds like Buddhist overtone chanting to me."

"Maybe it's Phurba's holy man?"

"More than one, I'd say."

CHAPTER 71

SIR RANDOLPH HAD gotten on his satellite phone as soon as Dane and Smokes had left. He called in the entire fleet of five rescue helicopters to come pick them up, along with the dead Sherpas' bodies. He wanted to get off Kangchenjunga and away from the bloodbath as soon as possible. It was just past noon, and much had happened since they had risen that morning.

"I can't wait to get off this mountain," Lance said. He sat with Armstrong and Harry, well away from the dead Sherpas. Sir Randolph had just finished his business with the satellite phone, and was standing near the others. Not far away, Phurba was looking up at Kangchenjunga's peaks, lost in his own thoughts.

Sir Randolph hoped the helicopters would not take too long. They had had a lot of early snow, and Phurba had said he was concerned about the stability of the landscape now that it was getting later in the day, even though they were not in a usual avalanche area.

While they waited, the men applied more sunscreen and sat around in their white-colored thermals, which kept them from getting fried in the midday sun. Sir Randolph almost felt breathless, with the sun beating down and reflecting off the snow, and light all around them. When they had begun this morning, the temperature was below freezing, but now the weather felt like summer by comparison.

A few steps away from Sir Randolph, Harry fiddled with his camera. He kept reviewing his shot of the yeti. After a while, Harry looked over at Armstrong. "We're going to be rich. This is Pulitzer material."

Armstrong laughed.

"Let me see what you've got," Sir Randolph said. He came over to take a closer look.

He crouched down. Harry played back his yeti encounter. Sir Randolph watched. Harry froze on a frame with the close-up of the beast's face, the image showing the beast's two grey eyes.

"Wow. Clear video. Nice job, fellas," Sir Randolph said, thinking a moment. *These people have been through a lot. They deserve to know.*

"Here is something to add to your story, Mr. Armstrong. I had some DNA tests run on the blood from a knife Dane used to wound the beast. A genetic specialist told my man that the DNA tested out as being very close to human. She said there were some *variations,* but she will be continuing to study the samples to see if she can find out anything else."

Armstrong looked at Harry. "Your Pulitzer joke may not be a joke after all. Human DNA? Do you know what that means?"

"It means we may have found our ancestors, gentlemen—alive," Sir Randolph said. "That's why we need to go back down there and capture a yeti."

Armstrong nodded. "Definitely."

"You guys go ahead. I'm going home," Lance said.

Sir Randolph laughed. "That's okay, Lance. Now that we know where they are, I can send down some actual big game hunters—a whole crew of them, in fact. And they can bring a whole yeti back for us. Maybe even a live one."

"I want to be there for that," Armstrong said.

"Me, too," Harry said.

Lance shook his head. "I'll take a hard pass on that one. Those other guys should never have gone back down there."

Phurba walked up. "No. They shouldn't have. But they are brave and feel they are doing what is right. Sometimes one must do what is right, regardless of the circumstances. It is better to do right and die once, than to avoid doing right and die every day while still living."

CHAPTER 72

DANE AND SMOKES followed the sound of the chanting, which led them down the tunnel out of the amphitheater room. Soon they came to a second, square-shaped room that had three more exits—one for each wall—to their left, their right, and straight ahead. The deep overtone chanting was getting clearer, and it came from the exit on the left.

They entered the left tunnel and soon came to the circular boulder room. The spherical rock was right where they had left it. They wasted no time in heading toward it. The sound came from the chamber below.

"Age before beauty," Smokes said, heading down the stairs first.

They trod lightly down the stairs and into the lighted square-shaped room below, alert to any movement, their shotguns ready, their Glocks holstered. Reaching the bottom of the stairs, they saw that the room was empty. They noticed there were four exits—one in each wall—but the sound, which was much louder now, came from the tunnel that led toward the center of the complex.

They crept down the tunnel, and the chanting became

louder and louder—almost hypnotic. They noticed some light about fifty yards down. When they were nearly at the opening, they saw two huge statues in the center of the room—the immense sculptures depicted two yetis standing back to back. What they saw next captivated them. Looking out from the tunnel, they could see much of the room while still standing in the opening. The seats were filled with yetis—lots of yetis.

"This place is crawlin' with these SOBs," Smokes whispered. He glanced back at his friend. "Maybe Randolph was right about gettin' more help. We are drastically short of ammo."

"Hindsight's twenty-twenty." Dane smiled and winked. "Listen. Something's wrong with this picture. They're doing a Buddhist chant. I don't think these are violent yetis."

Smokes looked skeptical. "So now yer a yeti expert?"

"When's the last time *you* heard a yeti chanting?" Dane asked. He started to creep toward the room.

Smokes blocked his path. "I don't give a shit, Lake. But don't be foolish. They could be singin' 'Dixie' and I'd still be thinkin' twice about interruptin' 'em."

Dane saw something over his friend's shoulder and pointed. "Look!"

Smokes turned and followed Dane's index finger toward the base of the statue. Sticking out from behind it were a dog's legs and a white tail. "Shit. It's Duke. Let's hope them yetis ain't chantin' grace." He turned back to Dane. "Well, blow yer horn, Gabriel."

Dane pulled out his dog whistle and blew into it. Immediately, the overtone chanting stopped. Smokes snatched the whistle away from Dane's lips—too late.

"Oops. I think we just rang the doorbell."

Duke started barking and ran over to them. Dane was so happy to see his dog alive, he gave him a big hug and let him lick his face. "Hi, boy."

"I hate to break up this tearful reunion, but we got other problems."

The yetis had all stood up from their seats and were looking toward the tunnel where the men were hiding.

But far from acting fearful, Dane was excited. "They didn't eat Duke. Maybe Lily's alive." Without warning, he ran past Smokes. "Keep me covered."

Smokes shook his head. "Crazy Injun."

Smokes followed Dane, who backed into the huge room, then circled the room, all the while staring down the yetis that were looking back at him. He could see that the room was filled with beasts of different colors. While the two men advanced, the yetis never moved, but stood there, silently observing.

Dane saw Lily lying supine at the base of the statues. He ran over and kneeled down to examine her. She was unconscious, and she appeared to have had a bloody nose which had stopped. More blood was on the floor next to her head. He reached out to shake her a little.

She began to come to consciousness. A few seconds later, her eyes opened to see Dane. She smiled then grimaced. She reached up to touch the back of her head and her hand came away with a trace of dried blood. "Ouch. I fell backward over Duke and must've hit my head."

"And your nose," Dane said. He pulled out a cloth and a water bottle. Wetting the cloth, he cleaned under her nose.

"I saw a yeti come out of the floor."

"Only one?" Dane asked.

"Yeah …" Lily looked past him and swallowed hard. "Oh, no …"

"Let me have a look at the back of your head."

Dane checked her head wound and cleaned it the best that

he could while making sure it didn't open back up.

Keeping his eyes on as many yetis as he could, Smokes backed up to Dane and Lily's position. "You two ready to go? Or would ya like to stay *as* dinner?"

"It's tempting," Dane said. Then, to Lily: "What do you think?"

Lily scrunched her nose. "We should go."

Dane helped her to her feet. The overtone chanting began again, slowly. All but one yeti from each section sat back down. The six yetis still standing walked to an adjacent exit and sat down facing toward the statues, thus blocking their escape.

"Looks like they're gonna insist we stay for at least a drink. Hospitable of 'em. In that case—" Smokes pulled out a Camel and lit up, "—think they'll mind the secondhand smoke?"

"Who's that?" Lily asked.

Dane and Smokes followed her gaze. Out of one of the tunnels came the porter with the wide streak of white hair who Dane had seen at base camp when he had first arrived with Shelly. *The friend of Phurba's brother-in-law is the holy man he talked about.*

The Sacrifist calmly walked past the yeti blocking that tunnel exit and came up to them.

"My name is Dzangbu." He spoke perfect English. "I recognize you. You are Dane Nielsen. Who are your friends?"

"Lily McCrowley," Lily said.

"Smokes Mitchell," Smokes said.

"You may put your guns down. You are in no danger here."

Smokes snorted. "No danger? Who you kiddin'? We seen what they can do."

"These are not the evil Mih Teh. They are Sacrifists. Each and every one of them is a Rinpoche."

"Rinpoche?" Lily asked.

Dzangbu nodded his head. "Yes."

"What's that mean?" Smokes asked.

"The term is usually applied to a notable spiritual teacher who has been reincarnated. Rinpoche literally means 'precious one,'" Lily said.

"Yetis are precious, all right. 'Bout as precious as a got-damn scorpion!"

Dzangbu responded tranquilly. "Actually, yeti is an ancient alteration of the original word for them, which was spelled j-e-j and pronounced *yā-yee*. It is the Kusunda word for 'father.'"

"I saw you in base camp. Phurba said you were his brother-in-law's friend. Are you the monk Phurba spoke of?" Dane asked.

"I'm a type of yogi, not a monk. Please. Sit down and let us talk."

Dzangbu sat down and waited. A few seconds later, so did Dane and Lily.

Smokes remained standing. "I'll stand. Thank you. An' I'll listen with one ear. My eyes an' the other ear will be busy watchin' the yetis ... uh, 'scuse me, the father-slash-rinpoaches. Just in case they get hungry. We don't wanna get et."

Dzangbu smiled benignly. "They are not going to eat you. There is no need to be concerned. They do not eat like you do. These yetis are only here to protect you."

"Yeah, I bet. We know they eat. We seen their leftovers."

Dzangbu spoke in a calming voice. "You saw how a Mih Teh eats. As I have told you, these yetis are also Sacrifists. They are different. In fact, they are eating now."

"What?" Dane asked.

"They're Breatharians?" Lily asked.

Dzangbu nodded. "That is correct."

Smokes looked confused. "What's a ... Brevarian? Ain't that

German? If so, it explains a lot."

"*Breath*-arian," Lily said. "Breatharians believe they can survive without food or water, and obtain everything they need from the air or from sunlight." To Dzangbu: "Most controlled tests with humans have proven Breatharianism is impossible."

"That is true—for a typical *Homo sapiens*. It should be apparent from looking at them, that these are not normal *Homo sapiens*."

Smokes blew out a puff of smoke. "Shoot. They ain't *sapiens* at all."

"But they are related to *Homo sapiens*. Their physiology is different. At some point in their past, each Mih Teh you see here combined with a Sacrifist to be the yeti they are today. These yetis are able to survive without food, and need only live on air and water. Their meditation and chanting creates a vibration of sorts which changes the physiology of the Mih Teh's body. Each breath turns into life-giving energy for their body."

"What is the difference between the term Mih Teh and yeti?" Lily asked.

"Yeti is the term we use after the Sacrifist has combined with a Mih Teh's body."

"Why is there more oxygen in here than outside?" Smokes asked.

Dzangbu paused then said, "I cannot tell you, for I do not know. Maybe the Lord Buddha has willed it so."

"Of what substance are these walls made?" Dane asked.

"Again. I have no answer."

Dane got the idea that Dzangbu might be holding back. "Okay. What is a Sacrifist then?"

"I am a Sacrifist."

"How does a Sacrifist combine with a Mih Teh?" Dane

asked.

Smokes grunted. "I hope it ain't like the statues we saw upstairs."

Lily looked puzzled. Dane whispered, "I'll explain later."

Dzangbu took a deep breath and pondered a moment.

"I will explain to you how I achieve my purpose. But what I am about to tell you must be kept secret. I must have your word on this by whatever you consider holy."

Dane answered first. "I'm not sure we can give you our word. Many people are dead. Someone must answer for their deaths."

"I understand. You have lost people you loved. But these creatures here—" Dzangbu gestured at the assembled yetis "—did not kill them. You know this. They have no claws."

It was then Dane and Smokes noticed that the yetis sitting there had no long claws like those of the albino Mih Tehs they had seen.

"Would you kill an innocent human being?" Dzangbu asked.

"Of course not," Dane said.

"What about the killings of about twenty years ago?" Lily asked. Dane realized she must be thinking of her late father.

"Occasionally, a beast has killed humans, but it has never been like this. What is happening now used to happen in ancient times."

"You are talking about the two albino Mih Tehs?" Dane asked.

"*Two* albinos?" Lily asked.

"Yes," Dzangbu said. "Twins. They represent the fulfillment of the Kusunda prophecy of the Qolom Qasigi Duktsi. Literally, 'white bad son.'"

Smokes guffawed and said, "Yeah. Same ol', same ol'. White people causin' problems."

"Something happened that had never happened before," Dzangbu said.

Dane took a guess. "Twins."

"Correct. This presented all the Sacrifists with a problem. We cannot break our sacred vow and kill one of the Mih Tehs. Each Sacrifist here *gave up* their life as a man or woman in order to subdue a Mih Teh. As I am here to do."

"You're here to give your life?" Lily asked, incredulous.

"Yes."

"Why? For what reason?" she asked.

"Do I have your word first?"

"Yes," Lily said. "I swear not to reveal what you say to anyone."

Lily looked at Dane, who said, "I swear it, also."

The three of them looked at Smokes.

"Okay. Me, too. But this better be *good*," he said.

Dzangbu nodded and began. "A Sacrifist is trained only by the High Lama of Diki Chhyoling Gompa in Olangchun Gola. The Sacrifist is located by a search and confirmed via an ancient technique of identification conducted by a legation of three monks that have been selected by the High Lama. He tells the legation where to go and how to identify the Sacrifist. The boy or girl thus identified as the true reincarnation of a Sacrifist is brought to the gompa at the age of five. All their secret training is supervised only by the High Lama of the gompa, and only the High Lama and his successor have access to the training texts. The training is actually only a re-familiarization of what they have learned long ago, perhaps from the Lord Buddha himself, or perhaps from even earlier. When a Mih Teh reaches adulthood, the Sacrifist is sent out to overcome them."

"How is that done?" Lily asked.

"Quite simply, it is achieved by getting themselves killed by the Mih Teh and then refusing to enter the *bardo*."

Smokes did a double-take. "Come again? I've only been listenin' with the one ear."

"The Sacrifist tracks the Mih Teh down, confronts it, and allows the beast to kill him or her."

Something did not add up. Dane looked at the others. They had blank looks on their faces, just as he did. None of them understood. They all had the same question: *If you're dead, then how do you overpower it?*

"Pardon us for being stupid. But I think we're missing something. You allow it to kill you, and then you refuse to enter the ... bardo? What's the bardo?" Dane asked.

Lily interjected. "It's the intermediate step between death and rebirth."

"Correct," Dzangbu said. "Yetis are not ordinary animals. They are Homo sapiens. Were they an ordinary animal, like, say ..." Dzangbu turned and looked at Duke, "a dog, we would not have to sacrifice our body. We would simply control the Mih Teh to keep him or her from killing animals, or harming anyone else for that matter. It is necessary for us to engage the Mih Teh. Their natural instinct is to kill and eat meat. But by killing a Sacrifist, the spirit guiding the Mih Teh is sufficiently weakened by the act of killing that it can be influenced. This weakened spiritual state of the Mih Teh allows us to control it, as we have been trained to *spiritually merge* with it. However, this can only be done within the first minute after our own body's death."

"That's a small window. What happens if it isn't done within that time?" Dane asked.

"The Sacrifist would become overwhelmed by the bardo, the in-between state, and would be forced to be reborn into human flesh again. This is problematic. Another reason we allow the Mih Teh to kill us is because a Mih Teh's body lives for over two thousand years. So even if we could control one without sacrificing our body, our human body would die long before the Mih Teh body, and we would return to the bardo, thus allowing the Mih Teh to revert to its beastly ways."

"How come when the yeti body dies, the Sacrifist inhabiting it isn't just reborn into a baby Mih Teh body?" Lily asked.

"Good question. For various reasons that I am not willing to divulge to you, a Sacrifist can only be reborn into a human body. Thus, the necessity of our act of sacrifice that enables us to complete our purpose," Dzangbu said.

Smokes, who had been looking increasingly skeptical, could not help himself. He started laughing. "I'm as spiritual as the next feller, but all this kinda sounds like a crock o' bullshit."

Dane found himself in agreement with Smokes. "You're asking us to take a lot on faith, Dzangbu. Do you have some way to prove what you are saying, besides giving us your word?"

Dane glanced at Lily, but she did not appear to question Dzangbu's story. *Maybe she can see that he's serious and being truthful,* Dane thought. Unfortunately, Lily had said that her intuition could be fooled perhaps one time in five, and Dane needed to be certain.

"Look around you." Dzangbu held up his hands and gestured, pointing out the obvious: they were surrounded by yetis, but none were attacking them.

Dane nodded. "Okay. I'm not going to say I'm not astonished that we aren't yeti, or rather, Mih Teh lunch right now, because, frankly, I *am* astonished. But how about some proof that it's because of … someone like yourself."

Smokes nodded his head. "Right. What he said." The two of them looked askance at Dzangbu, waiting for him to answer.

Dzangbu contemplated their request a moment then looked at Duke.

"Is that *your* dog?" he asked Dane.

"Yes," Dane said.

"Does he do what you tell him to do?"

"Yes. He's a highly trained search and rescue dog."

"If you tell him to stay, will he stay?"

"You bet."

"Then place him thirty feet from you, and ask him to stay."

Dane stood up and walked Duke to a spot thirty feet away. He gave Duke the hand signal for 'stay' and reinforced it with a verbal command. "Stay, Duke." Duke lay down and waited for Dane's next command. Dane walked back and stood next to where Lily sat with Dzangbu.

"Are you sure he will stay there?" Dzangbu asked again.

Dane had trained Duke for a long time. He knew Duke would not disobey his command. "I'd stake my life on it."

"Very well. Please watch your dog." Dzangbu closed his eyes and assumed a meditation posture.

Dane kept an eye on Duke, confident that his dog would not move even an inch.

Next to him, he noticed Lily watching intently. She appeared almost expectant, as though she thought she knew what was going to happen.

On Dane's other side, Smokes paid some attention to it, but the majority of his attention was still on the chanting yetis. But by the way Smokes had relaxed his posture, Dane realized that his friend had come to the same conclusion: these yetis, strange as they were, posed no immediate threat.

After a few seconds, Duke stood up on all fours.

"Look at that," Lily said, amazed.

"Stay, Duke," Dane said, sternly.

Duke took two steps forward.

"Oh, my god," Lily said.

Smokes turned to look as well. "Uh-oh. Seems to be a crack in ol' Duke's resolve, as it were."

Dane could not believe it. "Duke, stay!"

Duke began walking slowly toward Dane, without stopping. "Stay, Duke. Stay!"

"Maybe you should use some other word for stay," Smokes offered. "Duke, *wait*."

Dane rolled his eyes. "Thanks for the help."

"No problemo," Smokes said, and started laughing.

Duke was about five feet from Dane, who had given up on his dog. "Du-uke ... *stay*."

Duke reached Dane. Then, as if to ensure Dane got Dzangbu's point, Duke lifted his leg and urinated on Dane's leg.

"Hey! *Animoosh-zhish!*" Dane said, chastising Duke in Ojibwe. He turned to Dzangbu. "Okay, okay. I get it. I get the point."

Smokes and Lily were laughing. Dzangbu opened his eyes. Duke let out a little yelp, then went and sat down next to Lily. He had a guilty look on his face.

Dane looked down at his leg and stomped it on the floor to shake off Duke's urine.

He frowned at his dog. "Thanks ... man's best friend."

Duke lay down and whined

Smokes chuckled again. "Well, I guess now I've seen everything. You asked for it, Lake. An' yer lucky. My guess is that if he wanted to ol' Zangboo coulda made Duke go number two on ya."

CHAPTER 73

THE LEAD COPTER radioed Sir Randolph to alert him that they would be arriving, one after the other in ten minute intervals, in only a couple of minutes. Sir Randolph decided who would be traveling with whom.

"I want to be on the first copter," Lance said.

"The first copter will be taking Dawa back to Suketar Airport with one of his fallen comrades," Sir Randolph said harshly. "Then, Phurba, you can take another body with you in the second one."

Phurba nodded.

"Can I be next?" Lance asked.

"Do you want to go home, or don't you?" Sir Randolph asked.

"Yes. Home, please."

"Then you will wait your turn and come with me."

"All right," Lance said with resignation.

"Next we'll load the other two bodies to take to Suketar."

"Then Armstrong and Harry can go. Do you guys want to be taken to base camp, or to Kathmandu and then home?"

Armstrong and Harry considered it a moment. At last,

Armstrong said, "Home. We got enough footage. We'll need to get your testimony on camera, of course. But we can do that later."

"Fine. Lance and I will be the last ones out."

Lance looked disappointed.

The men heard the helicopters in the distance. Sir Randolph and Phurba watched them coming. As the first copter approached, they watched the slope for any signs of an avalanche. Fortunately, the rescue helicopter landed without incident.

They got Dawa and a dead Sherpa body aboard the first rescue copter, and it promptly took off. Phurba watched as his copter began its descent. He and the others prepared to load another fallen comrade. Each person anxiously waited for their chance to leave Kangchenjunga.

CHAPTER 74

"SO YOU MEAN to tell me that all of these yetis are being inhabited and controlled by someone like you—a Sacrifist?" Dane asked.

"Precisely," Dzangbu said.

Smokes scratched his head. "Hmmm. Kinda like the Exorcist—but in reverse."

Dzangbu furrowed his brow.

Dane smiled at Smokes. Then he said, addressing Dzangbu, "Don't mind him."

"You said there are a hundred and eight Sacrifists. Besides you, where are the other two?" Lily asked.

"One is a yeti who is currently nursing a newborn Mih Teh elsewhere in this complex. The other is being trained at the gompa and will be sent to subdue this newborn Mih Teh when his Sacrifist training is finished and the newborn Mih Teh has reached adulthood, which will happen in about twenty years," Dzangbu said.

"So when the next Mih Teh reaches adulthood, the Sacrifist training now will be sent to inhabit and control it?" Dane asked.

"Correct," Dzangbu said.

"By gettin' kilt?" Smokes asked doubtfully.

"Yes."

"How long has this been going on?" Lily asked.

"For a long time," Dzangbu said, not wanting to reveal too much. "The Lord Buddha was a *jej*—and the greatest of those who was a Sacrifist. Instead of continuing to be a Sacrifist, he chose a path of helping ordinary people attain enlightenment."

"So there are more than a hundred and eight Sacrifists?" Dane asked.

"Yes and no. There are a hundred and eight jej, and a hundred and eight *maj*. Fifty-four of each make up the Sacrifists."

"If jej is father, what is maj?" Lily asked.

"Mother."

"Where are the other hundred and eight?" Dane asked.

"This is not known, although the jej who was Gautama Buddha may return soon in the form of Jampa," Dzangbu offered.

"Who is that?" Dane asked.

Lily explained to Dane and Smokes. "Gautama Buddha prophesied his own return as Jampa, which is Tibetan for 'loving kindness.' Upon his return, he promised to teach again the pure *Dharma*—the original teachings of the Buddha—to help people achieve complete enlightenment. The prophecy says he will return at a time when the Dharma has been forgotten by most of the Buddhists on Earth. Some believe this time has already come, or that it may be imminent."

Silence reigned for a moment, as Dane and the others thought about what Dzangbu had said. Finally, Smokes broke the silence. "Well, why the hell not. Heck, before last month, who would have thought we'd see a yeti or a mit-tuh or whatever you call it. Science fiction ain't real ... *till it is*."

"Looks like you have one too many Mih Tehs," Lily said.

"Exactly. And we are honor bound not to kill a Mih Teh. The Sacrifist in training back at the gompa will not be ready for many years. And these twins have presented to us another problem. They *enjoy* killing and eating humans, and this has somehow changed them. Their savageness has spiraled out of control. I had a confrontation with one of them in the tunnels, but he refused to kill me."

"Refused? As in, *decided not* to kill you?" Lily asked.

"Yes."

"If they're thinking analytically, I see your problem," she said. "It means you can't fulfill your purpose."

"Correct again. This means, they will keep hunting and killing. Even if climbing on Kangchenjunga becomes forbidden, the twins have now tasted human flesh. They will seek it out, and sooner or later, both will be killed. I cannot allow that to happen. I must save at least one."

"How do you intend to do that if they won't kill you?" Dane asked.

"I will need your help," Dzangbu said.

This statement caught them all off guard.

"I knew there'd be a catch to keepin' my mouth shut," Smokes said.

"What do you have in mind?" Dane asked Dzangbu.

Dzangbu pulled out a book from his knapsack. He flipped through it, and Lily leaned forward and peered at the symbols on the pages. To Dane, they resembled the symbols they had seen carved into the tunnel walls and cavern rooms.

"Those symbols," Lily said. "Do you know their meaning?"

"I'm sorry," Dzangbu said. "I wish I did. I believe that once I understood their meaning, but that was long ago. The symbols may be the original written language of the jej and maj, but their significance has been lost in antiquity. This book has been in existence for a long time. However, no one knew it had anything to do with Sacrifist training until I returned to the gompa after my first unsuccessful attempt at subduing the beast."

Dzangbu turned to a page featuring a hexagonal diagram that resembled a snowflake. They all looked it over. "This is a diagram of the first level—just above where we are now. Here is where you entered."

Dzangbu pointed at the lower left arm of the 'snowflake.' Dane saw that it was the only arm that did not have a small circle at one end.

Smokes pointed at the first square room the entrance tunnel led to. "There's where we met ol' grey eyes."

Dzangbu pointed to a circular room just above and slightly left of the square room Smokes had indicated. The circular room had a black dot in the center. "This is the exit room leading down to level two."

He turned a couple of pages. Now they saw a similar snowflake diagram, except this hexagon had been shifted thirty degrees. He pointed to a small circle in the square room that was at the junction of the left-hand side of the hexagon and the left horizontal tunnel. "This is the entrance room of level two." Directly above the square was a circular room with a black dot in the center. "This is the exit room leading down to level three."

He then pointed to the large circle in the center of level two's hexagon. It represented the room to which all six arms (tunnels) of the snowflake led. "This is the room where we are right now. We are here," he said, pointing to a spot near the middle, "and the albino twins are on level three, below us."

He turned the page to a third snowflake diagram. Level three was almost a carbon copy of level one. The only difference was that it had two concentric circles in the hexagon instead of only one.

"That looks like level one," Dane said.

"Yes. They are similar. We don't know where the twins are on this level, but we have an idea that they may be in this area." Dzangbu indicated the upper left arm of the diagram and the accompanying offshoot tunnels and rooms.

"How many floors are there in this hotel?" Smokes asked.

"Six."

"Who built them? And how?" Lily asked.

"No one knows. Perhaps this book explains it. Perhaps not."

"What is to stop the twins from escaping to a lower or a higher level?" Dane asked.

"The other Sacrifists will be blocking their way."

"But if they're thinking analytically, then how are you going to get one to kill you?"

"We need something to make them bloodthirsty. Essentially, something to help them lose their wits."

"What does that?" Lily asked.

Dane knew. He had seen evidence of it. "Blood lust. Killing humans. Cannibalism, and their participation in it, has caused them to become more and more insane and bloodthirsty. Like we saw at the Sherpa massacre."

"Yes. I am afraid so," Dzangbu said.

"Sherpa massacre. What happened?" Lily asked.

"The twins killed all but one Sherpa," Smokes said.

Lily put her hand to her mouth. "Oh, no."

Dane turned to her. "We didn't expect to find you alive down here. We came looking for the two albinos in order to kill them."

"Those poor souls." Still thinking of the doomed Sherpas, Lily made the sign of the cross and prayed to Lord Buddha.

Dane explained to her what they had found after the massacre, and briefed her on why Sir Randolph had made the decision to leave. Dzangbu silently waited for them to finish.

"You mean no one waits for us above?" Lily asked, after Dane had covered the main points.

"Right," Dane said.

They were all silent for a moment.

Dane was about to speak when Smokes beat him to it. "Wait a minute. ... You want us to be *bait*."

Lily looked at the Sacrifist, horrified.

"Yes and no. There will be no danger to you. You will be protected by the other Sacrifist-yetis."

"But these other yetis won't kill their brothers, and I'm betting the twins have figured that out too," Dane said.

Dzangbu nodded. "That is a possibility. However, I am hoping that if they get excited enough to attempt to attack you, they will make a mistake and kill me when the opportunity presents itself."

"That's a big *if*," Dane said.

Dzangbu did not respond. The three of them sat there with Dzangbu for a few seconds thinking about it while the yetis continued their overtone chanting.

Finally, Dane said, "Okay. Say we help you out, and say you succeed in taking over one of the twins' bodies. Even then, there'll still be one twin left to deal with. What then?"

"Then I will take care of the rest. I plan to engage the remaining twin in mortal combat. He will be forced to kill me or die."

"I thought you said you'd taken an oath not to kill a Mih Teh?"

"*We* know that. The beast does not. Hopefully he will not look upon the attack of another Mih Teh in the same way he looks at a human sacrificing himself. And after he kills me as his twin, I will make the final switch."

"Has that been done before?"

"No. There have never been twins before," Dzangbu said.

"What happens if you fail?" Dane asked.

Smokes interrupted. "We start shootin' like John Wayne and Clint Eastwood. That's what."

"There will be no need for shooting. The Sacrifists will not allow you to come to harm. Later, once the transition has taken place, you may leave," Dzangbu said.

Dane didn't like the last part of Dzangbu's explanation, 'you may leave.' He looked over at Smokes and could see that Smokes was thinking the same thing.

Dane asked Smokes, "What do you two think?"

"I think we should talk this over," Lily said. She glanced at Dane, urgency flashed across her face before she looked back at Dzangbu, her expression impassive once more.

"Hell, I don't care," Smokes said. "The sooner he does his thing, the sooner we can get the hell outta here."

"Okay, Sacrifist. Where do we go next?" Dane asked.

"Let's talk about this," Lily said. Then, to Dzangbu: "May I speak with my friends privately?"

"Of course." Dzangbu got up and moved away, out of earshot.

"What's up?" Dane asked. Smokes crouched down to listen.

"He lied to us at least twice. He knows the meaning of the symbols in the book, and he probably knows who built this place. Plus, I'm pretty sure that when he said, 'you may leave,' something was off."

"You think they'd kill us?" Dane asked.

"No. I just don't think they'd let us leave. They have a secret here, one they want kept. The only way to do that is to keep those who know about it from leaving."

"How do ya know he's lyin'?" Smokes asked.

"It's a long story," Dane told Smokes. He thought about their predicament for a moment. "I say we go along with him and do as he says. They could have killed us easily enough already by overwhelming us. But if we have to, I think we can convince them to let us go. Remember, we still have the guns we brought, and the Sacrifists don't want their yeti bodies to be killed. That would mess up their whole sequential system."

Dane looked over his shoulder at Dzangbu, who was still waiting a short distance away. Smokes handed Lily's gun back to her.

Dane continued. "Provided all goes like Dzangbu plans—and I have my doubts—after he gets killed and performs the transition, we should hightail it out of here."

"And if he fails?" Lily asked.

"Start shooting," Dane said.

Smokes spit on the ground. "Roger that."

CHAPTER 75

SIR RANDOLPH WATCHED Kangchenjunga disappear in the distance, hoping Dane and Smokes would survive but he had his doubts. He usually had no sympathy for people who did not follow his advice, but he really liked Dane and admired Smokes for sticking by his friend's side. He picked up the sat phone and dialed his 707 pilot in Kathmandu.

"Jack, we're in the chopper and we should be there soon. Can you have the plane ready to go?"

"Okay. Anyone else coming along?" Jack asked.

Sir Randolph glanced over at Lance, who was staring at the chipped piece of tunnel wall he had picked up. "Just Lance, George Armstrong, and his cameraman."

"Destination?"

Still watching Lance, Sir Randolph said, "Bristol."

"Okay. See you in a few."

Sir Randolph hung up. "What's that?"

"Souvenir. I think it's a piece of the tunnel wall," Lance said.

Sir Randolph remembered how hard it had been for Armstrong to obtain a sample. "Let me see that."

Lance tossed it over to him. Sir Randolph looked it over.

The small greyish-black rock felt warm in his hand. He rubbed it between his index finger and thumb. The rock had no flaking or loose particles. He drew a line on the copter's window and was shocked when it easily made a small scratch. "Ooops." Instead of tossing it back to Lance, he asked, "How much do you want for it?"

Lance was surprised by the question. "Well, I don't know. It was quite an adventure, and I really wanted something to remember the event by. I don't think I could let it go for less than ... oh, say a thousand dollars."

"Done and done." Sir Randolph peeled off ten hundred-dollar bills before Lance could go back on his word.

Lance stared at the cash in his hand. The expression on his face said, 'I've been gypped.' "Why do you want it?" Lance asked.

"A souvenir," Sir Randolph lied, as he had obtained it for a much more serious purpose. To allay Lance's suspicions, he added, "I'm probably never going to get my son's remains back. So I wanted some memento of his final resting place."

This seemed to put Lance at ease "Oh. Okay. Makes sense."

Sir Randolph put the chipped rock in his pocket. *People believe whatever sounds reasonable.*

CHAPTER 76

DZANGBU AND A contingent of twelve yetis led Dane, Lily, and Smokes out of the amphitheater room to the square room that contained stairs leading to level one. Duke tagged along sans leash. Instead of going back upstairs, the yetis led their three guests to the tunnel on the right. Traveling down another dark tunnel, Dane and Smokes turned on their flashlights. Soon they entered another circular boulder room.

Two yetis removed the boulder and they all descended down into another square room. From there, they took a tunnel that led to the center of the level. It was another huge room, as big as the two upper amphitheater rooms, with six exits but with no seats or statues. Nonetheless, the three of them were amazed by what they saw.

In the center of the room was a circular pool of water about fifty feet in diameter. The pool was surrounded by stone benches. Duke walked between two benches and took a good long drink from the pool.

"Curiouser and curiouser," Lily said.

Smokes laughed, then said, "The yetis have a spa. All we need now is the Swedish Bikini Team."

Dane looked amazed. "It must be snow run-off. But the water must be piped in somehow." To Dzangbu: "Okay. Now what?"

"Now, half of our party will herd the twins into this room."

Six of the yetis left the party and headed back into the tunnel from whence they had come.

Dzangbu continued, "They will be ushering the twins through this entrance, and the twins will come unwillingly until they pick up your scent. You should stand on the opposite side of the pool from the entrance."

The three of them did as instructed. The remaining six yetis took up positions surrounding them. Dzangbu noticed the concern on his guests' faces.

"There is no need to worry. Once the twins arrive here, the other six will re-emerge and block all the exits. I will be standing with you, and when they approach, I will go out to meet the leading twin."

"And your metamorphosis must take place less than a minute after your death?" Lily asked.

"Yes," Dzangbu said.

They heard roars echoing from the tunnels. Duke growled, and then barked at the sound.

"Duke, quiet," Dane commanded.

Smokes leveled his gun at the entrance. "Get ready."

Dzangbu walked over to them. The six yetis tightened their circle, protecting the three guests. The roaring got louder and louder. Lily looked afraid, but Smokes and Dane seemed equally excited.

"You will not need that," Dzangbu said to Smokes, but his eyes were on the tunnel.

Dane and Smokes had gotten their shotguns out.

Smokes took no chances and gave his Remington 870 a

pump anyway.

The twin beasts burst forth from the tunnel, disoriented, and looked around. Following the twins walked the six yetis that had herded them into the area. When the six yetis came out of the tunnel, they immediately turned, and each of them blocked an exit.

The grey-eyed twin spotted the four non-yeti humans first. He made his way to his right and walked toward them, followed by his brother.

Dzangbu removed his knapsack and handed it to Lily, who was next to him, then went to meet the beast. Everyone's eyes were on Dzangbu as he assumed a meditation posture while walking. He closed his eyes.

Lily dropped his knapsack and pulled her gun out of her own pack. Dane's team circled back to their right in an effort to keep the pool between them and the twins.

The red-eyed Mih Teh noticed this and started to go back around the other way. The team stopped, and their yeti guard surrounded them to protect them.

The twins slowed down for a moment and looked around the room, seeing the exits blocked. They apparently knew they were trapped, for they roared in anger, which had no effect on the Sacrifists.

"They *are* pissed," Smokes said.

"I'd say so," Dane said.

With inhuman speed the grey-eyed Mih Teh ran around Dzangbu and headed for Lily, who was closest to him. Dane pulled Lily behind him, pumped his shotgun, and readied himself to shoot. Duke started barking.

"No!" Dzangbu yelled.

Three yetis stood in front of Dane with their backs to him, facing the grey-eyed beast. Dane did not know if they were protecting him or protecting the attacking beast. The grey-eyed Mih Teh growled menacingly at the Sacrifists blocking his path.

Dzangbu tried to engage the red-eyed Mih Teh, who had not moved. But the Mih Teh stepped away, circling the pool. Behind him, Dzangbu could hear the others talking.

"We have to do something," Lily said to Dane frantically.

"Why? The twins are trapped."

"Yeah. They aren't the only ones."

Smokes looked at the blocked tunnel entrances. "She's right."

The red-eyed Mih Teh joined his brother by attacking Lily from the other way around the pool. The three other yetis protected her using moves that showed they had years of martial arts training. This came in handy since they had no long claws like the albinos did.

"The yetis look like giant Chuck Norrises with slightly more hair," Smokes said.

The twins were outnumbered three to one. They kept rushing at Lily from various angles, but they were repelled each time by the swift moves of the Sacrifists. Grey-eyed Johnny almost slipped through once, swiping his clawed hand through a gap and narrowly missing Lily's legs. The others caught him from behind as she jumped out of reach. In the struggle, Johnny kept four of the six yetis occupied, leaving only two to defend against red-eyed Edgar.

The red-eyed Mih Teh made a flank move for Dane. Dzangbu tried to stop him, but was slapped aside and thrown through the air, landing roughly and smacking his head on a stone bench. A gash opened up on his forehead and he started bleeding. The two remaining yeti guards attempted to head off the red-eyed albino. The albino's ferociousness began to overwhelm the two, but they were joined by another yeti who had abandoned the exit he was guarding. All three repelled the albino, forcing him backward, though each yeti suffered deep arm wounds in the process.

Dane looked over his shoulder. "Behind us! The exit's open."

Lily did not need any urging. She was clearly terrified and took off running for the open exit as soon as Dane's words registered, followed close behind by Dane and Smokes. The yetis guarding the exits on either side of the open exit left their posts to stop the three humans.

"Das ago! Aga ista." Dzangbu said, telling the yetis in Kusunda to stop their pursuit of Dane and the others. They stopped and came inward to help the other Sacrifists.

Dzangbu knew that even if the three found their way back up a level, the other Sacrifists above would stop them from escaping. Dzangbu's main concern was with the twins. Their refusal to mortally harm him was the problem he most needed to resolve.

CHAPTER 77

DANE, LILY, SMOKES and Duke reached a square room that was torchlit, located at the first junction of tunnels they ran across. Lily was hyperventilating, and as they reached the open space, she began to break down crying. She fell to her knees.

Dane crouched down to try to calm her, putting his hand on her shoulder. "It's okay. We're safe."

Dane looked at Smokes, who was watching the exit tunnel they'd just escaped through.

"No one's comin'," Smokes said.

Lily looked up at Smokes and calmed down slightly. "I'm sorry." Her heart was racing. "I'll be okay."

"Which way do we go?" Smokes asked.

"I'm not completely sure," Dane said. "Wish we had Dzangbu's book."

"Oh! I took it." Lily hurriedly pulled the book out of her pack.

Smokes started to chuckle. "Lily Light-fingers. I'll watch my wallet." He smiled at her.

His playfulness calmed Lily further and she smiled back. Dane quickly flipped to the map depicting the third level. They scanned the snowflake diagram, which showed two concentric circles in the hexagon, the center one no doubt representing the pool. Six arm-like tunnels led out from the center, and the tunnels were each interrupted by a square room. Each square room had four exits—two leading to circular rooms, one leading back to the center, and one which continued to lead outward to five circular rooms—one at the end of each of the four offshoot tunnels and one at the end of the main tunnel.

One of the circular rooms had a big black dot in the center, and one of the square rooms had a circle in the center. Dane pointed at the square room with the circle. "That's the room we entered coming down from level two. We best not go back there. The other yetis may be there, and if so, they may be blocking the way." He pointed to the circular room with a black dot in the center. "That must lead down to level four."

"Wait a minute," Lily said. She flipped the pages back to level one, then returned to the map of level three. "Remember how he said that level one and three were similar?" Lily flipped from level two to level four and back again so the others could see that they looked exactly alike. "So are two and four."

She went back to level one and pointed at the lower left arm of the diagram. "That was where we entered underground this morning. See, it has no circular room at the end. Every other arm has a circle at the end to indicate a room. This lower left one has none." She flipped back to level three and pointed at the lower left-hand arm. "Look, no circle at the end on level three either. It could be another exit."

"Let me see that."

Lily handed Dane the book. He studied the map for what they presumed was level three, then handed the book back to Lily.

"That will be quite a few feet below where the climbing

ropes are," Dane said. "But I can free-climb up and send lines down to you two."

Smokes lit a cigarette. "Sounds like a plan to me." Then to Lily: "Well, let's not stand around. Which way do we go, Miss GPS?"

Lily glanced back at the map and pointed at the tunnel on their right. "That way."

They ran.

CHAPTER 78

THEY FINALLY MADE it to the exit tunnel of level three and reached the end where there should have been an exit. Instead, they found it blocked with snow and ice.

"Keep an eye out, Duke," Smokes said.

All three of them started hacking away with their ice axes at the snow wall that blocked their exit. All the while, they kept looking over their shoulders and listening for any pursuit. They knew they had reached the end of the tunnel because the tunnel ceiling had ended and only the floor had continued.

"If it's like the cave on level one, it should only go out about a few feet," Dane said.

Smokes threw his butt down and stamped it out. "Screw this. Get out yer scatter gun. Lily, step aside."

Dane got his shotgun out and said, "You hit right of center, I'll hit left. Ready? Shoot!"

BL-BLAM!

They blew two holes in the ice wall and saw daylight. Each hole was about a foot in diameter. "Again. A little lower. About two feet under the hole you made," Dane said. "Ready? Fire!"

BL-BLAM!

Snow and ice came crashing down onto the ledge, much of it falling into the crevasse. Dane climbed up the resulting mound of snow and looked up. He could see the ledge above, but could not see the ropes.

"Dane!" a familiar voice called out.

A brown head popped out over the edge of the top of the crevasse. Phurba was smiling and waving.

Dane yelled, "Good to see you!" He realized they would not have to free-climb without ropes. *Bless Phurba,* he thought.

"I told you I would see you later!" Phurba yelled.

"We need four ropes. Three people and a dog coming up. And we may have some demons on our tail."

"Right away."

Phurba got busy anchoring the ropes. Dane went back to Lily and Smokes, who looked relieved that they would have help.

"Thank the Almighty. I do believe I owe that Sherpa a churn of tungba," Smokes said.

"I'm buying," Dane said. "I'll have Phurba haul Duke up first. Then we'll get Lily going. You follow her, and I'll keep a lookout on the tunnel. Once you're under way, I'll start my climb."

"I want to thank you two for saving me," Lily said. She kissed each of them on the cheek.

"Let's not get ahead of ourselves until we get back to base camp. Scratch that. Till we're off this mountain," Dane said.

"That can't happen soon enough," Smokes said. "Get on yer crampons, girl."

They pulled out crampons from their backpacks and put on their outer coats. Each had two ice axes for climbing the wall. Luckily, the flat crevasse had a slight tilt to it, so gravity would hold them against the wall rather than letting them hang free—a big advantage for climbing out.

Phurba sent four climbing ropes down. Dane secured one rope to Duke's harness and Phurba hauled him up. Phurba had put packs under each of the four ropes at the lip of the crevasse to prevent the ropes from digging in. He struggled a little as he grabbed Duke's harness, but eventually pulled him up over the crevasse's lip.

Dane had them get what they needed for climbing the crevasse wall out of their backpacks. Then he had Phurba pull up their backpacks, which would make their climb out a little easier.

"Smokes, you go up first. I don't want Phurba struggling with Lily all by himself. She's not as experienced as you are at getting out of a crevasse."

"Aye-aye, Cap'n."

Smokes began to make his way up with crampons and ice axes, inching his way up the side of the crevasse. After he had gone up twenty feet, Lily began her ascent on her own rope. Dane waited for her to get about twenty feet up, then he went back into the tunnel and flashed his light back down the length of it. Seeing no movement of any kind, he thought, *Good. I hope Dzangbu did what he came here to do.*

CHAPTER 79

THE TWO SHOTGUN blasts had distracted many of the yetis who were trying to contend with the twins. Two of them had been badly wounded by the twins furious onslaught. Dzangbu sent one of them off for reinforcements.

Over the next few minutes, two dozen more yetis began to arrive. The twins growled and roared fiercely as they noticed the increase in the number of their captors. Dzangbu was at a loss as to what else he could do. He felt he needed to show fear in some way in order to attract their attention. He had been pretending to fear and made sure his bodily reactions mimicked that emotion but the twins had still not attacked him in any way.

The yetis surrounded the wild Mih Tehs in numbers that made it impossible for them to escape. Dzangbu walked past all of them in an effort to again try to goad one of the twins into making the mistake of killing him. He looked like a small gladiator facing two Goliaths. Every time he went forward to engage one of them, he was summarily and viciously slapped away.

The gruesome beating took its toll, but it was not life-threatening. He lost the strength to continue after several attacks. His face was bruised and bloodied, his clothes mostly ripped to shreds. He felt like a ball of yarn being played with by two humongous cats. His body throbbed with pain from all his wounds. His upper torso stung badly. But the agony mattered not.

He was frustrated and knew that if he did not do something quickly to provoke them, he would lose consciousness, and along with it, the chance to fulfill his destiny. Exhausted and breathing hard from his endeavor, he paused and stooped over, putting his hands on his knees to rest a moment and gather his wits. He spat, tasting the blood flowing into his mouth from his split lips. His broken nose bleeding, he watched the blood drip to the floor.

The small combatant pitted against two monstrous opponents, who obviously had no intention of killing him, looked around at all of the other yetis who were keeping the twins imprisoned within their makeshift arena in order to force them to compete rather than pursue Dane and the others. How to die, was his problem. He knew if he stayed there, he would never be killed by the albinos.

The solution became clear in an instant.

He yelled out to the yetis, speaking in Kusunda: "I will engage them only one more time. When I do so, I want you all to leave. Do not come to my aid. Go to the other Sacrifists and tell them to clear the way for me to reach level two but if the albinos try to exit the same way, prevent them from reaching level two."

The yetis nodded their heads. Dzangbu attacked the twins immediately. They easily beat him off, and he fell backward and feigned unconsciousness. The yetis exited, walking in single file. The twins were leery at first, but soon they realized they were free. As Dzangbu suspected, the twins took the exit that Lily and the others had taken to pursue the humans.

Dzangbu mustered all the strength he had left, rose from the ground, and began to run back toward the stairs leading to level two. The idea he had formulated to achieve his purpose was a desperate one. He knew if he failed there was no backup plan. He could not fail and he had no time to inform his brethren on what they should do if he should not succeed. He calmed himself as he ran. He envisioned his success.

The three humans may die, but he knew that their sacrifice may be necessary for him to reach his goal and the goal of the other Sacrifists.

CHAPTER 80

DANE GOT HIMSELF ready to climb using the last rope and started his climb upward. *We are lucky Phurba stayed behind to help us.* The thin air was noticeable after being in the oxygen-rich tunnel system. His breathing rate increased, but it was something he was used to. He had climbed out of many a crevasse—some harder than others. Because of its tilt and the smoothness of the wall, this one was relatively easy. *This crevasse is unnatural,* he thought. He didn't know why but he suspected that it had to do with the Sacrifists and their tunnel system. Before he knew it, he was even with Lily, who was moving much slower.

"Hey, Miss McCrowley. You all right?"

"It's been a while since I've done this type of climbing, that's all."

"Want some help?"

"No. I'll be fine. Don't let me hold you back."

"Okay. I think Dzangbu must have been successful. I didn't see or hear anything during my last check down the tunnel. See you at the top."

"I can't wait."

Dane continued on, and Lily climbed a few more yards up the crevasse. She took her time because she was tired from so much exertion in the thin air. The overwhelming fear she experienced while being attacked by the albino Mih Tehs had not helped to make her feel especially at ease. She stopped and rested a few seconds. *Don't rest too long, you'll lose momentum,* she reminded herself.

She looked up to see Smokes near the top and Phurba getting ready to help him over the lip of the crevasse. Dane neared the ledge on level one where they had first spotted the beast. For some reason, the thought of kissing Dane's cheek flashed into her mind. She felt a little thrill, and for the first time in her life, understood what it meant to be 'weak at the knees.' *Get a grip on yourself.* She got moving again. Slowly hacking away with her ice axes, she took careful steps on the crevasse wall, making sure her crampons made good contact and keeping herself anchored to the rope to prevent her from falling back down. *Don't make any mistakes now. Just be thorough.*

***

The two Mih Tehs made their way quickly down the tunnels of level three. Guided by Lily's scent of fear, they made their way around to the exit tunnel and saw the opening to the exterior world. They crept toward the exit, remembering the loudness of the guns.

Grey-eyed Johnny peeked outside and looked up, seeing two climbers—Dane and Lily. Dane was at the top and was actively being helped out of the crevasse. Lily was heading there, but had not quite reached safety. Johnny watched Phurba and Smokes help Dane over the lip of the crevasse.

Lily was all alone. The beasts began their climb.

CHAPTER 81

THE THREE MEN were congratulating themselves on having made it out of the tunnels alive and back to territory they were familiar with.

"Thanks, Phurba. Thanks for sticking around," Dane said. "I told you. You're a good man."

"I owe ya a churn, Phurb," Smokes said, lighting a Camel and blowing out the blue smoke mixed with his own frosty breath. "I do believe this is the best smoke I've ever had. Next to that one I had in Shanghai once after some ... strenuous activity with a girl named ... what was her name?"

They all started laughing.

A loud, desperate scream came up from the crevasse. They scurried over to the crevasse lip. Lily had just passed the ledge of level one. Looking past her, they saw the twins climbing up the ice wall like spiders.

"Dzangbu failed! Smokes, you're a better shot than me; grab your shotgun but get real wide. I don't want you hitting Lily by mistake. Shoot to kill."

"Right," Smokes said, and he ran to his pack to retrieve his shotgun.

Dane called down to Lily, "Don't look down, Lily. Focus on climbing."

"I am!" She swung one of her ice axes and took another step. Dane could see that she was shaking, but her face was a mask of determined concentration as she climbed upward. He could see she had about forty more feet left between her and the lip of the crevasse. From Dane's viewpoint, it looked like the twins were moving faster than Lily, but they were at least two hundred feet below her. Dane saw Smokes take up his position, weapon ready.

He yelled over to Smokes, "How does it look?"

Dane knew that Smokes could more easily see the rate the twins were moving compared to Lily with his wider viewing angle.

"Without our help, they'll catch her," Smokes said.

"Not happening. Phurba, let's haul her up. Rig up a belay and we'll pull her back up over the side." Then, to Smokes: "Smokes! Fire away!"

Dane called down to Lily. "Lily, get ready. We're going to haul you up."

Smokes had reloaded and pumped his Remington, and now he took aim at the grey-eyed twin, who was a little further up the wall than his brother.

KA-BOOM!

The shot hit the beast in the shoulder, but only got his attention. He snarled savagely at Smokes, who pumped his Remington again.

KA-BOOM!

This time his shot only hit the beast in the upper thigh. The beast swatted at the pellets sticking in his hide, but kept climbing. Smokes yelled to Dane, "I'm too far away! If we had slugs instead of shot—maybe. There's no tellin' how thick their skin is. Since they kill bears, I'm assumin' it's pretty thick."

Dane and Phurba began to haul Lily up as fast as they could. After several seconds, Dane and Phurba felt the nylon rope slip through their hands. Their belay blew up, injuring Phurba's ankle and they strained mightily to keep Lily from falling.

Smokes watched, unable to help, as Lily fell down five feet. Her instincts were good, however, and she dug her ice axes into the side of the crevasse, halting her descent. She lost her grip on one of them as she stopped falling, and the ax fell into the chasm.

"No!" she cried.

Smokes yelled to Dane and Phurba. "She lost an ax. One of the beasts has gotten a hold on her rope!"

"We need to get another rope down to her, *now*," Dane yelled to Phurba. Phurba grabbed another rope and threw it to Dane, who went quickly to the crevasse's edge and began to let it out. Lily was back down by the level one cave entrance, not falling, but not climbing either.

KA-BOOM!

Smokes hit Edgar's arm and the Mih Teh let go of Lily's rope. Roaring viciously at Smokes, the Mih Teh reached out for it once more.

"Smokes, keep distracting them while we get another rope down to her. Or else she might fall all the way down," Dane said.

"Right," Smokes said, and pumped again and again.

KA-BOOM! KA-BOOM! KA-BOOM!

Edgar forgot about the rope, momentarily infuriated by the loud noise and the stinging pellets.

Dane yelled to Lily. "Lily, traverse to the level one outcrop and cut the line below you. We're sending a second rope down to you. Phurba and I will pull you out with both lines. Hurry!"

Lily traversed the ice wall and landed on the ledge for level one. She got her knife and cut the rope below the prusik and it fell into the chasm.

KA-BOOM!

Smokes had struck Edgar three times now, but it looked like the beast only felt minor pain from the barrage. Edgar grabbed for Lily's rope again as it fell past him. Lily was attaching the new rope and readying herself to be pulled to safety. Johnny was a mere fifty feet from her, now, and still climbing.

"Lily, ready?" Dane asked.

"Pull me up!" she shouted.

Smokes saw Johnny closing in on Lily and took aim.

KA-BOOM!

Smokes hit Johnny in the side. The beast roared at him.

"Tell me how ya really feel," Smokes said to himself.

"Phurba! Let's go!" Dane yelled. "Smokes, come help us haul Lily up."

Smokes took one last quick look down at the twins. Edgar was catching up to Johnny, but had not yet succeeded.

Smokes hustled to help Phurba and Dane. Johnny was twenty feet away from her now.

"Hurry! Dane!" Lily screamed. She sounded hysterical. "Help me, please!"

Dane watched helplessly as she cried out. The beast gained on her, even though Smokes and Phurba were pulling on the rope as fast as they could. She was thirty-five feet from the top of the crevasse, but at this rate it would be thirty-five feet too much. Dane pulled out his Glock 21. He was not a great shot, but he had to do something. He dashed twenty feet to his left to try to get a clearer view of the beast. He took aim just as the beast came even with the cave opening. Out of nowhere, a body flew through the air and landed on the grey-eyed monster's back.

"It's Dzangbu!"

The Sacrifist had his arms wrapped tightly around the beast's neck. The beast snarled viciously and shook itself, trying to throw him off.

"Keep pulling, guys! Dzangbu is on top of the lead twin!"

"That's one brave sonofabitch," Smokes said.

Dane intended to go back over to where he could pull Lily up over the edge but Edgar had climbed to a mere ten feet lower than Johnny, who was still fifteen feet from Lily. Lily was twenty feet from the top.

"Dzangbu! The other beast is almost upon you!" Dane yelled.

Dzangbu ignored him. Johnny tried to shove him off. He held tight as the Mih Teh roared loudly. Finally, Edgar caught up to them and stabbed Dzangbu's legs with his claws. Dzangbu did not even cry out. The Sacrifist would not let go.

Dane took aim at Edgar. He thought about shooting him. He knew Dzangbu only held on to Johnny because one of the beasts needed to be fully responsible for his death. For the transformation to take place, Dzangbu could play no willing part in his own death.

Edgar moved up the wall and swung again. This time stabbing Dzangbu in the back of his neck and puncturing his upper spinal cord. Dzangbu's unfeeling arms dropped to his side and his limp body fell into the crevasse.

Lily screamed.

Dane watched him fall out of sight. He turned to Smokes. "Dzangbu's dead! Pull like hell."

Smokes nodded. "Roger that. Let's save the girl, Phurba." Smokes and Phurba pulled hard.

But it was too late. Johnny was upon her. He grabbed Lily's

leg and yanked.

"Aaaaaaaahhhhh!" she screamed.

The beast's jerk on Lily's leg made the rope slip from the two men's hands and the full weight of her body came down on Johnny's arm.

Johnny had to let go of Lily to keep from falling into the crevasse himself. She fell past the beast, and as she plummeted, she took the rope with her.

Lily felt herself stop abruptly as something caught her arm, nearly wrenching it from its socket. She looked up to see the red-eyed Edgar holding on to her. She fought to free herself, preferring to die in the crevasse. Her mind imagined being torn to shreds and eaten while still alive.

Edgar's claws dug into Lily's forearm and he spoke in a deep guttural voice. "Stop struggling, Miss McCrowley."

Lily stopped struggling, though still hardly believing what had happened. The monster smiled and his eyes told the truth. *It's Dzangbu!* Dane was about to fire. "Dane! It's Dzangbu!"

Dane hesitated a moment, still ready to pull the trigger. He watched Edgar-Dzangbu drop Lily safely at the cave opening, then turn his attention to Johnny.

Not far from Dane, Smokes reached for his Glock. He and Phurba went to the edge of the crevasse. Smokes took aim.

"Hold on, Smokes," Dane called out. "I think the red-eyed twin is now Dzangbu. He just dropped Lily on the outcrop. She even said it was Dzangbu."

"What?" Phurba asked.

"We'll tell ya later over that churn I owe ya," Smokes said.

They all watched as Johnny headed toward the cave. Edgar-Dzangbu would not let Johnny get past him. Johnny became more and more agitated. They began to grapple on the crevasse wall, each trying to knock the other from the wall. They landed on the ledge to the cave opening. Lily had already crawled inside.

Smokes began to take aim. "Why don't we just help Dzangbu a little and shoot the other one?"

Dane was going to answer Smokes, but in that moment Johnny got an advantage over Edgar-Dzangbu and clawed him in the throat. Edgar-Dzangbu fell and lay limp on the ledge. Johnny shoved him into the abyss. The grey-eyed beast watched his dead brother fall, then the Mih Teh tilted back its massive head and let out a roar. The men's blood chilled hearing the primal howl.

"Start shooting," Dane said.

They began unloading their weapons at the beast, and each got off two shots before the beast ducked inside the cave opening, heading toward where Lily was hiding. A moment later, they heard a roar, punctuated by Lily's terrified screaming which echoed off the crevasse walls.

Dane got up and hurriedly set up for rappelling down. "Help me down, Smokes!"

Smokes and Phurba scrambled to help, but Lily's shrieks ended abruptly.

Dane had just begun his descent down the side of the crevasse wall when the beast emerged carrying Lily. She was limp in its arms. Smokes and Phurba saw the monster first.

"Oh, no," Smokes said.

Phurba yelled, "Dane, look out!"

Dane looked down, and saw the beast holding Lily.

Above him, Duke began to bark.

"Quiet, Duke. Lie down," Smokes commanded.

Dane pulled his Glock out and pointed it toward the beast. Lily appeared limp and dead as the beast threw her over its shoulder and began to climb.

"It's coming for us," Smokes said.

Dane aimed his weapon. *This is for Shelly, Lily and the others.* He paused to make sure he would not miss this time or so he thought. He took a deep breath to steady himself and began to squeeze the trigger.

The grey-eyed beast stopped and looked at him. "You wouldn't shoot a friend, would you?"

Dane exhaled and relaxed his trigger finger, recognizing the cadence of Dzangbu's voice in the beast's deep and gravelly tone.

"Pull me up, you guys," Dane shouted. "That's Dzangbu."

Dane watched as the beast climbed effortlessly past him and up the crevasse wall with Lily over his shoulder. Phurba and Smokes helped haul up Dane. When Dzangbu arrived at the crevasse lip, Smokes went to help him get Lily up and over the edge safely. Phurba was visibly shaken by being so close to a yeti.

To Smokes's relief, Lily was breathing. He carried her away from the crevasse and laid her down, propping her up with their backpacks.

Dzangbu came over the top of the crevasse and stood at the edge, waiting for Dane. Phurba, who was nearby, kept his eyes on Dane, clearly afraid to look up. But the beast's grey eyes were no longer menacing, and the one time Phurba did glance up at the yeti's face, the sirdar saw kindness and compassion there.

Dane neared the top of the crevasse. But before Phurba could help him, Dzangbu the yeti reached down and lent Dane his giant hand. With his great strength he easily lifted Dane to safety.

Once Dzangbu had set him down, Dane ran over to Lily and kneeled down. Phurba walked over as well, conscious that the beast was right behind him, but not letting his fear prevent him from helping a friend.

Dane tried to wake her. He opened her coat a little and the amulet of Uncle DJ's necklace fell out.

A few seconds later, Lily woke up from her faint. She looked up at Dane.

Dane smiled. "You're going to have to stop fainting or you're going to miss all the action." He looked at her necklace. Lily followed his gaze.

"A little extra protection never hurts," she said weakly. She saw Smokes standing next to the yeti. "Either I'm dreaming, or that's Dzangbu."

The beast tipped his head at Lily in acknowledgment.

Smokes looked the yeti up and down, and whistled. "Damn, Dzangbu. That's a good look for you."

Dane, Smokes, and Lily laughed, flooded with relief at knowing their ordeal was finally over.

Phurba, who had been deliberately standing some ways away, appeared to come to a decision. The sirdar squared his shoulders and walked toward the beast. He got down and prostrated himself before the yeti. He looked up at the yeti.

The beast put his palms together in front of his chest with his fingers and claws pointed upward, giving the familiar Buddhist salutation. He bowed and said, in his deep voice, "Namasté."

All four of them returned the salutation.

Dzangbu turned and headed back toward the crevasse to join his brothers and sisters below. He was about to disappear over the side when he paused and looked back at them. He held his hand up to his mouth with his index finger extended. He put the finger up to his lips, reminding them all of their oath. Then he disappeared from sight.

They stood there a moment in silence, thinking about all they had been through.

Smokes said, "Dane, the next time ya have 'a little job' for me, remind me to ask for *more money*."

Dane chuckled. "Will do, Smokes. Will do."

The party of four headed back to base camp. That night they all slept soundly. The next day, when Dane woke up and exited his tent to get ready for their descent down the mountain, he nearly tripped over two body bags. He did not need to examine the contents to know that the bags were holding Rand's and Shelly's remains. *Thanks, Dzangbu. You're pretty unbelievable,* Dane thought.

Despite having four guards posted that night, no one had seen or heard a thing.

CHAPTER 82

WHEN SIR RANDOLPH got back home, Gus was already waiting for him in the library. Sir Randolph had received a full report from Courtney Kaufman. After looking it over, he asked Gus, "Is she trustworthy, and does she realize this is all highly confidential material?"

"Yes."

"Have you looked at this?"

"No. I glanced at it and it looked too technical. So I had her give me the summary—in proper English."

"We should bring her over here. I'm going to set up a research facility in Bristol. I want it close by so I can keep an eye on it."

"Okay. Anything else?"

"Yes. There's much more. I feel lucky to be alive, Gus." Sir Randolph detailed his entire adventure to Gus, which took over an hour. When he had all but finished, Sir Randolph pulled the chipped bit of stone from his pocket. "This is part of a tunnel wall. I want to look into it next." He tossed the rock chip to Gus, who looked at the grey stone with black flecks, then flipped it back to him.

"What's so special about the rock?"

"That is what I intend to find out. Also, Dane called. He's someone we may want to work with again. The damn kid went back into those tunnels and came out the other side without getting himself killed. He saved the girl, Lily, who we all thought was dead. And lastly, he's bringing back Rand's remains."

"Oh, good."

"Yes. This may mean there will be even more DNA for us to examine. He should be arriving here in two or three days."

"All right. It's all a good show, then."

"Yes. He and his partner are brave men. Dependable. I like dependable people."

When Sir Randolph received word of Dane's success, he was greatly relieved. He really did not think he would ever see the young man again. *Bless him. He's a daring kid,* Sir Randolph thought.

"What do you want done first?" Gus asked.

"Call Dr. Kaufman and offer her a job working in the new facility in Bristol. They'll be examining more DNA, and I'd like her as a project lead. Make it worth her while to accept. Arrange a laboratory space in Bristol. It doesn't have to be big, but it *has* to be secure. I want it up and running immediately. Hire a geologist or an expert in materials science and engineering to find out what this stone is made of. One who can keep his mouth shut."

"That it?"

"That's all for now."

"Okay." Gus got up and began to walk out. He paused at the door. "Good to see you again, Randy."

Sir Randolph smiled, then said, "You too, Gus."

CHAPTER 83

GEORGE ARMSTRONG SAT with his producer, Typhon, in Typhon's office in a Century City high rise. They had just finished watching the rough footage which Harry had shot.

The producer was downright giddy at the prospect of airing the show. "We want to build this up. Big. This footage isn't some shot from five hundred yards away. This is up close and personal."

"Yeah. Harry was wounded," Armstrong said.

"That's even better. It's great! We'll make a killing with other networks wanting to show the footage. In fact, maybe we can get the big networks to bid on a special."

"That's what I was thinking. There is nothing in our current contract that precludes that plan, is there?"

"I don't think so, but I'll check to make sure. Doesn't matter. We'll have them sign off on it just to get more promotion for their own channel, and they can always show the reruns."

"It's too bad those other guys lost their lives," Armstrong said.

"No. It's better. How many were there?"

"Nine. Three Americans plus six Sherpa porters."

"Nine dead. That's fantastic! We can have a dedication at the end of the program." Typhon giggled and waved his open hand in front of his face, indicating a banner headline. *"Big Game, Big Times' Finds the Bloodthirsty Yeti."*

"The Kangchenjunga Demon is what the locals call it."

"Catch-a-what?"

"Kang-chen-jun-ga. It's the third highest mountain in the world. That's why they call it the Kangchenjunga Demon."

Typhon frowned. "Oh, oh ... I don't know about that. That's a mouthful. And the *third* highest mountain? That's no good. Can't we make it Everest or even K2? People know about those places from documentaries and movies."

Armstrong shrugged uneasily. "I suppose so. If you think it will help sell the show. Come to think of it, the Sherpas would probably prefer it that way. They consider Mt. Kangchenjunga sacred, and wouldn't want to attract more people that were bent on looking for the yetis. They respect it too much."

"Great. We'll see which mountain plays better with focus groups. Too bad they didn't bag a yeti and bring it back."

Armstrong rolled his eyes. "We were lucky to get out of there alive. Poor Harry. Another few inches and I would have needed a new cameraman. However, Barrington said he had some DNA tested from Nielsen's first encounter with the beast, and get this—it turned out to be *human*. With some *'odd peculiarities,'* whatever that means."

"Really? When will you be interviewing him?"

"I have an appointment for next week. I plan to meet him at his estate in England after he gets settled."

"Fantastic. You really hit a home run this time, George. You're the master! Grounding and pounding! Nice job. After the focus groups, we'll get started on some high-quality mystery promos with ominous music. We'll send them out to all the big networks and see who wants it most. Hopefully, there will be a bidding war. Wouldn't that be great?"

Armstrong nodded.

Typhon laughed with glee. His greed was limitless.

CHAPTER 84

TWO WEEKS AFTER Lily's harrowing escape from the albino twins, she, Dane and Smokes were shown into Sir Randolph's library at Barrington Court.

When they had reached base camp, Dane had called Sir Randolph to let him know that they had made it out and had recovered Rand's remains. Sir Randolph was truly overjoyed at their success. Dane listened to him on the phone, and it sounded like the man was on the verge of breaking down. It made Dane happy to help the billionaire get some closure for his son's death.

They traveled down the mountain with what was left of their Sherpa expedition and made it to Taplejung and Suketar airport. They flew into Kathmandu just over three weeks after they had left it. Afterward, they spent a few days relaxing at the Royale hotel.

They sat in the library waiting for Sir Randolph, and Dane could not help being reminded of his first visit to Barrington Court with Shelly and Torleif nearly two months ago. Here he was again, with a good friend and another woman who, just like Shelly, had insisted on accompanying him to Kangchenjunga.

The coincidental circumstances made him feel kind of weird, but he felt blessed to have had a different result. The curse had been lifted.

He and Smokes had saved Lily's life. All three of them had witnessed something miraculous. But on their trip down the mountain, they had not even discussed it.

The three of them had shared an experience, it was safe to say, that no one else on the planet had ever shared. Since Dane had not talked about it with either of them, he did not know how they felt. He knew he felt closer to both of them, and he had already been close to Smokes.

We gave our word to Dzangbu not to speak about it, Dane thought. He intended to keep his word.

He watched Lily talking about Sir Randolph's library and all its books and remembered Shelly making similar comments. He missed Shelly, but because of his recent adventures, he had not thought a lot about the loss.

Being at Barrington Court under similar circumstances to those of his first visit brought his attention back to the great loss he had suffered. He felt melancholy, but the truth was that the whole adventure had changed how he felt about life as a whole.

If Dzangbu had not shown up, they would have killed the twins. Dzangbu's appearance, his subsequent death and his transformation were life-changing events, and Dane suspected he would be mulling over the implications for a long time to come.

In particular, it had changed how Dane felt about life, and it gave more credence to many things his grandfather had told him as a child. He did not know how Smokes or Lily felt about it. Smokes seemed the same as usual. Lily seemed different, though. Dane could not put his finger on it. She kept glancing over at him while Smokes flirted with her and kept her laughing.

"Oh, Smokes, stop flirting," Lily said.

"You can't ask a leopard to change its spots, now," Smokes said. "It's in my nature." Smokes beamed at her.

Dane laughed; glad to see his friends having fun with each other. He added, "Don't let him fool you, Lily. He's not a leopard, he's a fox. Sly, like a fox."

They were all laughing as Sir Randolph came in. "Glad to see you all in good spirits. I feared for your lives when you two went back underground." He looked at Lily and said, "And hearing of your miraculous return was most unexpected. I have something here for each of you."

Sir Randolph gave them each an envelope.

"Can we open it?" Smokes asked.

"Sure. It's your envelope," Sir Randolph said.

Smokes ripped his open and Lily did as well. Dane put his in his pocket without looking. Smokes pulled out the check and gave a long whistle, followed by a long, uncharacteristic pause. At last, he looked up at Sir Randolph. "I don't know what to say, sir. For once, I am speechless."

Dane laughed. "Well then, Sir Randolph's done the impossible."

Lily was still looking at her own check, her face warring between disbelief and embarrassment. "I don't think I can accept this, sir. I didn't do anything to get it. I don't deserve it."

"Miss McCrowley," Sir Randolph began, his voice genial but quietly firm, "you don't get to tell me how to spend *my* money. You keep it … or give it away, if you wish. It's your money now."

Lily sat down and just stared at the check. "Okay, sir. Thank you. Thank you very much."

Sir Randolph looked at Dane. "My boy, how did you make it

out of that tunnel system?"

Dane looked at his friends, but both of them remained silent. "Well, sir. It was a little touch and go. We thought we'd gotten away until the two albino beasts attacked us on the crevasse wall. Luckily, Smokes was able to pick both of them off while Phurba and I hauled Lily out in a nick of time. They fell into the crevasse. If Smokes's bullets didn't kill them, the long fall surely must have."

Sir Randolph looked at Smokes and said, "Nice work, Smokes." Then, to Dane: "I'll have to send Phurba a bonus."

"Yes," Smokes said, adding to Dane's tale. "They used to call me 'Dead Eye' in the army. Long-range sniper. I could pick off the enemy from a thousand yards."

"Will you plan a memorial service for Rand, sir?" Dane asked. He knew Smokes was a good shot in the service, but not a sniper, and Dane did not want him to get in over his head.

"Within a week or two. I can't thank you all enough, Dane. Thank you for retrieving his remains."

"It really was no trouble." All three felt a little awkward because they knew it had really been no trouble at all, since the bones had been brought to base camp in the dead of night by Dzangbu or one of the other yetis.

Sir Randolph continued, "George Armstrong was elated to hear that you all made it out alive. He wants to interview each of you."

Dane nodded. "Yes. He's left a couple of voicemails on my phone. If it is all the same to you, sir, Smokes and I prefer to let him have all the glory to himself."

"Lily, how about you?" Sir Randolph asked.

"I don't think I want to be part of that. I like my privacy. I don't need to be in the news."

"I understand. It's up to you all," Sir Randolph said.

Dane changed the subject. "We should probably be going. Where has Montgomery taken Duke?"

"He's feeding him in the kitchen. A driver will convey you to Bristol Airport. From there, my pilot will fly Smokes out to Helena, and you to Denver then take Lily on to San Francisco."

The three of them stood up and Sir Randolph came over to shake Dane's hand. "Son, what you did for me meant a lot more than the money I gave you. If you ever need my help—for anything—you give me a call."

"I will, sir."

"The same goes for you two," he said, looking at Smokes and Lily.

"Thank you," Lily said.

"Okay," Smokes said. "Can I ask ya something, sir?"

"Go ahead."

"What's it like to have all this money?"

"It feels magnificent," he said without hesitation.

Smokes frowned. "Did I just ask the dumbest question of all time?"

Dane and Lily said simultaneously, "Yes."

CHAPTER 85

ON THEIR WAY to Bristol Airport, Armstrong attempted once more to get through to Dane. Seeing this, Dane turned off his cell. Their flight to Helena was uneventful, and Dane spent most of it lost in his own thoughts, while Smokes told Lily some tall tales about his stint in the Armed Forces.

Once they entered American air space, the TV came on and they watched the news. They all quieted down when a commercial came on promoting a George Armstrong exclusive TV special. Brooding music set the mood.

The narrator began, "It's Jaws in the snow." Then the words 'Evil on Everest' dripped like blood onto the screen as the narrator continued.

Smokes snorted. "Everest? What the hell?"

"Why would they move the location?" Dane asked, addressing no one in particular.

"They moved it for ratings. Everyone's heard of Everest," Lily said. "Besides mountaineers and geography buffs, who's ever heard of Kangchenjunga?"

The voiceover finished by announcing, "See the first close-up footage of the Himalayan monster known as the

Abominable Snowman."

Smokes shook his head. "*Now* I've seen everything. Jeez, Hollyweird. No, thank you."

The fact that they had lied to Sir Randolph did not bother them. But the fact that none of them would talk about it, even with each other, sat like an elephant in the room. The TV promo had just put it out in the open.

Finally Smokes said, "Till the day I die, I'll never forget what that Tibetan feller did. I didn't believe him when he told us that he was gonna do it. And if I hadn't seen it with my own eyes and you'd just told me about it, I would have said yer full o' shit. So, I ask you, even if we told anyone, who'd believe it?"

"Right. Even at the end, when he was bringing Lily back up, and she looked dead. I was within a hair's breadth of shooting him anyway," Dane said.

"Lucky for me, you held your fire," Lily said.

"Yes. ... And I think about that. Why *did* I hold my fire? I wanted to shoot. For Shelly. For revenge."

They all paused a moment, thinking.

Lily spoke first. "Faith. You had faith. There's no other answer for it. It has to be why you did what you did. Voltaire said, 'Faith consists in believing, when it is beyond the power of reason to believe.' That fits."

Smokes nodded. "S'pose yer right, little lady. Guess we're not faithless after all."

Dane smiled at his longtime friend. "She's right."

They spent the rest of the flight in silence. They landed in Helena and began taxiing to where Smokes would disembark.

Suddenly, Dane did not want to go home. All the things he had at home would remind him of Shelly. He would have to pack things away, maybe even put pictures away, and it was something he did not want to deal with. *I need a vacation.*

Someplace else to be for a while.

"Smokes, you mind taking Duke with you for a couple weeks?" Dane asked. "I don't think I'll go home right yet. I need to stay away for a while."

Next to him, Lily's eyes went wide.

***

Lily's heart felt as though it had stopped. She had been trying to think of something to say to Dane to give him a hint as to how she felt, but she was afraid that all of her ideas were lame. So she had just stayed silent. Now it looked like Dane was going to leave, and she *still* had not thought of anything to say.

"No problemo. Come back when yer ready," Smokes said, answering Dane's query. "Take as much time as ya need. We'll go fishin'. Where ya gonna go?"

Lily realized Dane *was not* getting off the plane. She would have a couple more hours to think of something brilliant to say.

"Haven't made up my mind yet. Just not home."

"I get it. Too many memories," Smokes said.

"Right."

"Well, show up when ya feel like it. Me an' Duke'll be chillaxin' at the ol' homestead for a while, courtesy of Sir Randolph."

Dane hugged his friend. "Thanks, man."

"See ya, little lady," he said to Lily. She gave him a big hug and kiss on the cheek.

"Case ya can't tell, I'm blushin'."

Smokes gathered up his stuff and got off the plane with Duke. Dane let the pilot know his change of plans. Lily sat quietly across from him on the plane as it took off again.

Dane turned to her. "You don't mind me tagging along with

you a little while longer?"

Mind? Are you freaking kidding me? She smiled nervously. "No. Uh, I don't mind. Uh, were you, uh, where you going, uh, to go to ... where?" *Get a grip, numbskull,* she thought, scolding herself.

Dane sighed. "I don't know. Maybe someplace tropical. Hawaii, maybe. Kauai is kind of rural and secluded. Good hiking, I hear. Deserted beaches."

"Sounds great," was all she could think of to say.

They said little else. The hour-and-a-half flight was over almost before Lily knew it. Dane called Sir Randolph when they landed and got him to tell the pilot to re-fuel and take Dane anywhere he would like to go.

The plane's engines died down and Lily got up out of her seat, still not saying anything to Dane. Her mind was blank. All she could think about was that Dane's fiancée only had been dead for a month. *He's still grieving.* Lily gathered her things as the cockpit door opened up.

If Dane could tell that Lily had something on her mind, he apparently thought it best to keep quiet, because he said nothing as she finished gathering up her belongings.

The pilot came out and opened the cabin door. "Okay, Miss McCrowley. All set." He stood there and waited for her to exit the plane. Lily turned to face Dane.

"Well, I guess this is … good-bye. … Thanks for saving my life."

She melted when he said, "You're welcome. Stay out of trouble."

Lily desperately wanted to continue their conversation. She did not want to leave without saying something about her feelings. So she said the only thing she could think of. "I've still got that book of Dzangbu's. And I have a friend who is a linguist, and I'm going to see if she has any ideas about translating it." Lily had another wild thought and added, "Who knows, maybe it tells us where Bigfoot is hiding."

Dane smiled. "Still pining away for Bigfoot, huh? What, Mih Tehs weren't enough for you? Anyone ever told you you're a little kooky?"

"Sure. Lots of times," she said, wanting to prolong the moment. "But I don't care."

"Yeah? Why's that?"

"Because I like being kooky," she said, snobbishly. "It's my most attractive feature."

Dane laughed loudly. "Your most attractive feature, huh?"

"That's right," she said, nearly out of breath.

Dane nodded his head, surveying her. "Well, I'm not going to argue with that."

She bit her lower lip. Her ears buzzed and her knees were weak. She wanted desperately to prolong the conversation but she was out of things to say.

The pilot cleared his throat breaking the spell and the magic connection she felt.

Damn pilot. I'm having a moment here, she thought, then sighed with resignation. "Well, I gotta go. … Don't be a stranger." She turned to leave.

"Okay. Let me know what happens with that Sacrifist book. You have my cell."

"Right. Aren't you on Facebook?"

"Nah."

She turned to face him. "Jeez, Lake, get with the twenty-first century."

"Okay. Shelly always told me to … well, I'll join soon."

"Good. I'll *friend* you."

He looked at her quizzically. "Huh?"

She laughed and her jade green eyes sparkled as the light reflected off of them. She thought about explaining it to him but it would just be delaying the inevitable.

"You'll figure it out." She forced herself to smile then turned around and started walking out. "I'll see ya," she said, without looking back.

"Yeah. ... See ya," Dane said.

She hoped that fate would make it true. She stepped down the stairs onto the tarmac and walked toward the private terminal, resisting the urge to look back.

She began to cry.

CHAPTER 86

THE OVERTONE CHANTING of the Sacrifists filled the amphitheater cavern with varying levels of sound. Dzangbu chanted during the meditation as well. He perceived the minute changes occurring in his yeti body generated by the chant's fluctuating vibrations, changes not possible in his former body. With his assumption of the yeti body, his full memory of all his existence had returned. He was happy to be back with the others—*his* one hundred and eight.

He and the rest had handled the wrinkle of the albino twins adequately. Reminding all of them, again, that life was hard to predict. He thought about the other three *Homo sapiens* he had been forced to deal with. He had not minded misleading them. It would be for their own good. Even if they revealed the yetis' existence and location, it would not matter. If anyone came looking, their home would no longer be found.

Nothing was going to stop him or the others.

At the gompa, after achieving enlightenment again and returning to his extraordinary mental condition, he had spent the next five years scouring the gompa's library and other sources for the history of the last two thousand years, the time that he had missed during his previous existence as a yeti. He had found many items of interest, as well as news and occurrences brought about by the other one hundred and eight.

The ones moving forward with the other half of the Plan.

All of them would keep doing what they had been doing, no matter how long it took to achieve their goal. Of that, he was quite sure.

For a moment, Dzangbu contemplated his real name—*Za*. In Kusunda, it meant 'fire.' He was jubilant and at peace, knowing their future and where they were headed.

He had been chosen to perform a duty. He had been doing it for an unfathomable amount of time. How wise were he and the other beings who had devised their Plan. He admired their patience.

He and the others knew there was no such thing as time, only an 'infinity of nows' without beginning or end. If a person knew that, then patience was easy. They would achieve their purpose and reach their goal because they did not have to worry about running out of time.

Time was irrelevant to them.

Because the Sacrifists—all two hundred and sixteen of them—toiled in eternity.

***

SEE BACK PAGE FOR HOW TO CONTACT THIS AUTHOR

REVIEWS

If you liked this book then please review it online from whatever retailer you purchased it from.

CONNECT WITH THE AUTHOR

Facebook: https://www.facebook.com/TMasonGilbert or just type T. Mason Gilbert into your Facebook search bar.

Email: mjollnir.enterprises@gmail.com

Made in United States
Troutdale, OR
02/21/2025